HARLEM'S LAST DANCE

Peppur Chambers

Denver, Colorado

Published in the United States by:

Spaceboy Books LLC
1627 Vine Street
Denver, CO 80206

www.readspaceboy.com

Cover art by Benjamin Mills

First printed March 2023

ISBN-13: 978-1-951393-18-2

There is real value in Harlem's experience - a visible, invisible woman. Read it and you will understand why it's important for Harlem to be seen!"

— C. Elyse, author of *Lilies Bloom Lies Fester*

"Powerful and raw. Peppur captures all the vivid details and brings the story to life to show the 1940's burlesque scene and the struggles that a young black woman faces as she grows into a young adult."

— Aiyona Calvin, Comm '26, Marquette University

To those writers who are still in the trenches,
asking themselves, "When will I finish my book?"
Here is proof that you will.

To my family, friends and husband who
listened to me for all the years it took to
complete this one.

And, to those who have ever read
anything I've written. I am grateful.

PROLOGUE

From behind the velvet folds of the heavy purple curtain, Tilda watched the new girl. She was tall and pretty, no more than eighteen years old. Her creamy brown skin seemed to attract the magical glow of the chandeliers hanging directly above her. The light followed her as she walked, or maybe she absorbed it. Either way, she lit up the room. She was the attraction of the evening. With her hair swept up in a nice, neat cinnamon bun and her bare shoulders glistening as though rubbed with new butter, Tilda understood why the men in the room couldn't take their eyes off her.

'Course, that was the whole point.

The new girl had only arrived just that morning and Lady Magdalena had already made her a star of the evening. Curiously, she was in a special red dress just like the other Brown Betties—and the Brown Betties were the best of all the girls in the house. They were the "cremdulacrem" or whatever Lady Magdalena said when she announced them at each and every Lady M's Mysterie Party. Usually, Lady

Magdalena would stand in the center of the room, tall and mighty, green eyes blazing, and tell everyone at the party to 'hush' (but in a soft way where her words were warm like melted fudge—definitely not the way she shouted at Tilda when it was just the two of them around. Mean-like.) Then Amoura, Desire, Fury, and Honey would saunter into the dining room like the hot cocoa beauties they were. Everyone would clap, their white gloves a flutter, but their vigorous applause was no louder than the muffled sound that came when Tilda beat at the rugs to clean them—and sometimes she beat them pretty hard, 'cause they were the only thing that was hers to beat. Their white faces would stretch with big old grins that were wide as no tomorrow, showin' every white tooth they had in their awful mouths. Then some would bow and say *ooooh* or *aaaahhh* or *my my my* and the party would begin. Magdalena would float around the room, gently touching backs or leaning carefully on folks. Her jeweled arms would drape over the men in their black-tailed coats, and they'd hug on her just a little too long. She would do the same, acting like she was there for them to pet, or worse, to grab and pinch her bottom. Champagne would be passed around by butlers; the musicians would play something bouncy and light, getting everybody in the mood for some fun. That's what happened almost every party night. But tonight? Tonight was different. The *ooooh*-ing and *aaaahhh*-ing and *my my my*'s were the same and so was the champagne. What was different was that Honey was missing and in her place was this new girl.

When the girl had arrived yesterday, she'd introduced herself as "Ann Smith," but Tilda knew her real name was Harlem Winnepega Markeson. Tilda had been there when Magdalena had secretly messed about in the girl's suitcases and purse and things to find out the truth of her.

The girl was from Greensboro, North Carolina. Wherever that was. She didn't come from no New York like her name wanted to suggest. And she for certain didn't come from this neighborhood. Tilda figured the name Harlem was about something she was running from and this Ann Smith was who she wanted to be. Time would tell; it always did.

When Harlem had arrived earlier that afternoon wearing a smart navy suit, a petite hat that sat on her head just so, and her own pair of white gloves, she'd made an entrance. Tilda had decided right then and there that the air that swirled around Harlem was some kinda special. For one, it seemed like it had heat, the kind that made people take their time when they moved. And for twos, her air felt like the wavy dips of a smooth melody were mixed up in it—the kind Tilda liked to sing to herself when she was alone in the quiet of the Manor. Folks from this neighborhood didn't have that. At least not the ones she was accustomed to seeing in *this* place. Harlem most certainly had the sprinklings of something else on her. Tilda called it travel dust; lots of the girls who came to Lady Magdalena's had some type of it. And Harlem's type of travel dust seemed special.

There was something else, too. She talked funny. Not a lot funny, just a little. Like her tongue had gotten caught up in some caramel ice cream. Slow-like, but with a touch of sweetness and even a little chill. The girl had class. That's all there was to it, really. She was sophisticated and had some refinement about her. Maybe about the same amount as Lady Magdalena pretended to have. It was much more than any of the girls in the house and way, way more than Lady Magdalena's business partners, Ruth and Mary. They were two old, terrible girl-hunters, and they were the ones who had brought Harlem here. Dust and all. Those two seemed like they were permanently covered in doo-doo, or at least Ruth's face looked like it half the time. Always mad. Always looking like she stepped in it, or someone had dropped a bucket of it on her. Her sister Mary's face was nicer, but since she was kin to Ruth and they were always 'round each other, Tilda supposed there wasn't any other way but for them to have some doo-doo in common. Tilda didn't care for those two much. They were the two who brought all the girls to Lady Magdalena's Manor. They were important, she supposed, but they weren't no kind of good. They brought in Harlem, and Tilda wondered if they helped take Honey out.

Lady Magdalena led Harlem by the arm and swept her toward the high-class men in their high high-top hats and silly silk ties. Her doing that made their white noses point up in the air and their laughs become louder than Tilda thought was necessary. There were ladies there too. And their noses were just as high and just as white. As Lady Magdalena and Harlem approached, some of the women would hold onto the arms of the men who'd brought them there just a little tighter. Their gloved hands would curl around their men like growing green bean vines. Tilda spent just as much time studying those ladies with their permanently arched eyebrows and pale painted faces as she did the men. Blues at the eyes and reds at the mouths. Tilda wasn't sure what those ladies were thinking. They were all dripped in sparkling jewels. They all smelled of powdered roses and had on divine dresses that swept the floor and whispered when they walked. Didn't they already have everything they needed?

Sometimes Tilda wondered if the high-class lady was holdin' onto her high-class man for finders keepers or if she was grounding him. That way, he wouldn't fly up and away, only to then swan dive into that space between Harlem's bosom, which was made tight and alluring by the powerful red dress she wore. Lots of 'em looked down at that space like they wanted to drown in it: Harlem's and the other Brown Betties', too. When they tried to fly down Honey's dress, she used to "accidentally" step on their shiny shoes or knock into the champagne glasses they sipped from, making them spill all over themselves. She'd follow that move by a seemingly shy, 'Oops!' Tilda started to tear up just thinking of her, not because she was cleverer and prettier than anyone she'd even known, but because she was her big sister, and Tilda was worried terribly about her. She was missing from the house, and didn't nobody know where she was.

Tilda wiped her nose with the shoulder strap of her ratty apron and took a deep breath. She'd had many disappointments in her short, sixteen-year life, but this was a big one and she didn't yet know how to manage it. She'd have to figure it out. But she had to get through this evening first. Tired, she leaned her elbow on the wainscoting. She knew she was small for her age, but her chest now sat just above the paneling that had long been her measure for growth. She was thankful it was exactly at the right height for leaning. She sighed and shifted behind the suffocating curtain. She was getting hot, and her little brown feet were starting to hurt. *Come on, hurry it up,* she thought to herself. She was waiting for the dining room lights to flicker and for the real party to begin. The one that happened downstairs, in the speakeasy below where all these uppity people would sit at round tables with white cloths (that she had to clean) and white candles (that she had to light). It was down there in that gussied up basement with its red curtains and worn in stage where they'd whoop and holler all night long. They'd whistle and shout, *Wooo-weee!* when the Rainbow Girls came out. Tilda agreed that they should shout, really, 'cause the girls would shimmy and shake on the stage as hard as could be and do it with big smiles on their faces. The spotlights would make the itty-bitty beads of sweat on their foreheads glow and the grease on their elbows and knees shine. They deserved every howl.

After that, the four Brown Betties would come out. They were special. They didn't shimmy and shine. They sauntered smoothly and moved like silk. She loved to watch them flow through the crowd, dancing like they were a stream of delicious hot coffee being poured from the finest pot into the finest china. Just like that. Rich and liquidy soft. Her sister, Honey, had been the best Brown Bettie, of course. She knew how to sway just so, and lift her arms to the heavens just so, and step to the rhythmic beat of Joe's bass just so. Sometimes, Tilda would stand at the back of the speakeasy, in the shadows of the candlelight, and she'd move, too. Just so. She liked watching them be beautiful. But eventually their show would end and what happened after that was some kinda ugly that she did not care to watch. The dancing by the Rainbow Girls and the Brown Betties was just the warmup. It was the meat and potatoes before the dessert, so to speak. But the dessert wasn't so sweet.

Things would happen. Things that Tilda didn't want to see. Things that made some of the girls cry and others scream. All the while, Lady Magdalena would stand in the shadows and tally up the money that would come pouring in after everyone did what they did with the girls at her Mysterie parties.

Tilda knew that the new girl wasn't going to feel so new anymore in a very short while. And there was absolutely nothing Tilda could do about it.

CHAPTER 1

Harlem, New York, 1945

arlem lifted her trembling hand, leaned over into the tub, and turned on the faucet. It screeched in protest, but still allowed the water to explode out of it. She reached for the white rubber stopper that hung on a string of tiny metal balls, stuck it down into the drain like as she always did, and plugged it tight. She ran her thin fingers under the cascade of water, waiting for it to get hot. She needed the water hot, or it wouldn't work.

She wasn't sure what all had happened last night, but as she felt the water slide over her outstretched hand, she was sure that one thing had. It was the one thing she had been running from when she left Greensboro.

Harlem stood. She swayed and steadied herself. The room had begun waltzing but had forgotten to tell her it was going to do so. She didn't feel so good; in fact, she could not remember ever feeling (quite?) like this before. The one time she had been sick with influenza had been close, though maybe that time she'd eaten creamed spinach left on the counter to be thrown out was closer.

There was a dryness clinging to her tongue, and her mouth was crying for something to make it stop. She cupped her hands under the faucet and drank some water. It was warmer now, like tea. (She needed it hotter.) Its wetness dribbled down her chin, and she wiped her mouth with the back of her hand. She stared at the smear of red lipstick that was left behind, staining her brown skin. With disgust, Harlem rubbed the reminder of the night onto her thigh, still covered by the red dress she'd worn.

'You're so beautiful,' he'd said.

'Don't I please you?' he'd smiled.

Harlem remembered his lips touching hers. Softly. Her first *real* kiss. Her first kiss as a young woman of eighteen, out in this world, where so many things spoke to her for the first time. Her first real kiss that was implicitly all her own.

His hand had caressed her arm and warmth had danced pleasurably along her smooth, young cheeks and then moved much lower into her body, surprising her.

She had felt so beautiful. As beautiful as he had said. The night had been magical. Everything about the place felt special. She'd been worried, of course, having travelled so far from her home in Greensboro.

The Greyhound bus to New York City had been gritty and dusty, yet in some ways it had been exciting —even amidst the fear she'd felt over leaving home. It was her first time traveling unchaperoned and for such an incredibly long distance. When she'd arrived at Lady Magdalena's Manor she'd been concerned, naturally. It wasn't at all what she'd expected. But what can one expect when one hasn't seen much beyond the walls from where she grew?

Harlem was coming from a grand colonial home nestled off a long dirt road, cradled in the arms of ancient willow trees. Passed down from generations (some good, some not), her family home had two stories and eleven rooms—twelve if one counted the butler's room, which she didn't. That room was more for storage than anything else. From the great room, to the front and back parlors, to the dining room, everything had been redecorated by her mother and was up to the embellished standards of the time, as had been noted quaintly in the women's home section of the *Greensboro Times*. Harlem was used to grandeur. She'd been surrounded by it. Consumed by it. The size of Lady Magdalena's Manor was as though someone had sliced her own home into thirds, covered it in red brick and added a door to it. Harlem found nothing wrong with the size of it; everything she'd seen so far in New York seemed to be sliced and flattened and crammed together in some way. The Manor had its own style. It wouldn't have garnered the Ladies

Auxiliary's hushed tones of award-worthy adulation that her own home had, what with its handmade wallpaper from Paris and intricately woven rugs all the way from Morocco. However, none of that was of Harlem's concern anymore. This place was special because she had a place in it. At home, she'd often felt like a set piece, a small table in a far-off corner of the butler's room that everyone had forgotten to care for.

Here, it was something entirely different.

Here, she was adored, and that made everything exquisite.

She had stood beneath a hanging chandelier with hundreds of glowing, beveled crystal pieces all raining their admiration down on her. And she found herself pleasantly surrounded by the parlor walls, which were papered in a soothing crème color and had the texture of linen. Matching high-backed chairs nestled in the corners as though they were silent, welcoming guests observing her affectionately from the shadows. Other, more ornate rounded chairs, deep with colors of a pulsing heart, lined the walls and kept company with portraits both big and small of dignified-looking people, places, and things. All for her, it seemed. Music and more particularly jazz, which had been new to her, swirled about the room while butlers, precise and prompt, passed champagne in sparkling crystal glasses to groups of handsomely dressed women and men, all much older and paler than herself, with faces that told stories she did not recognize. Being amidst all of this, she had felt as though she'd walked into a marvelous dream from which she didn't want to wake.

The man had stood before her so admiringly. His oddly thin, pink lips. His smooth square chin. Slick black hair. Thick, coarse eyebrows. And piercing dark eyes, smiling at her, possessed with a manly charm. Someone this white had never been this polite to her. Her mother had always said Harlem, New York, was something to be seen, but never had she expected to see anything like this. His gloved hands had offered her a glass full of bubbles; they tickled her nose and fluttered gaily in her mouth each time she touched the glass to her painted lips and sipped.

'You look divine,' he'd said.

It was Lady Magdalena who had insisted Harlem wear the stunning red velvet gown, which his eyes travelled up and down. Nothing in Harlem's suitcase was suitable for this type of party, and both women had agreed as much when they'd gone through the things she'd carefully packed for her big move to New York. Neither her gingham day dress, nor the newly-made shift dress of cotton and white-lace, nor even the several elegant dresses she'd taken from her mother's decadent closet, including a jade-green silk gown she'd selected at the last minute for just such an occasion, were suitable. Her garments were of the finest quality, but not one of them was appropriate for this night.

As she had slid into the dress and stood before the mirror, she felt the garment was an understanding teacher she'd been missing her whole life. It simply asked her to be what she'd always wanted to be: sophisticated. It had instructed her curves to curve, her back to straighten, and her long legs to lengthen. She'd never before worn something that fit so well, leaving no room for dangling question marks or shy uncertainty. It hung on her perfectly so. She ran her fingers along the sweetheart neckline, admiring how her delicate shoulders, bare and alluring, were allowed to sing like spotlit torch singers lamenting lost loves. She glanced further down and smiled that her hips and legs did the rest. She slid her right leg through the peek-a-boo slit that ran up the side of the dress and slipped her hand along her sculpted thigh, divinely chiseled from thousands of *plies* and *grand battements*, and nestled in fine stockings and a lace garter. Both hands smoothed the dress along her hips, and she squealed with delight. 'I have arrived!' she'd said. Harlem had bounced away from the mirror to test just one more thing. The walk. With one kitten-heeled foot in front of the other, she found the rhythm of the dress. Like a pendulum on a clock, she tested how far she could tick and how far she could tock. Feeling like a student who had just received a perfect mark, she clapped with giddy confidence knowing she could most definitely walk in the way this dress demanded. 'My training has paid off,'

Harlem had shared with Lady Magdalena then. For, as girls her age and of her stature were wont to do, she'd spent her formative years in front of a mirror perfecting her ballet technique, learning to move with grace and precision. Lessons with books atop her head had helped too, naturally.

Then, just like a lady, she had lifted the cascading folds at the back of the dress and strolled from the room with Lady Magdalena encouraging her along, her eyes filled with surprised respect and even a touch of captivated awe. As Harlem made her entrance into the party that evening, she'd looked like one of those women you wanted to see. Or to be. And most definitely one you wanted to touch.

'I'll take good care of you, *ma chérie*,' he'd whispered closely in her ear.

Harlem raised her stockinged foot through the slit in the dress to balance on the tub's edge. Her fingers drifted along her leg to tug at her garter's metal clasp and release the hold it had on her stockings, now sagging from having been slept in. She released the first and then the second; then, grasping the sink with her right hand for support, she pulled them from her feet like putrid taffy as she listened to the water rushing into the tub.

She reached for the small hook on the side of the dress, the one Lady Magdalena had been around to help her with earlier. She spun round in a few dizzying circles before she got the hook to let go of itself. The dress, wrinkled and ugly now, fell heavily with a thud to the cold, dingy floor where it laid amongst the hexagonal family of black-and-white checkered tiles, which were too preoccupied with their design to care.

Harlem stepped over the dress and placed both hands upon the cool bathroom sink. She twisted the handle on this faucet, this time desperate for cold water. The waltzing room was swinging at high tempo now, and she could not keep up. She leaned down and drank directly from the tap, the coolness of the water welcoming on her tongue and almost steadying to her twisting stomach. She straightened up and looked at herself in the mirror, wiping the condensation from it. Her pin curls, smooth and well-placed before, were now frizzy and sticking from her head at odd angles. Mascara ran in streaks down her high cheekbones. The red lipstick was nearly everywhere, except on her bow-shaped lips. She looked a fool and felt like one. She turned from her reflection, unable to look at what she'd become: herself.

The tub sounded like it was ready for her. Water no longer echoed in the small bathroom; heat filled the space around her. She removed her rumpled silk underclothes. She laughed at the idea of them meaning to protect her most private parts. They had betrayed her, protected nothing. She unclasped her strapless brassier. It had not supported her. The clothes fell easily from her grasp down to the floor.

She looked at them, a piled heap. Useless. They'd been accomplices to all that had happened the previous night.

Now naked, she wanted to wash away the invisible.

Harlem dipped her toe into the hot water of the bathtub, "Jesus!"

It was too damn hot. But it had to be hot. Otherwise, it wouldn't work. A too-hot bath was her ally to fight the seeping poison that may or may not be inside her; fire against fire to calm the burning between her legs. It was a self-administered baptism. As Harlem immersed herself in the tub, the water stabbed at her flesh like sewing needles to stitch the wounds. Like it was supposed to. Like she'd done before in Greensboro, thanks to Roy, the man who had fathered her only to betray her in the worst way possible. She cried out lifting herself for reprieve from the water's stinging grip. It toppled onto the tile in her haste. She could take it. She had to. She slowly lowered herself back into the cauldron. A fine mist of sweat beads silently emerged from her pores, familiar allies to her anguish.

Harlem closed her eyes tightly and leaned her head back against the rounded lip of the white porcelain tub. This tub was smaller than the one she'd left behind in Greensboro, where her family home and family money had afforded nothing more than a haven for wrongdoing. She'd journeyed to New York only to have fallen into the same hell.

Her temples were pounding, beating like a silent, yet powerful drum. Harlem turned off the steady stream of water with her foot. The faucet dripped. *Plink. Plink. Plank.* Each drip a dare to remember.

When she'd opened her eyes, maybe only an hour before, she'd been confused. She had been in a bed she didn't remember, until she did. She had been in clothes she didn't remember, until she did. She had felt a throbbing pain below, one that she did remember, but didn't know how it got there this time.

Memories.

She wiped clinging tears from her long eyelashes and from her cheekbones with hands that shook.

The coffin box, the one to the left of her heart that held so many bad memories already, creaked opened. Snapshots fluttered out.

Harlem pressed her warm, wet hands tighter to her face.

Her throat tightened.

She remembered it all now.

She felt his fingertips pulling at her, kneading her, moving pieces of her aside as he moved with her but without her.

He'd gone too far.

In the darkness, then and now, she felt his grip on her throat, on her shoulders, her back, her arms, her thighs; she felt him everywhere. Fingers. Exploring. Wanting, taking what wasn't given.

He'd gone too far.

His touch had been different from Roy's. The only touch she knew.

But this one had gone too far.

"No!" she screamed. Her fingers gripped the rim of the tub as she hurled herself forward causing a tidal wave that crashed to the tiled floor below and soaked her underthings.

His name was Arthur. Lady Magdalena had introduced her to him. She had said that Harlem was in good hands and told her to enjoy the party.

Her stomach wretched.

Jumping from the bathtub, she fell clumsily to her knees and caught herself on all fours on the hard tile.

She crawled to the toilet and clung to it. Her stomach twisted again. She waited for the bile to come from her, but nothing came. Until it did. It all kept coming until, depleted, she doubled into a ball on the floor.

"Hello?" she cried out. She felt awful. "Help me. Someone. Please."

Pulling from her scattered memories the name of the one person she thought might help her right now, she gathered her strength and hollered with every bit of her being, "*Tilda!*"

CHAPTER 2

moura woke with a start. She had never slept very well before she had gotten to Magdalena's Manor, and now she slept even worse.

"*Tilda!*" she heard again. It was the new girl, screaming from the next room.

Amoura shifted her legs. She'd fallen asleep on the bedroom floor last night. All four of them had after working the Mysterie party. The wooden floor was hard beneath her, harder than usual, it seemed. That was probably why sometime during the night, Tilda had crawled onto her lap—just trying to find some kind of comfort. Amoura's legs felt like concrete and were full of tingles, but she didn't mind it at all. She'd do anything for Tilda. Amoura looked down at the young girl and touched her tiny shoulder. Tilda was small for a girl her age. She couldn't have been taller than a yardstick on top of a bale of hay, maybe five feet, if the crow were to say so. But the girl was mighty; Tilda took care of the Manor and everyone in it, whether she wanted to or not. Never in her own twenty-odd years had Amoura met someone so strong.

She hated to wake her; they'd only just closed their eyes. Still, Amoura shook her gently. Tilda looked up and raised her eyebrows in response.

Amoura whispered, "The girl. She's callin' for you."

Tilda stood slowly, adjusting her cotton frock, rubbing the sleep from her eyes. Amoura yawned. "Hurry back, Tilda. You look like I feel. Need to get some rest while we can, sugar." Amoura laid her head back against the wall she was propped up against and wrapped herself in the only thing in the room that resembled a blanket. It had been the topic of their conversation last night: Honey's flowered dress. Ripped down the middle like it was nothing.

Tilda tiptoed around the other two sleeping women, Fury and Desire, who were curled like kittens on the wooden floor. Things were very bad, and they had gathered just the four of them to have an emergency Brown Betties meeting; this time in Amoura's bedroom. They had all talked long into the night, asking Tilda over and over again what happened. She'd say the same thing, that Magdalena had sold off Honey, and off she went with Otto pointing a knife in Honey's back so she wouldn't run. He'd walked her down the stairs, and right in front of Ruth and Mary and the new girl too. She'd explain how scared Honey looked, though strong and brave at the same time. Then each of the girls would get quiet, trying to picture what Tilda saw and wondering what had happened to Honey. Wondering if she was dead or alive. Speculating what might happen to them too—if they'd end up the same. Too many questions had wrung them dry of what usually kept them going. They'd given in. There was a cot in the room, but neither had taken it. It wasn't very comfortable anyway. Sleep had simply taken them as and where they were.

Tilda quietly pulled the skeleton keys from her pocket, unlocked the door, and slipped into the hallway. As she relocked the door, she listened in the darkness. Nothing. To get the tired out of her, Tilda shook herself like the rags on a mop and trudged two paces toward the special bedroom where the girl was kept. She leaned her ear against the door and heard light whimpering, like a little dog. She knew that sound all too well. The girl was coming back to normal from the sleepy-time drugs the man had given her last night. It was time for more special tea. It was the only way to make the girls feel better at first, and Magdalena also wanted it that way.

Tilda marched slowly yet dutifully down the large staircase, her bare feet feeling the chill of the wooden stairs. Even though she knew there were nineteen stairs, and knew which ones curved here and got skinnier there and had a creaky dip in the center, she held onto the banister. There was no need to fall and break her neck. She wasn't going out like that.

Reaching the bottom, Tilda glanced toward the door of her own tiny room, tucked under those stairs. She stuck her tongue out at it. It was too small, and it was an insult, quite frankly. A broom closet. Everybody else important got a room. Wasn't she important? She'd been there her whole life, almost. Tilda huffed in disgust at it all and then wondered if she'd get Honey's old room, now that she was gone. Magdalena would do something mean like that: make Tilda sleep in that room, knowing she'd be missing Honey, and cause her to feel bad about something good, like having some space and a real bed.

Tilda walked seven more steps through the foyer and reached the heavy curtains that hid the sliding pocket doors to the main room. She pulled the curtains aside and snuck into their folds. She liked to hide in this space sometimes, like so many others in the Manor. With the curtains hanging around her like this, she felt safe, protected from all the bad stuff that went on, as though she were playing hide-and-go-seek with it all. She unlocked the pocket doors that disappeared into the walls when you wanted them to and then re-locked them behind her. She was an expert at that. She'd done it many times for many reasons, fast and slow.

As she made her way through the dark dining room, her foot squished on something. She flung it aside with her toe. *Prob'ly a piece of ham,* she thought as she quickly wiped her foot of the slime. She was so hungry, she wondered if she shouldn't pick it up and eat it. But she thought better of it. Who knew if some stupid party person from last night chewed on it first and spit it out? Even though those people were all dressed up, high and mighty, she'd seen them do nasty stuff like that. *Silly, nasty people,* she thought. In the morning, which she figured was probably only about three or four hours from now, she'd have to clean up after them. She'd also have to get the big dining-room table pieces from Magdalena's office, fit them all back together, and put the room back as it should be again in time for breakfast. It was a chore she hated, but she didn't get much choice in the matter no how.

Tilda turned on the light in the kitchen and slipped into the faded apron that waited for her by the door. Besides her room under the stairs, this room was hers, too, but this one didn't bother her as much. Plus, Magdalena hardly ever stepped into it unless she was barkin' at Tilda to do something, like to get the tea. Tilda had gotten tea enough times for the girls when they reached their achy time that she didn't need old Magdalena to bark at her to get it. She just went and made it. Like now. Tilda filled the tea kettle with water from the faucet, struck a match, and lit the stove. She yawned as she stood on tiptoe to reach into the white cupboard for the canister with its fading scarlet stripe, which contained the homemade concoction of tea that had a little bit of this and a little bit of that, with some of it bein' a little bad. Like arsenic. Tilda pulled herself up onto the counter and sat perched, legs dangling, while she waited for the water to boil. Her body ached with want of sleep. She leaned her head back against the cupboard and, to keep herself from drifting off, she ran her finger along the red of the diamond pattern inlaid in the old tile on the counter. The color reminded her of the treasure hiding in her pocket. Tilda glanced at the tea kettle. She had a little time before its whistle got loud.

She reached into her little pocket and pulled out the lipstick tube. It belonged to the achy girl upstairs. Tilda looked at the bottom of it and the words there said, "Iced Ruby Red." She'd already read it at least ten times since yesterday, but she liked practicing and making sure the words were still there. Just like what was inside. Tilda pulled apart the lipstick which made a little pop sound. Inside the tube wasn't any ruby red lipstick. What was inside was green. Something prettier. It was a roll of money squeezed real tight into the tube.

Tilda was still afraid to tug at it. The time hadn't come for tuggin'. She needed someplace to hide it if it all came tumbling out, and she didn't have any real place outside of her pockets to keep anything safe. Besides, nobody knew about this treasure, and she had to come up with a plan for what to do with it. On her own. As she held the tube, she felt her cheeks stretching over her face; this was something they didn't normally do too much. She figured it was a smile. Tilda positioned the tube between her little brown fingers and rubbed the paper money against her bottom lip and then dabbed it on her top lip, just like she'd seen Magdalena do hundreds of times.

"I must look real good," she giggled to herself. "Real good."

For maybe the first time in her young life, she was happy she had a voice that didn't work; she didn't have to worry about letting her secret slip out. Tilda returned the treasure to her pocket, slipped down from the counter, and grabbed the kettle before it started yellin' at her.

Then Tilda made the tea, turned off the kitchen light, retraced her steps all the way up to the top of the stairs, and unlocked the girl's bedroom door.

CHAPTER 3

Greensboro, North Carolina, 1939

Late-morning sun filtered through a stained-glass window nestled above an expansive bookcase in the sitting room. The bookcase ran the length of the back wall and was filled with sixty-four leather-bound books (she had counted them *all*). The books had been there for as long as Harlem could remember. Most of them had belonged to her grandparents and had been handed down, along with this house, to Harlem's mother, Susannah. Harlem loved the books, but not as much as she loved this room. It was smaller than their other great rooms, and felt tucked away from everything, like a secret. With walls covered in a paper of twisting green vines and soft white floppy flowers with little red tips— dogwood, she'd recently learned from a book in this very room—this place was special. There was one small round table in the room with two high-backed chairs. One for her and one for her mother. A chandelier hung from the ceiling and sometimes

Harlem felt like it was a princess, sparkling and delightful upon her throne. Dark green curtains snuggled against the windows, and a gigantic matching carpet sat on the wooden floor, comforting them from below.

Harlem was lounging there in the sitting room with her mother. They'd had their breakfast, and now, as they often did on a Saturday, they gathered in this room to read, just the two of them. Her mother was half-way through yesterday's *Greensboro Gazette*. A few feet away, Harlem lay on the carpeted floor with her children's book, *The Five Little Peppers and How They Grew*. It was a favorite of her mother's and sometimes she herself found the story about the five little children amusing. But today it was boring her. She rolled onto her back and stared up at the stained-glass window. It was shaped like half of the full moon and warmed the room with its purples, blues, and greens.

She rose from where she lay on the carpeted floor with her book. Slipping off her shoes and with the same expertise of a circus tightrope walker, Harlem tip-toed along a hazy beam of purple-colored sunlight. She stopped to twirl once, and again, and again. On the third twirl, she hopped off the beam and while holding the edges of her dotted orange and white cotton dress and bowed as though she were center stage with a full, grand audience.

"Harlem, dear. Do be careful. We wouldn't want you to twist an ankle, or worse," Susannah said as she licked her finger and turned the page of the newspaper.

"Yes, Momma," Harlem said lightly. She looked for something else to play upon. Something that would call upon greater ability. She smiled and ran toward the large picture window before her and bounded up onto the sturdy window seat, made plush with colorful beaded silk pillows. She crouched upon it like a frog, ready to jump back onto the floor.

"Harlem! Is that any way for a girl your age to be sitting? Stop that, please!" Susannah pleaded.

"Oh, you're no fun." Harlem plopped her bottom on the seat, leaned her forehead on the pane and peered out at the acres upon acres of their property. Willow trees dotted the lawn, blocking her view in some places. But, for the most part, she could see what she wanted—the big old main road. It ran parallel to their property, and she often felt it to have a life of its own. To her, it was like the palm of God's hand, just open, waiting, and willing for the next car, or bicycle, or sometimes the old neighbor on his horse to go somewhere on it.

Harlem often wanted to get on that road—to step into its life and out of her own. She hugged her knees to her chest, pulling the dress hem to her bare ankles. One day, she would. Sometimes, when George, their driver, had to run errands, he'd take her along for the car ride into town. The car would roll under the willow trees and down the dirt road out of the property, and as soon as they'd hit that big old main road, she'd always squeal, 'Turn right, George, *turn right!*' from the back seat. 'Let's have an adventure!' But George, in his old age and dutiful manner, would tip his hat with his wrinkly fingers and say, 'Got thangs t'do, Miss. Ain't got no time for 'venture, t'day. Maybe t'morrow, Miss. Maybe t'morrow.'

Somehow, it felt like tomorrow couldn't come fast enough. Especially lately.

Harlem turned from the window. "Momma?"

Susannah sighed, "Yes, Harlem, what is it?"

"When do you think I'll be able to go off to school like the other girls?"

Susannah put down her morning paper and folded it carefully. The sound of her soft fingers creasing the crisp paper filled the tiny room. Always the type of woman who thought before she answered, she rose tall from her seat. She'd worn blue today, one of her favorite colors. She tightened the belt at her thin waist and straightened the cuffs of the sleeves before arranging her cut flowers which rested in a vase at the center of the table.

Moving the bright yellow flowers about, Susannah said, "We'll talk about it."

"Momma, I'm almost thirteen now. You said that the last time," Harlem whined.

"Don't you like working with Miss Annette? She teaches you everything you need to know. And, more than that," Susannah said, wiping her hands along the folds of her patterned skirt, "your father and I have done so much to make it comfortable for her to come to you to get your lessons. I thought you enjoyed Miss Annette."

"Oh, she's fine, Momma. You know that she is, it's just that I want to go out there," she pointed through the window. "Out there. Away."

Susannah looked to Harlem, smoothing the loose hairs below her French-rolled hair. "This is the third time this month that you've asked me about getting away, and going out there, Harlem. Why do you want so badly to get away?"

"I just do," Harlem said, shifting in her seat.

Susannah sat down beside her, crossing her long legs at the knee. Harlem could smell the soft scent of her specially-made perfume. "I'm worried, Harlem. I'm worried about what's out there. People are doing all kinds of things these days that are just... unpredictable. I wouldn't want anything bad to happen to you."

Harlem twisted the thin, gold bracelet that dangled from her tiny wrist. "Momma, bad things happen inside the house, too—you don't have to go out there for bad things to happen."

Susannah paused, "Do they?"

Harlem avoided her gaze. "Couldn't I please go to a boarding school somewhere? Somewhere far from here, and you could come visit me on the weekends or the holidays? Wouldn't that be nice, Momma?"

"You would prefer to be away from me, Harlem? That's what you want?"

Something shifted in her mother's pale grey eyes.

"No, not really. Not you, Momma."

"Then why would you want to leave?"

Harlem looked up at the only woman she had known to love her so. She had no siblings like the five little Peppers children had. What's more, her mother had been an only child, just like she was. As a result, there were no aunts to look up to, no cousins to lay about with and discuss important things. She was alone. Harlem stared into her mother's eyes. They were deep and filled with a kindness toward her, but they also held something Harlem couldn't name. Her mother had been distant lately. Quiet. As quiet as the grey strands that peeked in and out of her momma's sandy-brown, straight hair.

Harlem reached for her mother's hand and pressed it against her own cheek, the two shades of brown mushing together. Harlem's heart began to race. "It's—just that. It's just that, sometimes—"

Susannah grabbed Harlem's trembling hand, "Sometimes what, darling?"

The door handle jiggled, making them both jump. From outside the heavy wooden door, Roy, her father, banged upon it and bellowed, "What the hell you two doin' in there?"

"Roy?" Susannah rose quickly toward the door. She tried to open it, tugging at it. "The door's locked —"

Harlem slowly reached inside the pocket of her dress. With fingers that shook more than she wanted them to, she withdrew the skeleton key to the door. "Here. Here it is."

Susannah, tall and thin, strong like the willow trees, turned and stared at Harlem. "Why would you lock the door, darling?"

Harlem shook her head. She shook it, and shook it, and shook it some more, her two long braids whipping her at the sides of her face. Driving her head to her knees, she covered it with her arms. She sobbed, "Keep him away, please! Keep him away!"

Roy continued to pound on the door. "Hey, let me in! Hey now—!"

"Harlem?" Susannah whispered, "*What's happened?*"

CHAPTER 4

Tilda opened the door and turned on the light. Her eyes nearly popped out of her head when she saw the girl, lying naked on the floor halfway between the bathroom and the bedroom.

Sweet Jesus! Tilda thought as she rushed forward, spilling a bit of the tea she'd forgotten she was holding. She turned and placed the teacup on the wooden spindle chair next to the bed and rushed to the girl.

Tilda had seen dead fish and dead chickens—food she'd had to cut up and cook—but she'd never seen a dead girl. She hoped she wasn't lookin' at one right now. Tilda touched the girl's neck with her pointer finger to see if the blood was still moving in her veins.

Thank you, Lord! Tilda exhaled. She kneeled down to the wood floor and smoothed the damp hair off Harlem's face. The skin was smooth and rich, like gravy when it turned out right. Still, Tilda couldn't decide if she should be mad at this girl or not for being the reason Magdalena sold Honey off to that awful Otto. What usually happened when a new girl came in was that an old girl had to leave. But the old girl who had to leave wasn't supposed to be family. It wasn't supposed to be her sister. Not Honey. Not the one who looked after her, who let her cry in her arms when she needed to, and who loved her for no reason other than that she could. *Not* Honey. And here was this girl lying on the floor, who hadn't really done nothin' but had done so much just by showing up.

Tilda shook her head. She had some figuring out to do, but all that would have to wait now. She looked at the girl again.

Even though there was a lot missing from her life, sometimes Tilda felt like she had some kinda funny blessings. One of 'em was seeing people the way they didn't always want to be seen. Tilda knew Magdalena was a spider backed into a corner with a big old broom waving in her face, in danger of being squashed at a moment's notice. Tilda knew Ruth and Mary were a pair of rats, stuck in a trap but still alive, with tails wigglin' like crazy, just out of reach of the piece of cheese that got them there.

I see you, Tilda thought as she smoothed Harlem's soft eyebrows, *I see you're just like me. Different.*

Harlem's eyelids fluttered. "My stomach," she moaned.

Tilda reached for the tea. Bringing the warmth to the girl's lips, Tilda admired her long eyelashes and a few freckles she hadn't noticed before. The girl sure was pretty.

Harlem sipped the tea and moaned. Tilda knew the tea was a touch of poison; it had caused the achy head and the stomach crampin' that had made all the other girls before her cry out, too. But when they drank more of it, all the suffering went away. It helped them in the beginning. The tea made them sickly enough to stall them on trying to get back to where they came from. It made it easier to hold them here, where they were kept. Tilda felt like she was helping; that she was doing some good. For a little while, anyway.

With closed eyes, Harlem drank some more of the stuff. The rest dribbled down her chin. Tilda stretched and reached for Harlem's clothes, which were still lying crumpled on the floor. They were damp. She didn't know with what, but she thought it was probably okay to wipe the mess from Harlem's chin with them. The girl calmed down. She'd be fine.

Tilda looked down at the naked girl out of curiosity. Then she looked down her own frock at the little brown mounds that were covered there. *Nothin' alike*, she thought. She was already sixteen; what if this was it? What if God was goin' to keep her whole body small and she'd never amount to anything like this girl or like the other girls in the Manor?

Tilda took another peek. She shrugged, *Don't matter no way. This face I got probably isn't goin' to change either. Even with paint.*

Tilda sighed. Heavy silence fell on her shoulders like Magdalena's massive fur coat that she'd tried on once and regretted immediately. She let the quiet shush the thoughts in her head. She was too worn out to do it herself. It was in this quiet that she heard the bathtub faucet drip into the tub. She knew the tub was full by the way the water landed with a full *plop* instead of an empty *ting*. That was one more thing she was going to have to tend to.

The girl started to snore. This was what Tilda was waiting for. She moved the cup aside, got to her feet, and squatted low behind Harlem's head and her smooth shoulders. She hooked her arms under the girl's pits (like she'd had to do many times before with the others) and gently slid the girl toward the bed. Harlem's body left a faintly glistening trail of water across the floor behind her. Tilda heaved as she crawled up onto the bed and pulled Harlem with her, getting the girl's top half up there in a floppy pile. She jumped back down to the floor, grabbed the girl's legs, and lifted them one by one up with the rest of her. Doing this kind of stuff made her appreciate the practice she got by hauling sacks of flour once a month.

Tilda straightened Harlem into a less-dead looking position and covered her with the thin blanket on the thin mattress. This bed was nicer than the cot in the room next door where she'd left Amoura, Fury, and Desire. It was supposed to be nicer for the new girl.

That way, when she came into the room for the first time she didn't suspect nothin'.

Reaching under the bed, Tilda found her "Fixer." She pulled the long pole out from its hiding place. Attached to the end of it was a Clabber Girl baking powder tin. Tilda moved a wooden chair in the center of the room, climbed on, and raised her contraption up to the exposed light bulb. She positioned the baking powder tin just around the bulb and turned slowly. She had made the Fixer herself and had spent a lot of time doctoring the insides with cloth and putting melted rubber bands around the edges 'til she got it right. She was too short to reach most of the bulbs in the Manor, and she'd gotten real tired of Magdalena tellin' her to figure something out when it was time to change them or take them out. So now she had the Fixer. The light bulb turned and fell square into her apron. She put it in her pocket. She'd broken many bulbs before, but she'd gotten pretty good at using it by now.

With the glow from the bathroom light to guide her, Tilda returned her Fixer to its secret hiding place under the bed. She quietly put the chair back next to the bed and placed the tea on the seat so Harlem would drink the rest of it when she next woke up. Tilda would keep feeding the girl the tea all week. Soon enough the girl wouldn't know what day it was or care where she'd come from. Magdalena liked it that way. She then quietly unscrewed the lightbulb from the floor lamp next to the bed and rushed back into the bathroom. She wanted to join the other girls and get back to sleep while she still had time.

Tilda pulled her sleeve back and plunged her arm into the bath water to take out the plug. The water was still warm. Warm as a flapjack with butter floating on it. Warm as the special tea. But something in the water surprised her. She pulled her arm out and left the plug exactly where it was. She kneeled next to the tub, leaned into it, and gently scooped the warm water into her hands. The water dripped through her fingers and sounded like music as it chorused back into the full tub. Tilda scooped again, rejoicing in the song. The girl must have made it sing.

See, I knew she was different. Just like me.

Tilda leaned forward and saw her reflection floating rhythmically. She scooped that up too and splashed her real face with her reflective one. It felt so good. Her skin felt so good. She cupped her hands to her face again, feeling Harlem's princess face mingling with her own once more. She felt her cheeks pulling tight again. She was smiling but wasn't sure why.

Tilda felt the questions in her head melt into music. She splashed more water onto her face. And then a little more. She dabbed some on her wrists like perfume. And before she could think, or tell herself not to, Tilda removed her apron and her dress with its torn hem and ant holes under the armpits. She wiggled out of her threadbare slip and out of her underpants that had both been stolen from a new girl's suitcase, just like everything else she wore.

Tilda took off all these things that didn't belong to her and stood in the skin that did. She climbed over the tub, her toes and knees and fingers and elbows happy to be in the water. She sunk her bottom to the floor of the tub, bent forward, and scooped the water onto her narrow shoulders and over her head, which was crowned with two plaits Honey had braided for her. The water fell down around her, and it was a delightful symphony of sound. She knew the source had to be the girl who had bathed here before, but this time she didn't care about secondhand. Somehow, Tilda knew that the pretty of that girl reverberated in this water, and that it would seep into her insides and she would become like her. That her parts would grow, that her nose would shift up a smidge to the right, and her lips would plump and settle a little to the left, and her eyes would brighten and glow like candle flames. She'd grow elegant, and she'd walk long and tall and floaty. Tilda straightened her knobby knees and before she knew it, she was under the water. Tilda swore that, from here, she could hear her own voice sing.

CHAPTER 5

agdalena rolled over in her bed. She was caught up in a layer of pillows that had gotten tangled underneath her thick satin blankets. She fought with them to find air. The night had gone late and was not all that chic toward the end, and now she was paying for it. She jutted forward in her bed, blinded by her inky black hair.

The body next to her moaned in protest.

Magdalena pulled her hair aside and blinked, her eyelids heavy, her brain slow to grasp that she was not alone; the ghastly amount of champagne she'd had the previous night was making her thoughts thick. She used her hands to steady her head as she looked at her companion. A hairy arm plopped greedily onto her lap.

"You have to leave," Magdalena said as she moved the arm aside. "Tilda will see you."

The large form in her bed shifted. "What d'I care Tilda sees me in here? Ain't you's the boss?"

"Yes, I'm the boss. So move it!" Magdalena leaned over and turned on the small bedside lamp, nearly knocking over the fringed, pea-green shade in the process. Maybe she needed more sleep. Or maybe it was this room, which was never intended to be a bedroom in the first place. It was too damn dark. There were four small windows on the wall above the bed, but even at the height of day there was never enough light. At this hour, which she was certain was just after dawn, the lazy pinks and purples of the new day weren't ready to do any lighting work.

Magdalena retreated from the bed, rescued her pink robe from the floor and tightened it against her bare body as she moved to the sink to splash some water on her face.

"Her room" had been her father's smoking lounge and private library, just off his office. Over the years, as things ebbed and flowed in the Manor, Magdalena had made it hers. She'd had a Murphy bed installed—which turned out to be big enough for two, even three on occasion—and a sink. Nevertheless, the tiny room had the regular accoutrements of a woman's boudoir; her petite vanity of mahogany and brass sat off the foot of the bed. Its mirror stood just tall enough for her to not be able to see herself while in the midst of lovemaking or otherwise. Its surface was filled with perfumes, some gifted, some lifted, and one or two purchased. The room held a floral scent that she knew to be a mix of jasmine, ylang ylang, and vanilla. The matching armoire was spared any witness of what happened in this room and lived in her office behind the desk. There wasn't room for it anyway.

The walls had been stripped of the grey and white pinstriped wallpaper she knew her mother had chosen for the room and re-painted a simple, egg-shell white. Aside from an oval portrait of either a stranger or perhaps a great, great grandmother near the sink, the only other art adorning the walls consisted of three gilded-framed paintings of vased magnolias, lilies, and peonies, which she'd found curbside alongside the two claw-footed bedside tables that flanked the bed. The matching green lamps that sat upon them had actually been purchased, chosen to match the floral greens in the paintings and, more importantly, her eyes. Her bedsheets were of the same color, for the same reasons.

Magdalena dried her face and strode toward the vanity for her cigarettes. "Get up, now."

Officer Brighton mumbled something Magdalena couldn't and didn't want to hear.

He rose from the sea of green covers and searched for his monkey suit. "You don't have to treat me like the hired help, you know," he said, retrieving his tuxedo trousers from under the bed.

"But you are, my dear." Magdalena lit a cigarette and exhaled. She glared at his slow-moving ass through the mirror. The smoke drifted into her cold green eyes. Razors had begun to cut through her head.

"Yeah, well," he scowled, "If you know what's good for ya, you'd better make a change in that department. Plus, I got feelin's too, you know."

"We are not in the business of feelings, Brighton," Magdalena snapped. "Ought'nt you put on your uniform rather than your tuxedo from last night?"

"Why'nt you remind me 'o that before I started puttin' my pants on? Geesh!"

"I'm not your mother, dear."

"You bettah not be!" He laughed as he walked around the bed toward his hanging uniform, smacking her hard on the bottom as he passed.

Magdalena whipped 'round to face him and grabbed her bottom. "*Oh!* Do that again and I'll knock your lights out, Brighton!"

He leaned into her, whispering into her neck, "But then who would you have to keep y' company?" He motioned for her to share her cigarette; she obliged, and he took a long drag, smiling at her with a pair of blue eyes that danced with a smirk.

She rubbed her achy knees, which were stinging more than her bottom. Her weary body was fighting her, resisting her like the pumps of a well. She took her cigarette back.

"Y' sore? Thought you liked bein' with a younger man. Maybe next time I should go easier on you," Officer Brighton laughed while he exchanged his tuxedo with his officer's uniform, which was dangling from a hanger on the butler stand near the bedroom door.

"You wish," Magdalena laughed and kicked up the Murphy bed, pushing it back into its hiding place and leaning against it. She drew hard on the cigarette. The tip of it glowed hot like her growing anger. Ashes dropped to the floor, just at the hem of her robe. She rubbed them into the carpet with her big toe. She watched him button his jacket with pink, meaty fingers and rolled her eyes, waiting.

"And hey there, Missy," he said, cramming his huge feet into his shoes. "Make sure yous bring me a cup o' coffee this time. I get thirsty out on that stoop guarding this place."

"Of course," she mumbled.

He came to her, kissed her roughly on the cheek, and sniffed like a bulldog as he left the room.

She called after him, "Brighton, I've a favor to ask."

"Another one?" He began to unfasten his pants.

"No, you dolt. I want you to keep your ears open for any sightings of Honey," Magdalena said, crossing her arms. "Otto is a slimebag, that much is certain, and I—"

"What, you gettin' a conscientious all a' sudden?"

"No, it's just that—"

"Whatd'you care? You got your money. 'Dis here is bus'ness. Just like yous always says. Who gives a flyin' fuck about that whore?"

"Watch your goddamned mouth," Magdalena rattled off before she could catch herself.

"Watch my mout' about what? 'Dis is a business, and she is a whore...?"

"The Brown Betties aren't whores."

"Just because she has a fancier title than the rest of the working girls you have, don't mean she ain't a whore."

"You know damn well the Brown Betties don't engage with my clientele in the way that the Rainbow Girls do—oh, never mind. Get out of here. Just get out."

"You're so touchy lately. 'Dis is why broads is only good for one thing."

"I could say the same about you. Barely."

"Now you watch *your* mout'!"

Brighton stormed off, muttering to himself as Magdalena turned her back to him. "Laces...?" she taunted as he left. He had not thought to tie his shoes. She rolled her eyes as she heard him trip over something in her office. He was making her head hurt even more.

"Y' really should clean up in here. It's dang'rous!" he called out.

Magdalena placed her cigarette in a round amber ashtray on her vanity and sat down on the cushioned bench with its faded satin, a reminder that more in this room than just her was getting older. She yanked a brush through her hair, her hand shaking with anger. "I'll be sure to do that, Officer!" she saluted the mirror with her brush. "And the word is *conscience!*" she yelled out after him.

"Shit. Shit. Shit," she whispered as her head fell forward into her arms. He was right. This was a business. She'd made a business decision to get rid of Honey. She knew better than anyone that sometimes hard decisions needed to be made in order to survive. This was one of those times.

She stared at her reflection. A fractured woman stared back at her. She was a rag doll sewn together with bits and pieces of her parents. Her father's green eyes sewn onto her mother's round nose, patched with her father's high cheekbones. Her mother's full lips sat above a chin that came from some other ancestor. Her skin was as pale as her father's had been. To those who didn't know, she was white. To those who did, she was as black as her mother had been brown. Colored. For those who knew how to look, especially black folks, she was black. She didn't fool those kinds of folks with their internal barometers for measuring the widths of noses and plumpness of pouts. But for the people she dealt with, those she did business with, she was one of them. White. She'd been playing this game of hide-and-seek for quite some time. Only lately she suspected that people had begun to talk, which meant she had another problem. A certain somebody, who had another game going in town, wanted to take her down. And to do so, the only ammunition that certain someone had was to shine a light on Magdalena and bring her ass out of the dark. She'd been paying to shut them up, but she'd been late a few times, thanks to business being down. And why was it down? Because they must have been out in the streets spreading rumors and making people suspicious of her. To thwart their suspicion, she'd been forced to get rid of the suggestive evidence: Honey.

Many didn't know Honey was her sister, and rightly so, because her skin was not as pale as Magdalena's. Hers had been touched by the sun or kissed longer by their mother. Whatever happened, Honey was brown and looked black. Colored. She had to go. Sold, like any other girl Magdalena owned.

For that, Magdalena had brokered a deal with Otto. They'd had many transactions over the years; while he was her least favorite customer, she knew he was the best one for Honey. Honey would, of course, fight off the big dodo because that's what she'd been taught to do. Magdalena knew the girl could escape, but with no money or resources of her own, she wasn't sure what her sister would do once she was free. Magdalena was ruthless, sometimes even heartless, but the girl was still family and not knowing her exact whereabouts was a new problem.

Maybe she had gotten conscientious.

She looked away from herself. She didn't particularly like what she saw in that vanity mirror;

but of course, this wasn't a novel thing. She exhaled heavily and attempted to blow out these thoughts and return to her present. Brighton.

"It's time for that jackass to go too!" she yelled aloud. Magdalena had had many lovers, some of whom hadn't been particularly loving, but they'd been experiences, nonetheless. Officer Brighton fell into the category of a "necessary experience." He satiated her physically, and she didn't believe in starving. He was also necessary because he guarded the Manor; he worked on keeping the girls in rather than keeping any burglars out. He'd been a repeat customer to her Lady M's Mysterie parties, along with other officers on the force. After a year or so, he'd started asking for a kickback to keep her operation secure. When business was good, she could afford to grease his palms, but lately, the grease was thin. This new, mutually beneficial security arrangement decreased the strain on her wallet, but it had also depleted her nerves, and he was getting on her every last remaining one.

"That's it!" she muttered, banging her fists on the dressing table. She'd had enough of him. Enough of lots of things. She told herself she could only handle one problem at a time. He would be the first, and she'd work her way back to the rest of the waiting pile.

Magdalena picked up her gold watch from the vanity and clasped it to her wrist. It was nearing seven o'clock in the morning. She finished her cigarette in three demanding drags, hoping to quiet the unruly tantrum that had started in her head, and then mashed the cigarette into a tiny, crinkled butt until her fingers turned white.

Magdalena rose and entered her office, blowing out a last billow of tobacco smoke. This room was dark as well, but rightly so; where there had been windows along the back wall, she'd boarded them up so that the girls couldn't get out without notice. Reaching across her massive, cluttered desk, she pulled the chain on the brushed metal art deco lamp; it had been a favorite of her father's, purchased in '31 before things in their home had gone entirely south. Warmth spilled from it, even though the room was not deserving of the kindness. Only yesterday it had shrouded Otto as he crudely cleaned his dirty fingernails with a pocketknife while Honey had stood tall and trembling behind him.

"Tilda!" she shouted and then regretted it. She held her temples with her fingertips and waited for the pain to subside. *Where is she!?* she thought. Magdalena didn't care how early it was. She was awake, so everyone else should be. There were important things to be done today. She walked toward the back of her office, just off the side of her armoire, and pulled the night covering from her birdcage. The parrot inside, simply named "Bird," was nestled awkwardly at the bottom. "Wake up, Bird."

She turned and faced the room, hands upon her hips. Piled high in her path were the disassembled pieces of her colossal dining-room table.

For the price of another "experience," Magdalena had convinced a carpenter friend to make a table that could be assembled and disassembled. The dining room with its dark wainscoting and built-in buffet could transform easily into a receiving room for parties. It would do so again on Saturday, when the Brown Betties in their red dresses and her courtesan Rainbow Girls would offer a good time to the highest bidder.

Magdalena crawled over the jigsaw of table pieces in her office. She walked through the shadowed dining room (currently a carcass left behind by partygoers no more polite than buzzards) and entered the dark kitchen, her robe flowing behind her. As she filled a glass with water from the faucet, she noticed the tea fixings.

"Good. Exactly on schedule," she said, swallowing the water and hoping it would drown the hammering in her head. After refilling her glass, she returned to her office. It was time to get back to business. The new girl.

Magdalena wiped the moisture from the bottom of the glass with her robe before setting it on her grand desk. She scanned the room for the new girl's treasures.

She smiled as she retrieved Harlem's things from under her desk, where Tilda must have hidden them. Harlem's purse was Magdalena's primary interest because her gift was inside it. She pushed her hair behind her ears. Excitement pulsed through her chest. Her breasts heaved beneath her thin robe. She'd touched the gift before, had held it in her hands yesterday, after everything had gone to shit, but she hadn't had the time to truly enjoy its presence. She'd been waiting for this.

Magdalena turned the purse around to open it and was momentarily startled. A smear of Ruth's dried blood on the blue and white leather of the purse caught her eye.

"Disgusting piece of trash," Magdalena dabbed a corner of her robe to her tongue and wiped the distasteful evidence away. "That'll teach her to try and steal from me." Magdalena huffed as she hastily forced the pearl clasp open on Harlem's purse. Shooting Ruth in the hand yesterday was not something Magdalena had necessarily intended. She hated violence, but over the years, she had learned that violence was often the only thing to which some people would respond. Yet, with Ruth and her sister Mary out of the picture, she wasn't sure how she would obtain any new girls. The three of them had been working together for over a decade. Despite this recent ugliness, they'd truly had a good thing going.

"Fifty thousand dollars!?" Magdalena stomped her feet and screamed as she stared at the check. *Was it real?* How could a girl like that have a check like this? She turned it over in her hands, raised it to the light to make sure it looked normal. She smelled it. Wanted to lick it. Magdalena had heard of Negroes having money, even lots of it, but she hadn't actually come across one who did. She'd heard some of them were bankers and some had invented gadgets and creams and so on that brought them incredible wealth, but, just like finding a four-leaf clover, it seemed too unlikely to be true. Yet here she was holding proof of it all.

Magdalena stood and paced. This was going to change everything for her. She screamed again; the elation reverberating through her body felt better than any excitement she'd ever felt with any man. "*Got tsu danken!*" she exclaimed in her father's language, kissing her self-claimed gift. She smiled broadly, "Thank you, God!"

She had to think. Cashing it would take some doing, but that would come. She ran her fingers through her hair, stopping to twist the ends of it between her fingers. For starters, Ruth and Mary wouldn't matter so much after all, would they? And neither would Officer Brighton. Neither would a lot of things.

"Til—!" Magdalena yelled as she gathered herself. The young girl had appeared in the doorway like an apparition. "Can't you knock or something? You're incredibly sneaky, Tilda, and I don't like it." Magdalena discreetly slid the check under the blotter. "Oh, for heaven's sake. Stop looking so sheepish and pick your head up. It's entirely too early. Whatever you have or haven't done, I frankly don't care. I do care that I have a headache and that this place is a disaster. Now let's get a move on. I have a lot to do today."

Tilda lifted three light bulbs to her questioningly.

"What do you want me to do with them, Tilda? Stick them where the sun doesn't shine? Would you kindly put them in the corner somewhere?" Magdalena shook her head as she sat at her desk. "I'm surrounded by imbeciles who can't think for themselves! How hard is it to think?"

The girl turned and put the light bulbs in a corner by the door.

"Why is the back of your dress all wet?" Magdalena asked.

Tilda spun round and shook her head quickly with shoulders hunched.

"Why I bother asking a mute a question is beyond me. Never mind, Tilda. Just never mind," Magdalena sighed. "Clean this place up." Magdalena hoisted Harlem's suitcase to her lap. Yesterday, she'd been able to look through it briefly. She'd discovered the small bottle of sage and lilac perfume, a silver-framed photo of a woman—likely the owner of the perfume—

and a journal. Magdalena opened the suitcase hastily, eager to look through it again to see what other sort of incredibly fantastic surprises might be held within.

Could there be more money hidden here? she thought excitedly. Magdalena fingered through some silk underthings and hand-made tailored dresses of the best cotton, wool, and linen. She lifted a strand of pearls. Magdalena wrapped them around her neck. Then she pulled out the journal bound in white leather and edged with pink satin. The bottom corner was monogrammed with *SM.*

"Now we're talkin'. Alright Miss Harlem Winnepega Markeson. Who art thou? *Who art thou?*" Hungrily, Magdalena opened the journal to the middle and read:

24, July 1939

> *My darling daughter. I can only admit
> here in these pages what I know. I am
> sorry. I am so sorry. And I have done
> nothing to stop this. What kind of woman
> have I become?*

"And I have done nothing to stop this," Magdalena read aloud, wondering what could have happened. Magdalena jumped in her seat; just then, a tumbling, thunderous clanging rang through her office. She closed the journal and looked up. Tilda held a leg of the table in her hands. It had released all the other legs, which had fallen loudly against the other pieces. The table lay in a mountain around Tilda.

Magdalena closed her eyes and rubbed her temples, "Didn't I just say I have a headache?"

Tilda nodded.

"Well, then, wouldn't that mean to be quiet? I need an aspirin and some bicarbonate of soda. Now."

Tilda stared at her. She blinked once.

"Stop looking at me like a damned fool!" Magdalena slammed her palms on the cluttered ebony desk. "Get me the blasted aspirin and *then* come back here and clean this mess up!"

Tilda scurried out of the room.

Magdalena grabbed the journal, closed the case, set it on the floor, and rose. She would read it in her room alone tonight, quietly. She could barely concentrate on it anyway, knowing she was going to be rich and that all her troubles would soon disappear. Magdalena called after Tilda, "And while you're at it, let the girls out and have them help you. I can't have this office in this shape all morning when I have important business —"

The phone rang, interrupting her. Magdalena scanned her desk for the phone; gripping onto the journal with one hand, she moved chair cushions, doilies, and Harlem's things about with the other. "Dammit to hell," she muttered. She got on her hands and knees to see if the phone was where Harlem's suitcases had been. It was not. Carefully, she backed herself out from under the desk and found the thick black telephone cord from the wall, following it along the floor, the shrill call of the phone egging her on. "I'm coming! Can't you see that I'm coming? Tilda! Where is the phone?"

Tilda ran back in and climbed over the furniture behind her as they both reached the closet. Tilda opened the door, whacking Magdalena in the head.

"*Oy!* You silly idiot!" Magdalena howled. "Get away from me. Just get away from me!" She grabbed the phone from Tilda and snatched the receiver off the hook, holding her throbbing head as she did so. The journal lay forgotten on the floor.

"Hello!" she barked.

"Maggie, darling," the voice cooed on the other end.

"Lucinda," Magdalena answered sourly. "I see you're up early."

"The early bird gets the worm, sister. Speakin' of birds, how are yours?"

Magdalena looked back at the bird. It hadn't moved, strangely. "My parrot is doing well."

"I mean the others, Maggie," the voice hardened. "The ones that make you all that lettuce you owe me."

Magdalena leaned her head back against the wall. She pressed the heavy black receiver to her forehead and exhaled deeply. This was the first problem that Harlem's money was going to solve. She brought the telephone back to her unpainted lips and then continued gravely, "It's time for this to end, Lucinda."

"I couldn't agree more. Pay up. Now."

The line went dead.

CHAPTER 6

reaking the seal on her crusted lashes, Harlem opened her eyes to slits. Darkness met her. As did her thoughts. They poured over her like wax, making her stiff in her sheets. Her body was heavy and thick and not her own.

Harlem wondered if she had died while she was sleeping. Maybe she was between worlds. That would be a better reality than the one she was currently living. Something warm trickled down her temples and into her pillow. Those were tears. So, she wasn't dead after all.

She sat up, using one elbow and then another. A heavy sigh fell out of her as she wiped her tears from her cheeks. Harlem slowly pulled her legs to the side of the bed, her toes finding reassurance in the familiarity of the wood floor. Her foot grazed what felt like, and should have been, the red velvet dress she'd left crumpled on the floor. She remembered now that she had taken a bath, one of her special, extra hot baths, but she didn't remember getting into the bed. Harlem held a corner of the sheet to her naked chest.

She stood on legs that resisted the request to hold her and stumbled over a thin wooden chair as she began searching for the bedroom light. Her fingers ran across the fine ridges in the wallpaper. Finally finding the switch, she clicked it on. Nothing. Instinctively, she looked up, then around, trying to remember if there had been a lamp in the room, trying to remember what the ceiling light fixture had looked like—as though, if she could only picture it, the light would cooperate with her and turn on. Harlem clicked the two-button switch again. Nothing. She sighed.

Something inside her stomach started wrenching. She felt like she was going to be sick. Dragging the sheet along with her, she shuffled through the darkness toward the bathroom. She stubbed her toe on the edge of the bed, cursing it for getting in her way. As she did, Harlem wrapped her arms tightly about her stomach, hoping to keep it in place. She found the toilet bowl and sat. The cool seat against her bottom reminded her that she existed, that she was still a human being. She relieved herself of whatever she had left in her body, thankful for the calming release. Harlem reached around in the dark for toilet paper, was quite grateful when she found it and used it generously. The chain to flush the toilet was where she imagined it to be, and she pulled.

The gurgle of the flushing toilet followed her as she found the porcelain sink and steadied herself against it to wash her hands. Harlem reached for the bathroom light and pulled the cord. Nothing. Again, she looked around the room, into darkness, searching for a clue that wasn't there.

There was a knock at her door. Startled, she gathered her sheets and fumbled her way to the door, which opened as she reached it. Looking out at the silhouette that stood between the light in the hallway and the darkness in her room, she saw what seemed to be Magdalena.

"Oh, hello," Harlem said, embarrassed.

"How are you feeling dear?" Magdalena said. "I've come to check on you."

"Not well, to tell you the truth. I think I've caught something. I feel quite awful." Harlem found her way to her bed and sat.

"Perhaps you simply had too much champagne at the party. Sometimes that happens," she laughed. "I've been on the receiving end of too many bubbles many times in my life. You'll get used to it."

Magdalena entered the room with a tray and set it down. "I know Tilda brought you some tea earlier. I've brought you some fresh water. I thought you might like a sandwich and some aspirin also, to help you feel better and get back to your presentable self. How does that sound?"

"Wonderful, actually." Harlem said, reaching for the sandwich, but nearly knocking over the tray in the darkness. "Something's happened with the lights in this room."

"I admit that is one flaw of this old house. Sometimes the electrical wiring goes kaput, I'm embarrassed to say. I apologize." Magdalena flicked the switch off and on. "Yes, the lights are out. You wouldn't imagine the problems I've had over the years. Running a manor comes with all sorts of surprises," she laughed. "I'll call a handyman in for tomorrow. For now, how about you rest? I think you could use a night of restorative rest, and tomorrow morning we'll start fresh. Do you think you'll be up to coming down and joining me for breakfast?"

Harlem sighed in relief as she chewed, swallowed and said, "That would be ideal. Thank you, Magdalena."

"Lady Magdalena," she said, backing out of the room.

"Thank you, Lady Magdalena. Good night."

"Good night, dear."

Harlem chewed her food in the darkness, thankful to have something in her stomach once again. She groped for the water and took a sip, enjoying its coolness against her throat. She found the aspirin and swallowed that down, too. Laying her head back down on her pillow, she felt some tension release from her shoulders. "I'm going to be alright," she sighed as her eyes closed. "I'm going to be alright."

CHAPTER 7

From her dark hiding place under the stairs, Honey had gone undetected. She'd crawled into this space deep in the night, during that stillness that comes between shifts in the city. One shift was stumbling home from places they probably shouldn'ta been, and another was waking up to head to places they probably didn't want to go.

When Otto had ripped her dress off with one quick flick of his switchblade in that back alley somewhere she couldn't place, she'd been thinking less about her modesty and more about her life. And she had fought for it, viciously, just like she'd been taught. Not having a dress was a very small price to pay for freedom. But walking through the streets in her underclothes would draw entirely too much attention. Keeping to the shadows gave her time to think, to plan. She navigated down several alleys, always clinging to walls and shadows whenever anyone passed by. Dusk turned to night like a beckoning finger urging her to come out from hiding, and she'd obeyed. Luckily, she'd found this place under the stairs, a vacancy for one.

Safe in her enclosure, Honey had fallen asleep; able to lick her wounds, get the rest she needed, and think about what the hell to do next. She'd woken early to the sound of people stomping on the steps, using them for what they were intended instead of as a makeshift roof. Her hiding place was under the back stairs of a tenement courtyard in a neighborhood that wasn't too far from Magdalena's. When she peeked out from under the stairs, she discovered the courtyard was a tall square box filled with a bright ray of sunshine. Small windows dotted each floor of the surrounding buildings and clothes lines crisscrossed throughout the opening, reminding her of spider webs.

She closed her eyes and a calm came over her, one like she'd never really known before, even at her well-earned age of twenty-three. She stretched her chin forward to rest it on her knees and allowed that ray of sun to embrace her happiness.

It had been hours since she'd run away. She was finally free to do whatever she wanted. She could sit there all day long if she wanted and simply do nothing. The thought of that made her smile.

Someone hollered and then whooped with laughter. The sound ricocheted off the brown brick walls and escaped through open windows to jostle the inhabitants inside. The courtyard and the apartments themselves seemed to be alive. Voices echoed endlessly—some joyous, others not as much—and each told a story she was too exhausted to follow. It was so different from home. There, the only voice heard so loud had usually been her sister's, and it was habitually laced with a harshness that was sharp enough to make your ears bleed.

She tried to move her legs, to stretch them out, but there wasn't much room for such acrobatics. She scooched her bottom a little to the left; the right cheek needed a break. It was tingly and falling asleep. Her bladder was calling for attention too. Honey rested her head against the rough, cool brick to make her think about something other than that. A cough sent prickles of pain through her throat. She pressed her fingertips along her neck gingerly, wishing she'd had a warm compress. She could still feel Otto's fingers wrapped around it, squeezing the life from her. She gasped for air from the memory and tried to swallow. Hot pain shot through her again. She lowered her hands, sighing. Honey reminded herself that this bit of discomfort had to be better than what Otto had had in store for her. Her thoughts drifted for the thousandth time since she'd escaped.

Magdalena must have known what he was going to do to her. How could she do this? How could her own sister sell her to that disgusting mud-sucking troll? She clasped her fist, wanting to use it again. But this time, on Magdalena. She winced, sore from that one good punch she'd gotten onto Otto's stupid face. She shook her hands to loosen the tightness there. She smiled, thinking back on how surprised he'd looked when she'd clocked him, and proud of her gumption. She shifted and settled her shoulder on the wall to her right. Something crawled on her arm; she yelped and flicked whatever it was off, banging her hand on the stair above her.

"Ouch!" she cried, angrily rubbing the sting. She scanned the area for whatever creepy crawler disrupted her thoughts. "Bug, if you want to keep on living, I suggest you not come back toward me in any kinda way!" She swept her hands across her meager clothing to make sure it hadn't settled in any crevices.

A window opened to her left. Honey held her breath. A woman leaned out and pulled a squeaky clothesline that stretched from her side of the courtyard to the other. A colorful scarf covered her hair and framed her brown, narrow face. With eyes squinted toward the sun, she hung the fruits of her labor fast and precise like clockwork, a clothespin stuffed in her mouth as she worked.

"A dress!" Honey whispered to herself. She tucked the hair on her face behind her ear with excitement. She watched her salvation march down the line with each squeaky tug of the white cord. Honey shifted to her knees quietly and watched the endless parade of shirts, pants, and cloth diapers. "My lord, she must have a family of ten up in there," Honey sighed to herself. The woman finally finished, wiped her hands of her work, and retreated inside. The morning sun baked the clothes, wafting the smell of soap and bleach toward Honey.

The dress, bright with broad yellow and white stripes, waved to her, a gentle breeze at its back. *How am I gonna get it?* Honey wondered. The dress hung from the first floor, nearly a foot above her grasp, even with the best jump. It was cheese in a trap. If she went for it, she'd be done for.

The door above her opened, and Honey skittered back and squeezed into the corner of her hole.

"That rat bastard! He'd better not show his face at work today," a young man snarled.

"How can you talk about your cousin thatta way?"

"Don't care iffin' that Negro is my kin. He done me wrong tryin' to take my gal," the young man continued. His voice, high with hurt, sounded as though he were no more than eighteen or nineteen.

Honey held her breath as the two sat on the stoop. Between the steps, she could see nothing but the thin striped socks of one and a hole beginning at the heel of the other.

The smoke of their cigarettes filled her nostrils.

"What're you so bent outta shape about? Wasn't like you were fixin' to marry the girl."

"What'dya call this?!"

"Golly!"

"Been savin' for a year for this piece 'a tin!"

Honey heard the ring ping against a far wall. It ricocheted with the force of the throw, boomeranged, and landed in the dirt just by her foot.

Honey caught her breath. *Oh no, oh no!*

"Ain't no need to toss out a perfectly good ring, now!" A brown hand reached down and fumbled for the discarded piece of jewelry. She tried to move her shoe, but the space was too tight, and she was too late. She clamped her eyes shut. "Go away! Just go away!" she pleaded. She heard the boy shuffle and land with a thud near her.

"Jeepers creepers! Uh... Petey. Com'ere. There's somebody dead under there."

"Stop playin' with me, Christopher. You know I am dealin' with somethin' serious right—"

Honey popped open her eyes. Both boys screamed and stumbled away from her.

"Momma! Momma! Come quick!"

Honey scrambled from under the stairs. She squinted in the bright sun, wiping the dirt from her hands and knees. She looked for a way to run, but the boys were in her way, blocking the only way she knew of out of the courtyard.

The woman who'd been hanging the clothes flung open the door and stormed onto the stoop.

"What in the name of Jesus are you boys yellin' about? I told ya'll the baby is sleepin'!"

The boys pointed. All eyes were on her.

"I don't want any trouble," Honey said, her voice raspy.

"Looks like you already been in a heap of it!" the hopeless romantic shot back.

"Are you hurt bad?" asked the boy who'd discovered her, chestnut eyes deep and wide. "Looks like somebody tussled you up real good," he said, his voice trailing.

Honey shook her head, "I can manage. I just—"

"Who do you belong to, young lady?" the mother asked, searching Honey's face for answers as she moved down the stairs toward her. "Where your people at?"

"They're all dead," Honey said quickly, almost too quickly. Her throat burned from it.

The three of them stared at her like she had three heads or something.

"All of 'em?"

Honey nodded.

The woman stepped near her, "Well. Come on in then. We'll get you cleaned up. Least I can do for you." She took off her apron and covered Honey with it. "Boys, cover your eyes. Show some respect."

Honey followed them up the stairs and into the home. She turned back to see the boys peeking through their fingers at her. They were the least of her worries.

CHAPTER 8

In peep-toe pumps of satin violet, Magdalena strode from her office and through the dining room. "Tilda!" she called out, adjusting the long pheasant feather that extended gallantly from her chapeau. Its dotted birdcage netting covered her cold, green eyes in a way that allowed her to hide from her opponents, yet still see them, and be ready to strike or evade their blows as necessary. Adding a fitted jacket over her silk dress, belted and figure-skimming, provided an additional layer of armor. She would need such accessories today.

Quickly scanning the room, Magdalena was satisfied with the work Tilda had done to get it back into shape post-party. The rich magenta curtains hung perfectly at the back of the room, and the matching parlor lamps had been returned to their four corners, next to cream-linen wing-backed chairs. Each of her hanging tapestries were straightened once more. She hated a crooked painting. A crooked painting, much like crooked teeth, signaled a crook—

and she didn't need anything betraying what she'd worked so hard to cover up.

Tilda popped her head out from under the massive dining room table, wrench in hand. She was tightening the bolts on the legs. She looked at Magdalena inquisitively.

"Yes, I'm going *out*. Don't look so surprised," Magdalena said, eyes steely, as she stepped past the girl. "Be sure to make the lunch—peas and ham again. It's all they deserve, and all my ration card will allow. And don't forget Officer Brighton's coffee!" she commanded.

As Magdalena closed the pocket sliding doors that concealed the dining room from the foyer, she felt a sharp jab in her temple again.

"Ooof!" she cried out. The aspirin she'd taken earlier was remedying her hangover with the utmost level of inadequacy. She pulled a pearl-covered compact from her purse and clicked it open to discover whether her face revealed how poorly she felt. It did. "For heaven's sake," Magdalena said. Hastily, she used her teeth to pull the deep purple glove from her right hand, swiped the little cotton pad into the compact and dotted another dose of "Ivory Snow" on the stubborn dark circles under her eyes. The shop girl had tried to sell her a darker, warmer "Sun-kissed Dawn," but Magdalena had insisted on Ivory Snow. She didn't care that it wasn't the right color; it was the color she needed to help her live the life she was living. She dabbed and dabbed, pressing the makeup deeper into her skin, coaxing it to work harder. Magdalena peered at herself and opened her mouth wide to slide one more layer of "Lantern Red Blaze" along her perfectly-thin, heart-shaped lips. She blotted them together proudly and, with a final glance, promised herself several champagne-free nights and some uninterrupted sleep this week; she needed to make better choices.

Magdalena felt a memory creep up her neck. She spun around and faced the very part of the wall where Otto had lifted her sister by the neck. The haunting image of Honey's heels dangling a foot off the floor sickened her.

"It had to be done," Magdalena said aloud as she returned her compact and lipstick to her purse and traded them for her house keys. She caught sight of Harlem's check in the purse. "And now, it's all going to be worth it."

Magdalena hurriedly unlocked and securely relocked the foyer door, decorated with beautiful stained glass, and then paused. Her home was a fortress designed to keep the girls from escaping or even thinking they had a chance to get out. The pocket doors to the dining room were always closed; hence any movement would send the sound as an echo throughout the house, an alert that they were being moved. The front door to her home was always locked and often guarded by Brighton, who was on the force but far from on the up and up. Back when she had been rolling in dough, she'd had two cops to guard the home, but finances had forced her to release the services of one, thereby forcing her to stay home more often and make an "arrangement" with Brighton. She waited on the tiled floor of the umbrella room as she heard the front door being unlocked from the outside.

"Hey, where d'you think you're going?"

"You are not my keeper, Officer Brighton: you are theirs," Magdalena said, pointing behind her.

"Unusual for you to head out in broad daylight," he said as he walked down the steps to hail her a taxi.

"I'm not a vampire. I merely prefer to go out at night. But there is something I must take care of immediately. On my own," she said from the height of the top step.

"Guess that's one thing that Honey was good'fer. Now looks like you's gotta do yer own dirty work. Unless y' want me to do it?" he said, returning up the steps. "Not a taxi in sight. Why don't I help y' out wit' whadever it is you're needin' t' do. You can stay here and tend t' the new girl."

"Since when do you tell me how to run my operation?"

"I'm not. I'm just tryin' t' help now's you're short-handed, Maggie."

Magdalena stepped to him and spoke closely: "Lady Magdalena; I am your boss. Have you forgotten this?"

"Alright, alright. Take it easy. Geesh."

Magdalena stormed down the steps. "I'll be back shortly. We'll be talking about the future of our arrangement when I get back," she said.

"Oh, speakin' o' that, while I was out here this mornin', a gentleman came by wit' dis for you," Officer Brighton waved an envelope at her from the middle of the stoop.

Magdalena recognized the envelope. It was from the electric company. She ran back up the steps.

"I hope you's ain't gonna have to make more business arrangements wit' udder fellas here in the near future," he snorted.

Magdalena shoved the envelope in her purse, "Mind your own business!"

With no taxi in sight and wanting to escape Brighton, Magdalena willed her legs to do what she rarely did. She walked down her own brownstone street, heels clicking angrily against the pavement.

"What chu doin' up here in Harlem durin' the day?" a hardened female voice shouted from a window above. "O'fay's like you only grace our part of town at night."

Magdalena didn't take offense to the term, often reserved for whites who liked to come uptown to play with blacks, but who may not have gotten 'round to allowing them into their lives otherwise. She flicked her hand at the woman. "This is a free country, last time I checked."

"News to me," the woman yelled. "Go back to your own damn neighborhood!" she said and slammed her window closed.

Magdalena picked up her pace to put more distance between herself and that encounter. "You can never find a taxi in Harlem when you want one," she sighed. Magdalena hadn't been out on the streets like this in a while. She wasn't a recluse by any definition, but she enjoyed the controlled privacy of her home in comparison to the unknown Petri dish of surprises on the streets. The only surprise Magdalena wanted today was to cash Harlem's check and surprise her dismal bank account balance with a few much-needed zeroes.

She sidestepped a group of three Negro women walking arm-in-arm toward her. Hats cocked to the side and skirts flouncing, they were too wrapped up in each other to pay her much attention. Magdalena thought how she and Honey should have been those women, worried about nothing more than luncheons, finding respectable work, and getting married. Their parents dying had robbed them of some of those normal things, but it was Magdalena who'd made things worse for the both of them—even though at first, she'd been trying to make them better.

Magdalena folded her arms tightly. She didn't enjoy feeling much of anything, especially guilt.

This is ridiculous, Magdalena thought. She's gone. It's over with—

"My dear, fine madam, if you're looking for a good time in Harlem, I know a place," a dandy of a gentleman quipped as she passed. His thin brown fingers tipped his hat.

"Excuse me?'

"Isn't that why you're up here alone in Harlem? So many white folks comin' up here these days to look for a good time, to see how we're livin', to, y' know, let their hair down and show how liberal they are. I, uh, saw you and bas'cly put two and four t'gether."

"I see. And what place would you suggest?" Magdalena asked.

"Joint over near 134th off upper Seventh Avenue. *Parlour Room?* Run by a white lady, same as you." He looked her up and down, "Maybe not as classy as you, but well-kept. Thought maybe you'd be interested."

"*Parlour Room?*" Magdalena pulled the netting lower as she rolled her eyes. That was Lucinda's place, where she was to go to "pay up." "What about Lady M's Mysterie down the street?"

"Mysterie? Stuffed shirts paying for dancin' girls over there; 'tis Negro-owned which is nice, o' course, considering. But *Parlour Room* has the straight dope and plenty of hooch to go 'round."

"Negro-owned?" she said. Her stomach dropped.

"Yep, heard it to be true from the lady of the house the other night when I was over at *Parlour Room* m'self—"

"The woman there told you Lady M's Mysterie was Negro-owned? She said this directly to you?" Magdalena blurted.

"Overheard her, I s'pose. The lady of the place was talkin' all about it to some other folks, you see. Ain't no problem for me, o' course. Seems like it is for you. Good day."

Magdalena stuffed her clutch purse snug under her arm. "Good day," she muttered. This was absolutely not a good day. "God dammit, Lucinda," she muttered as she slammed her balled fist to her thigh. "*God dammit.*"

Lucinda had gone too far. That woman was being paid to keep her ugly trap shut. "We had an agreement!"

The basis of their "agreement" was rooted in something that had very little to do with them. It had much more do to with the actions of their parents, many years ago.

"Your parents stole from mine!" Lucinda had screamed at her years prior, blond curls shaking under a fur cap and breath billowing in the cold night air. They'd been at the bottom of the brownstone's stoop. Jabbing her pointy finger behind her, she'd demanded, "That house is mine, and I want it back!"

"You've got no proof, Lucinda!" Magdalena had shouted back, shoved her aside and stormed up the steps. "Now beat it!"

Lucinda believed that Magdalena's parents had taken the home in some sort of silly arrangement that had then forced Lucinda's parents out over twenty years ago. Magdalena thought the whole thing to be a farce. There was no proof of it. Her house was her house and that was that. Especially since it was all that she had now.

Lucinda had become the biggest brat about the whole thing, really. She couldn't let the past lie where it was, and when lawyers couldn't help her get what she wanted, she turned to what she knew best, the big squeeze.

Lucinda was a gangster herself, no better than Magdalena, as it were. She had her own bevy of henchmen and hangers-on, whom she used to her liking to get what she wanted, just like Magdalena did with Officer Brighton. She knew how to force people to do what she wanted, by any means necessary.

The squeeze that Lucinda had put on Magdalena was deep; it was skin deep. And it was about exposing a secret that Magdalena had spent years crafting and maintaining.

Magdalena remembered the day she chose to start living a lie. "But why?" Honey had asked in the darkness. All three of them—Honey, Magdalena, and little Tilda—were huddled on one of the beds in a shared room upstairs. The windows had been boarded to keep out the bitter cold of a New York winter. They'd shivered in each other's arms, like sticks rubbing together to make a fire. "Negro or white, we still won't have nothin'. What would change? What?" Honey had whimpered.

"A lot would change. Just you watch," Magdalena had said. The next day, she'd walked only a few short blocks from their home and right into a butcher's and said, *"Her, meyn pa iz gefaln aoyf shver mol. kenen ir bite helfn aundz?"* (German for "Sir, my pa has fallen on hard times. Can you please help us?"). And he had. The next day, she did it again. This time she'd stood outside a synagogue and begged for coins, and the people gave them to her. They'd had more to give than the other side of her had. Perhaps because their giving had come from a different place. Had different history. The way they had dropped a coin to her, she had been invisible to them. Another street urchin.

The other side, which was her mother's side, had been struggling just as much as she was. Some would help with a pie or some clothing, but some wouldn't. Others had looked at her like she had scarlet fever or something and was going to infect them with it. Whether they had pity or disgust for her, she didn't need either one, especially when she was hungry. So, she made the invisible side of herself more visible was all. And once she'd done that, there was no going back.

After some time, Magdalena had been reinvented as Lady Magdalena. She had emerged from their decrepit, boarded-up home as a new woman, one who didn't live by the rules of other Negroes but instead with the freedom of those who weren't, and she started to thrive. When she started to make real money with her business was also when Lucinda had begun to put the twist on her to keep her dark secret —and that twist came with a hefty fee. Seemed Lucinda could no longer tell a little white lie.

Magdalena quickened her pace again. She needed to get to the bank. Now. With money in her pocket, she'd be able to make some real decisions. She'd be able to think freely and plan, 'cause not having money had made planning far from glamourous lately, and oh how she loved glamour.

With her head down, Magdalena barreled down the sidewalk like a bull. Anyone coming her way got out of it in a hurry. All she saw were rows of shoes sidestepping and leaping side-to-side. She turned the corner onto Lexington Avenue and rammed into a man black folks would describe as "brown-skinned"; rich, deep-dark, and liquid brown like molasses. "Can't you watch where you're going?" she snapped as she pushed him aside and out of her way.

"You need da lesson in da manners, Missus!" the man said as he stooped to pick up his newspaper. He mumbled something more, but in a language she didn't know.

—

"Aww, close your head," she said as she darted to the curb to hail a taxi. While she waited, she stared past the blue-painted letters of Dolly's Diner at the people hovering over their eggs and toast. The place was a Harlem staple and admittedly had the best malted milkshakes on Lexington Avenue. For a moment she thought about treating herself to one, but a stronger thought leapt into her head.

Uncle Mac.

His bar was right next door to Dolly's. Uncle Mac was her mother's brother and their only surviving family. Magdalena used to stop by the bar when things got really hairy, and Uncle Mac would take her and Honey next door for a sandwich or two. He had offered many times for the both of them to come and live in his one-bedroom apartment just above the bar. She had always rejected his offer, often saying, "We're fine, Uncle Mac." He knew they weren't and insisted his door was always open.

Magdalena walked forward and pulled the worn metal handle on the unmarked door of the faded brick building; Dolly's was boldly advertised, where Uncle Mac's was not. Those that knew about it slipped inside without notice, and those that didn't walked right on by.

As Magdalena stepped inside, her eyes adjusted to the darkness.

"Maggie? Is that 'chu?"

"Hey there, Uncle Mac," Magdalena said as she spanked the bar top with her purse. The place smelled of furniture polish and stale cigarettes.

"Somethin' got chu riled up, child?" Behind the bar, her uncle wiped his hands on a white towel and ambled toward her with a slight limp. Gravity was gradually pulling his shoulders down, but he was still a tall man and lean like her mother had been. He had always seemed to know more than anyone else in the room, and he looked at you that way, too.

"Nothin' a little drink can't fix," Magdalena said, sliding onto a bar stool. "Are you ever going to retire, Uncle Mac?"

"Maybe in five years or so. The good Lord has kept me going for these past eighty-odd years; no need to stop now. Why the sudden concern, Maggie? You haven't stepped a foot in here in ages." The old man poured her a shot of whiskey.

"Been busy, Mac," she said tightly and downed her drink.

"Too busy to visit your momma's grave?" He ran his gnarled hands, the color of oak, along his bald head as he spoke. She stared at his hands, reminded of her mother. Magdalena used to put her own hands next to her mother's and wonder why they weren't the same.

"Isn't that what I pay you for? To visit and maintain my mother's grave?" Magdalena answered.

"Because you're too highfalutin to do it? You live in Harlem, but you can't get yourself to the colored cemetery? Shameful. Carryin' on the way that you do. Plus, you haven't paid me in a terribly long while, Maggie, an' you know it. But you don't hear me askin' for nothin' because I seem to be the only one between us that knows the diff'rence 'tween right an' wrong," he poured her another, staring at her with contempt.

"Didn't come here for a lecture, Uncle Mac," Magdalena said, reaching for the shot.

Mac stopped her by placing his warm hand on hers. His dark-brown eyes, now rimmed with the pale blue cloudiness of age, were soft, "Maggie. I'm an old, old man. There was a time that if I'd had the chance, couldn't pay me nothin' to not do exactly what you're doin'. Skin-switchin' and whatnot. I was born into this one skin that's only got one tongue; speaks for me b'fore I even open my mouth. But y'see, this skin is where I belong, and for a reason I may nev'r know. But you? Your life—this privilege you're playin' with, it comes with a price. Can't hide. Can't be in the open, neither. After a while, can't exist. Is that what you want for yourself?"

Magdalena gently slid her hand from beneath his. Maybe this was a mistake, coming here to be filled up with something she was missing. She'd made a mistake. She grabbed the cool glass and drained the shot. Magdalena licked her lips to collect the last of the burn. "I'll be by next week with a check." She dropped some coins on the bar counter to pay for her drink and promptly headed for the front door.

"Don't want no part of your money," Mac said, sliding the coins back to her. "For drinks or otherwise. Forget the check, Maggie. My sister deserves better anyhow. Woman would turn over in her grave knowin' her own daughter was some kind of a harlot. Keep your money; maybe you can use it to pay the devil when you get to his door," he called after her sternly. "And I hope to goodness you are taking care of that sister of yours. Ain't seen her in forever neither. Girl probably doesn't even remember me. Family is family, and family's all you got, Maggie."

"It was good to see you too, Uncle Mac," Magdalena said, her back to him as she shoved open the door. Magdalena squinted at the sunlight as she ran into the street. Tires screeched from the traffic that she boldly interrupted as she stepped out in front of a taxi. She swung open the door and jumped in.

"Fifty-seventh and Seventh, please."

"Nearly got us both killed," the cabbie said as he made a careful U-turn to head downtown.

Magdalena closed her eyes and settled her head onto the leather headrest, "Yeah, well. I didn't." She wasn't even sure why she'd gone to Mac's. She could have gotten a drink anywhere.

"C'mon, Maggie, get it together," she whispered to herself. The whiskey was doing its work, but she wanted more. Another couple shots would help her not care about what the "good time" man had said on the street. Three more after that would stop the creeping feelings of guilt about Honey—what she'd done and hadn't done. She figured with just one more shot after all of those, she wouldn't feel so terribly… alone.

Too much thinking, Maggie. Too much. Magdalena clenched her eyes closed. She stopped daydreaming about shots and allowed the rock of the taxi swerving through the city streets to comfort her instead. She held her pocketbook in her lap with both hands. Inside it was the only thing that mattered anyway.

Twenty minutes later, they arrived at the Midtown National Bank. As she exited the taxi, she heard a low whistle from a passing young man.

"Whatta dame, whatta dame!" he exclaimed, looking back at her over his shoulder.

Magdalena drew her shoulders back and played the part. She smiled behind her veil as the man ran back and opened the bank door for her.

"Thank you kindly," Magdalena said.

"Pleasure's all mine, believe me!" His words were swallowed as she entered the cold, quiet tomb of the bank. Magdalena inhaled; the fragrance of the floor polish opened a vault of memories. This had been their family bank; she'd walk in with her father—her soft-soled white shoes not making a sound—and she'd look up, holding her father's white hand while he shook hands with everyone they passed. She smiled at the memory, having loved that private and very special time with him. She'd learned much later why her mother, Uncle Mac's sister, never went along with him to the bank and Magdalena had.

Magdalena looked around at the many unfamiliar faces working behind counters. It had been nearly fifteen years since her father's passing. Her father's banker Mr. Weiden was long gone, as were most, if not all who'd known her father and his money. She'd made different relationships with the bank staff. Her own way.

"Mr. Trieg, please," she announced to a waiting clerk.

"Of course, Madame," the clerk said dutifully and departed. Magdalena let her eyes linger on the crown molding decorating the high ceilings and soaked up the energy of the place. She loved money and any place that was associated with it. She tightened her gloves, tugging down on them at the wrist.

"Can I help you?"

Magdalena turned, "Mr. Trieg, darling, how are you?"

Mr. Stan Trieg froze; a plastic smile seized his handsome face. Magdalena relished his surprise. While this establishment was where she did her banking, her personal financial transactions with Stan Trieg happened elsewhere.

"Ms. Sapperstein, what a pleasure," Mr. Trieg motioned for the clerk to go and handle another customer. "Come this way, please."

Magdalena followed his broad shoulders through a row of desks toward the back of the bank. "So few friends refer to me by my family name," she laughed, scolding him.

"I doubt it would be very professional for me to call you 'Lady Magdalena' here, where my colleagues could hear me. Some of them know of your spot, but they don't need to know that I know," Mr. Trieg whispered as he escorted her through his office door marked "PRIVATE".

"I suppose you're right. Lady M's Mysterie is quite popular these days," Magdalena said, removing her gloves as she sat. "You enjoyed yourself last night, I trust?" she added coyly.

Mr. Trieg, easily nearing forty, straightened his tie and coughed uncomfortably. "What brings you to Midtown National, Ms. Sapperstein?"

Magdalena pulled Harlem's inheritance check from her purse, moved the "Bank Manager" name plate aside, and slid the check across the desk. "This."

Mr. Trieg picked up the check. His bright hazel eyes grew ever so slightly before he looked up at her. "Harlem Winnepega Markeson is a lucky woman."

"Yes, I suppose she is," Magdalena said, adjusting her hat's netting. "I'm here to assist her with that luck."

"Assist?" he asked, looking at the back of the check. "In what way?"

"By cashing it."

The room fell silent.

Mr. Trieg centered the slightly rumpled check on the desk and leaned back in his chair, adjusting his shirt cuffs, "Where did you get that check?"

"A little birdie gave it to me."

"Cut the baloney, Magdalena. You want me to believe one of those girls working in that house has this kind of money?" He stood, shoving his hands into his pin-striped pockets. "What kind of fool do you take me for? Why would this girl choose to stay and dance for you when she clearly doesn't need the money?"

Magdalena pulled her cigarette case from her purse and put one between her crimson lips. Mr. Trieg stepped forward and lit the end with a large crystal lighter from his desk. She could smell his aftershave.

"Women have secrets, Mr. Trieg." Their eyes connected, and he looked away. Exhaling, she continued, "These girls are fleeing families and lives with which they no longer want to be associated. They are fugitives who come to me when they have nowhere else to go. You see that I clothe and feed them and keep their creative spirits alive by allowing them to perform. We benefit one another."

"Benefit one another," he scoffed as he lit his own cigarette. He walked past her and leaned against the office door.

"Don't be a hypocrite, Stan," Magdalena said.

"Excuse me?" he said, eyebrows raised.

Magdalena turned in her chair to face him, "You heard me. We're all a big, bad machine that greases one another's palms and juicy buttocks. And everyone has been very, very happy. Including you."

"I think it's time for you to leave," he pointed to the door with his cigarette, his chiseled jaw tight.

"Does that mean you won't help me?" Magdalena turned her back to him and drew heavily on her cigarette. Her free hand gripped her bicep. Her eyes clamped shut. Waiting. She hadn't anticipated any opposition. This money was her only remaining defense against Lucinda. It was her ticket to freedom.

"This means I can't help you. I won't commit fraud for a little bit of chicken grease."

"Chicken grease?" Magdalena spun back around and suffered a laugh. "A little bit of chicken grease. Well. We both know you've had more than a little. And I can prove it."

"What?" he nearly shouted, moving to face her, his fists jammed onto his hips.

"You've had more than a little chicken grease is all I said."

"You know that's not the part I'm talking about. You think you can blackmail me into helping you? You're out of your mind. You have no proof."

"Don't I?" Magdalena peered at him while he started shuffling papers, his cigarette jammed in his clenched mouth. "After all these years, your ability to underestimate me still amuses me, Stan." She rubbed her cigarette out in a crystal ashtray, rose and swiped the check from his desk.

As Magdalena walked past him and toward the door, she tried one more tactic. "Did I mention I'd be willing to share? To make it worth your while?"

Mr. Trieg grabbed her elbow. "How willing?"

Their eyes locked again. This time he didn't move away. She broke their gaze, slowly leaned into him and whispered into his ear, "Name your number."

Mr. Trieg let her elbow go. Her arm dropped and nestled low between them. She felt the roughness of his summer wool pants shift as his interest grew. Magdalena didn't dare look into his hazel eyes as his fingers lightly smoothed a curl of her midnight black hair and tucked it behind her ear.

"Bring the girl in," Mr. Trieg said. His words deliberate, close to her. "She signs the check in front of me. We open an account for her. All on the up and up. You do your magic and persuade her to give you fifteen percent for you helping her and all. And then you give that fifteen percent to me. And maybe a little more."

"And what if I don't want to involve the girl? And I just want it to be between you and me?" she looked up at him and pressed into him further.

"I'll do some things for you, Maggie, maybe even to you, but I won't go to jail for you. It's this way, or you find another."

CHAPTER 9

As Magdalena stepped out of the taxi across the street from her Manor, she caught herself grinning, putting her hair behind her ear, retracing Stan Trieg's fingers, and feeling his breath on her neck again. Magdalena imagined his fingertips traveling to the other parts of her body that would just as easily welcome his tender touch. She straightened her skirt to avert her attention from the warmth pulsating below its material. She wasn't often attracted to her clients, but Stan Trieg was one with whom she could imagine a potential future, quite honestly. She'd flirted with him before but had never been as close to him as she had been today. When he attended her parties, it was the girls he was interested in, not her. They had, perhaps and quite unexpectedly, crossed a new frontier.

Bring the girl in. She signs the check. We open an account. Magdalena remembered Stan Trieg's words happily. This, she could manage. This would be done tomorrow and her business with Lucinda would be over. At thirty-five, her life, which had been shambles for over ten years, could go back to normal, but better. Ever since Harlem's check had fallen into her lap, she had been thinking about how that money could change things for her completely. She could use it to pay off her debt to Lucinda, or she could keep it for herself and remove what was allowing Lucinda to blackmail her in the first place: her whiteness. Uncle Mac was right; her privilege had come with a price and Lucinda was working to jack it up. But if she removed that privilege, what could Lucinda do? Nothing. She'd been hiding under a cloak of whiteness for long enough. She thought aloud, "I put this charade on when I had nothing, but by God, now I've got something! Time to take it off. Welcome home, Magdalena Sapperstein!" As she did, she was filled with a kind of glee that overcame her; she felt a weight being lifted and she clapped her hands joyfully. Freedom was on its way.

Magdalena heard a child laugh a few doors down. She squinted to see two Negro girls playing hopscotch on the sidewalk under a canopy of trees. The hems of their flowered dresses flounced gaily as they hopped about. "I am so glad I am not the marrying type," she murmured to herself with a crinkled nose. *Although, were Stan Trieg to ask, perhaps I'd be interested,* she thought through a thin smile. The question was, would *he* be interested in someone like her? Magdalena's smile faded as the girls' laughter fell about her like a sudden summer rain, strong enough to soak.

Stan Trieg had proven that he had an affinity for brown girls (or had no problem paying for them), but what might he think beyond that? What might he think should Magdalena introduce Honey to him as her sister? What might he do when they arrived at the gates of Saint Raymond's Cemetery, where her mother was buried with her father? And what might he say when Magdalena retrieved their family portrait from where it was hidden deep in a closet, pointed to the brown woman, and explained, "That's my momma"?

There was the chance that he might not do anything; Stan Trieg could come to love her, just as her father had loved her mother, when given the choice. Stan Trieg could choose to marry her, and they could be happy, just as her parents had been. But Magdalena had already colored his choice. If she was a white woman to him, maybe that's what she should remain? Was love worth it? Was he?

Uncle Mac's words kept crowding her thoughts like the oak leaves fluttering on the branches above her, 'Can't hide. Can't be in the open, neither. After a while, can't exist. Is that what you want for yourself?'

I want everything I deserve! Magdalena retorted. She wanted to thrive in Stan Trieg's world where men gathered in private rooms, shook hands, and blew cigar smoke that materialized into the word "yes." Her father had lived in that world. By birthright, it was where she belonged. Her father should have grown old, and she should have been by his side, a woman of means and education and inherited class, a true lady. When she was a girl, it was what they had spoken of, what he'd intended for her. He'd broken his promise.

She had to lie to become what her truth should have been all along. Before she became Lady Magdalena, she had nearly perished. She had wanted more. She had wanted other. In fact, she'd had to become other in order to live. And now she was stuck.

The girls laughed again; she scowled at them. "Must be nice for you that your mothers had it so easy," she said. She scoffed as she stood on her own solitary square of sidewalk, watching them, and imagined herself in bed with Stan, doing all that was needed to make girls who played so freely. She then imagined herself, pregnant with her secret, withstanding nine agonizing months of waiting to see what sort of surprise would be handed to her by a maternity nurse. Magdalena didn't like surprises. She figured that men like Stan Trieg didn't either.

The trees grew silent. The girls' laughter evaporated.

Magdalena crossed the street and stomped up her brownstone stairs rubbing her shoulder blades; they ached with the pain of far too much of this nonsense. A dull throb in her head jumped on the nonsense train and rumbled around her temples. She needed another drink and she needed it now. But just then Magdalena was halted by a green Thermos being shoved in her face. "Hello to you too, Brighton," Magdalena said as she grabbed it.

Officer Brighton sneered at her as he reached below the snake coil for a door handle to unlock the front door. "Coffee was cold."

"Sorry," Magdalena sighed as she walked past him.

"You's might want to watch talkin' to yourself. Folks'll start thinkin' you're looney."

"Thanks." Magdalena locked the foyer door behind her, leaving the key in the lock for Brighton, and walked into the home her father had cherished and her mother had built with bricks of love. It was the only place where she could just be.

The smell of baked ham wafted from the kitchen. "Tilda, I'm back," she called out as she walked into her office. She dropped the Thermos onto the floor with a clattering thud. "Bring me another aspirin."

Magdalena removed her hat pin and placed her purple hat on the desk next to a wooden box of cigarettes, collapsing into the leather desk chair. Her bird squawked loudly from its tiny cage. "Shut up, Bird," she sighed.

Magdalena withdrew one of her remaining cigarettes from the box and let it dangle between her lips as she checked her watch. It was just after two-thirty. She no longer had time to think about Stan

Trieg and babies and nonsense. There were larger issues at stake. Magdalena removed Harlem's check from her handbag, raised it high, kissed it and placed it carefully on her desk. *Later for you. Later.* Magdalena also removed the electric bill Officer Brighton had handed her when she'd left for the bank. She threw it in the side drawer with all the other service-disconnect notices and retrieved a large green ledger. "This, we deal with today," she muttered, lighting her cigarette.

Magdalena reached across the desk and pulled a hefty ivory statue of Budai the monk toward her. The statue figure, known as the "Laughing Buddha," was one of her prized possessions. She rubbed his big round iconic belly for luck, pulled back his smiling, bald head, and retrieved a large envelope from the statue's cavity. The envelope was thick with individual smaller envelopes stuffed with varying amounts of cash.

Magdalena blew out a stream of smoke as she opened the first envelope, labeled "Ann Smith." Its weight triggered a small grin. She counted the bills once and then once again before going to her ledger.

In perfect penmanship, she added a new entry:

Harlem Winnepega Markeson aka Ann Smith, 24 June 1944, $33.00

Then, thinking of her sister, she flipped back to the very first entry of the book and carefully crossed out what was Honey's first and only entry in the ledger:

~~Margaret Sapperstein aka Honey, 8 November 1932, $4.10~~

Magdalena browsed the yellowing pages of the ledger. Like a photo album, each page conjured up so many memories. Magdalena ran her blood-red manicured fingers over the dried blue ink living within the green and red grids of the pages. These were her certainties. These were the children she had worked hard to birth. Not the captured women themselves, of course; not the living and breathing beings that casually punctured her conscience with their questioning, haunting and pained gazes, but their soulless names entered here. Their names and their earnings, entered with precision here in her history book, were certainties. They were the indisputable proof of her hard work. Concentrating on them and this business was an endless sacrifice to stifle the kind of colorful surprise she might have birthed with someone like Stan Trieg.

Magdalena rubbed out her cigarette, opened her front desk drawer and retrieved a flask that she kept for "medicinal purposes". She tilted her head back and drank what she'd been craving—perhaps too strongly lately. Like earlier at Uncle Mac's, she enjoyed the burn that started on her lips and slid down her throat as the whiskey wound its way through her. She licked her lips, screwed the top on the flask and returned to business. The next envelope she opened was labeled "Ruby: Rainbow." Magdalena counted the bills twice before flipping the pages of the ledger. She entered Ruby's contributions on her individual earnings balance sheet, and then on another page that showed a running-earnings total for all the girls. Magdalena continued, accounting for all seven Rainbow Girl envelopes before moving on to the one marked "Brown Betties."

She placed the envelope on the desk. Her memories cried for attention. She rubbed her forehead softly with her fingertips. Her eyes closed.

The opening night of Lady Magdalena's Mysterie, back in 1935, had been a disaster and a dream. She'd been so naïve to business then, but she knew men. And she knew women too. She'd commandeered three streetwalkers from her neighborhood and showed them how to walk and talk in a way that was different from what they were used to. She'd thrown a party and invited folks and the rest was history. She'd been a streetwalker herself. After her father had died and 125th Street was feeling the effects of the stock market crash, she'd taken to the streets, just like everybody else. It was all she could do, and she'd needed to do something. She'd fixed her hair in pin curls and finger waves, like she'd seen the other girls do, stole a tube of lipstick from the corner store, and put on the best dress she could find. At thirty years old, there had been no need to make herself look older. That gig was up. She was a grown woman and she had hoped that would be a selling point. Somehow. (Even though she barely knew what to do when it came to selling.) She'd been so sheltered in her life, having worked at home for her father doing his bookkeeping. Being social had not been high on her priority list. Men would come to the home for meetings and such, but her father had never felt that any of them were good enough for her. In fact, her first and only kiss had come from a schoolmate, and that had been barely a peck on the cheek. There had never been anything more for her.

Magdalena cringed: her first encounter with a man had been with the first man she'd solicited. The experience had been awkward, painful, and exasperating. As he'd jammed himself against her in that dark alley, she'd wondered if he himself had known what he was doing. Banging into her like she was some wild horse he was riding but failing at his perceived task to tame. Magdalena sighed and shook the memory from her head. Never wanting to have an experience like that again prompted her to get off the streets and into her home. With the help of a young man who'd become a boyfriend of sorts, she'd created a real business—one that had dancing girls who did a little bit more than dance. One that also included Honey doing what Magdalena had done many times. After one terrible incident, she'd vowed to never make her sister be with another man ever again. The problem was, they'd both still needed to earn money to save their home and themselves. Something needed to be done. Magdalena had created the Brown Betties to keep Honey safe from doing the things that men paid for. The Rainbow Girls were created for that. Honey danced. Honey looked exquisite. Honey was a lure to get them to buy, and that was it—as were the rest of the Betties. Magdalena had done her best to take care of her sister then and now.

But then, Honey had become a liability. And it was Lucinda's fault.

Magdalena thought back to New Year's Eve, only six months earlier, when her life changed. She recalled standing on her front stoop in the chilly night air, after being pulled away from her party, and reading Lucinda's telegram that simply read, "THE GIG IS UP, SWARTZA. HAPPY NEW YEAR!"

Lucinda had pulled Magdalena's race card. And while Magdalena possessed coloring that had white men whistling and holding bank doors, Honey did not. Lucinda reveled in this and had begun telling people that Magdalena and Honey were sisters, and wasn't that interesting and deliciously strange, and what did it all *mean*?

Magdalena sold girls all the time. There was only so much room in the brownstone: she could only keep seven Rainbow Girls at a time. And she counted on the extra income from a sale. The Brown Betties had never been intended for sale. When she had decided, or rather arrived at the unavoidable conclusion that Honey must go, she'd chosen Otto. He was a fathead. This was key. Otto would be stupid enough to give Honey the breach she needed to run, to fight back— just like she'd been taught when they both first started out in this business. They'd taught each other how to fight back. Honey would find a way to fight.

"What have I done?" Magdalena mouthed. She and Honey hadn't been terribly close these last few years, but they were still sisters. Magdalena had known Honey her entire life, as is the case with being the oldest child. What was she to do without her? She reached for her flask and tried to drown the sob that was climbing up her throat. She clamped her eyelids shut to shield against the sting that fought to pour out of her. Clasping her knuckles in a grip that turned her fingers purple, she dropped her head to her fingers, "Momma and Papa. Watch over her. Give her strength. *'Helf mikh.'* Please give her strength. Wherever she is."

If only the check had come sooner! Magdalena thought. *Honey would still be here...* After raising her head and angrily wiping sadness from her cheek, she took another sip from the flask and returned to her work. Numbers and ledgers had always distracted her from feeling what she didn't want to feel. She opened the Brown Betties envelope, counted the contents, then counted again and entered the numbers in the book. The grand total for the night mocked her from its safe, unemotional place on the ledger. Even with the bonus she'd received from Arthur for Harlem and the nice bid from wealthy jeweler Mr. Rathbourne for the Brown Betties, the total was less than last week. And last week's total was less than the week before. On top of that, she'd lost money in the Honey trade. Magdalena leaned back in her chair and sighed heavily as she ran her fingers through her hair. It was the end of the month and even though she'd added last night's party to the schedule in addition to her regular Saturday night soiree, there was no way that she would be able to cover her financial obligations. Again. Not without that check being cashed. Business was slow, and Lucinda's demands were heating up; the pressure had really gotten to her, but it seemed God had sent her salvation. She didn't care to wonder if she deserved it.

She was going to need Harlem, and that meant the girl was going to have to cooperate, whether she wanted to or not. Because, if there was one thing she knew, Magdalena would see Lucinda in hell before losing Honey, and Harlem's money too.

CHAPTER 10

arlem drove through the back roads of her family's property. The majestic trees waved, the sun smiled down upon her and the tall grass seemed to run alongside trying to keep up. She laughed as she steered the car along the dirt road, dust flying just like the blue ribbons from her Sunday hat. The motor roared with as much excitement as she did. She turned to laugh with her passenger and saw that the passenger riding along was also herself.

Harlem jolted up in her bed. She licked her lips, expecting to taste the grit of the dust that had circled around her so gaily in her dream. There was no grit, just dryness living on wrinkled skin. She opened her eyes to see Magdalena standing at the foot of her bed.

"Oh!" she screamed out before she could catch herself.

"I'm terribly sorry," Magdalena said. "I didn't mean to startle you. You were so deep in your sleep that I didn't want to wake you."

"What are you doing here?" Harlem pulled the sheets to her chin.

"I thought we'd get a jump on the day!"

"Day?"

"Yes, you've been sleeping since I saw you yesterday. I thought it was best to not bother you. How are you feeling today?"

"Much better, I have to say. The rest must have helped."

"Delightful," Magdalena said as she propped open Harlem's suitcase, which was sitting at the foot of her bed. She lifted a black and white striped outfit, one that had yet a chance for wear. "What do you think about this dress?" Magdalena asked.

Harlem wanted to snatch the crisp garment from Lady Magdalena's hands. Instead, she offered a polite, "I think I can dress myself, thank you." Harlem didn't like the woman going through her things. She hadn't the right or her permission. Even Harlem's own mother had rarely done so.

"Of course, of course," Magdalena returned the dress to the suitcase and put her hands in the pockets of her floor-length pink chiffon robe. "I'll leave this here for you."

"And where was my suitcase? Under my bed?"

"Yes, it was. Tilda must have put it there for you. I'm sorry it wasn't somewhere in plain sight."

"I couldn't much see anyway, not when it was dark in here. Thank you for having the lights fixed."

Magdalena looked up at the bare ceiling light bulb. "It was nothing. Only the best for my girls," she smiled.

Harlem softened at the mention of 'my girls.' It was comforting to be included in such a thing. "Will I meet the other girls soon? The day I arrived I remember that one girl was leaving. You had said she'd had a bad toothache, I believe."

"Yes, that was Honey. That problem has been fixed."

"And the others, from the party?" Harlem asked, eyebrows raised.

"Did you enjoy the party?"

Harlem caught her breath. "It's all a bit of a blur, really. There... there are parts I'd rather not remember if I'm to be honest with you."

"Oh?" Magdalena leaned against the door. Her nightgown flowed about her. "Did something happen, dear?"

Harlem froze. For a split second, for a second as fast as the one that took her mother's life, she saw Susannah standing there in the door instead of Magdalena. Tall. Slender. Womanly. Questioning. Harlem couldn't help but think about what had happened to her mother once Harlem had confessed what had been going on behind closed doors. What Roy had been doing in their own home. Harlem squeezed her eyes shut and shook her head. Her words tumbled from her. "No, nothing happened.

Everything is so new here. So many new things." Harlem's hands began to sweat. She clung to her sheets.

"Well," Magdalena smiled again. "Ruth and Mary only bring the best girls here. They chose you, and that means you are supposed to be here, darling. You do know how special you are, right?"

Harlem swallowed. "Yes, yes. I do."

"You already fit in so wonderfully."

"I'd love nothing more than to fit in somewhere... here." Harlem felt tears filling her eyes and she wasn't exactly sure why. Her voice quivered. "I—I'd love to—to get dressed, and—and come downstairs. And perhaps you or one of the girls could take me about town. Show me New York City? I... I would really appreciate something like that. If you have time."

"Certainly," Magdalena said. "Take your time. I'll be waiting downstairs for you. I'm looking forward to us getting to know one another."

"Thank you," Harlem breathed.

Harlem wiped her running nose and waited for the door to click closed before she unraveled herself from the sheets that had cloaked her naked body. It was unlike her to sleep in the nude, and she found it jarring that she hadn't anything on. She quickly crawled forward on the bed and found her robe; it was modest, white, with a ruffle at the neck and cuffs. She had picked it out herself while shopping with her mother two years ago. Her mother had said that

Harlem needed something that would make her feel like a true young lady. The robe had sat mostly untouched in an armoire for some time at home. When she went to bed and when she awoke, she didn't feel like much of a lady. Still, for this new part of her life, Harlem had hoped to step into the role. She packed it, rather than leaving it behind.

Pulling on the robe, Harlem thought, *Is trouble going to follow me wherever I go?* The tears came again. "I want a new life! I want something new!" she said aloud. Taking her tears with her, Harlem walked in her bare feet to the bathroom. She pulled on the light and stared at her reflection in the mirror above the sink. "You'll have to forget all of this. You must," she said to herself. Her face twisted into a blob; she couldn't see clearly, just as when she'd look through the sitting room window during a summer storm. The rain would cascade across the window obscuring everything beyond it, leaving her to retreat to her imagination of what was happening outside. Same as now. She wiped her tears and turned on the faucet, letting the water run through her fingers before splashing some on her face. Then she cupped her hands to make a well from which she drank, hoping it would help her head and her stomach, too. "I can do it," she said.

Harlem returned to her suitcase. It was full of memories waiting to happen.

The shop girl had been just a year older than she and had told her so. 'I'm nineteen, goin' on twenty. I'm engaged to be married, you know.'

Harlem hadn't known. She smiled politely, shook her head no, and zipped the side of the rayon crepe dress she was trying on. Harlem had ventured to Lee-Lee's Couture downtown alone. George had dropped her off and promised to return in one full hour. The girl had not stopped talking from the moment Harlem stepped in the door and a soft bell tinkled to announce her arrival.

The girl, who was no more than five feet five, leaned against the gilded-edged full-length mirror. Her hair stood at attention in two very high victory rolls. Her eyebrows were plucked and drawn on her smooth round face with precision. Harlem could tell the girl must have had a subscription to LIFE Magazine. 'I'll be married and then we're going to live in my fiance's house over yonder on Harper's Lane, just a mile from here. And then when the time is right, we're gonna buy that house, and it's goin' t' be all mine. Mine y' see. And you know what I'm gon' do?'

Harlem had turned in the mirror to look at the back of the dress and shaken her head no again.

In two strides, the girl was next to Harlem. She knelt gracefully and straightened the hem of the dress with two swift tugs downward. 'For starters, I'm gon' paint the entire place robin's egg blue. Ev'ry single wall. And I'm gon' make me some curtains that match. That's whut I'm gon' do. Whut 'bout you?' She stood and gently swept her fingers across the gathered neckline.

'Me?' Harlem inspected the delicate keyhole button at the capped sleeves.

She stepped back. Solid in her engaged hour-glass frame. 'Well, yes. Not like you can get married.'

Harlem looked her in the eyes. 'And why not?'

She whispered, but not before tucking a wayward piece of Harlem's hair back into its finger-rolled place. 'You do know who you is, right? I mean, you are Harlem Markeson. I'm sorry t' say it, but you're tarnished goods in this town.'

Harlem gasped same as if the girl had accidentally stuck a straight pin into her.

The girl circled Harlem, stood behind her, and admired her in the mirror. Close to Harlem's ear, she explained, 'Don't mean t'be rude about it, but it's the truth ain't it?' She brushed Harlem's shoulders of invisible lint. 'Quiet as it's kept, I'm kinda wishin' I was you. 'Cause while I got a choice of paint, and any kind that I do want—you's got the choice to have any kind of life you want right now. Even if you are a criminal. Well. Sorta.'

'I see.' Harlem stood still. Letting it all sink in.

'I'd change my name, an' ev'rything. Sumthin' simple, like Ann Jones, or whatever.' The almost-twenty-year-old sage folded her thick arms and sighed. 'But, girl, if you have got one thing going for you, it's your figure. Look at this dress. Looks like it was made 'specially for you. You could do anything in that dress. Paint the town. Go t' a fiiiiine dinner. Strut up and down any main street in any city in these United States. The lavender compliments your coloring like nobody's business! And what's more? You can buy as many *of 'em as you want! The girl grabbed Harlem's arm, spun her 'round and laughed loud as a horse at feeding time. 'I'd say you was pretty lucky in an unconventional sorta way.'*

Harlem's face had turned fourteen shades of red that day in Lee-Lee's Couture. She had stood tall and listened to all the words the shop girl had said, and when she had finished giving her every last unsolicited opinion, Harlem had purchased three different dresses from her. (And two pair of seamed stockings, a slip, and a pale green polka-dotted head scarf.) As she'd left the shop with her boxes tied with string, she'd wanted to say, 'See ya, whuldn't wanna be ya.' Instead, she'd pulled her sunglasses down from her eyes, peered over her nose and said, 'Thank you. Kindly.'

Harlem zipped her dress of rayon crepe lavender. She undid the string holding the paper price tag and placed it in the elastic pouch in her Samsonite. As Harlem stepped into a new pair of stockings and clipped them to her garters, she repeated to herself over and over again—just as she had done back home to forget about Roy—"I'm a girl who is good. I'm a girl who should be happy, healthy and whole. I'm untouchable on the inside, where the good me resides." She had created a tune for this little poem in her head and she hummed it as she moved along.

Before the mirror in the bathroom, Harlem continued to hum while she brushed her hair, now thick with pomade, into a tight French twist. She pushed the last bobby pin into her head, careful not to stab her tender scalp yet again. While checking for that wayward strand that the shop girl had tucked aside, Harlem whispered again, "I'm a girl who is good, I'm a girl who is good..." She stopped moving her mouth long enough to apply a thin layer of lipstick to her plump lips. While blotting them together, Harlem made the bed, her white kitten heels clicking along the hardwood floor as she did so.

With her purse dangling from her wrist, she tapped the button for the light and switched it off. Harlem opened her door ready to experience something new and fresh. It was what she wanted more than anything. Except perhaps a warm chicken sandwich and a huge slice of strawberry rhubarb pie.

CHAPTER 11

arlem opened her door to find Tilda standing there, like a true servant. Having staff waiting on her was something she was used to back home, but she hadn't expected to have such luxuries here.

"Good day, Tilda," Harlem said.

The girl turned away and walked down the stairs without a word. Harlem wasn't used to such formality. George, her family driver, was more like another member of the family than someone who worked for them. He would never have been so quiet unless something were wrong.

Harlem followed the girl down the winding stairs, looking back at her door and glancing at the two unknown doors to the left of hers. "You're awfully quiet, Tilda. Is something the matter?"

Tilda looked back at Harlem with the widest eyes; the girl looked as though she wanted to hug her or something. Tilda shook her head no enthusiastically.

"Alright then..." Harlem grew quiet. This kind of silence wasn't entirely unfamiliar to her. That night a little more than a year ago when the police came to get her, they had led her silently through her family home and to their waiting police car, its headlights shining. Right now, she felt as she had then, walking along that path through the night while it stared at her as though she were a monster. Even the crickets had silenced themselves to allow for her procession. Harlem felt her arms crisscross and wrap themselves about her stomach again. She squeezed her hip bones, felt her rib cage moving rapidly. *I'm alright, I'm alright,* she said to herself.

She forced herself to focus on her surroundings instead of her memories. As she followed Tilda through the foyer, she instinctively scanned her eyes left toward the front door, and then to the right, toward a door under the stairs that she hadn't quite noticed before. They moved up to the ceiling, where an ornate gold light fixture hung, and back down again to the threadbare rug.

Their procession continued into the dining room, where Magdalena was seated at the head of the table. It was set with a similar tea service to when she first arrived. Where there had been biscuits last time (which were so dry she'd nearly choked to death), there were now finger sandwiches and fruit laid out upon a silver platter.

Harlem's heart sank, "I thought we were going to go out?"

"I thought about that, dear, and I became concerned that perhaps you wouldn't be able to endure Harlem's streets. You were feeling so sickly. It can get awfully hectic out there, what with all the people that have descended upon this place—much like yourself."

Harlem slid into her chair, placed her purse on the table, and grabbed the waiting linen napkin. "I see."

"You're disappointed. Don't be. You have tomorrow, and the day after that, and all the days following to go out. It wouldn't really do you any good to go out while you're weak, don't you agree?"

"I'm sure you have a point," Harlem said. She watched little Tilda pour coffee for Magdalena from a silver urn near her end of the table. Tilda then walked toward Harlem and began to pour her some tea.

"Tilda, would you mind terribly? I'd prefer the coffee that Lady Magdalena is having. Thank you." Harlem remembered her first tea at that table had been tepid, bitter, and tasted of almonds. There was no need to repeat that experience.

Tilda looked to Magdalena, who seemed to hesitate before nodding her approval. The girl retrieved the coffee and filled Harlem's china cup with the hot liquid. Harlem admired the dainty painted cherries around the rim as she took a sip. She was so eager to drink it that she nearly burnt her tongue.

"Careful, dear. Careful," Magdalena laughed.

"I've gotten ahead of myself," Harlem replied with a grin. Tilda served the sandwiches, and Harlem forced herself to take her time and be more ladylike while consuming them. As she swallowed her first bite, she realized that she could have waited an eternity to eat it. It seemed to be a sandwich of only butter, salt, and pepper. The bread was old, dry, and as disappointing as the biscuits had been. She reached for her coffee and swirled it in her mouth to help coax the offensive stuff down her throat. Harlem glanced at Tilda; if the girl was responsible for making and serving this drivel, she needed some stern talking to.

"So, tell me, dearest Ann, what are your plans?" Magdalena asked. She chewed her sandwich demurely, looking quite relaxed in a pale yellow, high-buttoned shirt in the crepe fabric that Harlem loved.

"Plans?" Harlem coughed, partly at the food and partly at remembering that she had indeed told these people her name was "Ann Smith." "I'm not certain yet. I've only just gotten here. I imagine there is so much to see and do in Harlem."

"That there is. So much. And do you have any skills?"

"No," Harlem debated having another bite. She was so hungry. Against all the manners she'd been taught, she tried dunking the bread in her coffee.

"Sewing?" Magdalena asked, with evident distaste on her face.

Harlem covered her mouth with her delicate hand as she chewed. "No."

"Cooking?"

"No."

"Did your parents not prepare you for this world, for a life?" Magdalena asked.

Harlem wasn't sure how to explain that days at her family mansion had prepared her one thing: a life of solitude. Dancing endlessly in the room of mirrors with the tinny music floating about like a forlorn apparition; walking on the grounds through the tall grass, collecting ladybugs for companions; taking drives with George to a nearby creek, where they'd share proper sandwiches of cured bacon and fresh tomatoes; or hiding in the attic to avoid her father's desire for her. "I'd wanted to go to boarding school, but I lived a pretty sheltered life back in Greensboro."

Magdalena sat back in her chair, holding her coffee cup to her red lips. "Sheltered?"

"Yes."

"I see," Magdalena said slowly.

"I can dance. I'm a good dancer," Harlem said. She motioned to Tilda to bring her the cream and sugar. She needed all the help she could get with this meal. She hoped dinner would fare better.

"I see. Some of the girls at my manor are also dancers; some make some money doing it, others, not as much. Perhaps you can chat with them."

Tilda clumsily dropped the spoon from the sugar bowl.

"Tilda, if you can't handle yourself, you may be excused," Magdalena said with a touch more anger than Harlem thought necessary. Tilda delivered the sugar, sans spoon, and retreated to what Harlem assumed was the kitchen.

"Perhaps I shall speak with the girls. Will they be around this evening? I've noticed it to be so very quiet here. Is that normal?"

"The girls here are very respectful of my manor. There's not a lot of carrying on here. And some are out, of course."

"Of course," Harlem said, stirring her coffee with her knife.

"I apologize to be so forward with this question, but what will you do for money, dear? Rent is due each month, you know. On time, I'm afraid."

"I have means. That won't be a problem at all," Harlem said, perhaps too quickly.

"That is a comfort to me, then. Thank you."

"Thank you for allowing me to stay." Harlem wasn't sure if she should confide in this woman. Of course, she needed to do something worthwhile in life, but concerning herself about means was not one of them, at least not at this point. Strangely enough, she hadn't thought beyond the Greyhound bus ride to New York. She hadn't thought about her future and what she would do with it; she just knew that she had one.

An idea came to her. "I was thinking about school, actually. That perhaps I would add to my studies somehow."

"Studies?" Magdalena laughed. "Women studying? Well, perhaps something clerical—"

"There are universities that accept women here, I'm sure. I could attend one. Perhaps go to a conservatory for dance. That's something."

"You'll need money for that, I'm afraid."

"I have money, as I said."

"Enough for an education? You must be a lucky girl."

"I suppose," Harlem said, forcing herself to forget the past.

"Your life is set, then. You will go to a dance conservatory, somehow. I will help you when you're ready. You just let me know." Magdalena rose. "I remember when you arrived you indicated that your family was deceased."

"They are."

"Why then—and again, please forgive my forwardness—how will you access these funds you've declared? Perhaps there is a benefactor or a distant aunt you've not mentioned."

"I would need to go to a bank. Mr. Hatch, our family accountant, said for me to set up an account—that it would be fairly easy. Even in New York."

"I'll introduce you to my personal banker, Stan Trieg. You'll get along fantastically, I'm sure."

"That would be kind of you, thank you. Shall we go tomorrow?" Harlem asked, now excited to be taking a first step toward her future.

"I'm sure that could be arranged. I'll put in a call."

"Splendid," Harlem touched the corners of her mouth with her napkin. "And the girls? It is so terribly quiet. Where are the girls, Lady Magdalena? I expected to see at least one of them by now? Perhaps running about, getting ready for work or for suitors?" Harlem giggled lightly. "I just—I don't know... I thought I'd see... Umm..." She struggled to remember anyone's name. She snapped her fingers. "Amoura! Amoura, where is that delightful woman today?"

"They are all at work, dear. They have full schedules, I'm afraid. You'll see them at dinner. How's that?" Magdalena smiled.

Harlem noticed her eyes had drifted to a small tapestry of a white hound standing at attention in front of a Victorian-looking castle. "Is that a favorite?" Harlem asked.

"A gentleman caller gave it to me. Tilda. Straighten that frame, would you?" Magdalena's face clouded; the smile had vanished.

"The piece next to it is quite striking," Harlem noted in reference to the huge portrait hanging next to the hound.

"It took nearly a month of sitting for that portrait. It is nothing if not striking!" Magdalena mused. "My home wouldn't be complete without it."

"I'd have to agree," Harlem said.

The room fell silent. Harlem looked around the room. It was handsome. The three empty high-backed chairs on either side of the table were outfitted in purple silk brocade. A stately, sparkling chandelier hung above the solid oak table. Where windows could have been were more tapestries: three of them, each depicting a scene related to the hound and the castle. A man atop a steed, holding a rifle and looking far off into the distance; the castle small and deep in the foreground; a forest of thick white and knotted pine trees with the hound holding a bloodied rabbit in its mouth.

I'm a girl who is good. I'm a girl who should be happy, healthy and whole. I'm untouchable on the inside, where the good me resides, looped through her mind as she stared at the ghastly art. She felt panicked. Her heart began to race, and her legs fidgeted underneath the table. Harlem nearly shouted, "Perhaps a walk! Perhaps I could walk down the block with Tilda? Just to the end and back?"

Tilda had disappeared into the kitchen. A pan dropped and clattered loudly.

Magdalena rolled her eyes and sighed. "Tilda has two left feet and three right arms, I'm afraid. She has no magnitude for the type of walks I imagine you are used to."

Frustration swirled in her sour stomach. Harlem grabbed her purse and slid her chair away from the table. "Would you mind terribly if I did return to my room for a bit? I think more rest is in order for me."

"As you wish."

Harlem stood and dropped the cloth napkin on the table. Her heels clicked against the hardwood floor as she continued back through the foyer and up to her room. Her stomach wasn't any better off than when she first sat down. She wondered if the butter hadn't been rancid or something equally awful.

Perhaps this seemingly glamourous place wasn't so glamourous. It was turning out to be pretty dull. She trudged back up the stairs, flinging the folds of her dress with her hand as she did so. Disappointment stung in the back of her throat, but she refused to cry, again. Perhaps she could search for another place to stay, she thought. She cringed at the thought of the first place she'd gone when she'd arrived in Harlem. Luckily, the sisters, Ruth and Mary, had been with her and advised her against the atrocity. The boarding house had been full of people quite literally hanging out of the windows, whooping and hollering. She'd made a note to tell her accountant, the old turtle-head Mr. Hatch, that his suggestion had been awful, and to see if he had another. She hoped he could come

through for her. In the meantime, Lady Magdalena's
Manor was going to have to do.

CHAPTER 12

As soon as Harlem was out of her sight, Magdalena jumped from her seat and danced around in a fit that even she couldn't contain. She clapped her hands joyously. This was going to be easier than she imagined. She was so glad she'd thought to change tactics. Late last night she had returned the check to Harlem's purse and brought the suitcase up to the girl's room. At the time, she wasn't sure how she was going to get that check, but today when Harlem suggested she do it *herself*— she could hardly contain herself!

The real work would begin tomorrow. Harlem would deposit the check and somehow, she was going to have to persuade the girl to hand over the money. She'd have to take her time with this. Maybe she could make the girl her partner and lead Harlem to believe that Mysterie was on the up and up. Then she could incrementally ask for more and more investments to cover bogus costs. Isn't that how people swindled people these days? If she were patient, a scheme like that could work. *But, Magdalena thought, I don't have that much time...* With Lucinda breathing down her neck, along with every bill collector in town, she couldn't wait for long-winded shenanigans to come to fruition.

Magdalena went into her office, carrying her coffee cup with her. She sat behind her desk and stared at the ceiling for answers. Her eyes followed along the crown molding, waiting for it or anything else to provide some guidance. She jolted forward and snapped her fingers. *Got it!* She would persuade Harlem to cash the check, deposit some of the money, and then carry a larger portion of it with her out of the bank—tell her the banks in Manhattan were corrupt and that the mattress was safer. Magdalena could steal cash. She'd done it before. She could steal the dough and kick the girl out. The girl would be left with some money in the bank and Magdalena would have everything she needed in hand. She could survive and then some. She could get back to being black.

CHAPTER 13

Harlem woke the next day and felt ten times better than she had the day before. Sleep really did do wonders for a person. She glanced hazily at the gold watch she'd brought with her to get a semblance of the time. It was stopped at five o'clock. She had no idea what the hour really was, nor the day to which it belonged. She looked toward the wall again, unable to understand why this room had no windows. Her room back home had French doors which led to a balcony overlooking the backyard. She had loved waking up to sunlight and using it to tell if it was dawn or dusk. This room was highly unsettling.

Getting dressed for today was easy; she chose to wear the same dress she'd worn yesterday. No one had really seen it anyways, and it was one of her favorites. Once she'd slipped back into it and was ready to go, she grabbed her purse, made sure her check was there, and walked out of her room to descend the stairs.

She slowly approached the pocket doors; they'd been left slightly ajar. Unsure if she should enter, she peeked inside first. What she saw made her draw her breath with a sharpness that hurt.

CHAPTER 14

Harlem gazed at the gaunt faces of several women who were scattered throughout the dining room. As different as they were individually, they all carried a palpable longing to be elsewhere. Dressed in drab, dirty lingerie, some sat upon the long dining room table and languished there. One leaned forlornly against the serving buffet, while another draped herself over the back of a chair. In one of two corner chairs along the back wall another sat slumped and distracted. Despondence was something she knew all too well, and it cloaked them all.

A sensation crept into her; it was the same sensation that had paralyzed Harlem when she'd step cautiously into her mother's bedroom looking for some comfort and instead would find an empty woman, frozen stiff at her vanity. Silver hairbrush held as though cemented in her hand. Unresponsive to life, and equally unresponsive to Harlem.

She stared at Magdalena and the nine women before her. She immediately recognized Desire and Fury; yet there was no consolation in this recognition.

"Shut up, you hussies," Magdalena said, opening a large ledger, similar to one she'd seen at Mr. Hatch's law office.

Amoura entered, wearing an apron over a set of thin undergarments. Gone was the glamour, the dazzle Harlem had seen before in the girl. Harlem was staring at a ghost.

The massive chandelier sparkled oddly above them all as Amoura set down a large platter of withered toast and what looked like thin, shriveled strips of fried ham. The girls clambered for the food like animals. Amoura stood back away from them and returned to the kitchen, with Tilda following behind her.

"I'm so incredibly tired of this," one girl said.

"What?" Magdalena said, looking up from the ledger.

"You torturing us with this slop you call food. You're lower than a dog."

The girls stopped; silence followed.

Magdalena leaned toward the girl; she had broad shoulders and hair that curled around her ears. "What did you say to me, Sapphire?"

Sapphire gnawed off a bite of bread and mumbled something into her plate. Magdalena reached across the table and grabbed the girl's jaw roughly with one hand and lifted her chin, "I said, what did you say to me?"

The girl shook her head, "Nothing," but as Magdalena released her vice grip, the girl spit her food at the older woman. Instantly, Magdalena slapped her. The girl reeled back in her chair and fell to the ground.

Harlem gasped; her hand flew to her own face, remembering the time she'd been on the receiving end of such a blow: Mrs. Whitscomber's vicious, redemptive slap on the courthouse stairs. The haughty socialite was her mother's friend and blamed Harlem for her death. Harlem jumped away from slit in the door, pulling herself out of sight. She turned back when she found her breath.

Fury stood and shouted, "Leave her alone!"

Amoura ran into the room, "What's happened?" she exclaimed.

Sapphire scrambled up from the ground and ran past Magdalena's office door, pulling a cord that hung from the wall. Harlem remembered the large, hideous painting of Magdalena as it split open, revealing stairs Harlem had walked down last night. Sapphire ran down them. "I hope you burn in hell!" she cried over her shoulder.

"Must you continue to beat up on us, Magdalena?" Fury said.

Magdalena said, "How I run this place is none of your concern, Fury."

That was the last thing Harlem heard. She turned and ran up the stairs to her room. Breathless, she grabbed her stockings that were hanging on the bathtub, found her toothbrush and robe, and stuffed them all into her suitcase. She closed the clasps, grabbed her second suitcase, which she'd found earlier that day in the closet, and ran back out.

She skittered down the stairs as quietly as she could, hoping to not bump her cases or make any noise. Her heart was pounding. She'd never been so scared to run. Harlem reached the door and turned the skeleton key in the lock. She managed to open it and lunged through the vestibule toward the front door. Harlem pushed on the lever of the wrought-iron handle with her palms. It wouldn't budge. She dropped the suitcases and, tugging with both hands, she jerked back and forth with the full weight of her body, desperately trying to open the door. Harlem found herself slapping at the windowpane, "Help! Let me out!" Suddenly the door swung open. She stepped back, snatched up her cases and charged through it, smack into the arms of a large man who was standing in front of the doorway.

Harlem wrestled her way out his arms clumsily. "Let me alone!" she screamed. She fell to her knees as he lost his grip. A woman passed by; she held her child close.

"Wait! Hello? Just a minute!" Harlem yelled to the woman.

The woman stopped, frightened, "What's happened?"

"Keep it movin' and mind your business, ma'am," Harlem heard.

Harlem turned toward the voice and finally saw the man she had knocked into. Relieved, she reached for the man and said, "Officer, help me. Please. I need —I—"

"We've got everything covered here, Miss," the officer said to the woman as he snapped handcuffs onto Harlem's wrists.

"No, wait a minute! What are you doing?" Harlem wailed.

"That's for me t' know and you t' find out."

Harlem craned her neck and called back to the woman, "Help! Miss, come back!" The woman turned away, picked up her child and hurried down the street.

"Shut yer trap!" Officer Brighton grunted. He grabbed her suitcases, lifted Harlem onto his shoulders and carried her back up the stairs.

Harlem's arms were cuffed in front of her and now were pinned between her body and the officer's. Her cheek slammed against his back, and the roughness of the wool coat scratched her face. Harlem lifted her head and yelled, "This isn't right!" Harlem kicked and screamed from over the officer's shoulder, "HELP!" She looked for someone else on the streets to help her but those that passed by did nothing.

Officer Brighton carried Harlem into the house and deposited her in the dining room.

"Ufff!" she exhaled as she collapsed to the floor and tried as best she could to grab her throbbing, cuffed wrists.

Magdalena shot up from her chair, "What on earth?"

"Caught her tryin' to escape is what on earth! Lucky for you, I caught her before she did."

"What exactly is going on here, Magdalena?" Harlem stared at all the women present, including little Tilda. They looked as shocked as she must have.

Magdalena clasped her hands like a priest and walked toward Harlem. "Where were you going, dear? What's happened?"

"I saw you. You slapped that girl—"

Magdalena stopped. Her eyes got very cold. She looked like a different woman.

Harlem continued looking at the girls, "And, and why are they all in their—where are your *clothes*? This isn't right at all. Something isn't right. And this!" She lifted her handcuffed arms as she stood up to face the officer. "You take these off me! I haven't done anything wrong."

The man shoved her into a chair. "Shuddup, I'm doin' nothing of the kind."

Magdalena turned her back to Harlem. The other girls, the ones she knew—Amoura, Desire, and Fury—dropped their heads as she looked at them. Magdalena strolled back to her position at the head of the table. "It is truly unfortunate that you didn't just follow the plan, *Harlem*."

"What?"

"Yes, I know your real name is Harlem. Harlem Markeson, I believe? Doesn't matter, really. You've let the cat out of the bag and now things have changed. You have yourself to blame for what's to happen next."

"I—I don't understand," Harlem said. She felt as though she were sinking in quicksand.

"Officer Brighton," Magdalena said. "Would you kindly help this charlatan to her feet?"

Officer Brighton pulled Harlem up roughly.

Magdalena sat. "Indigo, Violet, Sienna, go stand next to your new comrade."

The three Negro girls approached her. Their eyes were empty, their bodies like robots. They stood next to her as though she were a robot too. But she wasn't like them. Her skin was tingling; every cell was on alert. She was alive. *She was alive!*

"I've an idea. What do you think, Officer Brighton? Who looks most like this Harlem girl?" Magdalena sipped from her coffee cup like they were having high tea on any given Sunday.

Officer Brighton stepped backwards, silhouetted against the grotesque, fractured portrait into which Sapphire had disappeared. He crossed his arms. "How would I know? This ain't a real line up."

"Try."

"Well, Indigo's got the same brown color as her, but she's got the round nose an' her jaw's a little squarish, but she looks rough 'round the edges—like she'd cut y' in a minute and bake you yer favorite cake while y' laid there bleedin'. And Violet there, she's our movie star with them crazy-colored violet eyes and that curvy figure any driver would like t' race around, but we see she's a half-breed mulatto, so she ain't neither here nor there. And Sienna's got that long hair like nobody else and skin like somebody rubbed cinnamon all over it... to's the point I don't know where it's from. In fact, what are you, girl?"

"Doesn't matter what she *is*, Officer Brighton. Continue!"

"Alright. Alright! They're about the same height and all, but udder'dan that, I don't think they look nothin' likes this new girl and not a one of 'em acts like her neither," he shrugged.

"Oh, what do you know anyway?" Magdalena said. "In fact, you're excused for the evening. Thank you, Officer Brighton. I'll handle it from here."

"Yessiree. *Ma'am.*"

Magdalena walked closer to Harlem as Officer Brighton slowly backed out, watching them all. Harlem stared at him hard as he left. "How dare he pretend to help people?"

Magdalena grabbed her chin and bore into her with her eyes. "You'll watch your mouth. The freedoms you've been accustomed to are no longer."

"What are you talking about?" Harlem said.

Magdalena shoved her aside. She retrieved Harlem's suitcases, set them on the table and opened both.

"Those are mine!"

"Nothing you have belongs to you anymore. Not even yourself." Magdalena rifled around until she found Harlem's purse.

"You're deranged. Give me my things back. Let me out of here!" Harlem thrashed against her cuffs which only bit deeper into her flesh. "Let me out!"

Magdalena opened Harlem's purse. Harlem screamed, "Keep your crummy hands off my personal things!" She ran toward Magdalena, but she was quicker than Harlem, more prepared. Magdalena backhanded her square across her jaw, causing her to spin into the other girls with a force she couldn't control. Harlem fell into them like a bowling pin. She struggled to her feet. She stared at Magdalena with eyes so hot with anger she felt like her entire face was steaming.

"How dare you!"

Magdalena held up Harlem's check.

Harlem froze. "My inheritance."

"Ahhh an *inheritance*. Impressive," Magdalena laughed as she waved the check like a flag on Independence Day.

With raspy, hushed whispers the women seated around the table turned into a pack of coyotes and stared hauntingly at her. Quite alive now. Even as their prey, Harlem looked back at all of them defiantly. "My inheritance is none of anyone's business."

"It's my business now," Magdalena said.

"You've no right!" Harlem said, slamming her palms on the table, the metal handcuffs clattering. She felt like she was back on trial, back in Greensboro where the judge had toyed with her freedom just as Magdalena was now. "That is my money!"

"Splendid. Maybe we can help each other out."

"What do you mean? That is my check, *I* earned that money—"

"If you'll stop shouting, I can tell you what we can do."

Harlem continued shouting, "You will listen to me, and you will—"

Magdalena roared, "No, you'll listen to *me*! I'm the one in charge here. Not you."

Harlem flinched. She thought fast, thought of her Grandma Markeson. Grandma had said she was going to need a big stick to stop people from trying to take advantage of her. *Oh!* How she wished she had a big stick right now. All she had were her wits. Harlem collected herself. "What do you want?"

Magdalena stared at her. "You will go to the bank with me, cash the check, give me all the dimes, and I'll let you go free."

"I won't!" Harlem said.

"Arthur wanted me to tell you that he really, really enjoyed being with you at my party," Magdalena said as she smoothed her eyebrows.

"Arthur...?" Harlem's knees weakened.

"He's told all of his friends about you. They can't wait to meet you, personally."

The girls shifted in their places, making chairs squeak faintly like mice eavesdropping; no eyes would look at her now.

"What are you talking about?" Harlem reached for the back of the chair near her and held on with both hands. Her head was spinning. Arthur. Red dress. *Ma chérie.* Kisses...

"You and Arthur. Last night. Your little *rendezvous?*" Magdalena sauntered into her office. "Certainly, you remember your time with your friend?" she called out.

"How do you know about that?" Harlem slumped into the chair in front of her.

Magdalena returned with a small wooden box. "Because I arranged it," she mused as she set the box down near her seat and checked the green ledger, which was still open and resting near her coffee cup.

Magdalena's long finger traced along a page in the ledger. "He paid quite handsomely for you," she said, looking up at Harlem. "Something to do with you being so exotic and new."

The girls slowly pulled themselves straight in their chairs, as Magdalena reviewed the ledger. They dutifully clasped their hands on the table, looking straight ahead as though in a classroom. Tilda stood off from the table in a corner, a silent, tiny nun.

Magdalena picked up the box and walked with it toward Harlem, "In fact, I hate to break it to each of you girls, and especially you, Ruby," Magdalena paused and used her pinky to lift the girl's pale pink brassiere strap back up onto her freckled shoulder, "but 'Miss *Ann*' here was the highest bid last night. Imagine. A new and, might I add, younger girl, beating out each of you."

The girls groaned quietly; Ruby's head slumped to her hands. Her short, black curls flopped forward in defeat.

Harlem looked up at Magdalena now, the smell of cigarette smoke trapped in her clothing announcing her unwanted proximity.

"You must have some kind of experience, sweetie," Magdalena tapped Harlem proudly under the chin just as her own mother had done for perfecting an *arabesque*. Harlem jerked her chin away.

Magdalena carefully opened the box she held revealing a row of cigarettes and placed one on the table. "Your pay and reward for work well done," Magdalena's smile broadened; her green eyes lit up horribly as she set yet another cigarette on the table and winked. "Very well done."

"I hate you. You are an evil, evil woman."

"I stopped thinking I had a chance at heaven long ago, sister," Magdalena laughed and swooped her shiny black hair from her shoulder. "Now then, back to business." She turned toward the three Negro girls from the lineup. They were statues against the wall now, a string of cut-out dolls from brown, wrinkled parcel paper. "One of these girls will be signing over the check to me, just as though you'd done it yourself. Lucky for me, not a soul in New York knows who you are or what you look like, *Miss Markeson.* Nor do they care. Therefore, I no longer need you. Well, not for this."

"Have you lost your mind?" Harlem yelled. The girls seated at the table stared at her like cats soaked in the rain waiting to be let in.

"Perhaps!" Magdalena yelled back mockingly. "She's putting up quite a fuss, isn't she, girls?"

The soaked cats said nothing.

Huffing in disgust, Magdalena continued with a fling of her hand, "Girls show her downstairs and get her acclimated to how things are. I'll be down later to check on your progress."

Robotically, the three girls circled her and tried to latch on. They became a three-headed monster of gangly arms, hot, heavy breath, and eyeballs.

"Let go of me," Harlem screamed shrilly and struggled against their grip. "I said let *go!*" Harlem flung her shackled limbs and smacked the girl with the cinnamon skin's chest unintentionally.

"Hey, watch it!" Sienna scolded, holding her breast, "whad'ya think this is, some kinda boxin' match?"

Harlem glared at their three brown faces circling her, "Don't you dare touch me!"

Violet lowered her near-perfect face to Harlem's. She gripped Harlem's elbow and whispered urgently, "If you know what's good for you, you'll play along, sister."

"I said, don't touch me!"

"You don't want to get on Magdalena's bad side." Violet grabbed Harlem's elbow again.

Harlem squirmed, "I don't care about her bad side. She's not getting my money!"

Indigo's square jaw tightened; she pushed Violet aside and grabbed Harlem around the waist. "You're gonna find out fast that whatever you walked in here with ain't yours anymore. So that means we're all you got, and believe me, that ain't a lot."

Harlem started screaming, "Leave me alone! Give me back my things!"

Indigo cinched her brown, muscular arm tighter around Harlem's waist and clamped a rough hand over Harlem's mouth, muffling her cries. Sienna, with her long black hair almost reaching her behind, got in front of them all, stood between Harlem's legs and lifted them from the ground like the handles of a wheelbarrow.

Harlem thrashed against them, trying to catch her breath but Indigo's hot hand gagged her with the reek of sweat and fried meat. The split in the portrait swallowed them as they descended the stairs into darkness.

CHAPTER 15

"Let me go!" Harlem shouted; her words muffled behind Indigo's clamped hand, which gripped hard against her cheekbones. Harlem twisted and convulsed against their monstrous constraints. "Help!"

"Stop squirmin' like an eel. You want us all t' fall and break our god-forsakin' necks?" Sienna shouted from within the black tube that now shrouded them all in its darkness.

There was no telling what they were going to do to her or where they were going to take her. She truly didn't want to find out. She just wanted to go home. Harlem jerked again. A stinging pain shot through her calves. She kicked and screamed out, "Oww!"

Sienna dug her fingernails deeper into Harlem's legs. "I told you t' *stop* it!"

Harlem screamed and kicked again. Sienna slapped at her legs, "I'm warnin' you!"

"You can save yourself the trouble of screamin', too!" Indigo threatened. "No one can hear you 'cept for us, and we can't help you." Indigo released her grip on Harlem's mouth, "Understand?"

"Heeeelppp!" she screamed.

Sienna slapped at her again, "You are to stop that THIS INSTANT!"

"Ow!" Harlem eyed the girl's long hair hanging down her back and wanted to yank it, but she couldn't reach that far. "You! You horrible girls! Stringing me up like a hog. Let me alone!"

They reached the bottom of the stairs, "You're lucky I don't just drop you right here and now!" Indigo huffed while holding Harlem by her armpits in a wrestler's grip. "Sienna, let her legs down. Just let her down."

Instead, Harlem squirmed from their grasp and fell flat to the cold floor.

"Y' try to help somebody!" Indigo said as she walked away, massaging her thick wrists.

"You are one heavy pile a' rocks, sister. An' you look so slim, too. Good golly!" Sienna said, after getting in one good kick.

"Tyrant!" Harlem said as she kicked the girl back and missed. The rest of the girls filed down the stairs and stepped over her to form a half circle around her, staring down with the type of quizzical look one gets when inspecting something strange in a gutter.

"Do you mind?" Harlem said, looking up at their black, brown, and white faces. She pulled herself to her knees, placing her hands on the rough concrete floor to steady herself.

"Somebody get her a chair, would ya?" Indigo said, leaving the circle. "Let's pretend like we have some kind of manners."

A chair scraped roughly against the floor, and two girls lifted her to her feet and deposited her onto a wooden chair. She felt like she'd just stepped off a merry-go-round. "My head is spinning," Harlem said.

"It's the tea," one of the girls said loudly; her deep, scratchy voice matched her face, which was etched with scars. Her shock of curly, bright orange hair made her look like she'd been zapped by an electrical current.

"It's probably more than the tea, Topaz," Violet added, standing next to the scratchy, red-haired girl as they both peered at Harlem. "I'd call it shock!"

"I need some water," Harlem said. She dropped her head in her hands. The handcuffs clinked on her wrists. "Can't I please have some water?"

"If you hadn't noticed, this isn't the Ritz," Ruby said with a raspy cough that Harlem knew to come from smoking, rather than age. "Welcome home, just the same."

Harlem lifted her head. "Welcome home?"

Ruby shoved a chair under a table, "Sorry we didn't get a chance to tidy up for you."

Harlem looked around and licked her lips for any moisture she could get. "What's happened to the candles and the white tablecloths? It was so nice before." Rough, round tables dotted the room and loose saloon chairs were like errant children scattered about in places other than where they were supposed to be. To her left, the stage, which had glowed with animated beauty previously, seemed uninviting even with the flowing red curtain that draped the back wall of the stage. The gold curtains that had framed it with glorious glamour in the candlelight now hung lack-luster like soaked clothes left in the rain on a clothesline. The wooden floor that had been alive with dancing and movement was stark and ugly without stage lights; it was deeply scratched and looked as worn out as the girls who stood before her. The piano, situated on the floor to the right of the stage, looked lonely and practically afraid.

"Magdalena takes all the good stuff with her after our little parties. We do our best with what we've got, don't we girls?" Ruby said, pushing her coarse hair, black like coal, away from her forehead with her cigarette between her fingers.

Harlem looked around the room. "You mean to say you live down here?"

"And now you do, too, it would seem."

"What?"

Ruby wove through the tables toward another red curtain; this one hung from a rod and lined the back wall of the room. She pulled the curtain along with her as she walked, revealing several doors, each a different color. "These are our rooms."

"That can't be true."

Topaz stepped near her and bellowed, "Why would we lie?"

Harlem winced. The girl's voice was as painful to her ears as if they'd been boxed by the girl herself. "I'm—I'm not calling you liars," she stammered. "I just don't fully understand what it is that you're telling me. It's quite—It's not—It's not what I expected. At all." Harlem looked to the ceiling, it was lined with thick wooden beams that held the dank smell of a cellar and hung low. It was suffocating. Tears began to form in the corners of her eyes. Nothing at all had gone right since she left Greensboro. She wondered if anything had ever gone right in her life. What had she done to deserve being treated so poorly, over and over again? She wanted to ask God these things. Instead she wailed, "Why am I down here?"

She was met with silence, the same type that she'd experienced upstairs. Harlem raised her eyebrows, "Why?"

"Look at us. Why do you think?" Ruby asked, brown eyes squinting while she dragged on a cigarette.

They were like no women she had ever seen or met. Back home, her world of women had been small. It barely extended beyond her pert schoolteachers and private tutors in their modest black skirts and starched white blouses. There were also the women at church, of course (when Harlem and her mother went). They were sanctified in their holiness and walked with an air of piousness that seemed to lift their noses high toward Jesus and away from anything less. If they were ever downtrodden, they were so at home in their private rural houses, not out in the streets of Greensboro. These women, in their colorful hats brimmed with veils that created an air of exclusion, rarely focused on Harlem. They thought her to be tainted by wealth and other things they spoke about in hushed tones behind her back. Her mother hadn't had many womenfolk friends beyond the sour Mrs. Whitscomber, who came to their home less and less once Susannah stopped opening the door for visits—leaving the woman to stand on the porch, peering inside their dark home with its dark secrets. Even the little girls who stood by the side of the road selling peaches, with their hair mussed about their heads and tattered clothes that were either too small or too big for their hungry brown bodies, didn't seem like these six women before her. These women hungered for something, but Harlem didn't know what it was. They came from another world, another place of secrets and whispers created prior to life in this dank basement in Lady Magdalena's home.

Indigo pulled a chair forward and sat down in front of Harlem. She crossed one brown leg over the other and smoothed the wrinkles from her threadbare tap pants, riddled with so many mended stitches Harlem wondered whether there was any material left to them at all. A camisole with its one good strap hung from her nearly naked chest, highlighting a prominent collar bone, the kind debutants wished for and hung strings of pearls from. With hair in plaits that twisted about her head like a crown, she leaned forward, resting on her chin on her hand. Harlem noticed her right eye drooped a bit, giving her a fixed, demure wink.

"I'm going to give it to you straight, young honey. Because I can see that all 'a this is a bit new for you. But I want to tell you a story first. Alright?"

"Yes," Harlem said, feeling quite naked in front of this woman, even though she was fully clothed. Harlem relaxed her hands into her lap sensing this Indigo was to be her new teacher.

"I used to live in a cute little spot over on 118th Street. Me and my old man, Scottie. One day, I'm out getting some groceries, minding my own business, and this patsy come up to me and says, 'Don't I know you?' I says, 'No' and I walk around him with my bag of bread and bottle of milk and he starts to follow me. He proceeds to tell me that I look a lot like a dame he saw on the block who'd been hanging out the window, selling her wares to every fella on the street. I says, 'Wasn't me.' He pulls out a badge and says, 'I think it was.' Now. That was the beginning of a new life for me that I didn't ask for in any kind of way. And since you're new to Harlem, I'm gonna let you know that this sorta thing was occurring up and down every block. Especially to girls who look like you and me." Indigo leaned back in her chair. "Am I right, girls?"

Sienna and Violet, standing behind Indigo's chair, nodded their heads.

"That man was how I got into the business of selling goods, if you know what I mean. He brought fellas to me who didn't want to be seen with no streetwalker or get caught up in a raid at a flop house, see? I had to do all of that and pay him a bunch of lettuce for him to not take me down to the reformatory and lock me up for bad deeds done against society. What he was doin' was a racket and still is. But I got good on him. After a while, I got some muscle behind me and scared that stool pigeon off, and I started my own business. And I was making some real good money. Good money. I was enjoying my work. I was my own boss. I wasn't cleaning nothing for nobody. Understand?"

Harlem swallowed hard and nodded.

"I had it good. Only, my old man, Scottie, didn't know I had this little business. One day, he comes home for lunch unannounced and there I was, working. He didn't like that too much. He beat me up, gave me this beautiful eye, and threw me out on the street in not much more than what I's got on now. You follow me?"

"Yes," Harlem said.

"Good. Glad you're a smart girl. The work I was doing in my own home is the work we do down here. Got it?"

"But why?"

"The 'why' is for our darling Magdalena to know. That's above my paygrade. But if I had to guess, she was probably in a similar situation at one point or another, saw an opportunity just like that patsy did, and turned into a businesswoman herself."

Harlem thought about how she'd been an opportunity for her father, Roy. *What kind of a business had she been for him?* Her heart began to race. How she wished she'd gone to the address Mr. Hatch had recommended. Hooligans and loud music would have been a better option than what she had gotten into down here. Her mind raced with questions, "But why live down here? Certainly there are other choices?"

Indigo leaned back in her chair and Violet answered, her stunningly bright blueish-purplish eyes shooting darts of truth, "Look at us, do we look like we have a lot of choices in life? Choice has been removed from the equation, honey." Violet seemed tired with having to explain this to Harlem, and her thin fingers ran over her high cheek bones as she exhaled. "For one, most of us got rap sheets as long as little Johnny's Christmas list, and if we don't have that, we've got no other place to go. Probably just like you—"

"But I'm not like you—"

"I'll pretend you're not trying to be disrespectful by saying that," Violet said, narrowing her eyes which became steel blue with anger and pointed her finger at Harlem. (She'd never seen eyes like hers on a colored girl.) "You better understand right now that you are not any better than any of us."

"That's not what I meant," Harlem said, looking around at the six women. While they were of different colors and shapes and sizes, their faces were all creased with the same deep lines of annoyance, and all aimed at her. "I'm sorry. I—I—" she stammered.

Indigo shook her head and looked off and away from Harlem.

Sienna came forward and kneeled beside her, touching Harlem's knee, "Listen. I'm sorry I was so rough wit' you sweetie, but I had to do it," Sienna said, sweeping her long black hair from one shoulder to the next. "I hope you understand. I wanted this to be as painless as possible for you."

"This?" Harlem asked the girl.

"It happened to all of us, didn't it, girls?" Sienna called out to them.

Murmurs of agreement met her.

Sienna continued, "We call it initiation, basically. Listen, we all come from different backgrounds; once you get to know us, you'll see. But what we have in common is that we ain't leavin' anytime soon."

Harlem darted her eyes between the girls. "I'm not going to be a prisoner down here! That can't be what you're telling me." Topaz and her scratched face shook her curly head slowly. A pale-looking blond who had yet to say a word slowly dropped her chin. Ruby blew out a stream of smoke and hunched her shoulders.

"Well, I dunno exactly what's gonna happen for you," Sienna responded, twisting her hair into a loose braid. "I can tell you that I been here for three years —"

"THREE YEARS!?" Harlem jerked fully upright against the chair, knocking Sienna onto her round bottom. "What? You've been down here for *three whole years?*" Harlem gripped her knees, feeling the chill of her skin as she tried to contain herself. She jumped to her feet and began spinning around like a top. "Three years?"

"Sienna! Now you've done it, y' big blabbermouth. What'd you go and tell her that for?" Indigo said, going to Harlem's side.

Sienna stood, brushing her hands against her negligée. "What? It's the truth. She's gonna find out sooner or later that she ain't getting out. Not like this is some fancy hotel and we each have a god-damned key!"

"I can't do it! I can't. I can't be down here like this! Help! Help me, somebody!" Suddenly she felt like someone was kneeling on her chest and covering her face with a pillow. She gulped for air, wheezing with each gasp. She fell back to the chair; gripped her fingers for strength. "I can't breathe. I can't breathe..."

"Don't go and flip your lid," Violet said. "Put your head between your legs or something!"

"Harlem, baby," Indigo said, holding Harlem's chin gently, "Look at me. Look at me."

Between sobs that racked her body, she said to Indigo, "But I don't want to live down here! My life is upstairs. Magdalena has it. I want it back." Harlem caught her breath, blinked through the tears soaking her eyelashes. The girl's dark, experienced eyes searched hers; this close, Harlem could see the faint, jagged scar just above her eyelid.

"I want to tell you it's going to be okay; it is for the most part. You're not going t' die. We'll take care of you best we can. Got it?"

Harlem wasn't consoled one bit by Indigo's words and heaved, "I just want to go home." She flopped her head between her knees.

"We all do, believe me," Sienna said, gently pushing Harlem's shoulders back against the chair. "We all want to go back to something that was good before this. I'm sorry, I really am."

Harlem clenched her eyes shut; her breath was leaving her faster than she could bring it in, and she was starting to feel dizzy and tingly all over. The last time this happened was when she was in the backseat of her family car saying goodbye to the only home she knew as George dropped her at the bus depot to catch the Greyhound to this Godforsaken place.

"Listen, I get real mad each time this happens because it ain't fair in any kind of way," Sienna draped her thin arm around Harlem's shoulders. "Gosh. Each time a new girl is brought in, it is so terrible for all of us."

"New girl?" Harlem said, looking up at her.

"Yep. You're the new girl. We're the old beat-up ones nobody hardly wants," Sienna said, walking away toward the stage where the other girls had collected.

Harlem said, "Pardon?"

"Hey, speak for yourself, Sienna," Indigo said, hopping onto the desolate stage. With her hands on her thick hips, she swirled them round and round. "Everyone wants a little Mood Indigo."

"Maybe for two cents and a drugstore bottle of cheap perfume," Ruby laughed. She sat down at the foot of the stage, next to Topaz and the girl who had yet to speak.

"You're just jealous. Shut your trap," Indigo said.

"You're saying I'm to do what you do? Here?" Harlem asked, her voice barely strong enough to ask the question.

Ruby stood and walked with long strides to Harlem. From behind her ear, she pulled out and handed Harlem the two cigarettes Magdalena had placed on the dining room table upstairs. "These are yours. Better hold on to 'em. You're gonna need 'em."

"What am I to do with these," Harlem said, lifting the cigarettes. "Eat them?"

"I wouldn't. But, if there's something you can relish in, it's that you beat me out, new girl," Ruby said.

"Beat you out at what?"

Ruby's face softened. Her dark brown eyes, creased at the edges, drifted away. "It means... It means..."

"Just tell me," Harlem said, noticing now that Ruby was perhaps the oldest of all six of them. Harlem looked out at the other girls and they, too, found other things with which to occupy their eyes.

"It means some schmuck, Arthur the rat, paid the most out of what everybody paid for anybody. For you." Ruby pointed her finger at Harlem. "To be with you."

"To be with me." Harlem's stomach sank lower than it already was.

"Yeah. To be with you. Down here. During the party. You remember, sweetie. Us Rainbow Girls, dancin' up there. Each of us in our little costumes and colored masks. You were sitting right over there, right in the middle of it. I saw you. Drinking your champagne and whatnot. It's like this, see? People come to Lady M's Mysterie party down here, they bid on us silently, we go to our little rooms over there. We do our business. And when Magdalena feels like it, she rewards us for a job well done. You, cookie, did a job well done. I am truly sorry to break it to you, but you've already done what we do down here."

"You're the dancing girls from the party night...?" Harlem looked toward the stage, remembering once again how enamored she had been watching the girls glow in the spotlight, how they'd shimmied and pranced about in their colorful sequins and feathers, performers through and through.

With two hands, Ruby crudely cupped and plumped her ample bosom and said, "Ruby Red at your service, toots."

"The Girl in Orange awaits you," Sienna said, shaking her hips with an incredible undulating force Harlem had never quite seen before.

To her right, Violet pirouetted and ended with arms raised and elongated gracefully, "I am Violet with the Pretty Eyes."

"I'm Topaz; yellow is mellow, but I ain't..." and she lifted her middle finger in a way Harlem had seen Roy do once to a passing driver on their way into town.

The girl who had yet to speak, curtseyed and with a voice as light as her blond hair, said, "I'm Emerald. A gem for all to see and hold."

"Now just one minute!" Harlem shook her head, "I remember Magdalena said I was a Brown Bettie. The Brown Betties were in red gowns, they danced together. You all danced afterwards, I remember that. I was in the red dress. Doesn't that mean something? I wasn't dancing like you girls. I don't have *a room...*!"

With wrists straining against metal, she flung her hands toward the doors and tried to erase them from her sight.

Exasperated, Ruby flung her arms over her head, "Sometimes things change. *Things* get different!" She returned to the foot of the stage where she sat with crossed legs that bounced in frustration.

Different? Harlem thought. Her mind raced as her eyes darted about the room. Champagne. Arthur. Dancing. Girls dancing. Rainbow Girls. A stage. Music... Dancing. "So... each one of you knows about me and Arthur," she said aloud.

"Yes. Unfortunately, there are alotta Arthurs to come," Indigo said. With arms folded, she leaned against the wall where the gold curtain clung to the side edge of the stage. "Sorry, sweetie, but welcome to our grimy little club."

"You're one of us," Ruby added.

"But. I was special. I was a Bettie."

A door opened to Harlem's left. Sapphire, the girl who spit her food at Magdalena, stood in the doorway. The girl was stout with strong shoulders, little brown eyes and dark brown hair slicked tight on her head with finger waves. She leaned her arm against the door jamb. A blue sequined bustier hung on a wall behind her. "Don't be such a fathead. If you were a Bettie, you'd be upstairs with them right now where they're resting their pretty little heads. Things have changed."

Harlem looked at them and smoothed her cuffed hands along the folds of a dress that was meant for something far better than this. "I may as well have never left Greensboro at all," she said. "Nothing has changed. Nothing."

CHAPTER 16

From his jail cell, Jonas remembered.

He'd sat in the old, dusty bus depot and watched her from behind his newspaper. The heat was wanting his attention, but he was more focused on the girl. She stood in front of him, not more than six feet away. He noticed her proud, lean legs as she balanced on her white high heels like a ballerina. Imagined he could fit the hatband of his chocolate brown Fedora around her petite, hourglass waist. Appreciated her smart hat, monogrammed gloves and sophisticated navy suit; something a lady would wear. Her brown skin glistened in the North Carolina heat, which seemed to bake all the folks in the Greensboro bus depot into tasty chocolate biscuits to be enjoyed with an afternoon tea.

He could tell she came from money, didn't need the newspaper to tell him so, yet he was surprised by his own curiosity of her. But who wouldn't be? Her hallowed face was plastered all over the very same newspaper he was holding. Her mysterious eyes seemed to ask for help and condemn all those uncouth enough to stare. The headline didn't help none, ONE YEAR LATER, MARKESON MURDER/ SUICIDE STILL SHOCKS TOWN! Here in the flesh, this girl, who the papers said was only eighteen years old, seemed like so much more than what the newsprint made her out to be. A murderer? No. She looked to him like a young girl trying to find her way, one who was alone in the world and learnin' its ways without any kind of solid guidance.

She reminded him of his own daughter.

He'd stood and offered the girl a seat, which she'd declined. He'd introduced himself with a tip of his hat and an extension of his own brown hand, nice as could be. Told her he was Mr Jonas Stewart, which he was. She glared at him with velvet amber eyes, hot like he was the devil, and curtly introduced herself as Ann Smith, which he knew she wasn't. Her name was Harlem Winnepega Markeson. He admired her for being smart about not letting on who she really was, what she was really about. Nothin' wrong with you tellin' your own story 'steada always havin' to hear people tell you who they think you are. (Especially with a name like that.) Nobody has time for that nonsense.

Seemed like she was leaving town. He wasn't an expert on people, but he could tell a thing or two about most, and this girl was speaking that language of fear and courage and hope mixed all into one. He could tell by the way she kept lookin' for the bus to come. Leaning forward, peering down the road, waiting for a future, 'steada being anchored to the present. According to the paper, her trouble was in that town, and she was probably looking to get out of it. Only problem was, he was goin' to need her to help him get out of his.

His daughter was missing. Some said she ran away, some said she been helped along. He'd been after her for over two years now. Had been going it alone and getting nowhere and most recently had hired the help of a private detective, one that was local to his hometown in Kentucky. It was then that he got his best lead, and that lead pointed him here to Greensboro today. It was the sisters, Ruth and Mary.

They were there, too. Just three benches down. He'd been watching them from behind his newspaper all morning. They were a crafty two. Ruth, larger in frame and looking like she'd be in the first church pew each Sunday, was the head of the outfit. Her sister Mary was slight, flittered about like a canary and seemed like she'd run into a wall a few times 'til you pointed her away from it. His private investigator told him they lived in Greensboro, so he'd hightailed it here to watch them. He'd been trailing them for a week and during that time is when he learned that they had some kind of an interest in the girl. He'd followed them to when they managed a meeting with the girl's family lawyer; he'd spied upon them as they followed her to a dressmaker's shop. The girl was rarely alone, always with a driver, always sullen, quiet and withdrawn. Until today.

Over the course of his watchful week, whenever he saw Ruth's devious eyes light up at the sight of Harlem, he knew that look wasn't just about a curiosity around how a girl could kill her father and get away with it. That look was about greed.

The look had not left; if anything, it had intensified.

Even though the bus depot was full of folks—men in uniform tainted by war, mother's holding tight to wayward young children, young couples full of youthful love that had left him long ago—nothing was more compelling than Harlem. Nor more important.

When the bus had finally grumbled its dusty way down the lane toward all those who were ending or starting some kinda life, the young girl had accidently dropped her pocketbook while reaching for her suitcases. Ruth's eyes had nearly popped from her head, and she had jumped up from her seat to help like she was bumblebee 'steada his old ox. That's when he knew she wanted something; what it was, he needed to find out. He'd tucked that newspaper under his arm and swept in to help, too.

He was a father first; he hadn't protected his own daughter when she needed him the most. He damn sure wasn't going to repeat the same mistake now. He'd swooped in, like the man he was, and grabbed a hold of Harlem's suitcases, 'Lemme help y' with those, Miss Pretty,' he'd said. (Ruth hadn't liked that too much. Her eyes had said as much.) He'd put himself between Harlem and the sisters and got her onto the bus best he could. But once seated, Ruth had gotten herself next to Harlem, being the conniving woman that she was.

They'd all boarded the Greyhound bus, and all was fine and well until they arrived in their destination, New York City. Before he even got off the bus, he'd found trouble. Rumor went 'round that he was a fugitive wanted back in

Greensboro—which he was not. But didn't nobody want to hear what he had to say. Sometimes he wondered why God ever gave the Black man a mouth; didn't nobody want to listen to it when it really mattered. Turned out he had underestimated the power of those two women. His wife, God rest her soul, had always warned him against such a thing; guess his drive to find what was his had thrown him off a little. Clouded his own judgment.

From his New York City jail cell full of real criminals, it was all he could do to stop himself from thinking that he failed. He didn't know where Harlem was or if she was even safe. And the sisters were all to blame for it.

Jonas grimaced as he lifted his soiled handkerchief from his knuckles. His right hand had turned an ugly purple and was crusted with day-old blood. "Heathens," he sighed.

Ruth and Mary had done him a bad one saying he was wanted for murder back in Greensboro. It was a fine "How do you do?" when their bus finally arrived at the New York City bus depot after their long journey and all of a sudden he found himself face down on the grimy bus floor with someone stomping on his hand like they'd gotten the Holy Ghost. Looking back to the trip, he should've just followed his instincts. Simply let Ruth be instead of trying to be sly and make friends with her cunning self and her slightly daft sister, Mary. Jonas knew Ruth was behind the rumor that got him exactly where she wanted him: in jail and unable to get in her way.

He had to give it to her; she was smart. While he was fast asleep, she was able to mobilize all the men on the bus to detain him and give Ruth and Mary the opportunity they needed to break free of his watchful eye and run away with Harlem. Ruth knew that he didn't kill nobody, but misinformation is enough to ignite a mob, 'specially when fear is the fuel. That's why she told everybody on the bus that he was a fugitive. Probably told them all they were lucky he hadn't slit their throats overnight. The New York City police had no reason to believe his side of the story until they could match his words against Ruth's. They sure were taking their sweet time about it.

He'd never been in jail before, never once. And now here he was locked up for something he didn't do while trying to do some kind of good. The place was dank and dark and smelled like a hundred men had been through there, each one bringing in and leaving behind a stench. With each breath he tasted the sweat, fear, and the streets they had brought there. Even holding his handkerchief to his mouth, it was unavoidable.

Jonas leaned forward with his elbows on his knees; his hat dangled between his broad fingers as he angrily tried to smooth out the crumpled brim with his good hand.

"Shit!" He stomped his hard-soled shoe into the concrete. *All I had to do was watch her*, he thought. Jonas had vowed to keep Harlem safe from the clutches of Ruth and Mary because he knew Ruth and Mary were on that bus to take her and hide her somewhere in New York City, same as they'd done to his own daughter Arnetta three years ago. Jonas had paid good money to many a private investigator back home in Ohio and later in North Carolina to figure out this mystery. The problem was that none of them had found out *where* they'd taken Arnetta. Harlem had been his bait.

Never shoulda used that girl like that, Jonas thought, shaking his head as he stood. He was over six feet tall and drew unwanted attention from the handful of his fellow inmates.

"Whatya in for," one asked from the cell next to his.

Jonas was too preoccupied with his thoughts to answer.

"I said, whatya in for, boy?" the man repeated, rolling up his shirt sleeves from inside his own cell.

The men were separated in different cells—and not by crime, but by the more obvious reason that made all the difference: their color. Even in this place, privilege made second-class citizens.

With the bars between them, Jonas blinked rapidly to register what this man was asking of him. Jonas was taller than the man; he looked down to focus on the coarse white man and his pock-marked face. Jonas hadn't been called "boy" in quite a while considering he'd been in North Carolina around his own folk for the past month. He turned away from the man and gripped the jail cell bar in front of him to keep from saying something he'd regret.

"Mistaken identity," Jonas finally responded. His words deliberate. His breath restrained. Dammit if he hadn't had enough trouble already.

"That's a good one," the bastard laughed, slicking back his light brown wavy hair. "Ain't we all in here for that?" His fellow would-be criminals of the white persuasion, who were now staring at Jonas with mild interest, laughed along with him.

Jonas turned over his shoulder and looked at the row of colored men behind him. Most looked away, but there was one who didn't. He locked eyes with one youngster, about twenty years old, with a wide forehead and thick eyebrows. The young man sat up tall and nodded ever so slightly, confirming Jonas had an ally.

"I'm supposin' that could be true," Jonas said, crossing his arms slowly, his back against the bars and toward the white man who wouldn't let him alone.

"Who'd they mistake y' for—the Pope?" the man leaned his narrow face between the bars, his bloodshot eyes, small and set deep, challenged Jonas.

"A murderer," Jonas said.

This quieted all the men, both white and black.

"Me, too," the man said and then he spat toward Jonas's face. The spittle landed on the bar and on Jonas. "Maybe we ought to see who can kill the other first?"

The man jumped onto the bench and to the bars, reached through them and grabbed Jonas' neck. He was slammed backward into the steel and felt the inmate's hot breath on his head as the man crouched on the bench to get a better hold of him, "I'd like to get my hands on you without these bars, boy. I'd show you who the real murderer is. And it won't be you."

Jonas' knees buckled under the weight of the man's muscular arms. "Hold on a minute, now!" Jonas yelled as he struggled to break free.

Jonas's youngster jumped up and yanked Jonas away from the man's grip, "I suggest you find yourself another *boy* to bother, *Carl*."

The man looked surprised.

"Yeah, I know you, Carl, but you don't know me 'cause you're too busy running your mouth when you should be handling business, see? If you know what's good for you, you'll let this man alone or I will personally put in a word with your boss, Mr. Hoffstedder, over on 34th Street the next time I deliver his goods."

"You're that boy who runs for him," he sniffed as he jumped off the bench.

"Among other things," the kid said, as he straightened Jonas' jacket. "An' you and me know those things involve a certain level of protection. I'd hate to have to tell Mr. Hoffstedder a story that you tried to lay your hands on me in a way that was harmful to my well-being and, therefore, his business."

Carl sneered at Jonas. "Looks like this is your lucky day, boy."

"I guess it is," Jonas snorted as he scooped his hat from the ground. He nodded to the youngster, "I thank you kindly, son." Jonas studied his calm face looking for clues.

"My pleasure, sir. My pleasure," he said as he returned to his bench.

Jonas turned and allowed his forehead to find the cool of the cell bars. He wiped his neck with the back of his sleeve. He sighed. If it hadn't been for that boy, no tellin' what would have happened while that man Carl toyed with his goddamned life like a cat does a mouse.

As a boy, Jonas had heard many a sermon about the power of rage and the power of patience. One could destroy everything in its path. The other could destroy by leaving only what was useful intact. Rage could be like a wildfire, out to destroy. Patience could be the fall of a river, focused enough to clear a narrow route for its passage. Both could be allies to fulfill a worthy purpose. He'd seen it in a dog fight once out behind his neighbor's barn. How a dog could sit there calm and patient as could be, but if you looked close there was rage in that dog's eyes all along. Rage hidden in its skin with hair standing on end. Just waiting for the time to let it out. To get his opponent down and draw blood. Sometimes, once and for all.

Jonas closed his eyes and focused on his breathing.

Measured footsteps echoed in the corridor. He opened his eyes and drew his attention to the steps hoping they would bring good news.

"Portillo," a police officer with a clipboard commanded.

Carl rose. Jonas guessed that was good enough news for now. That low life was leaving. With a line of bars between them, he walked past Jonas without so much as a glance and shouted, "See ya later, suckers!"

The police officer pushed Portillo down the narrow hallway as faceless criminals cheered on the parade from behind their bars.

Jonas hoped he'd be doing the same soon. Harlem's life depended on it. And possibly his own.

CHAPTER 17

Honey slid the wooden chair out from the dinner table and joined the others already gathered there. A feast of corn, steaming mashed potatoes, and plump chicken baked golden brown loomed before her. She inhaled deeply, intoxicated by it all; she couldn't remember the last time she'd seen that much food in one place. Eager to dig in, she scooched closer to the meal and bumped the table with her knee—four sets of hands instinctively reached up to steady glasses of milk already set.

"Oh my!" Honey said, reaching to steady the turbulence she created. "I'm terribly sorry."

"Happens all the time!" Burle laughed as he tucked his cloth napkin into his shirt. "Nobody at this table has got time to cry over spilled milk!"

If ever there was a head of household, Burle's it! Honey thought as she smiled at the man who was both father and husband in the family that had taken her in. Big and tall, Burle had a chest like a whiskey barrel and tree-trunk legs to support it. She wasn't sure how his legs fit under that tiny table. His face was as chiseled as a wooden statue, but soft as custard at the same time. Honey had taken to him just as fast as he'd done her. The day the boys had discovered her under the stairs, Burle had barreled into the home, loud as could be. "I'm home, I'm home, I'm home!" he'd yelled with arms wide, and everybody had rushed to him and grabbed any piece of him that they could. While he'd washed his face in the kitchen sink and changed out of his work shirt, she was introduced as the girl they'd found under the stairs who didn't have nobody to call her own. Burle had stared at her, opened his arms wide again, just for her, and she'd walked right into them just as natural as could be. After that, his rough brown hands patted hers gently as he assessed her bruised knuckles. Nothing more had been said about it that night. He and his wife Marjorie had offered her a warm place to sleep, some clothes, and fewer questions than answers. She'd been comforted.

Burle continued, "One a' these days, I'mma get my family here one of those big tables; the ones you see kings and queens sittin' at and they have t' holler at one another just t' pass the butter."

Honey folded her hands in her lap and played with the lilac stitching on the napkin resting there. She was thinking, *Big tables don't solve everything.* But she kept that to herself and merely nodded.

"We'd need a bigger house to hold such a table, dear," Marjorie said, as she fastened their baby into a wooden highchair.

"Well, naturally, Marge. You think we gon' live up in Harlem our whole lives? In this here tiny apartment? Uh-uh. Not me. Not you. Not all 'a these kids."

"Pops, where you think we gonna go? Timbuktu?" Petey said while hunching up his shoulders at Honey. She noticed that the gold ring he'd thrown earlier was now around his neck. It dangled from a piece of string, with what she assumed was an altered state of hope.

Burle grabbed his knife and pointed out the window with it. "Som-a-where's other than here! Where there's trees and blue sky and dogs barking, steada' people all day long."

"Dogs? I don't want to hear no dogs all day long!" Christopher, the younger of the two boys, plugged his ears laughing. "What about peace n' quiet?" The boy, who seemed to be about fifteen, laid out his arms like he was resting on the best beach, and he bubbled with giggles that immediately activated his dimples. Honey covered her mouth with the back of her hand. Somehow that boy triggered her own funny bone, and she couldn't help but giggle too.

Their father leaned over and rubbed the boy's closely cropped hair, then pulled him into a loving headlock that sent him into more fits of laughter. "I'll give you peace n' quiet, boy!" The table jiggled again, and milk tumbled out from their glasses as they horsed around. Honey reached swiftly for Christopher's glass, as it was closer to her. Marjorie steadied Burle's, while Petey grabbed his own.

"Alright now, Burle. Settle down. Let's grab hands before this food gets cold," Marjorie laughed; the baby squealed as though to cosign the whole thing. Honey folded her hands in her lap again. Marjorie caught her eye. "Honey, would you like to do the honors?"

Honey looked at her. "Sorry?"

"Grace, baby girl. You *do* say grace at your house, don'tcha?" Burle said across from her as he reached for Petey's hand and the baby's.

Honey hadn't said grace in quite a while. The last time she remembered doing so was with her father and that had been in Yiddish. She coughed and cleared her sore throat. "Well, yes. We did. But... but, wouldn't one of you like to do it tonight?"

"You seems to be the one needing to say some words of thanks, maybe more than us tonight. Don'tcha think?" Burle grinned warmly.

"I guess I can't argue with that," Honey said measuredly. She pulled her tell-tale hands from beneath the table and reached for Christopher's hand to her right, and Petey's to her left, and bowed her head.

"Wait! Take some milk first, to coat your throat a bit so God is sure to hear you," Marjorie said.

Honey obeyed and swallowed a sip as best she could. "Dear Lord, thank you for the graciousness of the Artemis family. Thank you for this wonderful food. Amen."

"Alright everybody, dig in! Honey, if'n you're as hungry as you look, I suggest you grab you some vittles faster than my boys or you're gon' be left with lickin' crumbs from the plate!"

Honey knew a thing or two about grabbing for food; she stabbed at the leg of the baked chicken and then caught herself as she caught Burle glancing at her, eyebrow raised.

"Guess we don't need to worry about you fightin' for nothin'!"

"I'm afraid you don't," Honey chuckled, slightly embarrassed, as she placed the chicken leg on her plate.

Burle passed her the mashed potatoes, "Listen girl, nothin' wrong with fighting for y'self. I tell the boys that every day, right boys?"

The boys nodded and grunted politely in unison as they chewed their food.

Petey wiped his mouth, "I tried to tell her, Pop. I tried to tell her that she should be proud of her bruises. 'Cause it showed she didn't back down. That she knocked somebody into next week!"

"Petey, don't talk with your mouth full," Marjorie said as she looked hesitantly at Honey and fed the baby bits of mashed potato with her fingertips. The baby fought at her fingers for more.

Honey slowly chewed her own mashed potatoes. She prayed her throat would continue to cooperate. Over the past two days it had become a barrier to the food her stomach desperately wanted, and her stomach fought at her just like the baby. She swallowed painfully and quickly reached for the chill of the milk.

"I think it is alright to ask, now that we've spent some time together. Who were you fighting, again?" Burle asked.

Honey blotted the milk from her mouth as she watched Marjorie look at Burle.

"We shouldn't discuss it at the dinner table, Burle," Marjorie cautioned, looking back at Honey.

"If I learned one thing during my time on this earth, I learned that life ain't a box a chocolates for ev'rybody. Am I right, Honey?"

Honey nodded.

"Now, will you please tell me what man was coward enough to beat up on you like you was his punching bag?" Burle's face was red. His voice lowered, and it got very quiet in the very small dining room. The whir of a metal fan off in the kitchen window drew her attention. Through the window, she saw the clothes pins standing at attention on the clothesline in the deepening twilight of the evening, ready for their next batch of dirty work.

Honey coughed. "Um. Well," she said as she absorbed the stares from their curious eyes. She felt like a fraud taking kindness from these people. If they'd known where she came from, they wouldn't be so ready to help her. She knew they wouldn't. That bothered her more than admitting what Otto had done to her. She pushed herself back from the table, "I'm sorry, Mr. Artemis. I—I—"

"See, Burle. I told you, this is not dinner conversation!"

"Fine, fine. I'm sorry. Honey, please sit back down."

Marjorie rose from the table, came to her and sat her back down. She whispered in her ear, "You should go ahead on and eat. We'll talk later, alright?" As Marjorie pulled away, Honey noticed a faint scar across this woman's cheek. Marjorie covered the scar with her hand; and with that movement, Honey felt Marjorie might actually know more about her situation than she'd let on.

Honey placed the napkin back in her lap. Even with Marjorie as an ally, she found it hard to look at anyone, especially since they were all still looking at her. She stared at the corn kernels piled on her plate like gold nuggets instead.

"Honey?"

Honey looked up at Burle, "Yessir?"

Burle leaned across the table, his light brown eyes bright with what he wanted her to hear. "I just want'cha to know that I am proud of you. Just like I am my boys," he said, and he reached across the table for her hand. She gave it to him. He held onto her hand tightly, shook it as he spoke, emphasizing his every word, "Don't matter the details a' what happened. I'm sorry I pestered you. But I hope you know that you are a fighter. You are brave. No woman should have to go through what you done gone through." Water filled his eyes. "That much I know."

Burle released her hand. Honey stared at him. His words had filled her with something that loosened up the tightness she was feeling in her chest. So much so that a tear slid down her face and landed with a little plop on her lap. "Thank you."

They returned to their meal. Silence filled the room and sent each of them, even the baby, into their own thoughts. Honey slivered off a piece of her chicken, so thankful for it and the people who blessed her with it, and sent it down to nourish her as well as she could manage.

CHAPTER 18

Honey helped Marjorie with the dishes while the boys cleared the table. Burle sat on the couch and spent some time playing with the baby. The water from the faucet soothed her aching hands as she daydreamed out the window, looking into the moon-shadowed courtyard enclosed by rows of yellow-lit windows. The boxes of light contained dozens of people doing exactly as they were doing.

"Thank you again for all that you've done. I'm not sure how I'll ever repay you," Honey said, handing a rinsed dish to Marjorie.

"Well, you know what they say: the Lord works in mysterious ways." Marjorie placed her dried dish on a plate rack above the sink. "You've helped us appreciate what we've got even more than we already had. I'll tell you that much!"

Burle entered the room with the baby in his arms. "Boys, go to your room and change into your sleepin' clothes. And Petey, I'll be in to talk to you more about that engagement ring about your neck. I gots to talk to Honey now."

"Momma! You said you wouldn't tell just yet," Petey said.

"You know I can't keep nothin' from your father, Petey," Marjorie said.

"Go on, now," Burle said as he sat at the table. "Honey, come sit a spell."

Honey obeyed and joined Burle at the table, now clear of the tablecloth. She stared at the scratches in the wood surface, wondering how they'd gotten there and when.

Burle cleared his throat and said, "I been thinkin' about this whole situation."

"Yes?" Honey said.

"My wife tells me you said all your people are dead."

"I did," Honey responded.

"Well, I don't believe you. And that's okay because that is your bus'ness. I think you were runnin' from somebody who has that messed-up kind 'a controlling love for you, and I think you need a l'il help getting away from that person."

Honey lowered her head. He wasn't that far off; but Magdalena's face appeared in her mind's eye instead of Otto's. Her hands clenched into fists.

Burle looked at her hands and nodded over to his wife, "See there, Marjorie? I knew I was right."

Marjorie took the baby from him, "Yes, love, you were right."

"Get me the tin," Burle said.

With the baby on her hip, Marjorie retrieved a tobacco tin from a shelf near the small ice box. She handed it to Burle.

"We call this our emergency fund. You, dear girl, are in an emergency. We want you to take some of this money—"

"I couldn't!" Honey said, pushing away the small roll of bills Burle placed in front of her.

Burle pushed it back. "You will. You will take this money, you'll get on a bus to our cousin's house in Chicago, and you will start a new life there, far away from all this mess. Do you know why?"

Honey shook her head.

"Tell her, Marge."

"My husband before Burle, the father of my boys, he used to beat me something awful," Marjorie said, her voice coming from the past.

Honey reached for her arm, "I'm sorry, Marjorie."

Burle took Marjorie's free hand into his, "I took care of that mess and I'm takin' care 'a this one, too. You hear me?"

Honey took the bills. "I do."

"And this is under two conditions," Burle continued. "Number one, you get on that bus tomorrow. But before you do, you go down to that police station and you report the person that did this to you. Number two, you find a way to repay us within the year. That 'a way, I'll know you're on your feet and that we done good by you."

Honey knew she couldn't argue with Burle. She also knew that this was the best chance she was going to get to avoid running back to Magdalena for fear of starvation... Or whatever worse could happen out there in the Harlem streets. Something unwound in her and sprung her to her feet. She extended her hand with as much gentlemanly candor she could muster. "I'll do as you say, and I thank you."

"Good. Good," Burle clasped her hand warmly and with a soft grin. He then rose from the table, kissed the baby on the forehead and kissed Marjorie's too. He patted his broad belly, "I got an overcoat I grew out of; unfortunate for me, but good for you. You'll take that. You got the dress on your back and that's a start. Marge'll get you some more medicine for your throat."

Marjorie stood and went to the kitchen.

"You get you some shut eye on this here couch and in the mornin', you'll be off. I expect to hear good things from you, Honey," Burle yawned and headed for the boys' bedroom. "Don't let us down now."

"I won't," Honey said, holding onto the cash. "I won't."

CHAPTER 19

oney shielded her eyes from the morning sun as she checked the tall clock that stood guard outside the precinct. With its large face and stately black numbers, it told her she had two hours before her bus to Chicago would leave. The bus station wasn't far. She figured she had enough time to do what she needed to do.

She turned to Marjorie, who had accompanied her, "I've got time, right? I've got time to do this."

Marjorie held onto her arm tightly, "Time isn't the most important thing you'll be needin' right now, sugar."

"I know," Honey said, recognizing the truth of it.

Marjorie turned Honey to her by the shoulders, "And I know you can do this. You're goin' to go in there—"

"And find an officer who I don't know from Magdalena's, tell him everything I know—"

"And leave. And then you leave, hear? You get on that bus to Chicago and start over." Marjorie pulled Honey close and hugged her tight. "I've gotta go now.

My neighbor can only watch the baby but for so long. We'll be waitin' to hear from you." Marjorie smiled brightly for her, squeezed her arm, and left.

Honey listened to Marjorie's determined steps fading away and used the energy she left in her wake to walk up the steps to the precinct.

Last night, she lay awake for hours cocooned on the couch and searched for the courage to do what she needed to do. The glow from the streetlamp outside and the sounds from the street below had kept her awake, along with her thoughts. With the blanket pulled to her chin, she had stared out into the night. Unbelieving. Never in a million years could she have dreamed this. Never did she think *strangers* would be the ones to help her leave Magdalena's. She'd come to accept her situation in the house and that of the girls she lived with. As far as she'd been concerned, she was powerless over herself and Magdalena's actions. At least, that's what she'd come to tell herself. Leaving had truly ceased to be an option. And now... Now it was all she could think about. She'd been given a real chance to come alive and find a kind of life that resembled normalcy, like Burle and Marjorie's. "Or anything I want," she'd sighed aloud.

She'd also tossed and turned last night. The current relief she felt battled with her not-so-distant past. Like dozens of photographs, memories from her life had flipped over and over in her mind with nowhere to go. She'd swatted them away and rolled on her side. The memories were attacking the ugly, thick porcelain layer of acceptance she'd covered her life with, and it was breaking away into little pieces that fell and shattered on the concrete floor of her heart. The jagged pieces were calling to her; they wanted her to slice away at what had been keeping her confined: Magdalena. Or rather, her ties to Magdalena. She imagined herself slashing at her sister's octopus tentacles and being free. But she knew she couldn't truly be that until the root of the evil was destroyed. Her sister had to finally pay for everything that she had done to her and to the countless girls she had kept at the Manor. Burle was right. She needed to tell someone. To end this. But now that her porcelain armor was gone, she was left unprotected, and she was afraid.

Honey held onto the brown paper bag that carried a peanut butter sandwich and a piece of baked chicken, left over from last night's dinner. With haste, she tightened the scarf around her neck, one that Marjorie had given her to cover her bruises. Her hands shook. She wasn't afraid for this all to end. She wasn't afraid to speak of what she and her sister had done years ago and what Magdalena did now. She was afraid of who was behind the law-abiding doors she was about to walk through. Officer Brighton was an officer after all. That meant he could be anywhere. He knew her, she knew him. One encounter and it would be all over. She was smart enough to know that there were also other officers who came to Mysterie parties. They turned a cheek to the whole business, but they wouldn't be able to turn one to her once they saw that their own livelihoods might in jeopardy. By exposing Magdalena, Honey would be exposing them, too.

Honey turned and began to walk back down the steps, thinking, "I can't do it!" She'd have to think of another way. She'd worry about justice later, from the safety of Chicago, where no one could drag her back to Magdalena and that hellhole that she called home. She began to run.

"Hey, you! Stop right there," a voice commanded from behind her.

Honey skidded to a stop on the sidewalk and froze.

"Where do you think you're going?"

Honey turned around slowly, "Pardon me—"

Her heart plummeted. It was the man they called 'Officer Snow White,' for his white-blond hair and shockingly blue eyes.

"Aren't you the gal who makes the pie for the officer's fundraiser auction? We were just talking about you this morning!" He grabbed her elbow and escorted her back up the stairs.

Shit, shit, shit; this man thinks I'm someone else. Pies?! She thought. He clearly didn't recognize her without the red dress, outside of Lady Magdalena's Manor. Instead he thought she was some other black woman with some other service. She had to think fast, "I am, yes. That's me, sir."

"Well, what're you doin' here?" he opened the precinct door.

"I—I was… you know what? I think I've changed my mind. I'm going to deal with what I was dealing with on my own. Get back to my baking and—"

"I'll hear nothing of it; we are here to protect and serve, no matter the problem." He hugged her about the shoulders, squeezing her into submission as he walked her down a hallway that was overflowing with more men in their starched uniforms. "I just know you've got a sample of something *di*-vine in that paper bag. I just know it! *Whooo weee*, the boys at the desk are gonna be happy to see you!"

With her head smushed in his armpit, Honey thought how funny some white folks could be when they wanted something from you, like food. Or what was offered at Lady Magdalena's. She shuffled along next to him, her shoes scuffing the polished marble floors.

CHAPTER 20

A police officer with a clipboard called out his name, "Stewart. Jonas Stewart."

"Yes, sir. I'm Mr. Stewart."

"Come with me. You're bein' released." The officer, lean and efficient, barely looked at Jonas as his keys clanked against the jail's metal bars and unlocked the cell.

"Thank you, sir," Jonas said as he grabbed his hat from the bench and thanked God too. It had been a hard four nights in that place.

The officer used his clipboard rather than his words to indicate he should follow him. Jonas carefully slipped on his suit coat. He rubbed the sleep from his eyes, though he hadn't gotten much of it. His throbbing hand had kept him up most of the night, as did his chit-chatting cellmates. He'd had maybe an hour of sleep. He cradled his hand as he followed the officer down the corridor. As they walked past a few cells full of vagrants, villains, and vagabonds, Jonas felt relief for himself, but then a sadness too. He knew some belonged there and some didn't, just like him.

He said a quick prayer for their well-being and asked God to sort it out.

The officer said nothing as they walked; Jonas figured he was dealing with the type of man that tolerated the Negro for only so long as he could—or for as long as his job called for it. Before he'd left Ohio, the few friends he had left told him how Harlem was different from the rest of the country. That black folks damn-near ran the place and had a hoot of a good time doin' it too. He wondered if there was a jail in Harlem run by black folks. If that were indeed the case, he'd have felt much more comfortable in that one.

Jonas and his officer weaved through a river of chattering people. They arrived in a quiet, narrow room with a check-in area. A silver-haired desk officer looked up at them. "What have we got?" he asked as he was handed Jonas' clipboard. The older officer raised an eyebrow as the younger officer walked away without a word. "Cat musta got his tongue today."

"Would seem so, sir," Jonas replied, uncertain if he should or not.

"Can call me Officer Peterson. On behalf of New York City, I do apologize you were detained," the desk officer said as he reviewed Jonas' paperwork. He then rose and used a cane to help him disappear behind some filing cabinets. Officer Peterson called out, "But these things do happen, and we can never be too safe when Negroes are involved. Isn't that right, Mr. Stewart?"

Jonas snorted softly. He stretched his tired shoulders, trying to keep his inner chained-dog quiet, before answering, "I do s'pose you have a point there, sir. We can never be too safe."

"Yessir. Safety is our first priority," Jonas heard the reply come from over his shoulder. He turned. Another officer, tall with blond hair, waited behind him. "Ain't that right, miss?" The officer who spoke rocked on his heels authoritatively. Then he doubled over laughing, "I'm keeping the best pie-maker in town safe!"

Jonas looked to the officer's detainee. She was a young Negro woman of that fair complexion which often came from blacks and whites mixin'—whether they wanted to or not. Her face was covered in makeup that was doing a poor job of trying to hide a hefty bruise on her cheek, not much different from the one on his hand. Jonas nodded in allegiance to her, as the young man in the cell had done to him. She looked away.

"It's a thankless job we have here, isn't it Officer Verdanski?" Peterson said. "Take this fellow here. Paperwork says 'Mistaken Identity.' That he was wanted for murder back in Greensboro thanks to the word of two unscrupulous citizens named Ruth and Mary—if you can believe that! *Ruth and Mary*! Takin' names from the bible and acting unholy. Ain't that somethin', Verdanski? They lied on this man somethin' awful and sent him to jail!"

"You don't say, sir," Officer Verdanski deadpanned. He pushed the girl forward, "I got—"

"I do say. But thanks to our staff, our fine officers here, we found out it was all a damned, colored lie," Officer Peterson smiled and handed Jonas his valise, suitcase, and a paper bag with his personal belongings.

"Mhmmm," Jonas said, swallowing the words he wanted to say. He hastily retrieved his watch from the paper bag and fixed it to his wrist so he could get the hell up out of there.

Jonas turned and Officer Verdanski moved around him with the young woman. He was running his mouth about pie, and she was half-smilin', saying how she had to get back home in a hurry. It looked to him like she wanted to get away from whatever it was that was keeping her here. He caught her staring at him hard, like he was responsible for somethin'. Jonas walked past her out of the room and sat on a bench in the hallway to lace up his shoestrings. He had a rough time at it with only one good hand, but he was just about through when he saw a pair of turned-over shoes stop in front of his own.

"Excuse me, mister."

Jonas looked up and into the eyes of the young Negro woman "Yes?"

"Have you got the time?" she asked, her voice thin and low.

"Just after nine o'clock this fine morning," Jonas answered, standing slowly. He smiled cautiously at the girl again, still hoping for one in return—the kind that was often exchanged between black folks at home whether they knew one another or not.

"Thank you," she replied. Her eyes, big, green, and alert, surveyed his before darting to her left and right to take inventory of the many folks coming and going around them. The girl's jitters reminded him of how his wife, Julia, used to peek her head in the door and inspect their barn for skittering field mice before she'd venture inside to milk their cow. With a thin hand, the girl smoothed her golden-brown hair, which was falling out of its bun. She tightened her trench coat, which was easily two sizes too big.

"Is there somethin' else I can help you with, miss?"

She crossed her arms, stared him dead straight in the eye and demanded, "How do you know Ruth and Mary? And you'd better be quick with your answer."

CHAPTER 21

Honey wished she'd never come to this precinct. Everything had happened, except what was supposed to. When she'd asked this man about Ruth and Mary, she'd thought for certain that he was on the wrong side of everything—that he was after more girls. And she was about to turn him in to the police. Pointing a finger at him would be her small way of getting to Magdalena. But as soon as he started talking, she knew she had been way off. He wasn't after any girl; he was after one in particular. His face had tightened, and he'd told her how he had followed the sisters from Greensboro all the way to Harlem. Said he knew they were up to no good and he was out to stop them from doing more harm. Then his face had paled, and fear danced in his eyes. He'd said, "I think Ruth and Mary have my daughter."

Dammit! She'd opened a can of worms that could not be resealed.

They were outside by the steps, the same place where she'd been when Officer Snow White had stopped her. Jonas reached for her. "Please," he said, "Won't you help me? You might be the only person who can help me find my daughter." His question poured from his mouth like blood and soaked into her conscience as she watched the clock *tick* and *tick* and *tick*. If she left now, she'd keep her promise to Burle and Marjorie, and to herself. If she didn't... Painfully, she decided right then and there—she couldn't.

CHAPTER 22

oney brought the coffee cup to her lips and sipped. She held the cup there while the hot liquid found its own way down her sore throat. Marjorie's home-made menthol compress had done wonders, but there was still some discomfort. She winced as she studied the tired man in front of her.

"Sugar?" Jonas said, pushing the glass container across the table to her. "Mine's a little bitter."

She shook her head. Honey had only ever known the coffee Tilda made. She barely knew the difference between what was bitter or not, nor had the opportunity to choose otherwise.

"Would be nice t'think that coffee is coffee no matter where you go, but that just isn't always the case, I s'pose," Jonas offered.

"I'd rather suppose it's not," Honey replied.

Jonas scanned the dog-eared menus now resting between them, "Decided yet what you want to eat? You look—"

"I'm well aware how I look, Mr. Stewart. I can tell that, simply on how I feel."

"I wasn't meaning to insult you, Miss Honey," Jonas said, putting his cup down. "I—I don't know what I was meaning, really. We don't have to eat anything if you don't want." Jonas moved the menu aside.

"Soup," Honey said, tightening the scarf about her neck. "And two eggs. Scrambled."

"Soup for breakfast. Alright then. Should at least help that cold I hear comin' in your voice," Jonas said, smiling half-heartedly as he motioned for the waitress. He returned his attention to Honey. "You'll have to forgive me," he said. "I don't exactly expect you to understand all that I've told you about my daughter, or Ruth and Mary, or Harlem Markeson," he said as he stirred his coffee slowly. "I just hope you believe me—that you can trust me."

"At this point, I can only assume you are who you say you are, Mr. Stewart. Time will tell and time is... well, time is just about all I've got right now." She looked at the paper bag with her meal from the Artemises sitting next to her. Her unused ticket burned a hole in her coat pocket; Burle's voice echoed in her ears.-

"We're in the same boat, then, miss."

"It would certainly seem to be in our best interest to row together for the moment," Honey said, briskly smoothing her napkin on her lap.

"Agreed," Jonas said and reached his hand across the table to seal their deal. She did not take it, but only stared instead. He let it drop slowly. His face did the same.

"Let's be clear, Mr. Stewart," Honey leaned forward onto the table, careful to keep the bruises on her wrists covered. "You need me. I don't need you," Honey coughed. She took another sip of coffee and continued. "I've told you how ruthless my older sister can be. I've told you about Tilda. Now, I will try to help you find your daughter, but that is all. I will tell you what I know about Lady Magdalena's operations, and then I will do what I intended to do—and that is to get on a bus to Chicago and be gone from this place. I have no intentions to go back. You catch my drift, I'm sure."

Jonas nodded.

Honey straightened, cleared her throat, and finished her coffee. She'd never spoken to anyone like that before. When she was fighting Otto, she felt something come alive in her that she didn't know existed, and it was talking now.

"Can I please see the photo of your daughter again?"

Jonas retrieved his wallet from his jacket pocket. He carefully removed Arnetta's tattered photo and eagerly slid it across the table.

"How old is she here?" Honey asked as she folded her elbows onto the table.

"Ten or eleven," Jonas said. Honey heard him sniffle and looked up. Jonas' face was taut with an overpowering grief that hadn't been there before. He struggled against it. He wiped his eyes roughly with his handkerchief, trying to get rid of it somehow. She looked back down at the photo to give him some privacy. His sorrow had leapt across the table and gripped her heart like thick vines around an old tree. She wished it hadn't.

Honey's shoulders settled as she sighed, "So many of the girls change their names. I don't know any of them to be an 'Arnetta.'" Honey peered closer at the faded ancient photo of the girl captured in time. "With her being so young in this photo, I don't see much of a resemblance to anyone at all—" Honey gasped. Her hand flew to mouth.

"What is it?" Jonas asked.

"I—I—" Honey looked at him.

Jonas' eyes were wide. He stuffed his handkerchief in his pocket, "What?"

"The necklace. The 'A' around her neck. That 'A' is for 'Always'..." Honey felt like a boulder had dropped into the pit of her stomach.

"'Always?' No—it was for 'Arnetta'! What are you saying?"

Honey's voice got stuck in her swollen throat. The necklace had been in the office closet with all the other skeletons Magdalena had stolen. Honey had found the necklace years ago while foraging for the very dress Otto had torn off the day of her involuntary emancipation. The necklace had been tangled and stuck to the magnetic clasp of a forgotten handbag at the bottom of the closet. Like an unmarked grave, she didn't know to whom it had belonged, where it came from, or when it got there. When Honey had put the delicate chain with its dangling charm on herself, she had just thought it was pretty; but, when Honey put it around Tilda's neck the morning she left, it had become more. Honey had whispered that the lettered charm was for "Always." That they'd always be together, no matter what. No matter if they were in the same room, house, city, or lifetime. And now, here was this man asking after it, and so much more.

Honey sat back.

Jonas' eyes frantically searched hers, "I gave Arnetta that necklace for her ninth birthday. She never took it off. Never. That A is for *Arnetta*." Jonas grabbed Honey's arm, "You've seen it. Where? Where did you see it?"

"Please," Honey cried. "I don't know anything for certain—"

"But you do know," Jonas interrupted, his voice rising. "You do know!" Jonas was gripping Honey, "Where is she? Where's my daughter?" His voice pierced the din in the diner.

Honey looked about for help, "I've seen the necklace. But that's all I know. You must calm down!"

"Now just a minute, there, mister!" Their waitress appeared at their table. She loomed over them. She seemed almost as tall as Jonas and just as strong as she pushed him away from Honey. "What's the big idea?"

Jonas released his grip. He sunk into the booth and cradled his head, mortified, "I'm sorry. So very sorry."

"Didn't want the two of you's in here in the first place," the giant waitress grumbled as she pulled her rag from her apron waistband and hurriedly wiped down their table. "'Dolly's ain't the best joint in Harlem, but we at least act civil toward one another and try to dress proper. Just look at you!"

Honey looked away from the waitress. Her gaze was thwarted by a series of disapproving brown faces staring at her. Their breakfast forks were frozen in midair as they frowned at her overcoat and beat up shoes. They *tsk-tsked* her unruly hair and bruised cheek playing peek-a-boo beneath the makeup. They exchanged knowing glances with one another assuming she was something she wasn't. Honey tightened her belt.

"Now you already been in here nearly an hour, what's it gonna be?" The waitress's arms cradled her large bosom, "You standin'. He's sittin'. Did I just waste my time wipin' this here table off or not?"

Honey looked at the waitress and back at Jonas, who hadn't moved—a statue in his own museum of frozen thoughts. "I'll—I'll have...We'll both have the breakfast special, please. And some soup."

CHAPTER 23

Tilda pulled the cord on Magdalena's painting and walked down the stairs to the basement below. The light was still on, thankfully. She carried Harlem's morning dose of tea. She rubbed her eyes. It was just before eleven o'clock in the morning, but it had been a rough night. Tilda had had nightmares about Honey. She'd dreamt she was eaten by a giant cockroach and that she'd just stood there as it happened, screaming with no voice, helpless as the horrible beast ate up her sister. She had woken up in a sweat, tearing at her throat.

Tilda arrived at the bottom of the stairs and there was the new girl curled tight into a ball on the stage. She was up against the wall, using the curtain like a blanket. She probably wished she had that bed upstairs again.

No one else was around. The other girls were in their rooms, behind their narrow doors, sleeping on cots not much softer than a wooden board. Tilda stepped on a crushed cigarette butt. She pushed it aside with her shoe. She was goin' to have to sweep this place again before the next Mysterie party. She hadn't had much time to do anything she regularly did since the new girl came.

Tilda nudged the girl's bare shoulder. In response, the girl moaned and turned over some. Tilda let her alone, figuring the most she could do was to let her sleep a little more. She darn-well needed it. So did Tilda. The tea was already nearing lukewarm, but it wasn't going to matter if the girl drank it hot or cold. Tilda set it down a little ways away from her so she wouldn't knock it over if she woke up. Walking away, Tilda looked back at the girl whom she'd come to admire a little. It had been a long time since anyone had stood up to Magdalena, and even longer since a new girl made it as far as her in trying to escape.

Tilda looked up the stairs to where she'd come from. Magdalena wouldn't be calling for her for a half hour at least. *Maybe I can sleep, too,* she thought. Tilda tiptoed back to the stage. She stepped up on it and laid her head opposite Harlem, covering her own body with the curtain. She was out lickety-split.

CHAPTER 24

Harlem awoke to a jab in her shoulder. She flicked it away. "Leave me alone," she mumbled.

"Time to get up, Miss Money Bags," Harlem heard.

Harlem turned to her side. The cold wooden floor below her was no match for a bed. She burrowed herself further in the folds of the stage curtains, searching for warmth. She rubbed her eyes, noticing her tongue felt thick in her mouth. Then she raised herself up on an elbow and looked about her. She spied a teacup near her, and reached for it, gratefully.

"I wouldn't drink that if I were you."

Harlem looked up to see Ruby looming over her. "What?"

"That tea has a little something extra in it that you probably don't want or need anymore. I'd not drink it if you know what's good for you."

Harlem looked at the teacup cradled in her hands. She smelled it. "It's bad?"

"It's got a little kick to it to knock you out," Ruby said, her arms crossed. "Maybe Tilda here can get you some water, straight."

Ruby squatted down on her haunches and gently shook Tilda. "Tilda, Tilda honey. Wake up."

Tilda flew to her feet and looked around.

"You're alright, little bear. Relax," Ruby said, standing. "Do you think you can get this girl some water instead of the tea?"

Tilda shook her head.

"Tilda, I'm thirsty," Harlem said, raising herself to lean on her thigh and against the curtained wall.

Tilda shook her head again.

"Please?" Harlem said. "I'd be ever so grateful."

Petulant, Tilda shook her head again, before running from the stage and off up the stairs.

"Sometimes she can work magic, sometimes she can't." Ruby loomed above Harlem as she spoke, arms crossed. "I dunno, if you're terribly bad off, perhaps a small sip will make you feel better. I'm no doctor, but a bit will probably be better than nothing."

Ruby walked away, leaving her to decide for herself. Harlem took a small sip. "I guess I know now why it's a little bitter," she said aloud and sighed. She set the cup down and leaned her head back against the wall. "What I wouldn't do for some coffee... bread, jam... bacon... a hard-boiled egg..." Harlem's voice trailed off. The more she thought about food, the worse she felt.

"Keep dreamin' sister; you saw what we had up there, and that was a good day," Ruby said.

"When will we be called upstairs to eat?" Harlem asked.

Ruby laughed. "When Magdalena feels like feeding us."

"You can't be serious," Harlem sighed and laid her head back down.

"Can't I?" Ruby straightened her faded, rose-colored tap pants. "That's just one of the many benefits to boarding at Lady Magdalena's Manor; more and more infrequent meals with helpings barely fit for a child; it's all terribly great for your figure, actually. Baths once a week with just slivers of soap to share amongst us to help t' keep the wrinkles away. And absolutely no sunbathing to ruin your pure skin." She scoffed, "Truly, one of the better places to board in Harlem. You'll see, toots!"

Harlem stared at her. This woman, who couldn't have been more than twenty years old, seemed so much older than her own eighteen years in so many ways. Her skin was pale like bread dough and seemed just as mushy, but it didn't seem like baking would do her any good. In fact, when she thought about it more, she seemed more like the stale bread her cook would use to mix in with the cornbread to make stuffing. Harlem wondered if the girl had been hardened down here or came in that way. And if the same would happen to her.

Ruby began to whistle a tune as she walked toward the orange door, "Sienna, let's go. Wake up," she said as she knocked. Ruby continued to the next door, the yellow one. "Topaz! Rise and shine, toots!" She knocked on all the colored doors and the girls emerged from them, one by one.

Indigo stepped from her slightly darker blue door. Without a word, she walked toward the stage and began stretching against the wall next to the piano. Harlem figured maybe she wasn't a morning person. The others mingled in the center area of the room.

"You're named for the rainbow?" Harlem said, more to herself, but loud enough that Ruby heard her.

"Bingo. Magdalena is real original," Ruby laughed.

"Why else would I be called 'Indigo'? Ain't nobody in their right mind naming their child something like that," she laughed.

"My name is uncommon. I just thought maybe yours was too," Harlem said.

"Alright, I'll give you that one," Indigo smiled.

Harlem watched the six girls, thinking about their colors and what this meant.

"Sapphire still in a bad mood?" Sienna said, looking at the closed blue door.

"Probably," Ruby answered.

"Is she always in a bad mood?" Harlem said.

"She hasn't really come to grips with the hierarchy here," Sienna said.

"Have any of us?" Indigo said from her lone position by the wall. "I know I haven't."

"The difference is that you've accepted it, Indigo. You're smarter than Sapphire. You don't waste your energy trying to fight something you can't win against," Sienna said as she settled on the edge of the stage.

Indigo replied, "We all fight in different ways, Sienna."

Harlem watched them all, casually fascinated by their differences. Indigo seemed to be the most grounded of them all, almost like a favorite aunt she'd never had and wished for often. There was something about her that Harlem found comforting.

Indigo turned her head, "Harlem, there's one tip I'll give you right now. You'll be better off t' not keep anger in you. This is our life and until Magdalena wants somethin' different; this is the way it is. That's not giving in; that's not acceptin' nothing that happens down here. That's just acceptin' facts. You follow?"

"I follow," Harlem said. "Thank you."

Indigo smiled slightly. "You're welcome."

Harlem yawned. Sleep and a hot meal were both something she wished for. After her apparent induction into their club, the girls had gone off to their rooms. Some played cards, some read books or the tattered magazines they seemed to store in their rooms. She had watched them for hours, not saying much at all, until Magdalena had shouted 'Lights out!' down to where they'd arranged themselves, and the room became pitch black. Only then had she fallen asleep, but it hadn't been restful.

Violet approached her, stealthy on her long, light brown legs. They were the type that belonged to real ballerinas, not ones who simply studied dance like Harlem. "You gettin' acclimated, Sweetie?"

"Acclimated? Not really," Harlem said.

"Good. Then you won't mind moving," she said.

"Actually, I would," Harlem said.

"Leave her be, Violet," said a girl with large brown saucers for eyes and short, curly blond hair. She stepped onto the stage and extended her hand. "How do you do? I'm Emerald."

"Yes, the gem for all to see and hold. You were so quiet yesterday. Pleased to meet you," Harlem said.

"Likewise," Emerald smiled brightly as she settled onto the stage. Like a young girl with nothing on her mind but vanilla soda and her favorite summer book, she laid on her stomach, chin resting on her hands, her legs criss-crossed behind her. "So, new girl, what's it like on the outside these days?"

Violet sat down next to her and messed with Emerald's curls, "Why do you torture yourself? Why?"

Emerald pushed her away, and smoothed her hair, "I like to keep up with the times, Violet. You see, it gives me more to do than to be a horse's patootie, like you."

"So, is this how it is down here? You all just—"
Harlem asked.

"What would you expect we do? Make
appointments to get our nails done? Wait by the
telephone for our suitors to call?" Violet turned
herself toward Harlem, "You're certainly rich with
your comments this morning."

"I'd like to know how you'd expect me to be?"
Harlem said.

"That's the difference; I wouldn't expect
anything."

"Violet," Emerald said. "Your manners."

Violet stood and laughed. "Manners?" she scoffed.
"I haven't got any manners left!"

Harlem heard the others laugh with her. "I'm glad
this is so funny to you all," she said exasperated, and
then, "Can someone just tell me what's next in all of
this?"

"Next?" Sienna said, looking at her comrades and
pulling on a strand of her long hair. "Not much,
really."

Harlem peered at Sienna and her 'cinnamon' skin,
as Officer Brighton had described it. She noticed an
accent in the girl yesterday. Something slight, not
something she'd hear in Greensboro or in Magdalena,
and certainly not in Officer Brighton's choppy sound.
It sounded light and bouncy and made her think of
water bubbling from a faucet.

"Where are you from?" Harlem asked.

"Getting' personal, are we?" Sienna said.

"Sorry," Harlem said.

"Dominican Republic. My parents came here ten years ago. Big mistake that was," Sienna said.

"Are there colored people there?" Harlem asked.

"If you're calling me 'colored,' then yes, there are."

"I meant—"

Ruby laughed coarsely. "Save it. We've all got sob stories about where we come from, and I don't have time to hear any of them. We're the Rainbow Girls, not the Sob Sisters. Girls, c'mon, let's get started." They began to stretch obediently like the dancers they were.

"Hold on a sec, Ruby," Violet said, staring at Harlem. "A can of worms has been opened here; I'd like to see what's squirming inside. Your turn, *madame.*"

"Yeah. So, where're you from, money bags?" Topaz muttered; the girl seemed to pull sound from the bowels of a garbage dumpster.

"Topaz, that ain't polite neither," Indigo said from her solitary place at the wall. With one hand on the wall and the other holding steady to her foot, she gracefully pulled her foot, toes pointed, up to the back of her head and leaned her head back to meet it. The stretch made her look like a scorpion as she gently held onto the gold curtain for support with her free hand. "Leave her alone."

"What, we're dealing with pleasantries now?" Topaz responded, holding her arm across her chest to stretch her shoulder.

Harlem couldn't help but stare at Topaz.

"What are you lookin' at?" Topaz demanded.

"Nothing. Sorry," Harlem said, looking away. "Where I come from—everyone is... the same."

Topaz walked toward her, climbed on the stage on all fours, and crawled across it like a tiger. Her nose was inches from Harlem's. Her forehead and cheeks were marred with a constellation of scarred-over chicken scratches. Her breath was stale and hot as she croaked, "So you've never been this close to a white girl before?"

"No," Harlem said, inching away from her. "Not exactly."

"Topaz, give the girl a break. Can't you see she ain't used to all of this?" Ruby said.

"What, and I am?" Topaz spun away from her, stood, and jumped from the stage.

"Yeah, honey. You are. Give me a light, would ya?" Ruby pulled a half-butt of a cigarette from somewhere deep in the crevice that divided her large matildas.

Harlem looked down her dress at her own breasts. Even if she squished them together, they would never be as forthcoming at Ruby's.

"I don't appreciate you's talking about me that way, Ruby," Topaz said as she pulled a match from the strap of her shoe and struck it on the stage.

"Then act a different way so's we got something else to talk about!" Ruby leaned forward for the light and exhaled a thin stream of smoke. She turned her attention to Harlem. "Actually... I would like to know a little more about the darling who did better than me. What gives?"

Violet, Indigo, Sienna, and Emerald joined Ruby and Topaz in the inquisition. From their various positions in the room, they scanned her now with something more than simple curiosity. They were a pride of protective, ravenous lions, sensuously aware of the lone, defenseless, wounded zebra in front of them. Harlem felt their hunger. They sniffed at her with their eyes, wanting to pull information from her like meat from a bone. Harlem swore one of them licked her paws. Harlem realized she wasn't really one of them, even though she'd done what they'd done down here with Arthur. She was still different. Still alone. Still hunted. Harlem finally answered, "Greensboro."

"How old are you?" Emerald asked.

"I'll be nineteen soon," Harlem answered. They circled closer.

"Why do you have all that dough?" Violet asked coyly, taking the first bite.

"Why do you want to know?" Harlem retorted.

"Because I'm not a ding-dong and neither are these girls. For Magdalena to even *suggest* that one of us would leave this house means that check of yours has got to be really, *really* worth it. You follow me?" Violet said with icy blood dripping from her words. "So. I wanna know why you have all that money, because don't nobody I know who looks like you and me got any kind of money worth mentioning. And I wants to know how much it is."

"That's my business."

Sienna peered at Harlem while picking at her fingernails. "You seem sorta sophisticated. I remember my great aunt was sophisticated. She had money, too. A lot of it."

"Sophisticated?" Harlem looked at Sienna with a raised eyebrow. It was as though she'd spoken to her in a foreign language. Harlem had never felt sophisticated. She'd felt like chewing gum on the bottom of someone's shoe.

"Yeah. You got that hoity-toity air about you. Even in handcuffs you're sittin' pretty proper."

"Who gives a shit how she's sittin'? I want to know about the money. So, how much is it?" Topaz asked.

"I said—"

"I guess we'll find out soon enough, right girls?" Violet's eyes narrowed. She licked her lips, rubbed her hands together greedily.

"That money, like I said, is my own business," Harlem got herself up to standing; her legs felt a little wobbly. The handcuffs bit into her wrists. "I'll ask you nicely not to bring it up again." Harlem jumped down from the stage and made her way to a far table that had an accompanying chair. They all stared at her as she moved.

"Haven't you got something to do other than stare at me? I'm certain I am not that interesting," Harlem barked as she got herself into a chair and elevated her feet. She kept her back to the girls and exhaled. She smoothed the wrinkled stripes on her dress and tried to steady the anger that was rising in her, along with the bile that wanted to come with it.

"Hey," Violet said.

Harlem turned her head to listen to the tiresome girl, "Yes?"

Violet was sitting on the stage back-to-back with Emerald. Violet slowly bent her leg into her chest and then teasingly extended her light brown ballet leg straight so that her nose touched her knee. She reached up with long, strong fingers and caressed her slim calf. Violet cunningly turned her head out and looked at Harlem with her leg still in place. "Better hope it isn't me who's the lucky one that gets to be you at the bank."

"Ugh!" Harlem turned her back again, "Leave me alone!"

"You'd leave us behind, Violet?" Emerald asked flatly.

"You think Honey's out there thinking of us? You think any of the other old girls sold off to who-knows-what-hell are thinking of our sorry asses still being down here? I don't know about you all, but I've been waiting for a sweet opportunity like this. While I'm in my room tonight dreaming about it, I'd like to know how much I'll have in my pockets when I'm running like the wind."

"Keep dreamin', Violet. Darling Maggie ain't gonna pick you," Indigo said. From the corner of her eye, Harlem could see her move into a new scorpion stretch with her other leg. Harlem closed her eyes. She wanted to disappear.

"I don't see why she wouldn't," Violet said tightly.

"Because you can't be trusted," Indigo said squarely. "An' Sienna, don't go thinkin' it's gonna be you, neither."

"Don't worry, I wasn't," Sienna said. "I ain't anywhere nears as sophisticated as the rest of you's or like her. Maggie would never pick me."

Harlem turned in her chair and lashed out at them. "You can forget about it. Now! That money is mine, I earned it. Not a single one of you is getting your raggedy claws on it. Ever! Do you understand me? You can turn your greedy ideas onto something else and leave me alone!"

"Well, well. A little feisty, I see," Topaz gave her a good once over and then turned her back to Harlem. The rest of the girls settled into silence, shifting as predators do. Quietly, purposefully.

Harlem kept her eyes on them.

"Bravo, cookie!" Ruby clapped for her, cigarette hanging from her mouth. "It's not often someone can get these dames to shut their traps. Well done," she laughed.

Harlem looked at her, "Thanks. I guess."

"You're welcome," Ruby coughed. "One more thing. Why were you on the run?" Ruby demanded, taking the last drag on her cigarette butt. She blew out a cloud of smoke that settled around them like the early morning fog did among the acres on Harlem's family property.

"On the run?" Harlem stretched her neck to the side, waiting for the familiar pop to release the tension that was steadily clawing its way up it.

"We were all goin' somewhere," Indigo said, now massaging the arch of her pointed foot, which she had released from her shoe.

"Running from somethin'," Topaz said loudly.

"Or *to* somethin'," Emerald added wistfully.

"We were all runnin' before we got here. So. Why were you on the run?" Ruby said, rubbing her cigarette butt into the floor.

"I needed a change," Harlem said flatly.

"Who doesn't?" Topaz laughed.

Harlem's eyes narrowed as she stared at Topaz who now laid on her back, her leg extended toward the ceiling. Topaz flicked her bare foot in the air toward Indigo, who crawled to her, stood and began expertly massaging her foot in response. Topaz slowly turned her head to Harlem, her steely eyes demanding an answer.

Harlem rose, faced them, and spoke evenly and plainly. "People back home...? There's a game they liked to play with me. They kept me tangled up on a string on the end of a stick so they could dangle me around. They liked hanging me over a pit of fire, and they'd take turns dipping me into the fire and yanking me out again. They wanted to see how hot I could get before I would melt or scream. And that was just the townspeople. The ones who were *nosy?* Or who had some kind of power? Or were just downright mean and wanted to torment me? They would do it because they knew I was the girl who killed her father and got away with murder. They couldn't figure me out. But they continued trying to figure me out until I finally made them stop." The room got chillingly quiet. The dust falling casually in the stage light's beam was the only movement. Harlem's voice came out of her in a low and steady growl that felt as unfamiliar as it sounded. "They knew I shot my daddy dead and some of 'em could tell I was happy about it."

Harlem smoothed her hair away from her face, both hands doing the job of one. "People don't know what to do with someone like me. They like to start experimenting. Asking me questions. I didn't want to be around those types of people any longer. Does *that* answer your question?"

"Sure does, sweetie," Ruby said. She coughed again and turned away. The pride of lions shifted their attention away from her and back toward one another. Violet pulled herself up and helped Emerald to her dainty feet. Topaz massaged Indigo's broad shoulders. Ruby went to Sienna and helped her stretch her arms, holding them behind her back as she pitched her head forward, her black hair cascading as she got into the stretch. As they turned their attention to one another, Harlem wasn't sure if she felt relieved or shunned, but she knew she'd gotten her point across. Finally. She found her chair and sat down slowly. She rested her hands in her lap and tried to massage her wrists. Licking her wound. She smiled a little. The pain felt good. She felt good. Like someone else. *Something* else.

"Hey Harlem," Topaz said, looking back at her. "So, you shot your pops, huh? Wish I'd a' had the same guts." Her words landed heavily on Harlem like a scratchy wool overcoat. Harlem could only blink. They'd had more in common than she would have ever guessed.

"Alright, you lazy pieces of trash, let's get a move on. Darling Maggie is gonna make her way down here sooner than later, and I ain't in the mood to have my head bashed in because you good for nothin's don't know the routine for this week. Let's line it up," Ruby barked.

"Shouldn't we get ready for 'New Girl In'?" Emerald asked, pushing her blond hair behind her ears.

"Why would we do that? We don't know if Money Bags is gonna dance as a Bettie or a New Girl or what."

The women hurriedly completed their various forms of ritual stretching. Emerald bent forward and touched her nose to her knees like she was a spaghetti noodle. Violet dropped into an effortless split, with her legs seeming to take up the entire stage. Sienna bent forward to touch her toes, then back up to the ceiling, swished her hips side to side and in a wide circle, and then bent forward and back and forward and back. Harlem felt so stiff with all her aches and pains. It was impossible to watch them stretch and not want to do something as well. She straightened both her legs and pointed and flexed her toes.

"You're gonna have to do more than stretch your feet, honey. I don't know what Maggie has planned for you, so you better learn our Rainbow Girl number and the Bettie number, fast," Ruby said to Harlem.

"In case you've forgotten, I haven't really eaten nor slept. I've barely any strength to dance."

"Don't know, don't care. And neither should you if you know what's good for you." Ruby took center stage and extended her arms. "Alright, girls. Line up. Let's get those kicks goin'." The girls jumped on stage and joined her in the straight line. "When the Betties get down here, we'll pull out the instruments and go over the number."

They linked arms at the shoulders. In unison, they kicked their left legs, then their right legs, and then left again starting low to the floor, then up to their waists, then high to their chests and higher to their heads. Again, and again, and again. The rhythm of their feet hitting the stage sounded like the soldiers in Europe who'd solemnly marched off to battle. With each kick and its corresponding heel hammering into the stage, Harlem felt a resurging jolt of uneasiness and anger. *Why had Magdalena put her in the red dress and still bid her off to Arthur?*

"You're saying I'm supposed to dance?" Harlem asked.

"Stop asking questions and get to work," Ruby said.

"Hang on, what about Sapphire?" Violet asked.

"Sapphire! Get your butt out here," Topaz yelled between surprisingly high kicks.

From the right, Sapphire's blue door opened. She yawned lazily and walked with no sense of urgency toward the stage. She stopped and glanced at Harlem, "Still being special, I see?"

"*Special...?*" she said.

"You. The new girl. Getting to be a Brown Bettie on day one. I'm still wondering what you've got that I don't," the girl said.

"She's got money, that's what," Sienna shouted breathlessly from the stage.

Harlem crossed her legs and scowled. A lot of good her money was doing right now. It was as much of a prisoner as she was.

"Money?" Sapphire examined her with a suspicion that Harlem knew all too well. "That explains things."

"Does it?" Harlem asked. She hoped her sarcasm wasn't lost on Sapphire, who seemed so intent on tormenting her.

"The sisters probably lost their marbles when they got a hold of you," Sapphire said.

"The sisters? Ruth and Mary? What have they to do with any of this?"

Sapphire laughed, "You can't be that daft?"

"I don't think she knows, Sapphire," Indigo huffed between kicks.

"I don't know what?" Harlem said, stomping her foot to the floor. She hated being left in the dark. She wasn't a child.

"Maggie and the sisters are in cahoots, Money Bags. Those old hags are the reason we're here. They find us and bring us to Maggie and Maggie pays them for it." Sapphire continued to laugh, "I can see it all now. You all prim and proper, strutting down the avenue or wherever you came from; what'd they do, offer you a cookie and a teddy bear and you followed them to this hellhole?"

Harlem's stomach dropped and her face grew very hot. She thought back to the Greensboro bus depot; she'd been trying to disappear into a sliver of shade to get away from everyone with their newspaper held high, like a mirror to her face. Everywhere she'd turned, she'd been bombarded with that awful headline blasting the news of her murder trial. Harlem couldn't remember what the sisters had first said to her, but it was then that they'd approached her. At the time she'd thought them to be two harmless women past their prime without much in the way of means or anything else, for that matter. "They seemed so nice," Harlem said; her eyes cast down to her shoes and hot tears started to blur her vision. *Could she trust no one at all in this world?*

"Looks can be deceiving," Sapphire said. "Look at you."

Harlem bit her lip. She held her tears back, lifted her chin high, and stared Sapphire dead in her eyes, "What is that you have against me?"

"Sapphire, lay off," Ruby said, coming off the stage as the rest of the Rainbow Girls stopped kicking. Perspiration dotted her forehead.

"Why should I?" Sapphire said, up righting a chair and sitting on it backwards. "I want to understand why this trusting little chickadee got it so easy."

"So easy?" Harlem said. Her eyes hardened. The hair on the back of her neck rose again. "What's so easy about it?"

"You waltz in here—"

Harlem stood, raising her cuffed hands toward Sapphire. "Do I look like I'm waltzing? Do I look like I'm having a good time and eating caviar? I'm a prisoner same as you, and I seem to be the only one in handcuffs."

"All I know is, most of us get dumped here and then we have to work for the red dress," Sapphire strode toward her and stood eye-to-eye with Harlem. "I know I have been. As far as I can see, you came in here and took my spot. Lickety-split."

"C'mon Sapphire," Ruby stood between them. "We got work to do. Go on and get up there."

"Why're you coming to her rescue? Didn't see you move a muscle upstairs when Maggie was having her way with my face," Sapphire said.

"You know that's different, Sapphire," Ruby said.

"Is it? We used to stick up for one another. Now it's every woman for herself. This one here may as well learn the lesson sooner than later, right?" Sapphire looked at Harlem.

Ruby blocked her view. "There are rules, Sapphire. You break them, you go against them, you suffer the consequences. It's that simple."

"You can put your rules where the sun don't shine. All of you, you hear me?" Sapphire snorted in the direction of the other girls on stage before returning to Ruby, who stood her ground. "Maggie may have put you in charge, Ruby, but you're not the boss of me." Sapphire pushed Ruby roughly by the shoulders. "I thought I made that pretty clear the other night after lights out. I'm not here to follow any more rules."

"Aww, shuddup, Sapphire." Ruby pushed her back and jumped back on stage. "You're such a bully."

"So," Sapphire's eyes lit up with a renewed envy, "cat got your tongue, new girl?" Sapphire shoved Harlem. "I said I want to know why you're so special."

Before she could think, Harlem shoved Sapphire back away from her. The girl stumbled. "You don't know *anything* about me so keep your trap shut!" Harlem lunged at Sapphire and began swinging with her two bound fists. "You just keep your trap SHUT!"

Screams filled the room and Harlem felt the girls pulling her off Sapphire. "Leave me be," she shouted. "I didn't sign up for this life. I won't be disrespected by any of you!"

Their faces looked back at her in shock. "Sister, get a hold of yourself," Indigo said, concerned.

Harlem teetered, breathless. She shot her head back to whip the hair from her eyes. Rage continued to course through her veins and exploded, "I won't get a hold of anything! I'm sick of this. You hear me? Sick of it!" Harlem spun about; losing her balance, she pitched forward into a table. She banged on it and with both hands pushed it aside. It clamored noisily against another. "Now, how the hell do I get out of here?" she screamed.

"Sweetie, you don't." Indigo said softly.

"Maybe *you* don't," Harlem seethed, "But like Sapphire said, *I'm* special."

CHAPTER 25

Honey rested her head on her hands as she gazed out the large window at Dolly's Diner. A theatrical show of the comings and goings of neighborhood characters played out before her. *So many black and brown folks!* They vividly acted out their lives as they rushed from one stage direction to the next, so eager to parade in this dress rehearsal of life. She sighed. She was absolutely enthralled by everything about them: the way they walked, what they wore, how they wore it, how they carried their responsibilities and where. She wondered how she would make her entrance into their world. How would she handle the spotlight of this mainstage? What would she wear? How would she walk? She wanted to join them and felt ready to do so, but there was one prop she didn't want. It was heavy and kept her from her joy. And she wanted to leave that burden exactly where it was: at Magdalena's.

"You know, I've been thinkin'," Jonas said, returning from the diner's bathroom.

"Hmmm," Honey stirred her third cup of coffee. The spoon clinked against the insides of her cup and echoed her clinking thoughts as she continued to stare out the window.

"Honey."

"What is it?" she clanked her spoon on the saucer louder than she meant to.

"Are you alright?"

"Yes. Where were we?" She ran her hands along her head, smoothing her hair abruptly as she looked once more out the window.

"Are you sure?" he said hesitantly.

"Yes, please. Where were we?"

"Alright then," he returned to the notes he'd taken over the past several hours in his journal. "We were mapping out everyone's arrival to the Manor."

"Right. Okay. Yes?" Honey kicked at the table leg impatiently.

Jonas glanced at her. She stopped. He continued, "We know Arnetta went missing three years ago. Ruth and Mary could have brought her to Magdalena's any time after that, after 1942."

"Have you thought about if she weren't at Magdalena's? Have you thought that maybe she was never there, and this is all a wild goose chase?"

"Excuse me?"

"What proof do you have that she was or is there at all?"

"I have a lot of signs pointing to—"

"But real evidence. You're wanting me to go back to that house and you don't even know anything for sure, except for the necklace."

"Honey."

"Forget it. Forget I said anything. Let's continue."

"I'm not sure I should."

"Continue. Please. I can see that...oh, never mind. Please, just continue," she cried, throwing her hands over her face.

Jonas stared at her. She waved him to continue. He acquiesced. "Well. Um. You told me we can rule out all three of the Brown Betties," Jonas said quietly.

"Yes. Amoura, Desire, and Fury. They've been there longer than anyone, except Amoura who is newer, but she still came before 1942." Honey looked down and straightened her coat.

"Understood. And..."

"Yes?"

"Alright then, the girls who arrived at the Manor over the last three years are Emerald, Sapphire, Topaz, Sienna, and Violet. Right?" he said, tapping his pencil nervously by each girl's name he'd written down.

"Right," Honey confirmed. "Oh."

"What?" Jonas looked up at her.

"Topaz is white."

Jonas sent a line through Topaz's name.

"And Emerald is, too..."

Jonas sent another line through Emerald's name. "Well, that helps narrow things down, I guess. So. These last three are 'round about the same age as Arnetta from what you can remember or what you know to be true," Jonas continued, checking his notes, flipping back through several heavily-filled pages.

With his head bent down over his work like a schoolboy, Honey noticed gray strands of hair wound in with black strands that spiraled like a corkscrew. She wondered if he knew they were there, and what may have caused them.

"We don't really celebrate birthdays at Magdalena's, Jonas. Age is tricky, honestly. It's not like we're some big happy family like you read about in children's books," Honey coughed. She downed the last of her coffee.

"I'm sorry," Jonas said, putting down his pencil and looking up at her. "I hadn't thought about how hard this might be for you."

"Well."

"These girls are just names and numbers to me, but they must feel like family to you."

She looked away. Her foot tapped again.

"Listen, I can see there's something else, Honey. What is it?"

Honey couldn't look at him. "It's just that. I'm free. I'm free of that place. I'm free of—"

"Of them. And I'm bringing you back."

Honey focused on the life outside the window. "For years and years, I dreamt. I prayed to the souls of my mother and father, to their ghosts, to *please* haunt the house and mysteriously unlock a door. And to give me the courage to run when I had the chance." Honey glanced at Jonas. She spoke quietly. "I'd had chances, Jonas. Unlike the other girls, I'd been able to leave. To go to the market for butter or Magdalena's cigarettes. Or to the pharmacy when someone was sick with fever or worse. But I didn't have the guts to run. I'd felt so terribly responsible to the girls... terribly responsible. Especially little Tilda. I don't know if you know what that feels like. That *burden*." Honey wiped at the stinging guilt springing from her eyes. "God help me, I just want to use this ticket, get on the bus in these ugly shoes and this old coat, and ride all the way to Chicago—or Alaska even—and not look back!" Honey closed her eyes. She tried to rub away the conflict that was throbbing in her temples. "Is that awful, Jonas? Does that make me the most awful person in the world?"

"I think it makes you human. You've been a prisoner. What person wants to go back to prison?"

"I just want to live my life," Honey sighed heavily, "without all of them."

"Of course." Jonas reached for her arm, gently. "Of course." He leaned back in his booth. Honey did too. She wiped at her tears with her napkin and exhaled. They both welcomed the silence between them, which was quickly filled by the sound of other people's lives going on in the diner. Bits of conversations about this and that. That and this.

"I'll get you on that bus, Honey. I'm sorry I've been so selfish."

"Thank you for understanding, Jonas. I'll tell you what I know, and I'll get you to Magdalena's. But tomorrow, I leave." Honey placed the napkin on her lap and settled both of her feet solidly on the floor under the table. She reached for his journal and looked at his notes. "So."

Jonas slid the journal from beneath her fingertips and put it in his valise. "So. Enough about me. What did you think about your first night out?"

"Well," Honey smiled slowly and thought about her night under the stairs, "the stars never looked so good as last night." -

"Right," Jonas smiled back encouragingly. His eyes crinkled slowly at the edges. "And I myself had free room and board last night. Actually, we both did!" Jonas chuckled hesitantly.

"Right!" Honey pointed at him in jest and laughed. But the laugh swelled with a mind of its own and soon had control over her, spilling out in way she couldn't quite contain. It came out in large, cleansing waves. She grabbed at her bruised sides trying to catch it, but it continued to bubble in her and grew with each burst. "Free room and board!" they hollered.

"Alright you two jesters." The waitress had reappeared. She took a pencil from her shirt pocket that was stitched carefully to read *Gretta.* "You ready to hear the Blue Plate Specials comin' up for tonight? 'Cause you been here all afternoon and we been through your last drop of coffee refills. I ain't bringin' no more bread and you already shared a soup and half a sandwich and the breakfast special. What's it gonna be?"

Jonas stopped mid-laugh and grinned at the waitress. "We'll take the check, thank you."

"You got it," Gretta said, placing their bill on the table as she walked away.

Jonas reached for his wallet, smiling, "Honey, you know, I want to thank you for—"

Gretta returned, interrupting him. She placed her wide fingertips on the table and leaned into Honey, "You know, I been watching you. Both of you," she said looking deep into their eyes. "I been down on my luck, too. I want you to have faith that the Good Lord God is gon' help you get back on your feet, you hear?"

Honey looked at Jonas, then stared into Gretta's tired, concerned eyes. "Yes, ma'am."

"Good. I will see you all next time then." Gretta discretely took their bill from the table, put it in her pocket, and turned away from them without another glance. She paused abruptly. "Oh! My Lord," she said.

Honey looked to where Gretta was pointing, wide-eyed with her hand over her mouth. A group of soldiers was marching into the restaurant. Gretta's eyes rolled back into her head and fluttered. Jonas jumped up and caught her, just as she fainted into a heavy heap. Honey helped Jonas ease the waitress down to the tiled floor and knelt down beside her. As Honey rubbed Gretta's shoulder to soothe her, she caught the faint smell of roses and grease.

One of the soldiers rushed to and knelt by Jonas' side. "Thank you kindly, sir." He gently gathered Gretta from Jonas' arms and fanned her face with his garrison cap, "Momma? Momma?"

Gretta looked up at the soldier; her big brown eyes couldn't contain the happiness and relief that came pouring out of her: "Thank you, Jesus! Aloysius, is it really you?"

"I made it home, Momma," he beamed. A tear of his dripped from his cheek and reunited with hers as he bent forward to tenderly wipe his mother's face with his fingertips. "I made it home."

Honey moved aside as a sea of blue legs surrounded her. With murmurs of polite introductions and an outpouring of love—the kind that often comes from being around someone else's momma when you miss your own—the soldiers crowded around Aloysius and helped Gretta to her feet.

"Ev'rybody, this is my one and only boy. Back from the war!" she said, breathless, reaching for him. The restaurant erupted with clapping and cheers, filling it with such noise and pride that everyone felt like they were being held in a great and glorious hug.

"She's one lucky lady," Honey said, smiling brightly and clapping along with everyone else.

"She sure is," Jonas sighed.

Honey turned to Jonas. She touched his arm lightly. "We'll find Arnetta, don't worry."

He nodded in agreement and met her eyes. "I hope so. Shall we get out of here?"

"Let me help you," Honey said, lifting one of Jonas' suitcases.

"Now don't you dare, m'dam."

"But your hand," Honey said.

"I can manage," Jonas smiled, taking his suitcase from her and collecting his valise from the red vinyl booth seat. "What you can do to help *me* is to allow me to help *you*."

"Sorry?" Honey said as they reached the door.

Jonas positioned himself and his belongings so that he could hold open the glass door for her. "We should stop somewhere and get you some proper clothes. So that you can ride the bus outta here in style."

Honey walked through the door. With her hand, she shielded her eyes from the afternoon sun. "Thank you, but I can manage with what I have for a while."

"Well, now, I do think that if I've learned anything a'tall about you, it's that you can absolutely take care of yourself. But, well, miss, if I may be so forward, every woman deserves something nice on her birthday. Am I right?" Jonas grinned.

"It isn't my birthday," Honey said and looked away.

"Isn't it?" Jonas hinted, shrugging his shoulders playfully.

The sun warmed her face. Honey lifted her chin to allow it to welcome her. She looked back at Jonas. The magnificent hubbub that was Harlem filled her ears and eyes.

Unruly wisps of her hair floated in the breeze; the taut ties that bound her to the girls at Lady Magdalena's began to loosen and float as well. She'd get to Chicago as promised, but for now her spirit came alive in the currents of those who walked past her. She felt like she was in a whirlwind, in the midst of a new beginning. Happily on stage. "You're right, Jonas. Maybe it is," she smiled.

CHAPTER 26

Honey zipped the back of the pale-yellow dress with its white lattice overlay. It hung about her sculpted shoulders and curved along her hips as though it were made especially for her. It was a simple day dress, but it was hers and she couldn't have been more thrilled. She stepped out of the small closet that had been turned into a dressing room. Spinning about in front of the full-length mirror, she couldn't help but giggle. Honey faced Ms. Paola, the seamstress who owned the tiny store-front shop. Paola beamed. Her golden, rusty-brown skin glistened. Fine lines creased her face around her eyes and her smile, imprints of her kindness.

"Well, what do you all think?" Honey said, raising her arms as though she were a statuesque model.

"*Bien. Bien.* Good. Good! *Yo soy* happy I had something that would work for you, *Pequeñita.*" Paola's entirely white curls, cut in a smart bob, framed her face.

"You've always been so helpful, Ms. Paola," Honey said and hugged the woman fiercely.

"No. If I were really helpful, I would say something. I would have said something to the *policia* about you. But... I am a coward," she looked toward Jonas who stood quietly near the front door.

"You aren't the only one. It's alright," Honey said.

"They already watch me, you see. Magdalena makes sure of this."

"Have you seen the other girls, too?" Jonas asked from his corner. His voice was measured, like a schoolteacher's.

Paolo paused. She looked at Honey.

"No," Honey said.

"I make the dresses for Magdalena; the fine gowns she wears for her parties. I also make the costumes for the girls. But I do not see them. I get measurements and I make the pieces." Paola wrung her hands together.

"Jonas is looking for his daughter, Paola. I am trying to help him," Honey said and pulled Paola near her. "That is the only reason he is asking. And you must keep this secret also, yes? My sister must not know that we were here. She has thrown me out, Paola."

Paola cradled Honey's face and said, "My prayers have been answered, *Pequeñita*." The woman continued to speak in Spanish as she hugged Honey. Tears fell from her eyes. "*Yo comprendo*," she said, nodding her head, wiping her nose with a handkerchief she pulled from her dress sleeve. "*Mira*, let us finish here. And *señor*, I wish you the best. I am sure God will help you."

"Thank you, ma'am," Jonas said softly.

"I'd love to put this on Magdalena's account for you, but she's quite behind, you know," Paola confessed as she stepped to her cash register and replaced her glasses on the bridge of her round nose.

"Actually, it's Honey's birthday and I'll be taking care of the charges, Ms. Paola," Jonas intervened as he retrieved his billfold from his suit pocket.

Paola raised her eyebrows, then peered over her glasses at Honey.

"Mr. Jonas Stewart, ma'am. Apologies for not introducing m'self sooner," Jonas offered as he shook her hand.

"Strong handshake, strong will," Paola said, accepting the bills from Jonas.

"Well, *feliz cumpleaños*, Miss Honey," Paola smiled between them as she handed Jonas his receipt. "I see it has been liberating for you."

"It has, thank you Paola," Honey said.

Paola slid the cash register door closed and crossed her arms across her motherly bosom. "Ah, *un momento, Pequeñita*," Paola said, moving aside a dress form fashionably draped in a Puerto Rican flag. She opened a narrow closet door. "One moment. I want to give you something also. For your birthday."

Honey's eyes widened as Paola presented her with a smart pair of satin brown wedge sandals. "Oh, I couldn't!" Honey exclaimed.

"I cannot have my newest *secret* customer wearing one of my fine dresses while walking the streets of Harlem in a clunky man shoe. This is a problem. *Esto es un problema!*" Paola hugged Honey and whispered in her ear, "I am glad you are free of that house, *pequeñita.* And of whatever derelict put those bruises on your body."

Honey's hands flew to her neck; she looked down.

Paola lifted her chin. "Whatever happened to cause that, *esta terminado*, finished. I see this for you. *Sí?*"

Honey nodded her head, "Yes."

"*Ahora*, you let me know if you need anything else. Anything," she hugged Honey again, as tight as she could.

"I will, Ms. Paola. I will," Honey said softly.

Paola helped Honey out of the "man shoes" and into the pretty sandals.

"Now those are some handsome-looking shoes," Jonas smiled.

"*Sí,*" Paola smiled as Honey twirled about once more.

"Thank you, again, Paola," Honey said over her shoulder as Jonas held the front door open for her.

"You're welcome, *mami,*" Paola called out as the door closed.

Jonas paused as they walked down the street. "No one is safe from Magdalena, are they?"

Honey folded the overcoat over her arm. "I suppose not," Honey sighed. "We've never spoken of this, ever. Everyone is afraid, or embarrassed... or feels helpless, perhaps. I don't know. I feel relieved I told her what's happened though. She always treated me like a real person, and not... something else."

"Something else?"

"Never mind," Honey said and smoothed her hands along her new dress, brilliantly free of any wrinkles or someone else's history. "Alright. Shall we get back to business?"

"If you like."

"Great. Follow me. I have something quite nearby to show you."

As they walked, lost in their own thoughts, a summer breeze playfully shook the hem of Honey's dress. She turned to Jonas, "What did you want to be when you were a boy?"

"A farmer, just like my old man," Jonas said. "He'd owned land back in around 1870 in Mississippi, but as the story goes he lost it, or it was taken from him, dependin' on who's telling the story. He got us to Ohio where I was born and worked some land there. Hardest work a man can do, farmin'. But I like being connected to the earth. Seein' that what you put into the ground comes out as something nourishing."

"I see," Honey said. "And you were married and had Arnetta...?"

"Yes," Jonas trailed. "My wife—she died, right in my arms, actually. I never found a way to get past it, not really, and that's how I lost Arnetta too. Was too busy having my head down, drowning out my own sorrows, that I left Netta alone to fend for herself. I regret every bit of what I did to that child."

"Well, I'm sure you were doing the best you could at the time."

"I just hope God lets me make it up to her," Jonas said. "Enough about me, now. What did you want to be when you were a young pup?"

"A clown," Honey giggled.

"A *clown?*" Jonas said.

"Our mother was a vaudeville performer. Her act came into town, as the story goes, and my father went to a show. Saw her up on stage in those lights, just dancing up a storm. After my sister was born, she went back to the stage because she loved it so. Then I came along several years later, a bit of a surprise to them. They'd been unsuccessful with the business of child-making and didn't think they could have another. But even though she had me in tow, my mother still had the desire to perform—and she was able to do so, just a little less than before. I remember being at her rehearsals with all the performers and loving the clown acts the most," Honey laughed.

"You're never too old to be a clown. I think there's still hope for you, Miss Honey," Jonas laughed, shifting his suitcases around.

"Jonas, I can see that your hand is bothering you. Won't you please let me help you and carry one of those bags? I've been beat up, but not enough to where I can't help a fellow human being."

"Alright, alright. Here, you can carry the small one."

"Now that that's settled, back to clowning. You think I've still got a chance?" Honey said as she accepted the smaller valise and swung it around her head like an umbrella. She began walking around in circles like a duck. "Looks like rain, looks like rain, looks like rain. Quack, Quack!"

"Look everyone," Jonas cried, laughing, "it's the Honey Duck of Harlem. All hail the duck!"

"Soon to be the duck of Chicago! Quack, quack!" Honey squeaked. "The best duck anyone ever saw. Finally, my dreams have been realized."

"You see, dreams do come true!" Jonas laughed.

"That they do," Honey said, slowing her stride and careful not to scuff her new shoes.

"Did your mother go on to be rich and famous?"

"Influenza got her in the end. My papa was a doctor and, well... He tried hard to save her, but it was out of his hands," Honey's smiled dropped. "I guess my father was a little like you, Mr. Stewart. He was struck with grief and little by little he left us too. He started poisoning himself with arsenic tea to move the days and nights along. And then he died. 'Course, Magdalena remembers Papa and Momma the most. I was so young. I remember them off of pictures or fragments of memories."

"I'm sorry to hear that, Honey," Jonas said.

"It's quite alright. Things happen, you know. And I'm happy to be out here in this fresh air, remembering walks to the park with Papa."

"I'm sure he's looking down upon you now."

"Oh no," Honey gasped.

"What is it?" Jonas said.

"Officer Brighton."

"Officer Brighton?"

"He can't see me. He mustn't," Honey panicked.

"Pretend to tie your shoe. I'll block you."

Honey dropped to one knee and Jonas shielded her from view. She watched Officer Brighton carefully from the corner of her eye as he walked ahead and disappeared down 131st Street. After he was out of view, Honey rose, shaken.

"Who is that?" Jonas said, holding her by the elbow.

"He guards Magdalena's Manor; he keeps the girls in," Honey said, smoothing her bun with unsteady fingers.

"He's gone now. Are you alright?

Honey sighed, "I'm alright. I'm fine. I thought he'd be gone or inside. I thought it was a good idea to bring you here like this. I'm a fool."

"Here? Where are we?"

Honey turned and pointed across the street, "Lady Magdalena's Manor."

CHAPTER 27

Tilda placed the dripping cutting board onto the drying rack and blotted her calloused hands gingerly on a dingy dish towel. It had been an uneventful morning, thankfully. If anything had happened, it was that she'd been haunted by the fact that she didn't have the courage to take water down to Harlem. She wondered where her courage was at; it musta jumped out of somebody else's window.

Moving to the stove, she reached for the can of bacon drippings and looked inside it. There wasn't much left of drippings because there hadn't been much bacon lately no way. Tilda dipped two fingers into the can and scraped them along the ridged metal sides. She spread the grease into her palms, warming it into salve before massaging it into the cracked creases and raw, peeling skin around her fingernails. She returned the can to the stove and lowered the flame on the simmering, dismal chicken soup that would be Magdalena's dinner. She gently stirred the cast-iron pot of swirling dime-sized carrots, thin pieces of chicken, and slivers of onion while praying for a miracle that would taste good on her tongue.

Blech, she thought, grimacing as she sampled the soup. *Maybe time will do this some good.* Tilda placed the heavy lid back onto the pot.

Don't know why I'm tryin' so hard anyway, Tilda thought as she placed the wooden spoon on top of the lid. She turned and leaned against the sink, its porcelain lip cold against her back. Over the years, this room had been her playground and so much more. She looked down at the floor; the large black and white tiles had been her hopscotch. The small breakfast nook against the boarded windows had been her classroom where she had taken pencil to paper to draw or for practice lessons that often went uncorrected. The white cupboards had clapped for her when she'd pretended to sing and dance on her own stage.

Tilda silently asked the kitchen, her captive audience, *What am I gonna do? Die here? Be a Rainbow Girl?*

She lifted the lid from the soup again. The hot steam that hit her face seemed to say, *You don't know nothin' else but to do what you're doin' right now.*

Tilda stirred the soup angrily, *I know I don't know nothin' else. But can't I learn?*

Can you? the spoon seemed to say as she dropped it in the sink.

Yes. I can. Plus, Honey is out there somewhere and she'll help me. Tilda slid into the window seat.

The greying curtains, which hung listlessly from the windows that had seen as little sunlight as her over the years, whispered, *How will you find her?*

Tilda put her head down on the linoleum tabletop and spoke to the faded, tiny silver stars trapped in a perpetual swirl, *I don't know.*

The soup bubbled for her attention. She tasted it again. *There's no hope. None.* As she ladled a bowl for Magdalena, she wondered if she was talking about herself or the soup.

Tilda carried the bowl into Magdalena's office, where she found her with her head bent low over some kind of book. Tilda placed the soup on the edge of the desk and crept out before Magdalena could taste it and throw a fit.

"Come back here, Tilda," Magdalena called out.

In response, she squeezed her eyes shut, blew some air out in frustration, and turned on her heel. She presented herself in the doorway.

"'New Girl In, Old Girl Out,'" Magdalena said.

Tilda was glad Magdalena hadn't tasted the soup, but she felt her lip curl itself into a scowl before she could tell it not to, just the same. She wanted nothin' to do with those girls down there right now. She had other things to worry about.

"You know what? I don't care what you think, Tilda." Magdalena slammed the book closed and pointed a bony finger at her. "You can look at me like that all day long. I run this place, not you. Honey is out and she's never coming back. Ever. So get used to it. Now go get the Betties, the Rainbow Girls, and that piece of shit Sapphire, and get them ready to audition for 'New Girl In, Old Girl Out' like we always do."

Like we always do, Tilda mimicked in her head.

"And one more thing, Tilda," Magdalena pointed the book at her, which Tilda could now see was the journal that had been in Harlem's luggage. "Honey was a test for me. To see just how far I could go to get what I want. You're next."

Tilda swallowed hard. *I'm next?* she thought.

Magdalena seemed to have read her mind. "Yep. Next. Now go."

Tilda darted into the foyer and hurried to the door under the stairs. She turned the glass doorknob and skittered into the dark nook of her bedroom. She pressed her back against the door, her fingernails digging into the wood. In the darkness, Magdalena's words jingle-jangled in her head. *I'm next? Sold?* Honey's screams haunted her. Honey being sold to that slimeball Otto. Who would Tilda be sold to? Someone worse, probably. If that was possible.

Tilda reached above her and frantically pulled the long string dangling there; light easily filled each corner of the tiny room.

When they were a family, Magdalena and Honey and her, Tilda used to have the room upstairs, usually reserved for the new girl whenever one arrived. She'd been so young then, maybe four or five or so, but she remembered having that big room to herself. All to herself. When things changed, when things got bad, she got moved down here. Magdalena's shifty boyfriend at the time, Lonnie Listromski, had moved her down here to this dusty broom closet where her only friends became the spiders and mice that came and went.

A thin, lumpy mattress that was doubled over on a wooden plank sat on top of cement blocks served as her bed. On all fours, Tilda climbed onto the bed toward the end where her feet would usually go, just under the sloping ceiling. She was careful not to bump her head. She reached her hand inside a tear in the mattress that faced the wall, pulling out the lipstick. *I've got to try. I've got to try to get out of here.*

She stood. She slowly pulled off her apron and threw it on the bed. She looked around the room; there was nothing for her to take. The family photos were in Honey's room upstairs. She caressed the "A" for *Always* around her neck. It and the lipstick were all that mattered now. She put her hands on her hips and they started shaking. She held her wrists to make them stop. *This is no time to be shakin'.*

Turning off the light, she leaned her forehead against the door. *Please, good God above, help me out. Help me out right now. I ask you and I ask you again for good measure.* Tilda cracked opened her door and stepped out into the foyer.

Lon Listromski. His name had been said so many times and in not so nice 'a ways after a while, and that's how she could remember him. Couldn't place much in the way of his face, though. As she stood near the door and listened for any rumblings from Magdalena, Tilda wondered where that boy was now. *Course, he wouldn't be much of a boy now,* she thought. It had been so long since he'd found his way into their home and ruined what was left to ruin.

Tilda fingered the lipstick. She looked toward upstairs. *Betties. You're goin' to have to forgive me. I'll be back for you, I promise.*

Tilda stared at the front door and through the stained glass that looked like a vine of roses melting under water. *Alright, I'm gon' walk through those doors. Right now. Ain't no Officer Brighton there to stop me. Ain't nothing there to stop me!* She took a deep breath, lifted the "A" from her chest, kissed it for good luck, and ran to the door. Shoving her hand into her pocket, Tilda reached for the key. Her fingers shook like leaves as she quickly turned the big wrought iron thing in the lock of the first door. *Gon' find Honey and we'll be free together. Like we always talked about.* Tilda quietly closed the door and rushed to the main entrance. Glancing behind her hurriedly, Tilda laughed nervously and thought, *How many times I* opened this door for other people and now I'm about to do it for myself?

Tilda unlocked and swung open the front door. Air rushed over her like a tidal wave. She caught her breath sharply as though the breeze had punched her in the stomach. I did it! Tilda looked left, right, and then straight ahead to the park. She saw people walking by. She waved her arms at them, Help! Help! So many times she had tried to get her vocal chords to rub together to make a sound. So many times. She tried again. Help! Help me! Nothing.

A man was passing by. She clapped her hands and waved to him, her arm flapping wildly.

The man tipped his hat and waved back casually.

Wait! Wait! Tilda shouted in her head. She went to take a step, to run down the stairs to the man, but then all of a sudden, faster than the whoosh of the stove's gas flame coming to life, she felt like she was on top of an impossibly tall cliff. She felt that if she tried to take another step, that step would plunge her to her death. She blinked. The blues and the greens from the sky and the trees started to melt together. She placed her hand on the concrete banister to steady herself. A black car drove by. She wanted to wave it down. But now her arm wouldn't move, like the banister was holding her tight 'stead of the other way round. Chained. What if that was Officer Brighton driving that car? Or worse, Otto? What if those people out there, that man in the hat, what if he was the kind who *would do things to me?* Her mind filled with a bunch more thoughts. Quick, heavy, frightening thoughts that made her insides flip flop and her knees wobble. *Who will rescue me? Where will I go? Where will I sleep?* Each thought was like hot grease bubbling up and taking licks at her courage. The cliff was getting higher. She punched her legs to get them to take a step, but they wouldn't move. Her chest felt tight. She started gasping for air. Tilda looked behind her. Back to where she didn't need her voice. Where her legs worked. Where she could breathe. She was stinging and burning from the inside. *I can't! I can't,* she cried in her head and ran back inside.

Tilda doubled over, trying to smother the fire inside her. She fell to the floor of the foyer and covered her face. She wanted to scream to the high heavens to express how bad she felt. She pounded the floor with her tiny fists. She threw the keys she still clutched in her hands clear across the floor and lay there, surrendered fully to the ties that bound her to that place.

"Tilda!" she heard Magdalena scream from the basement. "What the hell are you waiting for? If I have to come up there, you will be very sorry. I promise you."

Tilda slowly pulled herself to her knees and crawled to where she'd thrown the keys and clutched them in her hands. *I already am sorry!* Tilda screamed silently.

CHAPTER 28

Tilda's key scraped in the lock. At the sound of it, Fury hooked her thumb in the frayed strap of her slip and turned onto her shoulder as the cot beneath her squeaked in response. Tilda was there to get her out of bed for something, but Fury didn't feel like going anywhere or doing anything. Her stomach was sour and her back ached, reminding her that another month had passed. Sometimes this coming and going was the only way she could keep time. She rubbed her back and wished for her great aunt Faye's special chamomile tea, which used to help her feel better. Women used to come from miles around to their family's sundry shop in Kentucky to buy the wonder medicine. She sure wished she had some now.

"What is it, Tilda?" Fury said, without turning from the wall. She was answered with a thud. Her dance shoes landed on the bed near her curled knees, having hit the wall in front of her. "Hey, what's doin', Tilda?" Fury said, rising onto her elbow and looking back at Tilda. Fury didn't like the look on Tilda's face. "What's happened?"

Tilda spun away from her, nearly knocking over the one possession Fury had, a dilapidated floor lamp. Fury had bargained and paid dearly for that sorry lamp because she couldn't stand being in the dark. The faded, blue-velvet shade was missing so many of its tassels. It reminded Fury of one of the old men who'd come to Lady M's Mysterie years ago. He'd only had three teeth in his head. When he smiled, Magdalena had shrieked so loud. She'd then pushed Tilda toward him to escort him out the foyer and back to wherever he'd come from.

Fury steadied the lamp as Tilda swiftly moved toward the closet door and unlocked it.

"*Tilda!?*" Fury grabbed her shoes, sprang forward, and wedged herself in front of Tilda. "What are you doing?"

Pushing Fury aside insistently, Tilda entered the empty closet. Fury followed her into the emptiness. Her and the rest of the gals only owned the clothes they were wearing when they'd been captured and, according to Magdalena, they didn't even own those. As a result, there was nothing to hang in the closets that each girl had in her room. Back home in Kentucky, Fury had a wardrobe full of dresses. Sometimes she would open the doors and bury her face in the crisp, starched linens and cottons that belonged to her and only her. Her cotillion dress had been the last thing of splendor that she remembered hanging. Her great-grandmother, grandmother, mother, and even her father had helped make the dress with its layers of white satin and delicate lace, all stitched with love. Fury thought of the dress and her family as Tilda pulled on a bare metal hook on the wall. As though pushed by a gentle breeze or a ghost, the back wall of the closet hinged open into darkness.

"Dammit, Tilda. Hurry up and light it first!" Fury said as she hung back behind Tilda, closer to the lighted bedroom.

Tilda pulled a small candle from her pocket. She struck a match and the flame burned the wick hungrily as it led the way.

The light filled the narrow passageway, which Fury had always supposed was about forty or fifty feet long, the length of two smaller horse stables like the ones she'd had back home. The passageway was more like a tunnel, with a ceiling that was low enough for Fury to touch if she raised her arms high above her head and stood on tiptoe. Of course, didn't matter what size it was, because when it was dark she didn't care about nothing more than getting out of it. Some of the girls believed this hidden tunnel—which led right into the basement that was now the Lady M's Mysterie—had been used for hiding slaves and that this house had been a stop on the Underground Railroad. Apparently Tilda had found some papers in Magdalena's office stating as much. Fury had never seen them so she couldn't confirm nor deny this. But she hoped it had saved some lives and had been more useful to them than it was these days.

"Tilda, slow down with that fast walking and tell me what the devil is going on!"

Tilda ignored her and continued on a few more paces. She stopped, turned to her left, and began fumbling on the wall. Fury brushed her away, "Here, let me do it. You can barely find the spot when you're not all worked up. You concentrate on that damn candle." With her fingers sliding across the rough wooden wall, she found the special wooden knot; four fingers to the left of that and six-fingers up from there, she found the invisible panel. It was about the size and shape of a jewelry box, maybe smaller. Fury pushed on the center of it and released a spring that opened the panel door. She reached in and pulled on a wooden switch hidden within. As she did so, a narrow door swung open into the passageway. Tilda handed Fury the candle and disappeared inside it.

"Hurry back, now," Fury said and held the candle at arm's length as though it was a cottonmouth viper that swam in the streams back home. She closed her eyes tight, counted to ten, and then did it again. Fury waited for the panic to drop down and out of her throat—or for Tilda to come back. She really wasn't sure what would happen first; each time was different. What never was different was knowing that she hated fire more than she hated the dark.

—

Tilda emerged from the doorway with Desire trailing behind her. Fury lifted the candle to her friend's face and gave it to her. "She tell you anything?" Fury asked.

In the candlelight, Desire's quiet, cold nature made her stunning. She was a year older than Fury, and taller, but where Fury was a sleek, powerfully-built Thoroughbred, Desire was a nimble gazelle. She moved with cunning ease, almost like she was invisible until she wanted you to see her. She was bold and unyielding. Just like her name. They all were like their names, which is why Magdalena christened them so.

"No, she has not," Desire answered, taking the candle. "Tilda, you can't just waltz into my room sniveling like your best friend died. Since I'm standin' here and Fury standin' right there, I know not one of us died. Unless Amoura's dead. She dead?"

Tilda rolled her bloodshot eyes and pushed past the girls.

"Okay, good. We know Amoura ain't dead. Is it Honey? You upset about her? We all are, you know that. C'mon Tilda, what's doin'?"

Tilda turned, walked ahead, and kept her head down low in response. Desire lifted the candle high as their guide.

"Guess we don't exist now," Desire said as she threw her arm up in the air and flung her shoes dramatically. They clattered against the ceiling and fell to the ground.

"Oh, we exist, sister. We exist," Fury said, stooping to retrieve the shoes. "Even with Honey basically being erased from our lives, we still exist."

Desire teased, "Tiillldaaaa... tell us what's wrong and I'll give you my dinner tonight."

Fury smiled a little, "Gonna have to come up with something better than that, Desire."

"How about my fox fur or my emerald necklaces?"

"You mean the ones Oscar Micheaux gave you when you worked on his last picture?" Fury joined in the jest.

"Yes, I am his *protégé* after all. But since I'm not off anywhere being famous, I have nothing better to do than to emphatically ask Tilda what's wrong and offer up my jewels. You see, this keeps me occupied, darling," Desire said, leaning melodramatically against the wall, her forearm against her forehead like a Lena Horne publicity photo.

"Looks like you're gonna be occupied for a long time. Let's keep a move on," Fury said.

They arrived at a third door. Before Tilda could push this door's panel, Desire reached for her tiny shoulder and spun her 'round gently. She lowered herself to meet Tilda's eyes, "Tilda, did Magdalena do something to you? You can tell us anything. You know we love you."

Tilda's eyes brimmed with tears.

"Don't'cha know you can trust us with anything?" Desire continued.

Tilda pulled herself away from Desire.

"You're wasting your time, Desire."

Fury pushed on the panel, released the switch, and watched as Tilda disappeared inside. She leaned against the wall and closed her eyes.

"You alright?" Desire asked.

"It's just that time," Fury answered.

"I'll rub your back if you want," Desire leaned her head on her shoulder.

"That's alright. I'll be fine soon." Fury looked toward the end of the hallway. They were almost at the end of it, near the staircase that led down to the basement. Even with whatever trouble was brewing, she was beginning not to care. She just wanted out of that dark, narrow tube that seemed to be getting narrower and narrower.

Tilda emerged with Amoura. She was cute as a button, but Fury knew that she would break a button in half and cut somebody with it if pressed. Amoura took the lead. Her behind swished to and fro in a way that Fury gave up trying to mimic. Amoura had come from the deep South and never let anyone forget it, as people from the deep South tend to do, but in Amoura's case she did it lest she forget it herself.

Amoura mumbled, "I was sound asleep. Sound. Dreamin' 'bout my grandmomma's peach pie. Was about to take a bite, Tilda. A big ole bite—"

Tilda clapped her hands angrily.

"Well, goodness! What is in your bonnet, Tilda?" Amoura asked.

Tilda rapped her little knuckles on the wall in Morse Code.

"Tilda, slow down, I can't understand you!" Desire begged.

"Can we just get downstairs, please, and talk about whatever this is some other time?" Fury inched along the wall.

Tilda kept rapping.

"Tilda, you what?" Amoura said, taking Tilda by the hands. "By yourself?"

"Oh, for heaven's sake. Amoura, what'd she say?" Fury demanded, closing her eyes. Amoura's husband had gone off to war, and she'd had to go work at the post office in order to take care of herself and their home, and it was there that she learned Morse Code. When Amoura realized Tilda had no real way of communicating with anyone, she'd secretly taught her, Fury, and Desire the taps and pauses that made up the alphabet so that the girl could talk. Fury hadn't caught on as quickly as the others had.

Amoura shouted, "What does Magdalena mean, 'You're next...!?'"

Fury flicked her eyes open.

Tilda placed her finger to her mouth and angrily silenced her with a "*Shhh!*"

Desire turned Tilda's shoulder, bringing the candle to Tilda's face, "You tried to escape? Without us?"

"Escape?" Fury felt paralyzed against the wall.

"Fury, keep up! Magdalena told Tilda that she was goin' to sell her out on the street, just like she did Honey. And so Tilda tried to escape."

"This clearly means none of us are safe," Desire said.

Fury looked at Desire, "Safe!?"

Amoura smoothed Tilda's hair, "But why would Magdalena put *you* out—"

"Save it," Fury barked.

"*Save it?*" Amoura's eyes widened.

The girl's shadows danced on the barren wall as Desire turned toward her, the candle spotlighting them. "Does it matter, Amoura? How long have we been here? How much have we seen that doesn't make sense? I'm through asking 'Why?' When I get outta here, Magdalena's gonna wish I gave her the chance to ask me why. The fact that Magdalena wants to put Tilda out there with Honey doesn't have nothin' to do with us, now does it? We see ain't nobody storming into this place and rescuing us now that they are out. Tilda would probably do the same. Survival of the fittest."

Amoura eyed her with contempt as she angrily wiped away a tear. "Tilda would come back for us."

Fury scoffed, "Just like Honey has."

Amoura glared at Fury.

"I see. So, you think Honey would scoop up Tilda and fly back in here on a magic carpet, whisking us all away to fairy-tale land?"

"Fury, stop it," Desire sighed.

"I'm just being realistic, Desire. Something Amoura doesn't seem to be too good at."

"Whatever it is that's botherin' you, besides all of this horrible nonsense, I suggest you find a way to take it out on somebody else 'steada me, Fury. I'm feelin' just as bad as you are and I don't need to feel worse," Amoura said as she stood with her hands on her hips.

Tilda rapped.

"Lay off it, Tilda. Stop makin' fun of me and siding with Fury. You do not have a magic carpet to get us out of here," Amoura stomped and crossed her arms.

Tilda pulled something from her pocket.

"Lipstick?" Fury felt a surge of something that lit through her body and pulled herself away from the wall. She grabbed the lipstick from Tilda's fingers. "Oh, I'm gonna fly on this? I'm gonna make it outta here because my lips are rouged? Well, if only I'd known that five years ago!" Fury threw the tube over her shoulder toward the stairs leading down to where they were supposed to be and where there was room to breathe.

Tilda barreled through Fury, knocking her over. Fury fell into Desire and the candle fell against the wall, pitching them into darkness.

"The candle, the candle!" Fury grabbed for Desire, pulled her near and fiercely buried her face in Desire's back to muffle her screams.

"Fury, calm down," Desire said, turning and holding her. "Amoura, find the candle."

"I found it," Amoura said, breathless. "Tilda, bring me a match."

Fury clamped her eyes shut so tight that shooting streaks of white and orange and blue and red flashed against the black of her closed lids. She felt a heat that wasn't there. Heard screams that were no longer there, from people who no longer existed. Their screams became hers and she wailed with them, her voice loud and shrill.

"What in the hell is going on up there!?" Magdalena's booming voice travelled up to them from the speakeasy that was only a few paces and one staircase below. "What is taking you so long to get down here?"

"We're comin', Magdalena!" Amoura shouted back as she took over for Desire and cradled Fury, "You okay, honey? You okay?"

"Six, five, four..." Fury counted as she found herself, remembered where she was, and got her breathing back to a normal pace.

"Candle's lit, Fury," Desire said. "You can open your eyes now. Coast is clear."

"You sure?" Fury whispered. Her fingers trembled as she reached for Amoura's hands which cradled her face.

"Promise," Amoura said.

Fury opened her eyes. Amoura's soft brown eyes comforted her. Fury smiled weakly as Amoura's fingertips soothed her eyelids. "I'm—I'm sorry, girls."

"Oh, honey, don't be sorry," Desire said, coming into view. "I will say that with the type of scream you got, maybe *you* should be the one in pictures."

Fury reached for them and pulled them to her in an embrace. "Thank you," she said. They all nearly fell over when Tilda jumped on to join in their group hug.

"Alright, alright. Let's break it up and get downstairs before Magdalena breaks our faces," Desire said.

Tilda rapped.

"Can we talk about it later, Tilda? We need to get Fury downstairs; Magdalena is waiting—" Amoura paused. Tilda waved her hands in their faces and shook her head fiercely, presenting the lipstick to them again.

"Okay, okay!" Desire said, taking the lipstick.

Tilda gestured to her crazily.

"Inside the case...? Open it?" Desire opened the lipstick case and caught herself, "Holy baby Jesus!"

"Oh my stars," Amoura said, her hands at her cheeks.

"Money?" Fury said, grabbing the lipstick from Desire. "There's *money* in here? How much is it?"

Tilda grabbed it back. She rapped slowly, for Fury.

"You don't know? Well, shouldn't we count it?" Fury asked. A race had begun in her mind and she was sprinting in it. "Where did it come from?"

Tilda rapped.

"Harlem?" Desire said.

Tilda rapped more.

"The inheritance?" Amoura said.

"GET DOWN HERE, NOW!" They all jumped out of their skins as Magdalena's hollered threat tore through the tunnel and practically strangled them.

"We gotta go. Tilda, put that lipstick in a safe place and—" Amoura spoke, interrupted by notes of Magdalena's clarinet winding up to them through the tunnel.

"Shit," Desire said.

"Magdalena is taunting us," Fury breathed, recognizing the haunting, sultry melody all too well.

Amoura clapped her dance shoes together. "Uh-uh, Fury. She's *mocking* us. And that's much, much worse."

Fury grabbed Tilda's hand and ran. "C'mon, let's go. That money is going to be our way out of here."

CHAPTER 29

From her perch on top of the upright piano, Magdalena belted Bettie notes from her clarinet like an angry snake charmer. It was a melancholy tune full of lusty sounds that had been composed especially for the Brown Betties. It was as signature to them as a woman's perfumed scent.

Magdalena hated to wait. They were making her wait. She blew harder into the instrument but the harder she blew, the more livid she got. She pulled the instrument away from her lips and dangled it from her hand as she crossed her knees, exposed by a high slit in her silver gown. She impatiently kicked the clarinet and was just about ready to drop-kick it like a football and watch it soar into the air.

Despite the *poink, poink, poink* sound of her foot against the hollowed instrument, the air was dead. It had been stabbed to death by the notes she had just finished playing. Magdalena stared at the graveyard of girls sitting like tombstones at the bare tables before her. She was disgusted by their very presence.

"Stop looking at me," she said vehemently. "Did I tell you to look at me? Look at something else."

The girls complied, except for one. "Harlem, have you gotten a nerve up?"

"No," Harlem said.

"Then do as I say." Magdalena heard steps coming up behind her, "Your highnesses," she said, laying the clarinet on the piano and bowing deeply as the Betties entered from backstage. "Thank you for gracing us with your silly presence. Minus one, of course."

"What do you want with us, Magdalena?" Fury said as she and the rest of the Betties stood on the stage.

"Since when do *you* ask me what *I'm* doing?" Magdalena snorted as she eased her way off the piano and stepped onto the stage. She faced Fury with only a few inches between their noses and glared down into the girl's blazing eyes. "I am not in a good mood. Do you understand me? You've already kept me waiting as though I don't run this place. If you want to see tomorrow, I suggest you remember your paltry position in life."

"You gonna slap me around like you did Sapphire?"

Desire and Amoura reached for Fury's arm and pulled her to them.

"That's right, protect her, you witches. And, yes, if you disrespect me like she did, I most certainly will, Miss Attitude," Magdalena sneered as she turned. She then picked up the clarinet and addressed Harlem and the Rainbow Girls, "Let's begin, shall we? You all look like a herd of dying elephants. Sit up. Sit UP!"

Tilda made her way toward the steps that lead out of the speakeasy. "And Tilda, I hope that you are on your way to punish yourself for serving me that God-awful piss you called soup. Don't you ever do that to me again."

Tilda kept walking. "DO YOU HEAR ME?" Magdalena roared.

A nod came from the girl; Magdalena waved her away with the clarinet, "Just go."   Magdalena now pointed the clarinet at the girls and stared each of them deep in their frightened, useless eyeballs. "Now. We know it's generally one of you obnoxious Rainbow Girls who is 'Out,'" Magdalena said as she walked into her seated audience; she weaved past Emerald and Ruby and brushed past Violet. She landed in front of and swatted at the hands of Sienna, who was busily biting her nails. "That is so incredibly unattractive. What man wants you touching him with disgusting nubs for fingernails? Stop it. Stand up."

Sienna stood.

"What was it I just said?"

"You said for me to stop biting my nails."

"Before that, you dolt."

"You said that it's one of us seven who's usually 'Out.'"

Magdalena circled past Sapphire and Harlem, keeping her eye on Sienna. "And by 'Out' we mean...?"

"Sold. Like Honey," the girl replied.

Magdalena winced mockingly and plugged her ears with her fingers, "But we don't like to use that term, 'sold,' remember? 'Out' is so much more efficient. And kind." She circumnavigated her way past Topaz and Indigo, "One of you seven who, unfortunately, is usually more expendable than the Brown Betties, is usually... okay, *sold*. And whoever is new to my manor gets inducted "In," but guess what, girls? Things are different now at Magdalena's. I've got to protect myself and my business. So I've decided to dip into the well of opportunity. Which means one of you is getting a ticket to first class. Which one of you wants to be really IN?"

"I thought I was the new girl and that I was already 'in?'"

Magdalena spun around to see Harlem standing, her hands still shackled from Officer Brighton's handy work. She looked her up and down as she walked toward her. Harlem looked frazzled now, her first night in the basement having taken its toll. Magdalena straightened Harlem's dress belt; it was quite oddly askew on her torso. "You still have to audition."

"What?" Harlem said, jerking away from her.

"Initiation," Magdalena said.

"This is ridiculous!" Fury said under her breath.

"I heard that; you watch it, missy!" Magdalena said.

"Harlem was a Brown Bettie," Amoura said. "You put her in a red dress."

"Yes, I did," Magdalena said, eyeing Harlem and thinking about that check that was going to make her troubles go away.

"Seems you made some kind of mistake," Sapphire said.

"Is that so, Sapphire? And you're better than her—is that it?" Magdalena laughed and looked at her own cuticles which were way more interesting than any of their jealous quibbles. "Amoura, which one of these—these... things can take Honey's place?"

"Well, no one can take Honey's place," Amoura volunteered.

Magdalena nodded in agreement.

Harlem interjected, "Amoura! You're saying I'm not good enough to be a Brown Bettie?"

"Hold your horses! I'm not saying that, what I'm saying is—"

"What she's saying is you're not good enough for anything here, even with all your loot and your entitled air," Sapphire said.

"I told you to stay away from me, Sapphire," Harlem snarled.

Magdalena looked up from her cuticles and raised her eyebrow. The Harlem girl had some spark. She liked that.

Amoura pointed a finger at Sapphire and said, "Sapphire, stop puttin' words in my mouth."

"I haven't put nothin' in your mouth that doesn't already belong there. You know what this is about, Amoura. It's about the precious Honey and her abrupt exit. Among other things." Sapphire flicked her hand at Amoura and crossed her legs, ending her side of the conversation.

"*What* other things?" Harlem asked.

"I'd watch your tone, new girl," Magdalena said and walked back to Harlem. From her pocket, she produced a key and removed her handcuffs. "At my party I put you in a dress to see how you would do. And you did what you did with whom you did it." Holding Harlem's hands, Magdalena led Harlem to the center of the stage. "Now take that dress off. You won't be needing it down here."

"I won't."

"You will, or there will be more trouble for you," Magdalena said, swinging the handcuffs on her fingers.

Harlem looked out at everyone and awkwardly removed her clothing as one struggles to remove a shell from a hard-boiled egg. Magdalena retrieved the dress and draped it on her arm. "Good decision." Harlem covered herself with her arms with the modesty of an ingénue. Her champagne-colored underthings glared in their newness compared to the other girls. That would change over time.

Magdalena continued, "You're practically useless to me as a Brown Bettie now. You'll make me more money as a Rainbow Girl, which was so nicely proven during the party. So now you're back to where any new girl is. At the bottom."

Magdalena smiled. "Happy, Sapphire?" she said as she put the handcuffs and dress on top of a table. Magdalena sat at the piano with Harlem shaking center stage.

"You see, anyone can spread their legs. Dance is the real magic that makes the merry go 'round. Dance is sin and savior down here in this church. Dance is everything, sister." Magdalena laughed.

"I'm a dancer," Harlem stated boldly.

"Is that so? Well, these girls are too, you know." Magdalena surveyed the girls and her gaze landed on the bossy Indigo. "Take Indigo. Indigo, you came here, what, three or four years ago?"

"Roughly," Indigo crossed her legs and rubbed a mark off her dance shoe.

"Indigo has a lovely figure. Favorable disposition. But she doesn't have that spark; that curious effervescence that makes her extra special. A Bettie."

Indigo rubbed harder at the shoes.

"But Indigo has accepted that. Right, Indigo?"

"Yeah, sure."

"So, when it is time to audition, which doesn't happen very often—perhaps once a year or so, sometimes more—she doesn't get her hopes up like

Sapphire over there. Indigo happily remains where she is. A Rainbow Girl. But she can play the hell outta the piano." Magdalena rose and swept her arm across the piano bench as a grand invitation for Indigo. "Come play for us."

Indigo walked to the piano, refusing to look at Magdalena. Magdalena stared at her just the same. Indigo cracked her knuckles and majestically commanded a sultry underscore from the piano keys that shifted the tension in the room. Magdalena lifted her arms and swayed her hips to the tune. "Right where she belongs," she crooned.

Indigo played the keys heavily, her head and shoulders bent over the row of black and white.

"Softly, now, Indigo. Softly. Who will join her?"

"I'll do it, you lousy has-beens," said Violet, and with her long limbs and narrow hips, she took the stage and readied the upright bass that was tucked behind the curtain, stored there by the bass man from the last party.

"Ahh, our rough, little Violet. Another one who has completely given up, knowing she, too, will never be a Bettie. Please play, you capricious girl, you."

Violet tried to give Magdalena an evil eye. Magdalena rolled her eyes. "Just play, will you?"

Violet dropped her head against the neck of the bass and willingly slid the bow across the waiting strings and made it sing low and smooth. Her notes mingled with Indigo's piano; Magdalena added her shoulders to her hip sway and smiled, "Anyone else?"

Ruby moved forward.

"Smart girl," Magdalena said.

"You're not gonna choose me anyway," Ruby sighed as she hoisted the sax from where it lay against the piano, brought it to her full lips and blew; a red-hot heatwave shot out of the instrument and leapt into the bones of anyone willing to listen.

"Ruby, if you didn't make me so much money as a Rainbow Girl, I just might be tempted to replace my sax man with you, girl!" Magdalena closed her eyes. Her arms moved side to side along with her hips that undulated with every beat of the music. "Magical, isn't it?" she said as she opened her eyes. She turned to address Harlem. "You can start dancing any moment now, Miss Ann."

"But I've—could I have some water to start?" Harlem said.

"Water. This isn't a time for excuses, *madame*," Magdalena stopped dancing. "The girls here have danced and performed with much less. I guess we know for sure which position you'll be in during the next Mysterie party," Magdalena said, snapping her fingers at Desire. "Desire. Show us what a Bettie can do."

"Wait, wait. I can do it," Harlem back-peddled.

"Too late. Desire, show us what a Bettie can do."

Magdalena went to the piano and picked up her clarinet. "Girls, go back to the Bettie number." Magdalena counted them in as she brought her clarinet to her lips, wet its rough reed with her tongue, and blew. Her fingers caressed the instrument's scratched silver keys as she began to play the Betties' signature number again. There was something about the blue melody of the tune that scratched an itch she couldn't satisfy on her own. It got deep inside her and she always got lost in how terribly good it was; she knew Desire felt it too because the girl danced it like she did. Magdalena watched Desire pull out the seductive soul of the song with her fingertips as Harlem stepped back out of the way. Magdalena stared at Harlem, disappointed in her lack of gumption. *Idiot!* Magdalena thought as she played on. Magdalena nodded sharply at Amoura and Fury to join in the dance with Desire. *Go!*

Amoura began where she was supposed to, right on beat with the break where the melody became real hot and real buttery. *Well, well, well; is it possible? She's actually getting better at her solo*, Magdalena thought as the girl ended her number. 'Course, she'd watched it so many times it could have been her imagination too. Fury's moment was coming. *Wait for your moment, hot pants!* Magdalena thought. She should have scolded herself because she must have rushed the notes; both Violet and Ruby looked at her like she did. *Shut up!* she shot back with her eyes as she refocused on playing

Fury's part, which was fast and furious just like the girl. Magdalena closed her eyes as they continued to dance and allowed the itch to be scratched.

When she got lost like this, she dropped into what was nearly an opium haze. She pulled pastel memories from her soul. As she blew into the haunted instrument those memories became a brush with which she painted a picture of the past. She shut out everyone and everything and stepped into the painting, forgetting for a moment that she was Lady Magdalena. She forgot about the mouths she had to feed, including her own. Forgot about all the palms outstretched that also needed to be fed in one way or another. Simply forgot. In this painting, she was innocent. She was Miriam, the name her parents gave her. She was fourteen again, the age when she daydreamed in smiling pale pinks, carefree yellows, safe sea-foam greens, easy pale blues, and encouraging purples. She hovered like a beautiful bumblebee, pausing to savor the colored nectar as she pleased.

Her fingers flew up and down the keys as she played. The notes filled her painting to its very edges. They soaked into every crevice in the canvas with the hope and the beauty and the happiness she'd had back then. With her baby sister. With her family. With hopes and dreams of being something. Of having a real chance to be something, someone, and to make a life for herself like everyone else. She felt tears start to line and seep out from her clamped eyelids. She crushed her eyes tighter together, keeping the seal intact. How badly she wanted to go back in time, to stay in that painting. To be given the chance again to choose that pastel path, to audition for that life, rather than be cast in the harshly-colored one she was living in now.

They had reached the part of the song that was Honey's intro. She played it on and on as she remembered how her sister danced. Even after things had gotten bad, after they'd become other and done horrible things, she had still moved with such grace, like a feather in the wind. No one was like her sister. Magdalena had loved to play for her, loved to watch her dance. They were together when she danced. It was their only time where they were one, in sisterly love.

'Play it again, Maggie.'

'Aren't you hungry? Shouldn't we go try to find something to eat?'

'When I dance, I don't think about food, Maggie. Play. Please... please play.'

Her thin frame barely held her dress that had become too big. Her cheeks seemed to take on the color the dress previously had. 'Thank you, Maggie,' she'd said, floating.

Magdalena heard only the notes, coming from her instrument... only that. She opened her eyes. The bumblebee immediately dropped dead to the ground as Magdalena left her pastel world and was quickly pulled back to reality by stares from motionless faces. Magdalena wiped away the wetness on her face, pretending it was merely sweat. But they had seen. The girls had seen what she'd been trying to hide. That she had lost a part of herself. "Why are you staring at me? I told you to stop staring at me! This is an audition. Someone should be dancing!" she shouted. "Somebody dance *or else*."

Magdalena flung her arm at the girls, motioning them to begin playing the number again. She blew hard as she dove into her own instrument, breaking only to glower at the girls as she played.

Harlem hopped onto the stage to take a shot. Her face was desperate with determination. Magdalena was about to tell her to save it when Sapphire's steam train of resolve charged onto the stage and pushed Harlem back and out of her way.

"Hey! It's my turn," Harlem said.

"Too late!" Sapphire danced—or moved in a way she thought was dancing. Magdalena watched as Sapphire chugged disastrously along the lines of Honey's invisible sheet music in some monstrosity of movement. She burned with the desire to be seen rather than a desire to entertain or entice. She grabbed at the notes with her body rather than opening her soul to feel them. With each move she tastelessly chased the spotlight. She kicked high when it should have been low. She stretched her arms out and then harvested the air to her bosom like she was gathering a bushel of spindly wheat, all before awkwardly rocking herself to the beat with it. Sapphire had learned all the Bettie steps, had studied how the Betties moved with and through one another. But watching her was like watching perfectly good poetry being poorly reworked into a foreign language; Sapphire just couldn't get the rhythm right.

Honey would have gotten it; she always did.

"Get off my stage. Off!" Magdalena yelled as she pulled her clarinet from her lips.

"But...!" Sapphire whined.

"I said get *off!*"

Sapphire stormed off the stage and glared at Harlem, who glared right back. *Too bad the new girl didn't bring that fire to the stage*, Magdalena thought as she watched Harlem whither in the shadows of the stage curtains.

Emerald approached the stage. Finding the rhythm of the bass, her agile hands rode up past her waist and along her torso to her neck, and then to the soft features of her little cherub face. Her hips took over the story. She beckoned to Sienna, who joined her and, in tandem, they moved. They danced a dance of seduction that had no beginning, middle, or end. Emerald artfully left the stage, unselfishly giving Sienna the spotlight. In that space, Sienna came wildly alive in her hips and elsewhere, and she whipped her hair in a cascade that intertwined with the wave of

Ruby's red sax. The two were like lovers; one visible, one visceral, as Sienna vied for the upgraded position.

"Next!" Magdalena cried. She hated all of them. "NEXT!"

Sienna smoothed her hair, unfazed; being daft kept her delighted to have these moments to dance. Topaz clawed herself onto the stage. She found the staccato in the piano and began a crazy tap dance that upped and upped and upped the fever emanating from Indigo's ivory keys. She tapped with all her might, arms flailing, head shaking in a frenzied whirl of orange, curly passion. She looked up and out at the girls. She'd shaken away whatever troll's expression it was that rested on her face and made her unappealing. A smile spread across her face. Her grey eyes exploded with a vivaciousness that radiated through her body and shot light from her shoulders through to her fingertips as she spun with her arms outreached like a perfect top.

"Goddammit, you are all worthless hacks."

Topaz stopped spinning; she stood staring from the stage. The light that sparkled in her eyes disappeared in a flash, leaving her face stony. She returned to her chair and kicked it as she sat down.

Magdalena rubbed the back of her neck with her free hand. From the moment she had walked down the stairs to begin this new girl business, she hoped that by playing music, playing Honey's song, she would be able to tie off her feelings about all of this...

that like a cinched corset, the cords that bound them all together would help contain what she felt. But the opposite had happened. She was unraveling, unleashing a bunch of feelings she had no desire to feel. Now she had a cloud of anger to deal with, thanks to these stupid girls trying to replace Honey.

"You sicken me. Each one of you. You're loathsome pieces of trash that can't do anything right and I should get rid of you all!"

She tore at the bodice of her clingy lamé dress. She needed air. She had to get away from them and their horrible stares and stench. Her clarinet clanged oddly on the floor as she threw it down. She ran toward the stairs not caring who was Rainbow or who was Bettie. The show would go on.

She needed a drink. Now. Something to calm her. To take her to a place where she could be numb from thoughts and cares. Maybe she'd drink the tea she gave the new girls and for once, simply feel nothing.

Someone pulled on her arm. Magdalena spun around, almost tripping over herself. "What do you want?" she breathed.

"What about me?" Harlem said, standing inches from her, breathing heavily.

Magdalena pushed Harlem out of her face. "What about you!? You had your chance," she hissed. "Get away from me."

CHAPTER 30

Harlem stumbled backwards from Magdalena's push and fell into a chair. She jumped up and walked toward Magdalena again; as she got closer she could see the veins in Magdalena's forehead popping out, ready to strangle her if released. Harlem put her hands on her hips.

"I want another chance," she said. "Do you hear me?"

"I don't care at all what you want. You had your chance and you messed it up. You made *excuses*. I told you what you're good at. You'll be doing that again at the next party. Get used to it!"

"I won't get used to it. You may have my money, but you won't take what's left of my dignity!" Harlem spun around and yelled to the girls who'd become the musicians, "Play something good and easy and play it now!"

The music began and Harlem closed her eyes. She filled her lungs with air. She exhaled. "Momma, help me..." she whispered. She was back in the room with the mirrors. In Greensboro. Where she danced with her mother. She felt her mother gently grab her wrists from above and they floated in time with the music like water lilies conducting dragonflies.

Her mother's arms wrapped about her as she spun in a contracted *pirouette*. Then her own arms flew out like butterfly wings as her leg slid seductively from *passé* at the ankle and then to the knee, before it flew to her nose and jutted back again behind her in *penché*. She lowered her leg into an *attitude*, collapsed into it, and allowed it to spin her like a corkscrew into the wooden floor. On all fours, she moved like a cunning cat to the stage, slinking along the boards, not caring that splinters snatched at her bare knees. She turned onto her back and arched herself to her shoulders, lifting her leg straight into the air and slowly lowering it to touch her nose with a flexibility that, in the past, had only come with her mother's hand guiding her. She brought her other leg up to meet its partner and, like dough, she elegantly rolled over her shoulders into a neat ball. She spun 'round to her knees, lifted her arms to the heavens, rocked back over her toes, and was pulled gracefully to her feet. She turned in *fouettes* until she met and fell against the wall, her hair falling messily in her eyes as she draped herself in the red silk curtain as though it were the luscious, comforting fur she used to lie on in the studio.

Harlem played hide-and-seek with the curtain, turning her cheek to the wall and allowing the red silk to tell the story she was too ashamed to tell. She wound herself in it, her shoulders and neck and back and hips speaking and retelling and sharing and releasing. Wanting to be heard. Finally. She disappeared in the fabric and in the dance, just like she had with Roy. She could disappear when she needed to. She disappeared from the pain of hunger, the pain of fear, and became the dance, like she was trained to. She moved with and through the notes; she allowed them to hold her and lift her and hold her again. The music continued. She felt alive and vibrant and whole, for the first time in a long time, or maybe for the first time ever. When she came to, she was on top of the piano, where Magdalena had sat. Sweat dripped from her brow, spent; her chest heaved and all eyes were upon her.

She looked out. They were speechless. Jaws dropped. Harlem looked to Magdalena. The woman looked frozen in time. A statue affixed to the stairwell railing. "Well?" Harlem asked, breathless.

"Sienna," Magdalena said as she gathered the folds of her dress and walked up the stairs.

"Sienna!?" Sapphire yelled. "You're picking Sienna to be the next Brown Bettie? She can barely dance, let alone walk and talk!"

"Sienna?" Harlem heard herself say. She couldn't believe her ears, nor what she heard coming out of her mouth next, "Screw you, Magdalena!"

"No," Magdalena retorted. "No, my dear, they will screw *you*. Good night," she reached the top of the stairs and turned off the light, leaving them in the dark.

Harlem laid back on the piano and screamed into the darkness, "I won't do it! I won't!" Someone patted her consolingly on her hips, "You'll be okay, Ann. You'll be okay!"

"My name is Harlem, and stop touching me!" she cried, kicking the person away.

"You'll do better to have what happens down here happen to 'Ann Smith' and not... to Harlem," someone said.

"'Harlem' has already had her fair share of happenings," Harlem answered. "I don't need Ann Smith. I don't need any of you and I won't be letting anything else happen to *either one* of me, understand?"

"*Ann*, you should come with us," Amoura said in the dark. Harlem heard footsteps walking away behind her.

"My name is Harlem, and I'm not gonna tell you again," Harlem said, rising onto her elbows.

"My stars, you're feisty," Amoura said, coaxing Harlem off the piano. "We'll call you whatever you want. Just come with us."

"What for? Where're we going?"

"Back to where the Betties perch," Sapphire said, blanketed by darkness.

"Don't be jealous, Sapphire," Desire called from behind Harlem. "You said so yourself—

no one is good enough for anything here."

"Don't patronize me, Desire," Sapphire sniffed. Harlem heard Sapphire walking away and heard a door slam.

"Good riddance!" Harlem said to Sapphire as more footsteps led to more opening and closing doors.

"Sienna, congratulations on your win," Emerald spoke, her soft voice sounding like a whisper in the darkness.

"I feel like I should be glad I'm *la crème de la crème* now, but I don't feel any different," Sienna said. "What'm I supposed to do now anyway? I'm heading right back to my hole in the wall with a door and that Harlem is going back upstairs with the Betties. Ain't nothin' different in my eyes."

"You'll see the difference once the party comes. And you'll know it, too," Topaz croaked as another door closed.

Harlem felt a hand guiding her on her elbow, "C'mon, Harlem."

"Tell me why I should trust you, Amoura. Everyone seems to look out for herself in this place. What gives?" Harlem said.

"Nothing gives. We're all you've got, so you might want to be nice to us."

"Girls."

"Fury?" Amoura said. "Fury, are you okay?"

"No."

"Where are you?"

"On the stage."

"What's wrong?" Harlem asked.

"She is not fond of the dark. Fury, just breathe."

From upstairs, a door opened. Someone came running.

"Tilda!" Desire said.

A match struck and there was light.

"Thank you, Jesus. Thank you, Tilda," Fury said, her voice shaken.

"You've got it bad, huh?" Harlem sighed; somehow that sigh let loose a string that was holding her all together. Her knees buckled. "I'm afraid I'm going to need a bit of help also."

"We'll help both of you," Desire said. "Amoura, you get Fury. Tilda, come over here and grab Harlem's arm to help her and we'll get her up our stairs."

"I'm done for. I've got nothin' left."

"You'd never guess by the way you were dancing back there," Desire said, leading her to the steps of the secret passageway. "Didn't know you had it in you. I've never seen anything like it."

Harlem held onto Desire and Tilda as she hobbled up the stairs.

"Is that the way they dance where you're from?" Amoura's voice floated from behind her.

"It's how my momma taught me to dance. But to be honest, I don't fully know what I was doing up there. I've never really danced like that before. I never had such a reason to. I just heard the music and let it move me. Let it let me forget," Harlem sighed.

"We're going to have to call you 'Forget-Me-Not Bettie' from now on," Amoura laughed.

"Lift the candle higher, Tilda," Fury whispered.

Harlem turned behind her to look at Fury as Tilda followed the instruction. The girl looked as thin and fragile as the shadows cast by the flickering light. *Surprising, to be afraid of the dark,* Harlem thought. But then, she figured everyone had something they were afraid of.

"This is the last step," Desire cautioned. "Now take your hand like this and follow along the wall. Pay attention to the nicks and holes and grooves in it. It's like a map. That's how we know where we are."

"Where are we, exactly?" Harlem asked, feeling along the wall which was made out of a lot of uneven concrete, wood, and plaster.

"Tilda says it's the Underground Railroad, right Tilda?"

Harlem heard two stomps. "But Tilda can't speak."

"You just heard her—didn't she, Miss Tilda?" Amoura said.

Harlem heard two stomps again.

"We taught Miss Tilda our own version of Morse Code and a few other things. She communicates fine when she wants to."

"I see," Harlem replied as Tilda squeezed her hand. "Well, good for you, I suppose." Harlem had never known a mute. She was experiencing so many new things in such a horrible place. They continued on. "But, where does this hallway lead to? Does it lead out? Can't we use it to get out of here? Slaves must have used it to get away."

"All we know is it runs behind our bedrooms and down into the basement. The basement, from what we've been able to find, has got one way out, and that's the stairs you saw Magdalena go up."

"And those stairs lead right into the dining room," Harlem groaned.

"Exactly," Desire said.

"This is my room," Amoura said.

Harlem heard a scraping. A faint swish of colder air hit her cheeks. Tilda led her into a room.

"Welcome," Amoura said. Candlelight filled the room.

"Watch that flame," Fury said.

"We've got the candle safe over here, Fury," Desire said. "It's probably our last one, for a little while anyway, so believe you me, I'm being careful with it."

Harlem looked behind her and realized she'd just walked through a closet. "My room is like this. Does that mean my closet has a special door also?"

"It does," Amoura said.

"I guess it's all the same then, sort of. Only I don't have any light at all. No electricity, nor a candle."

"You'll see. Magdalena's gonna make you work for your lightbulb. Well, that's if she lets you stay up here with us," Desire said. She sat on the bed while holding the candle, "We use these sparingly. Tilda can only steal so many from Magdalena before she notices. So we have to ration them."

"Have a seat on the floor and try to get comfortable," Amoura said, settling next to Desire on the bed. "We all should rest, really. Who knows what Magdalena is cooking up for us next."

Harlem lowered herself to the wooden floor and lay down on her back, meanwhile Tilda helped her gently put her feet up onto the small cot. She let out a breath to calm herself, placing her arms under her head—like she used to when she'd rest under the willow trees and look up to count the stars in the sky at night. She took three more deep breaths. "I'm so... tired."

Little Tilda sat on the floor near her and massaged her feet. Fury sat with her back leaned up against the bedroom door. Their shadows danced on the walls.

"How can you all stand it?" Harlem asked, her eyes closed.

No one said anything for a moment as they settled into their spots and their thoughts.

Harlem opened her eyes and tried to look at each one of them closely in the darkness. She saw or maybe felt something new in them that she hadn't seen before. Suddenly, she saw them for what she thought they were: four young women with a whole lot to give but nothing to lose. Just like her. "Truly? How can you stand it? I've been here such a short time and already I want to go mad."

"We've got each other, that's how," Fury said after a moment.

"And you've got us now, too," Amoura said.

"I'm sorry," Harlem said, closing her eyes again. "But that just isn't enough. How could it possibly be?"

"Who else is there?" Desire asked. "Who else out there gives a damn or knows that you're in here besides the sisters?"

"What about Honey? She knows!" Harlem said, rising on her elbows abruptly.

"What about her? Do you see her?" Fury kicked off her dance shoes. "If it were me, I'd be long gone. We were just talking about this. Hell. This sort of thing has never happened before. Usually, it's a Rainbow Girl who's the one to leave and we never hear from her again."

Harlem's moment of hope dissipated; she laid back down and felt herself drifting, felt her mind going to the place where she was safe. "I miss my momma," she said aloud, without really meaning to. But there they went; her words floated in the air and fell on each girl for her to catch however she may.

"What was her name?" Amoura asked softly.

"Susannah."

"How'd she die?"

"How'd you know she was dead?" Harlem said tightly.

"For us Betties, all our mothers are dead. Most of our fathers too, except for Desire."

Harlem opened her eyes and looked at Desire.

"I ran away. Because I was bored. *I* was going mad living in the same four corners of Chicago where my mother had grown up. Where my father had grown up. They been together since they was sixteen! My daddy's family lived on one side of the hallway, my momma's on the other. They're still in the same building. It's alright they felt safe there, but isn't there a whole life to live? No one had any gumption to think they could leave! I wanted to go see something else of the world, so I cut off all my hair, dressed up like a boy, and jumped on the back of a train. Figured if I looked like a boy, nobody would question me. And they didn't. Kept to the shadows and got myself to Los Angeles. Then I became a girl again. Cleaned toilets at first, then I got a waitressing job over on Central Avenue. Grew my hair back into this cute little 'do. I was a dish, girls! Thought I was going to be a big movie star. Meet Oscar Micheaux. Only thing I got to be was broke. On my way back to be with my family is when the sisters got me. Boy, did I feel lousy for my ever even wanting to leave home," Desire sighed, stretching her legs out in front of her and crossing her ankles angrily. "My family probably thinks I'm dead by now."

Amoura shifted on the bed and laid her head on Desire's lap. "My momma died bringing me into this world and I was raised by my daddy. Then, about seven years ago, he said something wrong to a white lady outside the grocery store and... well. You can imagine the rest. I got married to the first man I could find, and would you believe it? My husband died in the war! Truth be told, his sergeant shot him. They said it was an accident. That was just about two years ago. Sisters got me when I ran away from going damn-near crazy working war relief at the post office."

Harlem glanced toward Fury who rubbed at the floor with her heel. Harlem looked to Tilda, who simply shook her head slightly and looked down. Desire and Amoura avoided her look, too.

"Fury?" Harlem asked anyway; her question seemed to wait patiently for its answer. Fury grabbed her knees and placed her chin on them. She spoke slowly. "We had horses in Kentucky. One of 'em kicked over a lantern and set our barn on fire," she looked up at Harlem, laughed sarcastically, and returned to playing with her toes. "Ask these girls and they'll tell you I don't do so well with fire today. Or the dark. I was trapped in the barn for a while with everybody and everything dead around me. Couldn't see anything. Anyway. Both my parents died trying to save the land my family bought once they were freed.

Was my fault they died because I'm the one that left the lantern there," she sighed. "Sisters got me when they'd asked me for directions one day as I was walking on our dirt road. Just minding my own business and trying to clear my head of all the bad stuff that had collected in it. My guard was down. I got in a car with them; Ruth had a gun and said she'd shoot me if I said anything or ran. I believed her. And next thing I knew, I was here."

Harlem turned away from Fury to give her some privacy in her thoughts. They were quiet again. Tilda, who was resting against the bed, rapped on the floor.

Amoura said, "Tilda wants you to know that she was left here at this house, on the doorstep. She never knew her real parents, but the parents she did know were the mister and missus of this house."

"Here?" Harlem said, turning on her side to face Tilda, eyebrows raised.

Amoura continued, "Here. Used to be normal here. Magdalena and Honey are sisters. Tilda was raised like their sister. Then, everything fell apart."

"Well, what happened!? I simply can't believe that in this horrible place, with Magdalena the way she is, there was ever a family around. I simply can't believe it," Harlem said.

Amoura sat up, "What's so hard to believe? Look at all of us. It's a domino effect. One thing happens from which folks just can't quite recover and the demons take over. It happens when folks don't see no other choice!"

"Happens all the time," Desire said.

"Yes, but... still," Harlem said.

Amoura slapped her hands on her thighs. "Well, then, what happened to your parents, Harlem?"

Harlem heard the words. Heard the question, but the question made her sick to her stomach. She couldn't tell them what her father did to her. She couldn't tell them what her mother did to herself. "I'd —I'd rather not talk about it."

"Well, isn't that a fine how do you do?" Amoura said lightly, lying back down on Desire's lap. "We all told you about ourselves. Even Fury who never talks about anything."

"Maybe she'd rather talk about what Tilda has hidden in her pocket..." Fury said.

Tilda kicked Fury.

"What?" Fury said, leaning forward and crossing her legs beneath her like a schoolgirl. "She might as well know we have it. That's what we should be talking about anyway. Instead'a what the hell happened to our dead relatives."

"Have what?" Harlem said.

Tilda placed something cold onto her bare thigh. She reached for it and gasped, "Oh my goodness." Harlem pulled her elevated legs from the bed and pitched to her knees. "What in the world!" Harlem looked to each of them, angrily. "*We have each other!?*

You'd like me to believe that when you've had this all along?"

Desire moved to the edge of the bed and put her feet squarely on the floor, "Now hold on a minute, sister."

"Hold on for nothin'!" Harlem shrieked.

"Keep your voice down. You do not want Magdalena coming up here," Amoura warned.

Harlem opened the case; her money was still rolled up inside. "How did you get this?"

"Tilda found it in your things," Fury said, standing up.

"My things?" Harlem looked at Tilda. "You can get to my things?"

Tilda rapped on the floor. Amoura spoke, "She found this your first night and she thought it was lipstick. She wanted something pretty for herself. And then—"

"And then, what?" Harlem said, struggling to stand. "What about my check? The real money? Can she get to my inheritance check?"

Tilda rapped. No one said anything.

"Well, what did she say? What did you say?"

"She said that you had a chance to get it back."

"Magdalena said she wanted me to go to the bank with her and have me cash it and give her all the money! That is not my idea of getting my money back."

"Why do you have all of that money?"

"Because my grandfather left it to my mother," Harlem began to sob. She struck at her own tears trying to make them go back inside where they belonged. "And when she shot herself, it came to me —"

"Your momma shot herself?" Fury said.

"How could she? That's a... that's a *sin...!*" Amour gasped.

Harlem's breath stopped dead in its tracks; no one had ever said that to her face before. "You are not allowed to talk about my mother."

"Harlem, honey—" Amoura rose from the bed, her hands reaching out for her. Harlem could see the concern in her eyes, just like the police officers had in their eyes when they sat her in her jail cell the night she was arrested.

"You don't know what I had to endure to get that money—"

Harlem shook her hands vigorously to get the feeling back in them. They were stuck full of pins and needles, and it felt like they both wanted to fall off her arms. She had to catch her breath to keep it from flying all the way out of her body. The room was starting to spin. "You just don't know! And, and, and it's... mine. That money is *mine!*" she cried. She was stumbling and pacing. She backed herself against the wall and threw herself into a corner. "Mine!"

"*Was* yours," Amoura said softly.

Harlem spun around. "I don't want to hear those types of words coming out of your mouth, Amoura. I won't stand for it. I won't!"

"Calm down," Fury said. "Calm down."

"I'm getting out of here." Harlem paced along the wall. She pointed the tube of money at them, "I swear to God I'm getting out of here! And you're going to show me. You're going to show me this place. And all its mazes and back alleys. Where is the front door? Where is it?"

The girls pointed.

"So, all I have to do is run. I have to run out this bedroom door and I'll see the front door?"

The girls nodded.

"But Brighton will catch you again."

"I'll fight. I'll expect him this time. I'm leaving. I'm leaving right now!" She fell to her knees. The crying wouldn't stop, and she really wanted it to. "This is all your fault. All of it. If you weren't so— If I wasn't so—" Her words and their meaning got all jumbled up. She didn't know what she was trying to say, so she stopped. She just cradled the lipstick in her hands and rocked.

Amoura knelt to her; her freckles jumped from her face. "Harlem, honey. Are you alright?"

"I want to go home," Harlem said, looking into Amoura's eyes. "But I don't have one."

Amoura wrapped her arms around her and held her tight. Harlem let those arms hold her, because it was what she needed. And she cried tears she was used to crying when she was alone.

"*Shhhh. Shhhh...*"

Tilda rapped on the floor.

"Tilda, are you certain?" Fury said.

Harlem sniffled; what she wouldn't do for a handkerchief. "What—what did she say?"

Fury stood. With hands on her head, she began to stride about the room. Her eyes were closed, and she looked like a scientist trying to understand something new. "We'll be alone...?" she whispered.

Tilda answered her with a nod.

Desire stood up too. Only she didn't look like a scientist. She looked scared. "What should we do?"

Amoura had released Harlem and sat heavily on her bottom; Harlem reached for Amoura's shoulder, "Tell me. Tell me what's going on."

"We think we might have a chance," Amoura said, her eyes distant.

"At what?" Harlem asked.

Fury stopped her circling. She kneeled to Tilda, "So, she'll be gone—for a while at least. Right?"

"Who?" Harlem asked, wiping her nose with the back of her hand.

"Magdalena," Amoura answered.

"Where's she going?" Harlem's eyes darted between Tilda's knuckles knocking on the wood floor and the recognition on the other girls' faces.

Desire explained, "Magdalena's going to Lucinda's, Harlem. Lucinda throws parties too. We think, well... Tilda thinks that Lucinda wants something from Magdalena. That something has happened. Lucinda told Magdalena to come by the house tonight for her party."

Amoura whistled low and long. "Girls, maybe this *is* our chance."

"Do you really think we could do it?" Desire asked.

"Actually escape from this place?" Fury said, wringing her hands.

"Why haven't you done it before?" Harlem said, understanding now. "Surely she's gone out before?"

"We didn't have anywhere to go. We've been afraid—" Desire said.

Fury moved to her, cupping Harlem's hands. "We never had what you have."

Harlem held open her palm. The lipstick case glowed in the candlelight. "If this is all it takes, then we're getting out of here. Tonight!"

CHAPTER 31

Magdalena pulled on the chain for the kitchen light. She leaned over the white porcelain sink, turned on the faucet, and splashed water on her face. "Dammit," she whispered. She reached for the tea kettle on the stove, filled it, and placed it on the burner as she wiped her wet face with the back of her hand. She lit a match and watched as it ignited the burner with a *whoosh* and a blue flame licked the black kettle. She turned the gas up; she had no patience to wait for the water to boil, and no patience to let another idea, a better idea, seep into her head.

She moved to the cupboard slowly and reached for the metal canister that had the special tea. Magdalena's fingers shook slightly as she popped the lid off the container. She wet her finger on her tongue and dipped it in the canister.

Her mind wandered. She was Miriam again.

'Papa? I have your tea...?' she said in front of his closed bedroom door at the end of the hallway upstairs.

'Bring it to me, tayner, my dear one.' She entered the room with a tray, careful not to spill. Her father sat up weakly and propped himself on his pillows.

The room was dark. He had built a wall to cut off the part of the room that had the windows. 'The windows were for your mother,' he would say. 'I live in darkness now.'

She watched him sip the tea greedily, drinking it as fast as the temperature would allow.

'Papa, I don't know that this is helping. You look worse,' she said.

'Ahhh, looks can be deceiving. Believe me, Ikh bin geting beser. I am getting better.'

Magdalena reached onto the top shelf of a forgotten cupboard. She reached for and pulled down the teacup and saucer her father had used. She rinsed the cobwebs and dust from it. It had been a part of a set. A wedding gift for her parents from her mother's cousin, she'd been told. Both adored the set and used it as much as they could until each piece had broken, one by one. It was the most delicate china Magdalena had ever held. Its pale yellow and pink flowers still whispered of elegance.

In the beginning, when she'd made the tea for her father, he'd requested two scoops. Then three, then four, and as he reached the end, what she eventually realized was the end, he was up to five and six. His teas replaced his meals; his desire to die replaced his appetite to live. And soon he got his wish.

For the girls who Sister Ruth and Sister Mary deposited in her possession, Magdalena had added opium to the concoction, and significantly lessened the arsenic. She'd no desire to be responsible for killing anyone. Not again.

Pulling the bottle of arsenic from a drawer, she sprinkled just a tiny bit into the wedding cup.

She laughed. "The things people do for love." She was well beyond the age where women were supposed to either find or be forced into companionship. She had never known the type of love her parents had. She thought she'd been close with that miserable Lon Listromski, but that turned out to be a horrible lesson in misjudgment. And what a joke for her to have thought Stan Trieg would actually want anything to do with her. She caressed her pale, bare ring finger. "I don't know what happened," she whispered. Maybe she didn't love like everyone else. Maybe she didn't know how and that's why it never happened. Maybe that's why the people she loved left. Magdalena looked at her kitchen. They were all gone. *Maybe she'll come back. Maybe.*

The kettle whistled. Magdalena added a teensy bit more of the special tea mix and poured the boiling water over the entire mess and stirred. The spoon clinked against the china chillingly.

She took a very long sip. Her tongue tingled with its bitterness.

Magdalena heard a knock. She jumped. "What the hell are you doing here, Tilda?"

From the doorway, Tilda pointed to her wrist.

"I'm not going to Lucinda's tonight. She can kiss my black ass," Magdalena said as she took another sip of tea and brushed past Tilda.

Tilda reached for her elbow and Magdalena swatted it away. "I'm not going, and that's it!" she said while looking at Tilda, who was strangling her neck in pantomime. "Lucinda's not going to kill me, Tilda. Get a grip on your imagination."

Walking through the dark dining room, Magdalena slid her fingertips across the gleaming maple table. She thought of the dinners her family had had there.

The chandelier sparkled brilliantly and lit up their Thanksgiving dinner.

'Amen,' Magdalena had said, finishing their prayer, proudly.

'Papa! Pass the mashed potatoes!' Honey had squealed.

'Dear, she's going to melt into a puddle of fits if you don't give them to her,' her mother had laughed.

"Tilda," Magdalena stopped. "When you were a baby, the first November you were with us, that was the Thanksgiving we had where Honey dropped the entire bowl of mashed potatoes right here on the ground. It was right here."

Tilda stood stiffly.

"It was the best Thanksgiving we ever had. I never laughed so hard. I remember it like it was yesterday. We were happy. You were too, I think. You were a happy baby once you got used to us. I had a hard time getting used to you. But I did."

Magdalena walked into her office. She turned. "Tilda," she said. "Don't stand there like a wooden doll. Come in here." Magdalena took a sip, laid the cup and saucer on her desk and opened the closet door. She rummaged through the lost and found closet, "Tilda, starting tomorrow, we're doing away with these things. They're weighing me down. I must be free of other people's memories and trinkets and clothing and so on. You can't take it with you, after all. That's what people say. We're starting anew." Magdalena foraged in the closet, she pushed aside worn suitcases, loads of mismatched shoes, stuffed animals, and travelling hats with their brims crushed and netting mutilated. She waded toward what she was looking for—there, standing tall against the back wall. "Tilda," she shouted. "Go and find a hammer and nails. And probably a ladder."

Magdalena kneeled before a huge portrait; she touched the penciled signature on the brown paper that covered the back of it. She grabbed the gilded edges and pulled it through the muck and out of the closet. It was almost as tall as she was, and three times as wide. She carefully leaned it against her desk, picked up the teacup, and hiked up her gown as she sat on the floor in front of the portrait. Her mother's deep brown face shone out at Magdalena with pride; her hands rested upon her and Honey's shoulders, both seated with backs erect, shoulders square—like ladies. Tilda, a baby in a mass of white cotton ruffles, was in their father's lap. His eyes danced with joy even behind a stoic expression so common in still paintings. The painting was begun when her mother got sick and was completed just before she died. It was true, 1931 had been a terrible year and 1932 had proven to be worse. Magdalena stared at the portrait for a long time, replaying years of memories that she had previously left unattended, stored in the back of her mind. Her wristwatch ticked through the silence of it all. A reminder of time that had passed. "You people were the best time of my life!" Magdalena saluted the photo with her tea and swallowed every last drop of it.

"Tilda! Did you find it?"

Magdalena heard Tilda gasp behind her. She looked over her shoulder, "Probably the only picture we have of you, and definitely the only one of all of us."

Tilda handed her the hammer absently.

"Nope, nope. We are doing this together." Magdalena reached for Tilda's arm. "Help me up... Whoa, whoa, too fast!" Magdalena steadied herself on the desk. "Whoa!"

"We need music," Magdalena spread her arms to find her balance; when she did, she went into her bedroom and came back with a very large radio which she plopped on the desk. She plugged it in and found a station. A blanket of big band music fell over them. She swayed side to side with the rhythm of it. "This song here is 'Dream of Life.' Lady Day is singing it of course, but Carmen McRae wrote this song, Tilda. She came here once. Came here and turned right back around the minute she got hip to what I was servin' here. Turned right back around. Will you just listen to that arrangement?"

Magdalena fumbled for a cigarette while humming. "'*My life was empty when you went away...*' Beautiful song. Where is my lighter, I wonder?" she spun around a bit too quickly. With the cigarette dangling from her lips, she said, "Tilda, the room is moving much faster than I am." Magdalena shuffled back to the portrait. "If you find the lighter, will you bring it to me?"

The doorbell rang.

"Who could be here at this hour? We know it's not the sisters!" Magdalena felt a giggle course through her. She spit out the cigarette and covered her mouth and her laughter. "Go get the door, Tild. Tild-ah," she slurred. "Tiiiilda. Goooo get door. Go."

Tilda ran off and Magdalena dragged the portrait to the fireplace, looking above the mantle to the empty spot where it used to hang. She pulled a chair to the fireplace, pulled herself onto it, and tried unsuccessfully to wiggle out the old bent nail that was still there, "I see you been waiting for me, little nail. But I'm going t' need some a-a-a-ssistance from you. Come out now! Come on out!"

"Wha' th' hell is that?" she asked as heavy footsteps sounded from downstairs.

Magdalena turned over her shoulder, "Off'cer Brighton. What're you doing here?"

"Lucinda is asking for you."

"Lucinda, pfffft. She just wants my money and I'm not giv'n any, anymore," Magdalena said, swaying on the chair. She motioned for Office Brighton to come near, "Can you come 'ere. Tilda and I want to hang this and we need you. A strapping man such asth yourself to help. Us."

"I'm not touching that thing," Officer Brighton said.

"That *thing* is my family," she pointed clumsily to herself in the portrait. "That's me. See the long black hair? It's the same. That there ith Honey, my sister. You know her too. Over here is little Tilda. She was abandoned like a runt of a litter and we took her in. So, also a sister. This handsome man ith my father and this be-aut-i-ful woman ith my mother."

"Your mother was a got'damn nigger?"

"Well. We didn't call her that, you asth—*asshole*. We called her 'Momma'."

"Get your pocketbook. Lucinda wants you at her place. And she said to bring what you owe her."

"Hang on. Hang on one cotton-picking minute. How do you... you know anything about *anything*?"

"I work for Lucinda."

"Noooo you don't. You work for and on *me*. Right here in my offith and over there on that, that um, lumpy mattress. Not for that witch, Lucinda. You've gotten yourself confused!" Magdalena grabbed the mantle to keep from falling as she stabbed a thumb to her chest, "*I'm* not going anywhere. 'Cept right here to talk to my momma and papa." Magdalena turned back around to wiggle the nail and heard the familiar click of something to which she should pay attention. She turned back toward Officer Brighton.

"Now," he pointed his gun at her.

"It's like that, is ith copper?"

"Yeah, it's like *that*."

"You no good, two-timing... low-brow, low-down selfisth... schmuck! How did thith all come about? You, did you go over there and jump into her bed, too? How much, how much ith *she* paying you?"

"More than you. And on time. And she brings me coffee. That's hot."

"You rotten weasel!" Magdalena grabbed a goblet from the mantel and threw at him.

"Hold on just a minute!" Officer Brighton yelled, ducking. "Now, get offa that chair and come on. Now!" he raised the gun higher and pointed at her chest.

Magdalena stepped down from the chair and fixed her hair. "Alright, I prefer not to be shot today, so I wilth go with you. You idiot." Magdalena walked toward the door.

"And don't forget the money; Lucinda said to make sure's I bring the money."

"Money!" she laughed, "I'm not paying her another red cent, you hear me? She can go jump in a lake. I'm not bringing her anything—"

"My gun is gonna start talkin' if you don't stop and do what yer told," Officer Brighton said.

Magdalena figured she'd better do as he said. She found her way to the Budhai on her desk. "Turn around, you oaf."

Officer Brighton turned around and she pulled back the head of the statue and retrieved the envelopes of money. She left one behind for herself. Along with the check. Lucinda would have to take what she was given. Magdalena glanced at Tilda who was plastered against the wall near the desk, "Tilda. It seems... I will be going out. Can you get. My wrap?"

CHAPTER 32

The clock above the cubby-hole mailboxes chimed seven o'clock as Jonas signed the check-in card and slid it across the desk to the hotel clerk. "Mister and Missus Jonas Stewart," the hotel clerk read and looked up at them. Jonas thought he looked like a lizard. His face was long and his skin was rough.

"That is correct."

"When you called to make your reservation, didn't say nothin' about a 'Mrs.' Stewart."

"She decided to join me on this trip last minute," Jonas said, reaching for Honey's shoulder. "Women do change their minds frequently these days."

"Don't see any bags for her, so musta been pretty quick changing. Room 17. And I don't want no trouble tonight. And no loud noises. This ain't no sportin' house."

"Wouldn't think of it and I should certainly hope not," Jonas said. "Ready, dear?"

"Certainly am," Honey smiled.

They walked up the stairs in the direction the man pointed. "Guess there's no elevator in this place," Jonas said.

"I can't imagine why you'd think there would be one. This is hardly what you'd call a hotel," Honey said, holding her parcels from Ms. Paola.

"I s'pose you're right," Jonas nodded. They reached the landing and he looked for Room 17. "Aha, here it is," he hummed, turning the key in the lock. Jonas looked at Honey; she looked away. "You still okay with this?"

"I'd have to be unless I want to sleep on the streets again."

"Means to an end, Miss Honey. Means to an end," he swung open the door and they both stopped.

"Oh my," Honey gasped.

"Maybe the street would be better," Jonas groaned. The room had a single bed with a weathered grey spread that was older than his barn. It was thin and frail and lay across the bed like a dying widow. A solitary window covered by a tattered beige shade tried to welcome them but fell quite short in its delivery.

Jonas stepped into the room and straightened the faded, thin rug with his foot, "Well, I'd say I would never want to be a fly on these walls," he laughed lightly.

Honey stood steadfast in the doorway. "We'd have to wash your mouth out with soap, that's for certain."

"Thankfully, this here is only temporary until we figure out what it is that we are doin'." Jonas rested his suitcase on the armchair underneath the dismal window. He opened the leather case and pulled a bed sheet and a pillowcase from it. "Here you go. I learned early on to pack my own linens."

Honey stepped into the room and took the sheets timidly.

"I'll sleep here on this armchair."

"That won't be comfortable at all," Honey said.

"I don't see an alternative at this moment, do you?"

Honey looked at the bed and then down at the floor. "No, I guess I don't."

"And that's just fine. Let's get ourselves settled." He walked into the bathroom to check out the rest of the place. "This bathroom may just be our saving grace!" Jonas clapped his hands. "A tub—and a clean one at that—is right here and ready for the usin'."

"Now that is a splendid thing!" Honey said. She stood next to him in the doorway and congratulated him with a hand on his shoulder, "You done good, Mr. Stewart. Real good."

"Thank you, madam," he said.

"Mind if I go first?"

"Not at all. You go ahead on. Enjoy yourself. You've certainly deserved having a nice bath, even if it's in a crummy hotel, m'dear. Maybe there's some

Epsom salts in there to help take down some of your bruising."

Honey rubbed her wrists and said softly, "That would be nice, wouldn't it?"

"I'm going to go down to that all-night shop we passed on the corner and get us a few things."

"Can I please make a request?" Honey asked, smiling.

"What would that be?" Jonas reached into his suitcase and handed her his bar of Ivory soap, still fresh and in its wrapper.

"A candy bar."

"Candy bar? You've come all this way and you'd like a candy bar?"

"I truly would. It has been an awfully long time."

"What sort?" Jonas asked, his hand on the front doorknob.

"Anything chocolate," she clasped her hands with excitement.

"I'll surprise you then," Jonas said as he left.

"Oh, and Jonas?"

He poked his head through the door, "Yes?"

"Maybe some chewing gum. If you can manage," she said.

"My pleasure," he smiled. "Make sure you lock this here door and don't let a soul in besides me. But I'll have the key, so you won't have to open it. I'll be right back." Jonas closed the door, waited to hear the lock turn, and walked down the narrow hallway. It smelled of old hair grease, dust, frying oil, and watered-down vinegar. "My humble abode, ladies and gentlemen," he said aloud to himself, sweeping the fedora from his head in a deep bow.

Jonas walked down the stairs and past the lizardly hotel clerk. "Sir, do you happen to have any extra towels—"

"We are not that kinda joint, fella."

"Yes, yes, I see. I'm not sure why I bothered to ask."

"Place down the street that charges double and takes greater notice of who it lets a room to might have some of those extra towels you're askin' for," he said while snapping his *Amsterdam News* to the next page.

"I'm sure we'll be perfectly fine."

"That's what I thought," the clerk said and didn't bother to look up again.

Jonas pushed through the double glass doors out into the street, which was bubbling with Friday night partiers. Folks were arm-in-arm, laughing and walking with that youthful anticipation that he called the "jitterbug bounce." He side-stepped a group of young men carrying on about which establishments would let them in. "I fought in the war. They better take my green!" Jonas tipped his hat in agreement as he turned right from 116th up Seventh Avenue. He thought about Arnetta. He'd hoped, like he'd done a thousand times before, that she was actually out and about with people like these dapper folks and was living her life a free, happy woman. Maybe she had simply chosen not to reach out to him. That reality he could handle, unlike the looped fits of panic and worry his imagination had him going through. He had to admit that now that he had seen the Manor, the place where she may or may not actually be, his imagination was going all haywired again. But he'd tried to remain calm and normal in front of Honey. He hoped he could continue to succeed.

He arrived at the corner shop. A neatly scripted sign with red letters in the window advertised for Coca Cola. A bell tinkled as he pulled open the glass door to the tiny shop. He tipped his hat to the fellow behind the counter. "Good evenin'," Jonas said.

"Good evenin'. Let me know if I can help you at all," the young man said.

"Just need some shoe polish, toothpaste, and so forth," Jonas replied as he walked down an aisle that felt only about as wide as his shoulders. He reached for the boot black. The dank-smelling hotel reminded him to get some Murray's hair dressing pomade as well. Then he walked around the corner and found some ointment for his hand, before locating the tooth powder and then selecting a toothbrush for Honey. If she needed anything else, she'd probably welcome the chance to come get it herself. He headed for the counter.

"Find everything you need?"

"That I did," Jonas placed his items on the counter and reached for a Hershey's chocolate bar. "I'd like to add on this chocolate bar, and I'll take some Wrigley's chewing gum, if you have any."

"We do," the young man said.

Jonas looked at the fellow. He seemed to be in his early twenties. He had a thin mustache and a chiseled jaw. Jonas was certain he must be popular with the ladies. His brown eyes looked as though they told the truth, so Jonas asked, "Tell me young fella, what do folks do around here for entertainment?"

"Not from around here?" his brown eyes briefly looked over Jonas as he slid the gum to him.

"Nope, nope. Visitin' from down south," Jonas nodded toward the streets outside as he reached for the billfold in his suit pocket. "I feel these folks all runnin' and goin' to places and I was startin' to feel a little left out!" Jonas chuckled.

"Well, depends on your taste, sir," the young man said as he bagged Jonas's things, glanced at his bandaged hand, and clearly made some conclusions about it. "Take me; I'm a musician, so I need to be playin' and out around the jazz crowd. So, me personally, I like to get to the Lenox Lounge, Victory Gardens, and maybe The Cotton Club, if I'm lucky enough to get in. And tonight, I'll be playin' at the Cornett Lounge over near 118th and St Nick's."

"I see, I see," Jonas said as he paid the young man and then dropped his hand below the counter out of view. "And what about other folk?"

"Don't judge me now if what I'm about to tell you ain't your thing. But. If you're lookin' for the cat's meow—"

"Cat's meow. You mean ladies?"

"That I do. Then you might want to try Lady Magdalena's Manor. See I play there, too, on occasion —"

Jonas stopped. His heart had jumped into his throat. "Lady Magdalena's?"

"Yes. They got dancin' girls down there; sort of a high-class speakeasy, if you will, and I play my upright bass in a band there sometimes." The young man leaned forward, his face grave, "You didn't hear this from me, but from what I seen down there, you can also maybe buy yourself a girl if you want to. Low-life activity. I ain't never seen it *actually* happen, so, as far as I'm concerned, it don't happen," he said. He leaned back again and closed the till with a ding. He crossed his arms. "Now, don't everyone know about that place —well, they didn't use to—but now people have loose lips and it ain't as secretive and as exclusive as it use' to be."

Jonas cleared his throat. "What's your name, fella?" He could barely breathe. Here was another confirmation that this place truly operated and people, normal people like this young fellow here, went there regularly.

"My name's Joe."

Jonas gingerly shifted his bag to shake his hand. "Nice to meet you, Joe. I'm Mr. Stewart. Jonas Stewart. I'll be in town for a few days. Maybe I'll see you around."

"I'll be at Lady Magdalena's tomorrow night and playin' the Lenox Lounge on Sunday, Mr. Stewart."

Jonas rushed to open the door, eager to escape into the night air. "Thank you, Joe," he said over his shoulder. "Thank you." Jonas looked down as he hurried back to the hotel. His imagination raced with morbid thoughts; they sprang out of his head and onto the concrete where the hard soles of his shoes crushed them there like bits of hard candy.

Arriving at the hotel, he pushed through the doors and raced against the black and white tile as he hurried up the wooden stairs to the door of Room 17. Once there, he leaned against the wall and caught his breath.

Think, Jonas. Think! he demanded of himself. He needed a plan. Lady Magdalena's Manor. He thought through the situation as he stared ahead and searched the pinstriped lines on the dingy hallway wallpaper for direction. He had to get in there. *Had to!* By the time he used the skeleton key to open the door, he had an idea.

"Honey?" Jonas said as he entered the room and tossed the bag on the small desk in the corner.

"Still in here," Honey called out from the bathroom.

"How's it going?" Jonas said, methodically taking the items out of the brown paper bag.

"Di-vine," Honey said.

"Wonderful. I've got what you asked for."

"Jonas, I haven't come out exactly because I do need something else."

"What's that?" he said, moving closer to the door. The light from underneath the door shone through as he leaned his head in to listen.

"Would you happen to have any pajamas I could borrow..." she asked.

"Of course!" Jonas said. "I've got an extra pair of pajamas that I'd be happy to give to you. You'll probably swim in them, but they are my gift. I'll leave them right here by the door—when you're ready, you can just reach out and grab them. How will that do you?"

"That would do me fine. Thank you very much, Jonas."

"My pleasure," he said as he pulled the blue, striped pajamas from his suitcase and laid them at the foot of the bed, near the door for her. He then retrieved his journal from his satchel and sat down hurriedly at the miniature desk.

Honey sang melodiously from behind the closed door.

He tried to catch the unfamiliar tune while he scribbled down his thoughts.

June 22, 1945

Dear Arnetta,

I've finally arrived in New York City, and call it Father's intuition, but I feel I am desperately close to finding you. I've met someone that has escaped from Magdalena's. I've considered this a big, big break. I'm doing everything I can to reunite us. Tonight, I am taking real action. I hope to see you soon.

Love, Father

Jonas tightened the cap on his fountain pen and returned it to its place in his leather journal. He replaced the journal carefully in his attaché, then rummaged through his suitcase and found his shaving mirror. He propped it on the desk, opened the lid of the shoe-polish tin, and dabbed some black, oily polish on his chin, rather than onto his shoes as originally planned when he bought it. Jonas checked his reflection as he added a bit more. Pleased with himself, he returned the lid to the tin and wiped his greasy hands on the brown paper bag. With as much speed as he could, he changed out of his travelling trousers to something a little less nice. He loosened his tie and pulled his fedora low over his eyes. He added some ointment to his hand and was thankful the bruising would add to his character. Then he checked himself out in the hand mirror. He hoped he was convincing as a low life type of man, the type who would buy someone's daughter.

"Honey, you take your time in there. I'm goin' to, uh, run out again. I might be awhile," Jonas said, unwrapping a stick of gum and nervously chucking it into his mouth.

"You're going out again?" Honey said.

Jonas heard the bathroom door open, and he quickly turned his back as he opened the front door. He didn't want her to see his face. "You'll be fine. Will be good for you to have some peaceful time alone, anyway."

"Jonas? Where are you going?" Honey asked; fear mingled with her curiosity.

Jonas stooped down and pretended to tie his shoe. "I'll be back later."

Honey hesitated, "Alright, then. Goodbye. And hey —Jonas? Be careful."

Jonas turned and looked at Honey.

"Oh... !"

Her expression was as serious as his. "I will."

Closing the door behind him, Jonas looked down the mangy hallway. He turned right this time instead of left. There had to be a back stairway somewhere. Jonas slouched his big shoulders as he walked. He imagined himself to be some sort of straggling bear. He snuffled and snorted. Practicing for when he would maul Magdalena.

CHAPTER 33

Harlem propped herself against the bedroom door. She wished her stomach would stop. She felt like it had grabbed a hold of itself on wash day and was wringing out every bit of water that could have been in it. Her skin was sopping up anything her stomach wrung out, making it slick and cold to the touch. Parched on the inside, wet on the out. She swallowed hard, hoping to grab a sip of anything wet. She closed her eyes. Tried to concentrate. "If we keep going over this, we're going to run out of time."

"We won't make it anyway if we don't do it right." "Since when is there a right way to escape, Fury?" Harlem opened her eyes and stared frankly at the girl. They'd been going over things for nearly an hour already. "Do you think a rat starts strategizing how he's going to bite off his leg to get out of a trap? No! He just starts biting!" Harlem said.

"We aren't as experienced as you, Harlem," Fury snapped. "We need a plan."

"Do you want to get out of here or not?" Harlem asked.

"But we have to take the others...!" Amoura protested.

Harlem slammed her fist on the door behind her, "We can*not*! We'll be caught for certain."

Desire protested, "Just because you don't know the—"

Harlem grabbed for the doorknob for support and stood shakily, her stomach steadily wringing. She willed missing clarity to shine its bright light on them. "Listen, listen, listen, listen... NO!"

The bedroom door swung open, knocking Harlem off her balance. She staggered to catch herself and fell into Amoura's waiting arms.

"I've got you," Amoura reassured her, getting her to the bed. "Tilda, you nearly killed Harlem barreling in here like that!"

Tilda's arms were full of clothes. Her face beamed above the pile.

"You got them!" Desire said.

Tilda inhaled deeply while shaking her head with disbelief and laughing silently. She deposited the armful of clothes on the floor. From the center of the pile, she carefully retrieved a teapot, wrapped in a sweater. She handed it to Harlem.

"Thank you, Jesus," Harlem's hands shook as she drank directly from the pot. Tea dribbled down her chin and she didn't care one bit about it. She took a breath and drank more.

Desire pulled the pot down gently. "Not so much! We need you to be coherent, sister."

Tilda knocked.

"It's mostly water, Tilda? Good," Desire's eyes were filled with concern. "Still, Harlem. You should be careful. Take it slow."

"Harlem, you'll feel a little better in a bit," Amoura said. "Maybe then you'll be able to think more clearly."

"My thinking is crystal clear, Amoura. Oh—!" Her stomach twisted hard, and she turned toward the wall to hide from them how badly she was feeling.

"Harlem?"

"I'll be alright," she croaked. She wanted to rip her stomach out. Anything to stop the pain.

Amoura rubbed her back some. "Give it time, just give it some time."

"We haven't got time." She lifted herself to a more upright position. "We should get dressed."

"She's right girls," Fury said. "Let's get a move on." The girls turned their attention to Tilda's bounty and sifted through the dresses.

Tilda rapped again.

"I sure bet you thought you were going to die, Tilda!" Desire responded, "You dove into a danger pit for us!"

"What do you all think of this black and white striped shirt?" Fury asked, modeling the top.

Harlem held her stomach; she wished that time would hurry up and start making her feel better. "Don't you girls think we should—just... This isn't a fashion show." Her words went unheard.

"Since I've got the skirt to match it right here Fury, I think you look all the rage," Amoura beamed as she slipped into a pale pink shift with a fitted bodice and hugged Tilda. "You've really saved the day, sweetie."

Desire stepped into a green dress with polka dots. "Real street clothes! What a dream."

Harlem watched as they admired one another encouragingly, using each other as the mirror they didn't have. They filled in the holes for one another, like friends are supposed to. They were truly Brown Betties and she was just... brown. "If the girls downstairs are named for the rainbow, what are you all named for?"

"Love," Amoura said.

"Hate," Fury added.

"Want," Desire finished.

"And Honey?" Harlem asked.

"She is the original; she came before all of us. Magdalena chose it, just like she chose our names," Fury said. "Good thing we're leaving. You won't need a Bettie name from Magdalena."

"Good thing," Harlem said,

"C'mon Harlem, pick something out!" Amoura encouraged.

Harlem rose and solemnly pulled a light blue dress from the pile. It was pretty enough. The blue reminded her of the afternoon sky after a quick rain shower. She didn't care about it one way or another, except that it covered her body and that it would help her get out of there. As she reached around to her back for her zipper, she felt someone's fingers helping her.

Harlem turned. Before she knew it, Amour's cheek was against hers; Desire's arms were wrapped around her waist, Fury cradled their shoulders, and Tilda wiggled her way in between them all. Harlem was smothered.

"We couldn't do this without you, you know," Amoura said.

Harlem smiled at her and whispered, "Thank you." She hugged them tighter and then let them go. "It's nice to be needed."

"And you sure are!" Desire said.

Harlem reached for Desire's hands and gave them a squeeze of gratitude. "We really should get going. There's no telling how long Magdalena's going to be out."

The girls finished dressing with silent urgency and helped one another with remaining zippers and buttons.

"We don't look half bad," Desire smiled.

"We look normal enough to be walking down the street, that's a start," Fury said.

"Who knows how far we would have gotten in our unmentionables," Amoura laughed nervously.

Harlem turned and gently held Amoura's hands, which were shaking more than her own. "Nothing worth having is easy. I'm living proof of that. We can do this." They locked eyes. Amoura nodded bravely.

"Alright girls," Harlem said, retrieving the Iced Ruby Red from the bed and placing it in her front pocket. "Everyone ready?"

Tilda rapped on the wall frantically.

"We're not taking the other girls, Tilda." Amoura held the girl's shoulders. "We're going to get out safely, find someone who can help us, and come back for them."

Tilda blocked the door.

"We've already been through this, Tilda," Harlem grabbed Tilda's arm. "We *have* to do it this way. If I'm willing to leave my inheritance behind, we can afford to leave them. We'll come back!"

Tilda crossed her arms and shook her little head.

"I don't know," Amoura said. "Maybe she's right."

"No!" Harlem said.

"Tilda, you tried to fly outta this coop solo without us. Why're you so worried about the girls now?"

Tilda rapped.

"You made a mistake?" Desire said.

"Fine. Have it your way; give me the keys. I'll be outside waiting for all of you," Harlem said.

Tilda shook her head.

"You're being so foolish!" Harlem yelled. She felt the tea wanting to come back up the way it had gone down. She swallowed hard. "Give them to me!" she lunged for Tilda.

Tilda was quick and ducked out of Harlem's reach, running away into the secret closet.

Harlem shrieked, *"Tilda!"*

CHAPTER 34

Magdalena stumbled up the stairs to Lucinda's brownstone.

"Whaddya doin'?" Officer Brighton exclaimed as he caught her.

"I'm tripping—what does it look like?" she stammered.

"Well, get ya' selves together," he grumbled. "It's okay you passed out in the taxi, but I ain't carrying you in here."

"Ohhh... don't be such a drip," Magdalena said.

They reached the top of the stairs and the front doors opened to release previously muffled jazz notes. They were met by a tall, striking Asian woman who was on the arm of a lanky, handsome white man. The two cut between Magdalena and Officer Brighton as they passed them, snuggling and laughing as they went. They made no eye contact with Magdalena, as was the norm at this stage of a party. Before you went through the doors and after you want out them everyone was anonymous. Inside the party though, that was another thing.

Brighton grabbed Magdalena's arm and pushed her through the open door. "You don't have to escort me in, *Officer* Brighton," Magdalena said, pulling her arm away from Brighton, her purse dangling from her wrist.

"Yeah, I do. It's my job to do it. So, I'm doin' it."

"Idiot!" Magdalena said under her breath as she entered the home she'd visited so many times before.

Lucinda's manor was similar to Magdalena's, in that there was a formal foyer that led to a front hall. Lucinda's home had a center staircase that separated two great rooms, parting them like the Red Sea. At the top of the staircase, four musicians spoon fed the party people a dizzying kind of jazz they cooked up like liver and onions and gravy on a hot griddle. *These people are soppin' it up, too,* Magdalena thought as she scanned the musicians.

Magdalena paused. "Hey, where's Joe?" She wanted to speak to Joe about his next set at her Mysterie party.

"I hear he got a spot with some band over at The Cornett Lounge," Officer Brighton said.

"Hmmph," Magdalena muttered.

To the left and to the right of the foyer, the rooms pulsed like a beating heart, and people spilled into the foyer in a sanguine river of bodies. Doctors, lawyers, musicians, poets, military men and women, writers, dancers, bankers, all of them craving a good time. She was immediately smothered by their captivating heat

---

and mesmerizing pompousness. Magdalena could hear and smell them. They disgusted her. They laughed louder than they needed to. Smoked more than they needed to. Dabbed more rose water perfume behind their ears and in their cleavage than they needed to. They debated headlines in the *New York Times* longer than was humanly necessary. Others quoted Langston Hughes and Zora too often to be natural. But it was all needed here. These types of parties wouldn't be the best type without these indulgent, gorgeous, slinky, angular, obtuse, incessant, openly sensual beings. A butler passed by with a tray of champagne cocktails. Magdalena grabbed one sloppily. *She* only needed every ounce of courage to fight Lucinda.

"Be careful, *sis-tah*," scolded a brown woman whose hair was braided intricately like an African Princess.

"My apologies, darling," Magdalena said, flicking the spilled champagne from her fingers. "Quite sorry!"

The African princess swiped a napkin from a tray and walked off mumbling something about *'mann-ahs!'* as she wiped the spattered bubbly from her vibrant orange dress.

"Some people are so damn sensitive," Magdalena said.

Officer Brighton grabbed her elbow. "Let's go find Lucinda."

"Keep your mitts off'a me! That's my drinkin' arm you're manhandling!" Magdalena wiped the champagne from her chin and hunched her wrap back onto her shoulders.

"This way," he said as he led her toward a drawing room to the left.

"Traitor," she said, walking ahead of him through the tightly-nestled revelers. Magdalena blinked, trying to focus through the haze of cigar and cigarette smoke that hung over the crowd. With each blink she felt her mind collecting images, putting the pieces together, like a puzzle that would later be fixed in her memory. A flash of a sleek black mustache, molded with thick pomade. Red lips parting to expose gleaming white teeth. Netting over an eye that was rimmed with charcoal black. A chocolate fedora raised in greeting. A prism of light reflected from square-cut diamond bangle. A gold ring, flat, with the triangular Masonic emblem etched upon it. A necktie, striped with lines of black and white. Magdalena filed the images as she threw back the last of her champagne and grabbed another. She spotted Lucinda.

Lucinda waved to them demurely; she was seated center on a camel-back couch. She was a socialite, high on charisma, but still low brow. Like a crocodile in a marsh, she was easily the center of attention. Her silk tuxedo pantsuit was gleaming white and pearly like exposed teeth.

"Pontificators and bullshitters. All at your beck and call, Lucinda," Magdalena said sourly, crossing her arm and sipping her cocktail as she landed in front of Lucinda.

"Which category do you fall into, Maggie?" Lucinda's eyes sparkled with mischief.

"Neither, thank you." Magdalena held Lucinda's gaze.

"Maybe liar and thief," Lucinda said and handed her martini over to a young woman who lounged on the arm of the couch. The girl's eyes were cunning; she wore a black pixie bob and was draped in a yellow gown with a front cowl that dipped to her navel, which Magdalena found quite stunning. Lucinda whispered to the girl, who rose, gave Magdalena a cursory once-over, and walked away. Lucinda stood and embraced Magdalena for what was a bit too long... and a bit too close. Magdalena pulled away, faltered drunkenly in her footing, and smoothed her hair.

"Maggie. It's a pleasure to see you and I am delighted you finally made it." Lucinda said, smiling like crocodiles do.

Only a few people got away with calling her Maggie. Lucinda took her liberties with it. "It has been far too long," Magdalena said, clutching her handbag, which contained Lucinda's hush money.

"Feels like an eternity when you're waiting for what you're owed."

Lucinda rose and led them deeper toward the back of the home, where it was darker. Cave-like.

Weaving through more pleasure-seekers, Magdalena caught their sparkling, haunting eyes searching hers, hungry for answers as to who she was and why she was with Lucinda. Magdalena was herself accustomed to being the Queen. She was usually the one smiling with stretched lips, kissing cheeks, patting shoulders. But now Lucinda was the one in charge. She didn't care to be the one who followed someone else's lead and she didn't care for the stares. Magdalena stared back at these faux *artistes* with their ascot ties and velvet hair ribbons and arched eyebrows and mentally reminded some of them that they'd be going back to their one-room shacks in just a few hours.

"Officer Brighton, thanks for fetching Maggie," Lucinda called over her shoulder casually. "I don't think she would have made it otherwise."

"Glad t' be of service there, Lucinda," Officer Brighton said, his words brushing over the top of Magdalena's head.

They entered a secluded parlor. It was a handsome room, outfitted outrageously with a circular bed, mirrors, chandeliers, and a bear-skin rug. The girl with the pixie bob lay on the bed near a cocktail tray with a silver shaker and two martini glasses placed upon it. She quietly poured two martinis. Magdalena had never been in this room before and rapidly felt the notion why. She shifted in her heels.

Lucinda sat down on the plush bed full of satin pillows, accepted a martini from the girl who quietly sipped the other, and patted the bed. "I don't bite, honey."

"I don't believe you, Lucinda," Magdalena said as the door closed behind her, muting both the jazz and the people enjoying it. She looked back over her shoulder; Officer Brighton leaned against the door authoritatively. Just like he did at her house. She frowned and wrapped her mink tighter about her shoulders. "This ends tonight, Lucinda."

"Is that even possible?" Lucinda laughed. Her blue eyes lit up maliciously as she looked at Magdalena.

"Things have been rearranged," Magdalena said, holding onto each word to steady herself. She smoothed her hair again. The room was getting smaller by the minute, its edges seeming to melt as she focused on the slithering crocodile before her.

Lucinda lit a reefer that had been resting on the tray, took a long drag off it, and exhaled a cloud of pale-blue, chalky haze. She smiled as she offered Magdalena some and said, "It's your masquerade party. I'm just the one holding up your little mask, darling."

Magdalena waved the marijuana smoke away from her. She couldn't stand the sweet, sticky smell of it. Her stomach flip-flopped. It had been hours since her dose of tea. The high had worn off, and now the sickness that came after had arrived. The champagne she slammed was sneaking up on her too. Her gut twinged in wringing bursts that felt less than pleasant. She had to get out of here. Magdalena opened her clutch and offered Lucinda the cash. Lucinda nodded for her to hand it to Officer Brighton.

He counted it and shrugged. "This could be every'ting and maybe it ain't. I'm learning Maggie here likes t' keep secrets."

"That's everything I've got," Magdalena said, thankful for Harlem's check.

Lucinda pulled from the joint again. "Not exactly."

"I told you before. I'm not giving you my father's house."

"You mean *my* father's house," Lucinda exhaled.

"My papa bought our house fair and square—"

"Lies. And you know it. They kicked my papa out because he was a Jew," Lucinda said.

"You know mine was too—" Magdalena crossed her arms indignantly and swallowed hard, keeping whatever was frothing up down.

"You should see the family portrait she's got!" Officer Brighton scoffed.

Lucinda scowled at Officer Brighton.

"Ain't no normal lookin' family."

"You've seen her mother, then?"

"Right I have!"

"Well, her papa pulled his Negro wife out of his back pocket when the property fella came knockin'," Lucinda said.

"What kinda property fella likes colored folks?"

"One that *is* colored folk," Lucinda smiled as she passed the joint to the girl. Lucinda sipped from her martini.

"You don't say," Officer Brighton said and whistled. "When'd they let a colored man do that?"

"Do you have to sound like a numbskull too, Brighton?" Lucinda said.

Magdalena licked her suddenly-parched lips. "Your family could have stayed, Lucinda. Your family didn't want to be mixed in with what was sure to be coming."

"There wasn't an opportunity for mixin'. That property man put us out on the street like we were dogs. All so that he could sell every piece of his property in Harlem to your kind."

"My kind," Magdalena laughed. "This is Harlem, Lucinda. What are all of those 'kinds' you got in your living room right now? Sipping your wine, lounging on your couch, kissing your 'kind'...?"

"You're right. This *is* Harlem," Lucinda said. "People want to get to know each other. Touch and feel something they might be forbidden to in their everyday, humdrum lives. I'm the fuckin' sorceress of 125th Street over here. Brewin' up a bubbling mixed-match of everything. But one thing I haven't forgotten is that when lots of these businessmen *O'fays* come uptown to get away from their vanilla lives downtown, they still want to deal with *vanilla*. It's what they trust. You know that or you wouldn't be pretending to be what you're not all these years. And paying me to not blow your goddamn whistle!"

"You've got loose lips, Lucinda. I'm done pretending," Magdalena growled.

"Then I'll get that house for sure. Downtown won't pay top dollar to a whorehouse run by a—"

Magdalena stood tall and pointed hard at Lucinda. "Watch yourself. You watch your fucking mouth."

"By a *shvartse*."

Magdalena grabbed the money from Officer Brighton and threw it at Lucinda, "I'm finished with this. And with you. You've been blackmailing me long enough about my family. And don't think I don't know that you've been telling every Tom, Dick, and Harry everything anyway. I'm done with you. Consider my debt paid, Lucinda!"

"Your debt has deep roots, Maggie. Very deep," Lucinda approached Magdalena as the girl gathered the money.

Magdalena stumbled backwards, "No one will believe you. My sister is gone."

Lucinda caressed Magdalena's chin. "I'll admit, Honey's one drop of color was important to me too. It's too bad Otto is such a nincompoop."

"Otto?" Magdalena asked, watching Lucinda as she took off her white jacket, threw it on the bed, and walked to the bedroom window. Lucinda pulled the curtains aside and opened the window wide. Her hair moved gently in the night breeze.

Lucinda ran her fingers through her short bob. "He's family. Like Brighton here. But he fucked up, as you know. Now none of us has Honey," Lucinda sat on the window ledge and lit a cigarette from a case resting on a small table. "I want your house. I want the girls in it, and I want all of it by the end of the month."

"I will burn that house down before I give it to you."

Lucinda laughed horribly and blew smoke out the window. "Maybe that would put us all out of our misery."

"I'll do what I have to." Magdalena lurched forward, grabbed Lucinda's half-finished martini from the tray on the bed, and downed it. "I always have."

"You don't have to confess your sins to me—" Lucinda laughed, throwing her cigarette butt out the window.

"I saved myself and my sister when no one was around to help us. To feed us. I saved us with the resources we had," Magdalena felt something swelling in her. Something like rage and she wasn't sure if she could contain it.

Lucinda sat on the ledge, crossed her legs, and laced her fingers around her knee cap. "Oh, Bravo, honey!"

Magdalena glared at her. "You stupid *bitch*! Sitting in here all comfy and cozy and complaining about how your daddy didn't get his property. What about what happened to my papa? What about what happened to me? They left me with nothing!" she screamed. Magdalena charged at Lucinda like a locomotive, wanting to shove her right out the window onto the pavement below.

Lucinda darted away from the window, her blue eyes wide. She flung her words at Magdalena, "The fun part is, you coulda stopped. But you didn't. *You* didn't. Not even after you got locked up for it. You brought more in. Kept it goin'. Face it. You're addicted to it, Maggie. You need it. And now you're screamin' about what happened to poor little you. Darling, you're pathetic. You sold your own flesh and blood! Now you want to lead some sort of normal life. Is that it? Well, 'normal' don't come free, sister. You should know that better than anyone."

"It's just me now—" Magdalena said.

"With Honey outta the picture, you think you got rid of your goddamned proof? You've forgotten about one new, very important witness," Lucinda said as she grabbed her jacket from the bed and put it back on. The girl in yellow stood beside her—a loyal soldier.

"Who? Him?" Magdalena followed Lucinda's gaze. "Officer Brighton and I, we already have an understanding."

"An understanding?" she laughed. "I don't think you get where the understanding is. It's Officer Brighton and me who have an arrangement." Lucinda walked toward Officer Brighton who was still posted by the door. "You see, you thought he was working for you, guarding your girls. But I've had the bigger picture in mind for a long time. He has been working for me, watching my property. *My* house and everything in it. Weren'tcha, big fella?"

"That there's a correctly stated factoid," Officer Brighton said, picking his teeth.

"What...?" Magdalena said slowly. She landed squat on the windowsill. *All those times she'd been with him, thinking she was appeasing him. Doing him a favor.* Her hands travelled nervously against the nape of her neck, smoothing the thin black hair there. She wanted to throw up. And felt close to it.

Lucinda kissed Officer Brighton lightly on the lips. "Maybe you can persuade him to kiss and not tell."

Officer Brighton reached for the buttons on his pants.

"Jesus H. Christ. You can't be serious," Magdalena said, shooting to her unsteady feet.

Officer Brighton walked toward the bed. "I'm gonna pretend that I don't knows I've been wit' a—wit' a nigger woman all this time. And I'm gonna need some help right now to feel better that I was lied to, by both of you's."

"Why don't you make Lucinda pay?"

"She don't like me the way you like me."

"We both know there's nothing he can do for me," Lucinda reached for the girl's hand. "Except humiliate you. Like your family did to mine."

The two other women walked toward the door hand-in-hand and Lucinda paused to open it. The sounds of the party, of life being lived raucously, wafted into the room. "By the end of the month, Maggie."

Magdalena sprung awkwardly from the window's open offer to escape or lose her lunch and tried to follow them. "Lucinda, you can't do this. I'm going to —"

"Going to what?" she paused.

"Come clean. *I'm* going to tell everyone, everyone, I'm a Negro."

"You wouldn't dare. You're not that smart. Plus, who would believe you? You've gotten rid of all the evidence, right? Tah-tah!"

Magdalena froze in her tracks as Officer Brighton blocked her path. His eyes cold, his face filled with a hate that hadn't been there before. She heard the familiar sound of a pistol being cocked into place for the second time that evening. She felt a cold chill in her shoulders and knew that this time she wouldn't be appeasing anyone.

CHAPTER 35

Harlem skipped down the dark, underground-railroad hallway. Her breath rushed from her body rapidly as she yelled again, "Tilda! Come back!"

The wall became her guide as she reached the stairs which led down to the Mysterie room.

Shouts rose to meet them. The Rainbow Girls had been alerted.

"Cat's out of the bag!" Desire said.

Harlem's head wanted to explode from anger. "I never would have made it out of Greensboro if I'd had to deal with all this chaos. And now I've got to get these women and me and you all out of here? I swear this is the first time I'm happy to have been an only child. Do you hear me? How are we going to get them *all* out?"

"I don't know," Desire said. "But we're going to find a way."

"That's the last step down, Harlem. Watch yourself now."

"I've got it. Where are we?"

"We're just getting backstage, remember. Bit of a maze back here, but it's easy to navigate once you've found your way."

"That is *not* going to be on top of my list of things to learn!" Harlem shouted.

Fury and Amoura pushed back the hanging curtains for her to hobble through. Even though they were the ones on stage, the show in front of them was in high gear. "What is she *doing*?" Harlem asked as she watched Tilda trying to mime to the girls from the stage.

"What's the big idea getting' us outta bed?" Topaz growled with her arms crossed angrily. "We ain't got no idea what you're tryin' to say, Tilda."

"We're leaving!" Amoura yelled in a burst.

Harlem grabbed her aching head. "This is a disaster."

"What!?" Topaz exclaimed. The rest of the girls exploded into disbelief with her.

"Girls, girls! We don't have a lot of time to explain," Harlem spoke up, trying to take some control. "We have to leave right now."

Tilda ran toward the main stairs that led upstairs to the dining room. She raised her ring of keys high like a beacon and clanked them against one another.

"Let's go!" Desire shouted as she jumped from the stage.

"Where are we going?" Violet asked, wringing her hands.

"What's going to happen to us out there?" Emerald wondered after her.

Sienna wasn't convinced either. "Magdalena is sure to catch us. She'll kill us!"

"Shut your traps, you silly birds, and just move it!" Sapphire yelled and ran to follow Tilda.

From the stairwell, Desire yelled like a drill sergeant, "You heard me, folks, *let's go!*" The girls jumped into gear and ran through the tables, pushing chairs aside as they went. Worried murmurs punctured the air.

"Where're the clothes for us, too?" Topaz said, running after Sapphire. "We ain't just gonna blend in with everybody wearing these rags."

Harlem raced with Amoura and Fury. She groaned, "Clothes? I told you! We can't stop to get clothes for them."

"Listen, if we did risk getting the girls some clothes, oughtn't we try to find your check, Harlem?" Amoura said.

Harlem looked at Amoura. "And if the check is gone? Me wasting time on that would be like shooting myself in the foot. We should just get the hell out of here!" She stopped to catch her breath.

Amoura sighed. "I just don't think I could leave all that money behind."

"My grandma and grandpa worked hard for that money," Harlem agreed. "But you think they'd want me chained to a bed because of it? They'd want me free and able to make more of it. This little bit in my pocket will be enough to get far away from this place. It's all I need. I promise you."

"Whatever you say," Amoura said as they reached the stairs.

"These stairs are too narrow for all three of us to fit. You two go ahead of me," Harlem instructed them. She shook her head to get the feathers out.

"Are you alright? We never should have given you the tea," Amoura worried.

Harlem closed her eyes. "I feel a little loosey goosey. Like I did the day I came. Sitting there with Magdalena and the sisters."

"You'll be fine; mind over matter. If you don't mind, it won't matter. Just focus on getting out," Fury spoke as she and grabbed Harlem tight around the waist and helped her.

From above, they heard loud squeals from the girls.

"Oh my God," Harlem sighed.

"I guess they went for the clothes," Fury said.

"Run up there and make sure those girls are getting what they need and then get them out. And hurry. I can get up the stairs," Harlem said.

"Are you sure?"

Harlem nodded in reply.

Fury and Amoura ran up the stairs. With voices hushed, their shoes scuffled loudly against the wooden steps as they hurried up. The hair on

Harlem's arms stood on end with excitement. The charge in the dark stairway was as real as the electric storms back home in Greensboro, the ones where jolts of energy ran through the clouds and illuminated the summer night sky. Harlem wasn't sure how she was going to make it through this. Her head was buzzing, and she couldn't give any thought to her stomach. But the thought of getting out was all the pain killer she needed to climb up the stairs.

She pitched herself through the door and into the dining room. Her breath came like wild horses as she nervously looked around, half expecting Magdalena and the sisters to be sitting at the dining-room table leering at her, with forks and knives in hand ready to eat her up. There was no sign of either of them. But who knew for how long. Harlem shook the chill from her spine. "Girls! Girls! *C'mon!*" Harlem yelled out as she hurried to Magdalena's office.

Good gravy, she thought. Arms and legs stuck out of the closet like a bunch of trout caught in a net. Every single Rainbow Girl was jammed into Magdalena's huge closet grabbing whatever garment she could find. Some cried at being reunited with their things. Harlem saw her own suitcase: open, barren, and discarded against Magdalena's desk. She felt her feet wanting to move toward her belongings, but she seized the doorknob to stop herself. "Please. Please! You all! Have some sense," Harlem pleaded. "We have to leave!"

"Harlem," Amoura called out from behind Magdalena's desk, "We went ahead and tried; I just can't find the check. It's not here!" Amoura's hands flew up in exasperation.

"I told you to leave it, Amoura!" Harlem felt disgusted looking at all of it. She could barely stand it. The carnage. The waste. The wanting. "Please! Please, we must *go*!"

Fury grabbed Amoura's hand and pulled her away. "C'mon Amoura. And watch you don't trip over Magdalena!"

"What!?" Harlem shouted.

Fury pointed.

And there it was. A portrait like she'd never seen before. "I knew it! Magdalena's momma is a Negro just like us," Harlem exclaimed, looking at Amoura.

Amoura looked back at the portrait as they reached Harlem. "Tilda told us long ago! Makes all the sense in the world, doesn't it? Well. As much sense as we can give."

Amoura and Fury ran past Harlem and out of the office. Desire came out of the closet, pulling Emerald and Violet with her. "Drop it, just let it go!" she yelled at them as they tugged back and forth on a dress.

"Desire, take them to the front door!" Harlem shouted to her. Desire and the two girls ran past her. Their voices, now heavy with panic, filled the room.

"Tilda!" Harlem called out over the din. "We need the keys, right now!" Tilda emerged from the closet, frantic and frazzled with Topaz and Sienna. The girl's arms were full of clothing. "What kind of fools are you?" Harlem seethed. Ruby, Indigo, and Sapphire emerged and ran past her sheepishly. Harlem slapped the clothes out of their hands. "Let's go!" she jabbed her thumb over her shoulder and out the door behind her, before she ran out herself.

"Tilda, get those keys ready!" Harlem warned as they scrambled. She trudged past the dining room table and through the huge pocket doors. Just as she reached the foyer, she heard Magdalena scream, *"Jesus Christ!"*

CHAPTER 36

agdalena covered her head with her hands as she ping-ponged off one frantic body and into another. She crashed into the wall of the foyer like a bowling pin as more bodies charged passed her. She couldn't decipher who or what was coming toward her as she spun around and reeled backwards. Her arms flung out like a cyclone as she lost her balance; her heel had gotten stuck in the folds of the fabric of her gown and she fell hard to the ground on her tailbone. "*Goddammit!*"

In the dark, she scrambled to her feet and crouched. Ready. She held her pocketbook like a baseball bat, prepared to swing at whatever came near her. Shrieking and confusion surrounded her. She whipped her head toward the sounds, trying to make a visual accounting of the chaos that was whirling around her.

"Hurry, hurry!"

Her eyes adjusted, as did her understanding. She flung her bag at the door. "You ungrateful wenches! You can't escape me!" she bellowed. She could see them now, a many-limbed mass surging toward the front door. Magdalena snorted like a bull and ran her fingers through her hair angrily as she charged for the exit. "You won't get out!"

Someone yelled from the foyer, "Tilda! The front door's locked! We need the key!" Magdalena thought it sounded like Fury.

"Tilda! If you open that door, I will *kill* you!" Magdalena shouted in the darkness as she kicked off her shoes, threw her wrap to the ground, and buried her own keys deep in her pocket. "I swear to *God*, I will do it!"

The girls had gotten through to the foyer door because she'd unlocked it while coming in. But she knew they were trapped by the street door, which she had re-locked behind her after stepping inside. Magdalena grabbed the first body she reached and yanked it away from the door and to the waiting ground. Whomever it was landed with a thud.

"Oh! Oww!"

Magdalena went for another girl, trying to throw her down to where her sister was too. In the moment, everyone seemed an unrecognizable tangle of parts. This one whacked her good in the nose. "You...! Bitch!" Magdalena huffed and became more enraged, grabbing the girl again harder.

The girl struggled back. "Help! She's got me!"

"Get her!" someone yelled.

Hands grabbed for her calves and then around her waist. Magdalena kicked the groping hands away and freed herself from the encircling claws.

"I knew this day would come! I knew it!" Magdalena said as she sprinted away from them and toward the staircase. "But I'm smarter than you."

"Hurry!"

"Run!"

They sounded like tortured dogs yelping for their lives. Glass shattered. She turned her head toward the foyer. Those stupid harlots had smashed the windows on either side of the front door. *Oh, someone is going to pay!* They were breaking free, chewing their own legs off to do so. For two seconds, Magdalena thought, *What if I just let them go? What if they leave? This will all be over, and I can start new like I want.* Then reality hit; she couldn't let them leave. She'd go to jail. Again. "I will not let you *dimwits* ruin me! I promise you that. Not today!" she growled at them.

Magdalena felt for and pulled the wooden finial off the top of the staircase banister. Digging inside its secret cavity, she retrieved a small pistol that had been hidden there. This was her emergency fund and was perhaps even more important than Harlem's check right now. She pointed the gun toward the front door and fired.

Their screams pierced the night.

She'd rather one of them were dead inside the Manor than alive outside it. Out there they were able to harm her like Lucinda did, like Officer Brighton had, like Honey probably would. Each one of them could destroy her. She fired again.

"Get away from the door! NOW!" she roared. The room became silent.

With the windows knocked out, the very faint glow from the streetlamps outside offered some light. Magdalena could see two forms huddled in a corner, and another by the doors leading into the dining room. She could feel others near Tilda's broom closet bedroom under the stairs.

"If anyone dares to move a muscle," Magdalena said, "you'll be sorry."

Magdalena kept the gun pointed at the clumps of girls before her. Her shadow menaced them as she slowly walked to the foyer door and closed it, its latch clicking into place and signaling a certain finality. She ran her fingers along the wall and found the light switch.

Magdalena felt charged, ferociously crackling with something that was beyond anger; she was high on hatred thanks to the opium tea, Lucinda's martinis, and Officer Brighton's demeaning violation of her. It had been an eternity since anyone had done the things he'd done to her in the way that he did. She wiped the back of her hand against her mouth to rid herself of him. Her wrath surged as she paced and looked at each one of their pathetic, idiotic, guilty, grimy, ugly faces: her captive audience. "Pathetic!" she spat.

With her gun as her enforcer, she pulled the keys from her pocket and locked the foyer door. Magdalena faced them. Amoura, Desire, and Fury were holding onto each other in the corner near the door. Harlem and Tilda were clinging to the wall near the dining room. Emerald, Violet, Sienna and the others were scattered about like strays.

"You're no better than a pack of mangy dogs," Magdalena reprimanded as she peered at the other girls. They stood frozen, unsure what to do. "I'd like to say that I'm surprised, but I'm not. I feed you. I shelter you." Magdalena pulled at Desire's green polka-dot collar, nearly strangling her, "I *clothe* you." She released her grip as Desire slapped her hands away. "And this is the thanks I get?"

"Well, thanks for nothing!"

Magdalena spun toward the degenerate who risked her life to say such a thing. It was Harlem. Magdalena laughed. "What did you say, you spoiled brat?"

"I said, 'Thanks for nothing!'"

CHAPTER 37

Before Harlem could tell herself not to, she took off her shoe and threw it at Magdalena. The shoe knocked Magdalena square in the head and the *whop!* sound it made was all the distraction Harlem needed. She screamed like she'd never screamed before and charged into the woman, tackling her by the waist. The two landed in a tangled mess and howled in pain as the gun Magdalena held flew across the floor.

"You witch!" Harlem yelled. The feeling that had possessed her to swing at Sapphire downstairs reared its head again, only ten-fold now. Harlem pummeled Magdalena. She barely saw the woman before her; instead, she saw a writhing mass that stood for everyone and everything that had hurt her. She wanted to reach inside Magdalena's throat, grab her awful soul with her bare hands, pull it up from its depths, and whip it against the wall. Just like what had been done to her. Harlem clenched both hands around Magdalena's thin neck and squeezed it like she'd seen her grandad do to chickens on his farm.

The woman thrashed under her grip, flailing and jabbing at Harlem's arms. Harlem kept her hold and looked deep into Magdalena's bulging green eyes, her pupils wide with surprise and fear.

"I won't let you get me. I won't!" Harlem squeezed tighter.

"Harlem! Stop! You'll kill her!" Fury shouted.

Harlem kept her grip and looked back at Fury; she snarled, "Get the hell out of here. Go!" As Harlem turned back to Magdalena, she felt a sudden sting peel across her face; and found she was reeling toward the ground. She landed hard on her shoulder and skid clumsily across the floor from the force of the blow.

"Oh my God!" Amoura yelled.

Harlem groaned and rolled to her stomach; the side of her face pulsed with a hot pain. Harlem hunched on all fours and pulled her knees to her stomach to stand. She faltered and fell back to the floor and sat on her bottom, dazed. The room was spinning. She felt something warm and sticky and foreign on her face. Harlem reached her hand to her face and pulled it away; blood covered her fingertips.

"You...!" Harlem spotted the gun near her. She dove for it and grabbed it before Magdalena could.

Harlem stood with the weapon in her hands, which she found did not shake as they had the night that she shot her father.

"You wouldn't," Magdalena said, her eyes full of disbelief, just like Roy's had been.

"Yes. I. Would," Harlem said calmly as she pulled the trigger.

Harlem waited for Magdalena to fall to the ground like Roy had. Maybe she had missed. Harlem pulled the trigger again, and again. There was nothing but a loud click.

Magdalena laughed.

Harlem hurled the gun at Magdalena, wanting to stop the wretched laughing that was coming from that awful mouth. She missed.

Magdalena rushed to Harlem. Harlem fell to the ground and tried to shield herself from the blows coming her way. Her forearms weren't the best shields, nor were her shins. She swung and kicked and fought back as hard as she could, but she was no match to Magdalena.

"Help!" she cried. There was a reprieve in the blows; she looked up to see that Tilda had jumped on Magdalena's back. Magdalena spun around, trying to get her off.

"Won't you stop it!" Magdalena growled as she flung Tilda hard against the wall, batting her off as though she were a rabid dog. Tilda fell to the floor; after she hit the ground, she didn't move.

"Tilda!" Harlem crawled for the girl, but her momentum was interrupted. Her head yanked backwards. Harlem clawed upwards as she was pulled up to her knees. Magdalena had her by the hair. She squealed and slapped at Magdalena's hands to break free of the gripping pain. From her knees, she spun around and stared up into Magdalena's eyes, which bulged with fury as she hissed, "You are going to be very sorry."

Harlem turned her head and looked for someone, anyone. "*Help!*" she pleaded to them.

With her fist gripping Harlem's hair, Magdalena pulled Harlem to her feet and dragged her through the foyer toward the dining room. "Nobody move!"

"*NO!*" Harlem screamed out in painful protest. "No!" she shouted as Magdalena dragged her into the dining room. Harlem kicked her heels into the ground. Screaming. She caught sight of Indigo, Ruby, and Violet. They stared, statues, doing nothing. Tears streamed down her face; she felt her hair ripping out from her head as Magdalena pulled harder, lifting her from the ground and dragging her toward the basement.

Harlem kicked more and hollered louder. Her legs banged into things that toppled over and flew out behind her. Each step Magdalena took away from the front door felt like another nail in Harlem's coffin.

Harlem turned and looked behind her again just in time to see Sapphire run to Magdalena and push her hard. Harlem fell forward onto the dining room table and tumbled to the ground. She was thankful for the help and scrambled to her feet to join Sapphire in the fight against Magdalena with hopes of making another run for the door.

Sapphire raised her fist for a right arm hook and hit Magdalena again. A loud pop rang out again, an explosion of sound in the small foyer. The girls screamed in response. Harlem covered her ears, shaken to the core.

Sapphire staggered backwards out of the dining room and into the foyer, then slumped to the ground.

Harlem ran around the dining-room table and into the foyer. "Sapphire!" Harlem screamed. She sprang to the wounded girl. "Sapphire!"

Magdalena staggered into the room. She swung the gun around her head, breathless. "Get back. Against the wall, all of you. Get back!"

All the girls scurried to the wall. Harlem landed against it with a thud, she'd moved so fast. She stood between Amoura and Emerald. The hair on her arms was as alert as every other part of her body.

"Help..." Sapphire said. She was balled on the rug in the center of the foyer. A pool of blood was forming beneath her.

Harlem moved toward the girl. Magdalena pointed the gun at her. She froze in her tracks.

"*Help,*" Magdalena mimicked as she stepped to Sapphire and looked down upon her. A tear slid down Sapphire's smooth brown face and disappeared into the rug. Magdalena whined unsympathetically, "*Help me, I've been shot.*" She pulled the slit in her gown aside and showed everyone her scar. "This is what I got for trying to rob a corner market."

Magdalena looked at Sapphire. "Welcome to the club, dingbat. That's what you get for trying to betray me. Consider it payback for being so mouthy lately." Magdalena nudged Sapphire with her foot. "Get up. Get UP!" she yelled.

"I'll not have you bleed all over my father's rug. It was a gift to my mother! Now get up!" Magdalena reached down and pulled the rug from underneath Sapphire, causing her to scream out in pain. "Oh, shut up, already. It's only a measly flesh wound."

Violet slumped down the wall, an accordion of legs. Harlem thought she looked green. Had she not already seen Roy's bleeding body, she might have been the same color.

"Don't like the sight of blood trickling from one of your comrades? Should have thought about that before trying this stupid stunt," Magdalena scolded. Swinging the gun toward Sienna, she continued, "Get her out of my sight. Now." Sienna crawled to Sapphire and hauled her, moaning, from the room.

"Revolting piece of trash," Magdalena said, watching them whimper off. "You disgusting pack of vermin."

Magdalena turned toward Harlem. "This is you. This is your doing. I know it." Magdalena pointed the gun at her and came toward her. "How dare you point a gun at me and pull the trigger. How *dare* you!"

Harlem walked backwards, through the pocket doors and into the dining room. She raised her hands. "Magdalena—"

The woman raised her hand and backhanded Harlem across the face.

Everything went black.

CHAPTER 38

Jonas pulled his hat down low as he marched up the last brownstone step and pushed the doorbell. He heard the chime far off into the house; in the still of the night, its sound was more like a deep, echoing gong. Back home in Ohio, you ring somebody's bell this late and loud, a few lights flicker on over at the neighbor's. But he had learned pretty quickly that New York was no Ohio.

He jiggled the snake handle on Magdalena's front door and stepped back to look up at the windows, waiting for any indication of movement. His shoes crunched on broken glass. His matchbox rattled as he pulled it from his pocket. Deftly, he struck a match against the rough wall and used the flame like a lantern, squatting down to get a better look. He picked up a piece of colored glass. Jonas stood, examined the front door, and quickly found the source of the glass in a broken windowpane.

"Well, I'll be," he whispered softly. The hair on his arms rose. He flicked out the match in quick movement as it burned his fingers. "Hello? Hello?" he rang the bell again in spite of the late hour; then slammed his fist against the door. If some neighbor did come, maybe that would be a blessing. "Hello!?"

Suddenly, the door opened. A woman, who he presumed to be Magdalena, stood before him. Her black hair fell around her face and shoulders in a disheveled mess. Her dress didn't know if it wanted to be off or on and seemed to be hanging onto her body for dear life. Her lip was bloodied, and her face was swollen.

"What the hell do you want?" she spat, her knuckles blotting her split lip.

"A, a-a-a girl," he stammered, groping for words. "I want the cat's meow."

"Come back tomorrow, *putz*."

Jonas jammed his foot in the door to stop it from slamming in his face. His mind raced. Had to get in there. Had to. "Wait," he held up a large roll of bills. His savings. Most of it.

Magdalena grabbed it and shut the door. "Hold on."

He peeked through the hole in the glass. It was too dark to see anything. He could hear something. Some movement. He knew something was wrong. *But what? Was he too late?* His mind rattled with the unknown. "Hey! Hey in there!" he pounded on the door. "Hey!" Suddenly, it reopened.

"*Mazel tov!*" Magdalena said as she shoved someone through the door at him and slammed it so hard the door frame shook.

His arms were full of a body. He looked down at the face of a young girl. Her eyes were wild with panic. She clambered from his arms and banged on the doors with all her might.

Not knowing exactly what to do, he reached for her and held her tight. "You're alright. You're alright!"

Her mouth gaped, yet no sound came out. He knew then that he was holding Tilda.

CHAPTER 39

Honey cradled and rocked Tilda in her arms. She washed the tears from Tilda's face with a warm washcloth and placed an ice bag they'd found in the bathroom on her head. "Shhhh, it's going to be alright," Honey soothed. "I promise."

Honey glanced at Jonas. He had not stopped pacing since he returned with Tilda.

"Jonas, please. You're going to wear another hole in the rug," she sighed, rubbing the sleep from her tired eyes.

"I can't help it. I simply cannot," he said and looked back at her as he raised his arms and clasped his fingers behind his head. "What the hell are we going to do now?"

"Keep your voice down, Jonas. We don't want to be thrown out of here, especially at this time of night."

"How can you expect me to be calm? What if that girl who's been shot, Sapphire, is Arnetta? My baby girl could be bleeding to death in that hellhole."

"And what if she's not? What if Sapphire *isn't* Arnetta?"

"Then worse!"

"*Shhhh!*"

Jonas attempted to lower his voice and failed. "She could be slipping further away from me. Right this minute."

"Would that really be worse? She could be free. She could be running home," Honey said.

"Dammit it to hell," Jonas muttered, punching his fist into the wall.

Tilda flinched and grabbed Honey tighter.

"You *must* calm down, Jonas. We have to think through our next move and do it with clear heads."

Jonas groaned. He sat in the lone chair in the room; it sighed under his weight. He leaned back reluctantly, massaging his hands. "And Harlem. Who's to know how she's faring."

Jonas squeezed his eyes shut and turned his face away from her. Where Tilda's shame and sorrow flowed freely down her face, Honey knew Jonas was keeping his own at bay. Honey looked down at Tilda and lifted the ice bag. There was a nice knot forming on the back of her head. Honey smoothed Tilda's fuzzy plaits and reapplied the pack. The ice settled in the bag, eager to do its healing work.

Tilda shifted in Honey's lap. Her eyes were troubled. She rapped harshly on the wooden bed post.

"What more could you have done, Tilda? You can't blame yourself," Honey soothed.

Tilda continued.

"And if you had left them like Harlem suggested, then what?"

Tilda paused; she reached up to Honey's shoulder questioningly and then rapped more.

Honey shifted on the bed. "I *was* planning to come back for you all. Jonas and I were both planning. Why do you think Jonas showed up at the Manor?"

Tilda answered.

"For his daughter. Of course, for his daughter, but to get inside so that we could get you all out."

Jonas looked at her.

Honey kneaded her knotting shoulders with her free hand. They were twisted and desperate for a relief she couldn't quite supply. She sighed. "Of *course* I planned to go back for you girls and get you out; you're my family. There just wasn't enough time to do it between running from Otto and finding Jonas. And who could I trust? I'd been just as alone and just as afraid as anyone. I'd needed a plan, Tilda," Honey said.

Jonas looked away from her.

"You believe me, don't you?" Honey looked down at Tilda; the girl merely looked back at her for a better answer. The truth. Honey closed her eyes and leaned her head against the wall with its cracked, dingy plaster. "Tilda, we'll talk about this later. Right now, you need to rest."

"Maybe we should go to the police," Jonas said.

"No," Honey said tightly with her eyes still closed.

"Every officer can't work for Magdalena."

"There are more than you think."

"We need help."

"Not that kind."

"You expect me to sit here and do nothing—"

"I'm expecting you to think quickly, quietly, and rationally. That is all. If you must go *do* something, then please, run off somewhere and do it. *I am thinking.*" The kindness from her voice had disappeared, along with her patience.

"Sorry," he said after a moment, his voice clipped.

"It's alright."

They sat in silence. She welcomed it. Silence didn't judge. It didn't ask for anything. Didn't get angry. It just was.

The muscles in her face relaxed. The knot in her shoulders unraveled a tiny bit. She exhaled softly. During the late nights at Magdalena's, after the last partiers had gone, the last champagne had been sipped, and the last girl had completed her Rainbow Girl duty, Honey would lie awake in her bed. In the silence, in the dark, she would listen for the sounds that used to be in their home. Her mother laughing. Her father telling one of his many stories. In her mind, those sounds were trapped in the walls, trapped like she was, and if she only listened close enough in the silence she'd hear their voices, hear her freedom.

She still craved that freedom, even now. In the hallway, a door closed. Honey jumped; it pulled her from her memories. Opening her eyes, she focused on her current surroundings. Dawn was cautiously stirring outside of their window. She yawned.

"We should rest, Jonas."

Jonas clicked off the desk lamp curtly.

She'd hurt his feelings. "I'm sorry, Jonas. It's just that—"

"You needn't apologize."

The room fell silent again. Jonas shifted in the armchair. She knew it wasn't comfortable for him. He flipped his suit coat from the back of the chair and used it as a blanket. He probably wouldn't sleep; she, on the other hand, would try and Tilda was already snoring softly, dead weight in her arms.

Honey lifted Tilda from her lap and positioned her against the wall. She placed the ice pack on the rickety nightstand. She fought to fit into the sliver of space left on the twin bed and pulled the thin blanket to her chest. With her head laying on her hands for a pillow, she sighed deeply.

"Jonas," she said carefully.

"Yes."

"My sister is predictable even when her actions seem incredibly unpredictable. She's not going to turn down money. She can't afford to. That means there will be a Mysterie party Saturday night. As always."

"So—"

“So… We will be there.”

CHAPTER 40

With her crystal decanter in hand, Magdalena stumbled from her office and sank into the chair at the head of the dining-room table. Lifting the heavy vessel for a huge swig of its dwindling brandy, her bracelets jangled against one another as the brown liquid stung her lips. As she wiped her mouth with the back of her hand, she lost her grip; the weight of the decanter thundered with a single clap of applause, slamming into the table. She rubbed the spot where the two connected and found that the crystal had indented the wood. "What's another battle scar?" she shrugged and massaged her red, swollen knuckles before running her hand back down her arm to play with her bracelets.

She hadn't slept very well, if at all. Her dress from the evening still cloaked her. She hadn't bothered to change into bedclothes. She could feel last night's makeup crusted in her eyes. She blinked and blinked again. Even with the blaring brass symphony in her head, which was thankfully starting to fade with each sip of brandy, it was eerily quiet. Magdalena looked at her watch.

"Tilda!" she yelled. "Til—"

Moving her eyes toward the open portrait, she remembered. She rose, grabbed the bottle, her only friend, and yanked the cord abruptly to close the doors. "Miserable shits, you are. I hope you all die!" she yelled into the portrait and down to the sleeping girls below.

Magdalena tripped on her gown as she turned and walked to the foyer. "And you're all going to pay. After you die, you're going to pay." She paused a moment before continuing. "First thing, you're paying for the gown you made me trip on and rip," she said as she passed the balled-up rug. "And you're paying for the cleaning bill for my mother's rug." Then Magdalena leaned down, scooped up her pistol, and sneered, "Harlem, you horrid troublemaker. You're paying for more bullets."

The stairs were like quicksand as she trudged up them. Magdalena waved the gun toward the front door. "And all of you are paying for that glass window. That is going to be a hefty sum, I tell you." Magdalena passed Harlem's door, out of breath, and arrived at Fury's to unlock it. Fury was pacing.

"I'm hungry." Magdalena said.

"What?"

"I'm hungry. It's damn near eight o'clock. Make breakfast." Magdalena turned to walk away.

"Where's Tilda?"

Magdalena pulled one key off the key ring and threw it at Fury. "I need pancakes. Tell Amoura. She makes good ones. Hurry up."

"Where the hell is Tilda!?" Fury screamed.

Magdalena cradled the brandy under her arm and rubbed her neck, soothing the area where Harlem had choked her. She then lifted the gun and pointed it at Fury. "Don't make me shoot you too. Do you want me to shoot you? Because I will. Pancakes. Now."

Magdalena loved the power of a gun, even when empty. She didn't think herself to be a common gangster, but she marveled at the thought of how many people she had shot recently. They'd both been accidents, really. With Ruth, she had pulled the trigger, but hadn't thought she'd pulled it so hard as to shoot the woman. Sapphire, well, it was her own damn fault. She should have known by now not to mess with anyone holding a gun. "The irony," she said, smirking in her haze of thought. "You try to keep a household running, and you turn into Jesse James." As she made her way back down the stairs, she could hear Fury opening the doors of Amoura and Desire's rooms and the urgent whispers that followed. They had a lot more to worry about than Tilda's whereabouts.

Getting rid of Tilda had, perhaps, been more cathartic than she'd imagined it would. With Tilda gone, so too was her last tie to her immediate family.

It was also one less reminder of who she'd become. Yet, for the past several hours she'd been haunted by the image of the man who took her away. She knew nothing about him. Except that he was a Negro man in a hat who threw a roll of money at her—money that was now stuffed in her cleavage. The man was a ghost, a phantom. Magdalena sensed the man was nothing like Otto, but she had learned from experience that sometimes the nicer looking ones were worse. Otto. Honey. She rubbed her neck again. Her entire body hurt. And not just where she'd been kicked or strangled or entered or punctured with poison. The pain, of course, was her conscience, which she had mostly been able to ignore over these years, like an annoying rash that came and went. But an irritation was growing now, worse since Honey left. And now, Tilda... Tilda. The itch was becoming more persistent. Unmanageable. Uncle Mac's words were ringing in her ears again, *Can't run, can't hide. Can't exist.* The sting had mostly been in her knees before, but now it was starting to weave itself further into her. It was seeping in and spreading like an incurable disease. It was making her do things like drink the special tea—and want more and more of it. She needed to cut it all out. Now.

She stumbled into her office, steadied herself against the door jam, and surveyed the mess. "Heathens," she said. "Through and through." Magdalena stepped over piles of clothing and kicked a suitcase as she swallowed the last of her brandy. She set both the gun and the decanter on an empty space on her desk. The Budhai, askew from its normal position, caught her eye. "If they—"

Magdalena opened the Budhai. The check was still there. "Good," she said. She pulled the roll of money from her bosom, threw it in the Budhai, and closed it.

Straightening her back, she stood in the center of her office and massaged her temples; her head was spinning. A warbled growl emanated from her stomach. "Where are my pancakes!?" she yelled. Even the force of yelling was too much for her body. She steadied herself on the side of her desk. The portrait of her family loomed in front of her, leaning against her desk. Magdalena stood in front of it. She swore the reflection of her younger self was jeering at her. The innocent eyes didn't look so innocent. The pert mouth transformed into a snarled grimace. The thin fingers pointed at her accusingly. "Aw, shuddup!" she groaned at the portrait and hastily slid it back into the closet where it belonged. "What was I thinking?" she said as she kicked aside more junk and closed the closet door. Besides not being able to look at her former self, she couldn't take the fact that all those people, the only ones she knew as any kind of family, were all officially gone.

She'd been punished for what she was and what she wasn't. Brighton thought he could take her dignity by doing what he'd done to her, but much of that had vanished long ago. He'd called her so many names last night, each venomous word a lash trying to erase his weakness for liking a Negro woman. She'd laughed in his disgusting face. "*You're* the repulsive one," she'd said. "Your lack of self-control is astounding!"

So now, she had something on him. He thought he could manipulate her, fiddle with her mind, but it was his silly mind that was fucked. He'd have to live with his thoughts.

She hungered for more tea. A cigarette would have to do for now. Magdalena rummaged through her desk and found and lit one of her last. Her hands shook desperately as she sat on her desk and sucked the life out of it.

Her office was quiet. Too quiet. She slowly looked toward the birdcage. There was no squawking bird. It was dead. She blinked. *When had she fed it last?*

Smoldering ash fell into her lap. She gazed at it as it slowly burned a hole into her silver lamé. Her leg stung, but there was something about the burn that almost felt good. Something else fell into her lap. It was wet. She wiped her face. The last time this happened, where the tears fell freely, she was getting into a Ford with a strange man for the first time.

She spun around, grabbed the decanter from her desk, and threw it at the mantle. It shattered into pieces. With a sweeping arm, she hurled everything from her desk. She became a tempest of howls and guttural shrieks. She whipped about the room, swiping at lamps and chairs and curtains. Nothing in her path was spared. The storm raged on until she found herself spent, on the floor, amidst the mess she'd created.

Her door opened. Magdalena looked through the strands of hair that covered her eyes. "What do you want?"

"Your, your pancakes are ready," Amoura stammered.

Magdalena blinked, bringing herself back to her reality. She got herself to stand. With her arm, she moved her matted hair from her face, "Clean this up and get rid of that rotting bird," she rasped. "When you're through, we're going to the bank."

CHAPTER 41

moura wearily eyeballed the disaster that was now Magdalena's office. She stooped to pick up a pair of stockings which were hiding underneath a pile of papers and had been skewered by the overturned fireplace poker.

"What a mess," she sighed heavily. Everything had become a big mess, not just this room, which had become a tomb of their past, but everywhere in the Manor. Their escape in the foyer had been a chaotic disaster of a mess. Magdalena, surely pouring syrup on her pancakes by now, was disorderly and damn near unrecognizable. Downstairs, in the basement, Harlem was a battered and disheveled mess. Amoura had snuck down there while Magdalena had been up in here throwing her god-awful tantrum. Harlem had been sprawled on the cold concrete floor; probably in the same grotesque position she'd landed in when Magdalena hurled her down the stairs. Amoura had awkwardly dragged Harlem's uncooperative body over to the stage to make her as comfortable as possible. She'd checked on Sapphire next. That girl

---

was an even bigger mess. Someone had tied a makeshift tourniquet just above her thigh, which she tightened, but the dark red blood that covered Sapphire's cot said she needed the type of attention Amoura didn't know how to give. If that didn't get taken care of, Amoura feared things would get much, much worse.

Amoura wrung her hands in the stockings. Somebody was going to have to do something, and she figured that somebody was probably going to have to be her.

But what could she do?

She had given up fighting for herself long ago. She was powerless against Magdalena, but last night Harlem had taught her, shown her, that giving up was no longer an option. Harlem had pointed a gun at Magdalena and pulled the trigger. Harlem was willing to *kill* for herself and for all of them. What had Amoura done? Make pancakes?

She'd been a coward last night. She'd been an awful coward and a spineless friend. "I've got to make things right. Got to!"

Amoura pitched the stockings in the waste bin near the desk. She thought about the check. "It's gotta be here, somewhere," she said to herself. Amoura ran to the desk and looked in the drawers again; she felt along the underside of the table and touched something cold and solid. Amoura knelt. There, under the table, a gun was strapped plain as day. "My stars,"

Amoura said to herself as she pulled it from its hiding place and shot up to standing. Maybe this could be the thing. Maybe this gun was more powerful than the check could ever be right now. Amoura held the gun in her hands and pointed it at the closet door. She knew how to shoot; she didn't know if she could actually do it, but at least she knew how. *What am I doin'?* Amoura thought as her hands shook and she hid the gun inside the waistband of her dress. It was cold against her back. *You're doin' something, Amoura. And it's about damn time*, a voice inside her answered.

Amoura righted the armchairs that were toppled over like furniture in a doll's house. "Jiminy cricket!" Amoura huffed as she clapped her hands together angrily. Harlem had been right! So right. She and the Brown Betties should have left the Rainbow Girls and simply come back for them later. They'd be free right now. She would be free. She would be outside on the street thinking of something other than her own regret. Doing something other than cleaning up after a woman she despised. Feeling something other than divine guilt.

She grabbed an empty suitcase and bulldozed through the mess with it. She shoveled papers and clothes into it, sat on it, and snapped it closed before throwing it in the big closet. She swiftly flung the rest of the mess in behind it. She laughed sadly. These were the very things Tilda and the girls had so urgently rummaged through earlier; these things, remnants from a life to which none of them would truly return, hadn't mattered then and they clearly didn't matter now.

While bulldozing, she tip-toed around broken glass, careful not to pierce the soles of her thin shoes. She sniffed. "Somethin' smells off..." She looked around and remembered what Magdalena had barked at her.

Amoura walked toward the bird cage in the far corner. The cage, with its delicate wrought iron design that had been painted white, rested on a marble pedestal. As a result, it was as tall as she was.

"Poor thing," she said, holding a finger under her nose. The parrot's lifeless body lay awkwardly atop a pile of its own filth. The bird's glassy black eyes were cold and stared past her. A black tongue, hard and useless, extended from its beak, which was opened wide as though it may have squawked some final thoughts as it keeled over and died.

"Good gracious," she sighed as she noticed its food and water dishes were painfully empty.

Amoura retrieved the stockings from the waste basket along with some paper. She unhinged the squeaky door and reached in for the bird with the paper as her protective glove. Its body was rigid and hard beneath the lined sheets. With its wings, easily as wide as her hand, frozen tightly against its body, it was like a colorful war missile. Its many tail feathers were as long as her forearm. They bent repulsively against the thin bars of the cage as she wrestled the large bird from its small quarters. Amoura drew the bird closer to her; she was in awe of how, even in death, its feathers were still morbidly bright. She realized they contained at least one vivid hue for each of the Rainbow Girls wasting away downstairs, possibly awaiting a similar fate. "I'm sorry," she whispered as she gently wrapped the bird in paper and cocooned it with the silk stockings.

Amoura's jaw was set as she marched from the office with the dead bird. "This is the last thing that is going to suffer in this house. I swear to God!"

CHAPTER 42

In the darkness, Harlem rocked back and forth. She was churning a fire that moved deep inside her like lava, and she let it bubble up and explode from her throat in a vindictive scream. Searing pain shot through her in response. Coughs followed, spilling from her uncontrollably.

"Harlem!" someone said.

Harlem wheezed as she fought to catch her breath. Someone touched her shoulder. She flicked it away. "Get away from me," she whispered harshly.

"Harlem?"

"How dare you," she shouted, coughing again. "How dare you—caring for me *now*? You should have helped me up there! When she was beating me. You're too late!"

"We—"

"I can't stand to be near you," she rasped. "Get away from me."

Suddenly she was bathed in light.

"Breakfast!" Magdalena yelled at them from above, having flicked on the light. "Get up here now."

Harlem wanted to spit at the sound of Magdalena's voice. She pulled her knees tighter to her forehead, clutched her arms tightly around her legs, and screamed again instead.

"Harlem!" Violet kneeled in front of her. "We're so sorry."

"I hope you're happy with your new dresses," Harlem said, staring into Violet's bloodshot eyes.

Violet stood and turned from her, wiping her eyes on the hem of her dress.

"You needn't be so harsh, Harlem," Indigo said.

"No?" Harlem looked up at the girls who'd gathered on their hands and knees around her. Their faces recoiled at the sight of her, confirming that her face must have looked as bad as it felt.

"You're all cowards. Leave me alone." The huddle mass moved away from her silently. Harlem returned her head to her knees.

"Get up here, *NOW!*" Magdalena yelled again, her voice flinging daggers into them as she flicked the lights for their attention.

"I'm afraid to go up there. What's she going to do to us?" Violet cried.

"What if we just don't go?" Sienna said. "We're already in trouble."

"Won't matter if she does somethin' to us up there or down here," Indigo said quietly.

"C'mon girls. Let's get this over with," Ruby said as they filed upstairs, one by one, as commanded. "It'll be worse if we make her wait."

Alone in the cavernous speakeasy, Harlem slumped over into a puddle of nothingness. Her sobs echoed in the prison. Her cheek lay against the cool wood of the stage that harbored so much lust, spotlighted and disguised as entertainment. With her eyes so close to the illusion, she saw clearly that it was nothing more than old wood, scratches memorialized into it from high heels that had been forced to dance. Tears fell across a cut on the bridge of her nose and seeped into the stage. "I was so close," she sobbed. Harlem turned her gaze out to the chairs and tables resting in the graveyard before her. They were skeletons. They held no soul, no life. Harlem stared at them, but the longer she stared, the more she felt they were her jury. They were judging her, like the people of Greensboro had. They whispered, gossiped, mocked her:

You deserve this.

You brought this on yourself.

Worthless.

Failure.

Murderer!

This is exactly *where you belong.*

"It's not! It's not where I belong. Shut up! All of you!" Harlem rolled over and turned away from them, hoping to silence them with her backside. She pulverized the stage with her fists. "Just shut *up!*"

The coughing exploded again; while she waited for it to calm itself and with the chairs taunting her from behind, she stared at the red silk curtain in front of her that hung from the ceiling and covered the back wall. Its lush color could have been comforting to her, like a warm blanket. Instead, its folds stared back at her cold and unyielding, just like everything else. Harlem closed her eyes. Her mind was drowning with thoughts that had plenty of beginnings and no ends. She disappeared. She was back home, running through the tall grass. Grasshoppers leapt as high as her head, clearing the way for her. Little yellow butterflies flitted about her face. *'Harlem! Come inside, now.'* She ran into her large kitchen with its high ceilings and butcher block table where she used to sit alone to eat. George was sitting at the table alone reading a paper. He turned to her. His face vacant. He couldn't see her. She wasn't there. He didn't exist because the kitchen no longer existed. But his voice lingered, the words he'd said to her came back to her: *'And, even though there ain't no more physical home to call home, that this place is your home and I s'pose I'm kinda your only family now, if'n you ever wanted to b'lieve I was...'*

"What am I going to do, George?" she said aloud. Could she go back to Greensboro? She'd sold the home and the family assets. Where would she go? What could she do? She was without anything that belonged to her. Not even her strength. Not even—she sat up. Harlem shoved her hand into her pocket.

"Oh my God," she cried. "Oh my God!" she held the lipstick in her hand. She cradled it to her chest and sobbed in relief. "I still have this. I—I can try again."

Harlem heard a loud moan. She sniffed and ran her hand across her runny nose as she painfully hoisted herself up on her sore elbow.

"Help. Help me."

"Hello?" Harlem called out. She swiped at her tears.

"Help me..."

Harlem returned the lipstick to her pocket and lifted herself slowly. She stepped from the stage toward the voice. It was coming from Sapphire's room. Using tables and chairs as her crutches, she worked her way through the room.

"Sapphire," Harlem froze in the doorway.

"I need a doctor," Sapphire said. Her dress was soaked with blood that had turned black. Her face was pale, voice weak.

"I—where are you hurt...? What, what... can I do?" Harlem faltered. She stepped away from the girl; she absently rubbed her foot on her leg, reminded of stepping in the blood that had pooled around Roy's body. Harlem wanted to run from the room. Run from what felt like death. One she hadn't wished for, but may have caused. Again.

"Please help me."

"Harlem!" Magdalena's voice jolted them both. "You are not exempt, you silly cow! Get up here now! Or I will come down there and get you."

Harlem paused, looking toward the stairs and back into Sapphire's frightened eyes. "Sapphire, I'll get help. I promise."

CHAPTER 43

Harlem clenched the side of Magdalena's portrait as she steadied herself and labored through the opening into the dining room. When Amoura's eyes landed upon Harlem's emerging form, she gasped as her hand flew to her mouth. Harlem looked her straight in her southern-belle eyes until she looked away. Harlem had no time or space for pity. But blame was another thing entirely, and she shot Amoura full of syringes loaded with it. Desire and Fury, seated next to Amoura, weren't excused. They got pricked with the same and looked down at their laps in unison.

"Sapphire needs a doctor," Harlem said from the doorway.

"It is so good of you to be concerned about your fellow deserters," Magdalena said with irony, shoveling food into her mouth. "But I don't give a damn about that stupid girl down there."

"You're just going to let her bleed to death?"

"I'll look to her when I'm ready."

"She needs a doctor!"

"*You* don't tell ME what to do. Sit down and shut up!" Magdalena roared.

Harlem moved like a hunchback to the opposite end of the table. Her body ached with soreness in so many places; she felt as though she'd done a million calisthenics and walked a thousand miles. She passed by the silent girls. Their heads were bent low and seemed to drip with guilt pulled up from the dirty pools of it welling inside them. She couldn't look at any of them. They all knew they were responsible. For Sapphire. For her. She lowered herself into the chair; her insides howled and she tried to suppress her coughing.

"I thought you might be hungry, Harlem. It has been a while since you've eaten anything."

Harlem glanced at the empty plates in front of each girl. Their plates were clean; it didn't look like they'd seen so much as a crumb. Her plate had a pancake on it. She was so hungry she was almost beyond it. The girls stared at her.

Harlem pushed the plate away and stared back at them. "I'm not hungry."

"Uh-huh. Suit yourself," Magdalena said as she rose and snatched the plate from Harlem. Magdalena returned to her seat. "Syrup." No one moved. "*Syrup*," she repeated with a growl.

Sienna passed the syrup. "Smart girl," Magdalena said.

Magdalena's cutlery scraped against her plate as she sopped up the syrup with the solitary pancake and shoved it in her mouth. She chewed greedily with her mouth open. The sound of Magdalena smacking her food filled every inch of the silent room. Harlem cringed and glared sideways at the hag opposite her. Magdalena had morphed into a witch who was shrouded in tattered glamour. Her face was drawn and pale. Her hair needed a comb. Her battle scars, bruises and choke marks around her neck, exhibited themselves clearly. Gone was the seemingly sophisticated woman who had greeted her that fateful day Harlem arrived at the Manor.

"Pathetic," Harlem whispered to herself.

Magdalena looked at her with eyes blazing. "Did you say something?"

"No," Harlem held her ground.

"You better not have," Magdalena leaned back in her chair, keeping her eyes locked with Harlem as she wiped her mouth with a cloth napkin. "I wanted to commend you all on a job *almost* well done last night. Bravo."

The girls hung their heads in silence. Harlem did not.

"I suppose that if I were you, I would try the same thing. What a pity. I can only imagine how it feels to be so incredibly unsuccessful. I've been thinking about what type of punishment you deserve." Magdalena pulled something from under her. Something she had been sitting on. It was some sort of a book. Magdalena placed it in front of her for all to see and smirked at Harlem. It was her mother's journal.

"That is not yours." Harlem wanted to spring to the table like a tiger and swipe the grin off Magdalena's face.

Magdalena laughed, menacing her. "Aren't we a family here? Aren't we here to love one another—just like family?"

Harlem continued to sneer at Magdalena. "I said, *that is not yours.*"

Magdalena put her elbows on the table and looked at Sienna. "You. You're sitting next to your sister."

Sienna looked blankly at Indigo. "Her?"

"Yes, her. She's your sister."

"But we aren't actually sisters," Sienna said flatly.

"Pretend, goddammit!"

"Alright," Sienna said quietly, taking Indigo's hand in hers. Harlem could see Sienna's hands shaking.

"Aren't we supposed to take care of each other? Of course, sometimes family lets you down. Family turns a cheek and does nothing to help you. Does nothing to take care of you," Magdalena stared at her. "Right, Harlem?"

Harlem stood. Her ears were ringing. The coffin box with her bad memories flew open.

"Don't I take care of you?"

Harlem trembled. "You know nothing about taking care of anyone. Not even yourself. You don't have the will in you to—"

"I have the will to live. Unlike your mother."

"Don't you dare talk about my mother."

"*I* have a spine. Unlike your mother."

"You shut your mouth."

Magdalena read from the journal, "*It is happening again. Right now—*"

"Stop it," Harlem whispered.

Magdalena continued reading, "*I sit here. In the shadows. Disgusted.*"

"Stop it..."

"*I am the vile one. It is me. It is me.*" Magdalena looked at her. "June 12th, 1944. Just about a year ago today."

"I said STOP IT!" Harlem couldn't contain herself.

"Girls, I don't know if you've caught on to all that I've just read about the little girl sitting before you. Get a good look at her. You're looking at a real hero."

"Leave her alone," Fury said.

"And you all think I'm so bad. I'm a saint compared to her mother."

"*You* have willingly given me to the devil, just like my mother!"

"There's no devil here, only paying customers. There is a difference between what goes on here and what went on in your perfect home tucked away in the... the... how did Susannah write it? The 'arms of the willow trees'? So don't ever compare me to your darling, depraved, weak, mother."

Harlem gripped the table. The coffin box was pulling her inside it. She was slipping. Back to North Carolina. Back to her home darkened by deceit. She could see her mother walking down the hallway again, on her way to the bathroom. The gun in her hand still glistening in the moonlight. "No!" she cried, grabbing her head, not realizing the words had escaped from her mouth.

"'No' what? I don't know who you think you are, but this is still my Manor. I run this place. Not you. I do the talking here. *Not you.* You don't seem to realize that I can do anything I want."

"No!" Harlem cried again. She was slipping.

"If I want to shoot someone, *poof*, done. Shot. If I want someone to go away, *poof*, done. Gone. Don't forget that if I want to get rid of any of you, I will. Tilda is gone. I threw her out the front door like a sack of garbage. *Poof.*"

They all gasped. "What?" Sienna said.

"You needn't all be so artificially concerned. She was paid for, handsomely. Just like Honey."

"You sold her?" Amoura whispered.

"I know, it *is* surprising that someone would want a stupid girl like her, but yes. I sold her."

"No..." Harlem whispered again. She felt hot. But her hands, her hands were damp. She clutched at her dress. She looked out at the girls. She felt sickened

—

397

that they'd probably had mothers and fathers who tucked them in at night and sang them silly lullabies. Sickened that they were cared for and loved with love meant for children. Harlem shook her head. 'No.' She heard herself speak from within. '*No!*' She wasn't going to spiral to that place. That place was dead to her. Dead. That part of her needed to be dead. '*No!*' She didn't care about things like that. Love and such. Did not care. She ran her fingers through her hair, her tingly scalp, and pulled herself from the memory of that night when she became an orphan and all the helpless nights that led up to it. "No!" she screamed and fell to her chair. "NO!" She pulled herself from that place that kept her lying on the fur jacket in the dance room for so many days without moving.

"I said, NO!" Harlem lifted her head and placed her hands on the table. "I'm not going to that place. You can't make me. I won't go." She stood. A new strength powered through her. "You tell me. You tell me *right now* what you want from us. What do you want from us? What!?"

"What do I want?" Magdalena stood and threw her plate against the wall. "I want some goddamn RESPECT!"

"Respect is earned!" Harlem yelled.

"Shut up!"

"I won't! I won't shut up! What are you going to do with us? Are you going to keep us rotting here while you turn into an old, miserable hag? Are you going to sell us all off to the creeps of the world or are you going to kill us all? What!?"

Magdalena leaned onto the table. Thick veins bulged from her neck. "Before Honey and Tilda left, when we were a complete family, you all were like the twelve disciples and I, I was like Jesus," she raised her arms wide. Her head was thrown back, possessed. "Jesus! I liked it better that way, and now you are a bunch of infidels. A rotten, horrible, table full of Judases!" Magdalena pounded her fists on the table, and the table shook. Her voice boomed, "You work for me! For ME! I sacrifice for you each and every day and I want some respect! You *will* respect me!"

Magdalena began throwing the remaining dishes off the table. The girls jumped away from the table, screaming and ducking to avoid being hit. "This is your doing. YOU alone are going to pay for this, you hear me?"

They all looked toward Harlem. Harlem gripped the lipstick in her pocket. "I won't take this anymore. I'll do it again. And again. Until I get out of here."

Magdalena threw a fork at her. "I don't give a flying fig what you do, because you know what? You're going to pay! Do you know how?" Magdalena walked toward Amoura and pulled her head back, grabbing a hold of her chin.

Amoura whimpered, "Please... please, stop."

"Amoura is going to go to the bank with me. She is going to pretend that she is *you*, and I'm going to take your money. Your mother's guilt money. All of it. And then I'm going to sell all of you to Lucinda. And I can assure you she will NOT be anywhere near as kind as I have been."

Harlem looked at Amoura, who stared back at her, frightened. "I don't care," Harlem said, sitting. She slammed a nail into the coffin box.

"Maybe you'll care that thanks to you, Harlem Markeson, the *crème de la crème* just got creamier." Magdalena threw Amoura aside and she fell to the floor. Snatching Desire and Fury by the collars, Magdalena said, "You girls will be delivering on promises. You'll get to see how your Rainbow Girl sisters have been living. Tomorrow night you're all paying bidders in the same goddamned way."

"What the hell does that mean?" Fury said, jerking herself free of Magdalena's clutches.

"The Brown Betties are over."

"Over?" Amoura said.

"What about 'New Girl In'? And I was going to be a Bettie..." Sienna said.

"No longer relevant, sweetie pie. You're back to being a color and that rich girl over there will be in the red dress again. That's what you get for betraying me." Magdalena grabbed Susannah's journal and pointed at Harlem with it. "And you all have that mastermind right there to thank for it."

Harlem stood slowly. "Do you think I'm going to feel guilty? Do you think I'm going to cry? Crumble on the ground and ask you for forgiveness? You can't hurt me anymore, Magdalena. You can't do anything else to me or make me do anything more that's humiliating or leaves me feeling like less of a human being. You can't win. You won't win. Rainbow Girl or Brown Bettie. What does it matter? I've already done it all," Harlem laughed.

She sidestepped from the table and labored toward the portrait, ready for whatever was coming next for her. She paused, looking once more at Magdalena. "You're such a very, very sad woman. I feel sorry for you."

CHAPTER 44

Jonas used the side of the bed to push himself to his feet. His knees cracked as he rose from the floor and flicked the light switch on the wall. Dusk was settling in and with only one window, their hotel room was becoming crowded with shadows.

"Honey, you're certain there is no sort of exit in the basement? Perhaps a door or chute that was used for coal?" Jonas asked.

Honey sat cross-legged on the bed and was hunched over the makeshift map of Magdalena's Manor, which they'd drawn on the paper bag from the corner store. "Not as far as I remember."

"I'd imagine it could be possible," Jonas said as he stretched himself tall and then returned to crouching on the floor at the bed's side. "Homes had to get their fuel somehow."

"Perhaps there's something," Honey said and rubbed Tilda's back. She was hunched on the bed next to Honey. "What do you think, Tilda?"

Tilda reached for the wall and tapped.

"Yes. It is a big, strong vault," Honey said. Tilda returned to leaning over the map, pointing at their drawn squares. "Even if there was something, a chute or whatever, it would be boarded up, Jonas. Just like all of the windows. You can't really get in or out except for the front door."

They had been thinking over a plan for hours. They were to attend Magdalena's Mysterie party tomorrow with the intent of rescuing the Brown Betties and the Rainbow Girls. Jonas was beginning to worry how they were going to pull off such a feat; it would not only mean plucking a bunch of girls from Magdalena's clutches, but also caring for and escorting them to safety afterwards. When he'd started off from Greensboro just five days ago, he hadn't anticipated a coup when he'd envisioned finding Arnetta. Not at all. He rubbed his forehead in his hands. A headache was knocking, and he was trying not to answer.

Jonas glanced over to Tilda. "Tilda, when was the —" Jonas caught his breath. He couldn't believe what he was seeing. "Where did you get that?" He reached for the necklace dangling from Tilda's neck. Jonas stared at Honey.

"What is it?" Honey leaned forward to see what Jonas was looking at. "Oh my," she said, leaning back.

"That necklace," Jonas's hands were shaking. "It's Arnetta's."

Tilda looked at Honey, frightened, "Please, Tilda. It belongs to his daughter."

Tilda gently removed the necklace and handed it to Jonas.

"Where did you get it?"

Tilda shook her head and pointed to Honey.

"You?" he said.

"I found it in the closet, with all of the girls' things... I... I'm sorry, Jonas, I didn't know what to say before. At the diner. I wasn't sure who or what you were. Are..." Honey said.

"You lied to me. You should have told me. You said, you asked me if I had any *evidence* that she was there. You let me continue to wonder if she'd been there and you've known all along that she has. *You knew!*"

"Jonas, try to understand," Honey rose from the bed.

"Get away from me. You aren't who you say you are."

"I was afraid. I... I," Honey looked at Tilda.

"You have no idea how this feels," Jonas whispered, standing and gazing at the only thing he had left of his daughter. He traced the outline of the 'A' with his fingers. "You have no idea!" he wailed. "I miss her. I—I want her back." He looked back at Honey. He felt like he was drowning. Like he had stepped off his front porch in Ohio and plunged into a deep, dark well.

"Jonas," she said softly. "I'm sorry."

He couldn't hold it in any longer. Sobs poured out of him, from places he didn't know they'd been trapped. He fell forward; his knees seemed to have vanished.

Honey and Tilda rushed to him. "You're going to be okay, Jonas. We'll find her."

Jonas pushed them away. "Leave me be. Just leave me be!"

CHAPTER 45

Desire sat in her chair and shuffled her shoes noisily along the wood floor.

"Desire, you're driving me mad with all that scraping. Please stop," Fury said, pacing back and forth on the stage.

"Sorry," Desire said.

Amoura had gathered the Brown Betties and the Rainbow Girls into what she called an emergency council meeting. They'd pulled their chairs into a circle in front of the stage and held a forum. They'd been like this for what seemed an eternity already and there'd been a whole lot of nothing accomplished except a new pile of confusion.

"Girls, I've got something to show you that I think will help us," Amoura said. She retrieved Magdalena's gun from under the stage where she'd hidden it and showed it to them all.

"A gun?" Sienna said, with eyes wide.

Ruby leapt up, hurried to Amoura, and swooped the gun from her lap. Admiring it, she said, "Where'd ya get this bean shooter?" Ruby breathed on the tiny gun and polished the dull silver barrel with the edge of her silk shorts. "Looks like an old Derringer. If we're gonna use this buster, you get one shot, so you'd better be good."

"How do you know so much about guns, Ruby?" Fury asked.

"Let's just say I been around the block, and the block has got some dark corners with dark people lurking in them. Where'd you nab this honey piece from?"

"It's Magdalena's," Amoura said. "It was in her office."

Ruby whistled and handed the gun back to Amoura. "Holy moly. You're a brave one. What happens when she finds out it's gone? Then we're all dead!"

"That's why we've got to come up with a plan," Amoura said.

"That ain't the only reason," Desire chimed in. She was seated in one of the chairs holding onto her knees and rocking back and forth. "Magdalena said the Brown Betties are over. What are we going to do?"

"Desire, you've asked that five times already. Can't you see we're trying to figure that out!" Fury shouted.

Amoura turned toward Fury. "Keep your voice down, Fury. Shouting isn't going to solve anything." Amoura faced the girls. "Does anyone have any concrete ideas for what we can do to save ourselves?"

"Harlem, do you think we could try to run for it again?" Desire said, turning to her where she sat off in the corner on the floor.

Harlem shrugged. Her eyes were empty.

"Let her be," Violet said softly. "She hasn't been the same since the fight. She needs some time—"

"We don't have any time," Desire said just as softly.

Amoura leaned in. "Even if we only have one shot with this gun, we need to use it."

"Sure, that's the ticket. We've seen what guns do," Emerald said, rising from her chair to check on Sapphire. As soon as Magdalena had banished everyone to the basement, they had pulled Sapphire's bed from her room so that she could get some fresh air. They didn't know what else to do for her. Fury had the most experience with medical care since she had taken care of her horses back in Kentucky. Desire had stood back and watched as the girls found some rags and sanitary napkins to hold the bleeding at bay; that seemed to work okay, and she wasn't bleeding too, too much. Fury stitched her up with a real needle and thread. She didn't know if it was the right thing to do or not, but she sure did it. Desire had never seen that type of thing before. So much blood and the bullet had torn through the skin like nothin'. It had left a cratered trail of burnt flesh that had made Desire's stomach turn.

"Do you all think Lucinda will move us to somewhere else or do you think we'll stay here?" Desire asked aloud, turning away from Sapphire.

"Don't you see that we need to be on the move before that even happens?" Fury said, scratching away at some dried blood on her dress.

As one of nine children, Desire had witnessed many family council meetings. She liked the one they'd had about their future pet the best. Deciding what type to get and what to name it. The one when they'd had to move to a new apartment with only two bedrooms was bad. Deciding who was going to sleep with whom, in what bed, and in what room. It was a mess. In the end, they all drew straws. The longest and quietest meeting was when their cousin got caught up in running numbers and the family had to decide how they were going to get him safely out of Chicago and off to Milwaukee. Desire was the third youngest of the kids and often kept her mouth shut, or was told to do so if she didn't. This council meeting was different.

"What if we just don't dance? What if we stand there and don't move or do nothin'?" Desire asked, holding her stomach. "What if we scream out to everyone that we want to leave and that we are prisoners here and that this is all wrong?"

"Yeah, and what if nobody cares?" Ruby said, rolling her head about her neck.

Violet added, "She's right. People want this to go on. They want the opportunity to do this. To be with us. Why else would they come here?"

"Maybe at the bank," Desire said and turned toward Amoura. "Maybe at the bank, instead of you trying to run away, like we thought about—"

Fury interrupted her. "Don't go back to the bank idea, Desire. We can't get help there."

"But we could, Fury. Don't be so quick to shoot down all my ideas! Amoura, instead of you trying to run away, maybe you could tell someone. There are security people there. Maybe you could drop someone a secret note and someone there could help us." Desire kneeled by Amoura's chair.

"I don't know, maybe. This is happenin' so fast. I'd have to know what to say. Magdalena's bound to be shouting for me soon. What d' you think, girls?"

"I think they'll think you're a crackpot. I'm startin' to wonder why anyone would help us. Maybe that's why we been here so long," Sienna said.

Amoura leaned over and whispered in Desire's ear, "I'll try, I promise."

Topaz got up out of her chair and kneeled next to Emerald who was holding Sapphire's hand. "Gals, we've got to help ourselves."

"Are you even capable of it?" Harlem said. Her voice sounded mean and sharp like the edge of broken glass. Desire didn't blame her. She'd be mad too if she were Harlem. Desire had cowered by the wall last night when it had been time to really do something to get out. She didn't know what had come over her; she'd felt like her feet were cemented to the floor. And even when Magdalena was beating up on Harlem, she hadn't moved. She'd never felt so scared. If she had done something, maybe she'd have been shot too, just like Sapphire. And now, here they all were... no closer to anything being better. In fact, everything was closer to getting a lot worse.

Desire stood and faced her. "Harlem, I'm sorry I didn't help you. I'm real sorry, and I hope that you can forgive me. It won't happen again."

Harlem waved her away, coughed, and put her head in her hands. "The show must go on. I'm running the first chance I get. You all can do whatever the hell you want. In the meantime, I need to learn this dance and look like everything is normal until then." Harlem raised her head. She looked horrible. "Which one of you can teach me this dance?"

Amoura said, "Harlem, you can barely stand up; how are you going to dance tonight?"

"I'll find a way. I always do," Harlem said, standing.

"I can't do what you all do. I can't. It ain't fair," Desire said, biting her fingernails.

"All of a sudden you're concerned about what's fair?" Indigo asked, crossing her arms.

"Rainbow Girls been doin' all the work while you Betties sit back drinking champagne, and now that it's your turn, you want to say 'it ain't fair'?" Ruby said, flicking a cigarette butt and blowing her smoke angrily.

"That's not what I meant. It's just that that's the way it was, and that's how it has been, and—"

"I am just about tired of you," Indigo said.

Desire wrapped her fingers at the base of her neck, "It's just that, I'm—I'm..."

Topaz floundered to the floor and leaned against Sapphire's bed. "Too good for this?"

Desire took in their horrible accusations; she shook her head. "I... I ain't never been with no man."

"Never?" Violet sat up from the stage where she'd been lying down.

"How is that possible?" Ruby lit another cigarette.

"Well, I never had a boyfriend. No room or time for that. And my daddy woulda killed me. And then, for a long while, I lived as a boy on the streets. Then when I got here, I was immediately a Brown Bettie... and well, I just never been with a man in that way."

"My first time was here, and I don't wish that on nobody," Violet said, crossing her legs.

"You see, I can't do it. I can't. It just ain't fair on top of everything else. I can't!" Desire cried.

CHAPTER 46

R uth pulled herself up the last concrete step. With no real money for a taxi, she and Mary had walked the past twenty blocks from the bus station this morning. Her feet were on fire and thanks to the late-morning summer heat, her dress was wet in more places than it was dry. Her chest felt like it was being squeezed by the snake that coiled on Magdalena's front door handle and she leaned on the brownstone banister to let out a cough to ease the python grip. Her head felt a little feathery, like she wanted to faint. It wasn't the walking that was making her feel weak. It was what was pulsing and growing beneath the bandage on her hand.

She peeled back the dirty gauze from her hand. *"Oh..."*

An electric jolt singed her stomach; she was scared. Her hand had swollen to nearly twice the usual size and the colors she saw swirling on her palm didn't belong there. She looked closer to where the bullet had gone through; it looked black with mold. The doctor who stitched up the hole in her hand was one they'd found in the attic of a low-rent boarding house near 110th Street, and was little more than a backyard vet; he had hacked into her palm like she was an animal. And with nothing to really help the pain except some cheap whiskey, she had screamed and writhed about like one the whole time. He'd been recommended to them because he was supposedly good at "helping women." By the way her hand looked, he couldn't have been good at anything, let alone cutting out women's problems. She retightened the dirty bandage around her freakish wound and coughed again.

"Sister, are you alright?" Mary asked, her hand holding Ruth's elbow.

"Fine, fine. Just catching my breath is all."

Ruth heard a scoff behind her.

"You don't look fine."

Ruth turned and looked behind her at their new conquest; the girl looked worse than the New Jersey gutter they pulled her from and was one to talk.

"You 'bout the size of my great aunt. That heifer keeled over from a heart'tack when she was 'bout fifty-five. You might want t' get yourself in some better shape."

Ruth gave the girl a look. "I appreciate your concern, Emma Sue." She turned away from her and knocked on Magdalena's door and then rang the bell.

"You are going to love Magdalena's Manor, Emma Sue," Mary droned. Mary had lost all enthusiasm for the girl, just as Ruth had.

"You sure they got hot food up in there?" Emma Sue said.

"Yes, plenty of hot food," Mary answered.

"This place don't look like they got nothin' good; looks like they got a whole 'lotta nothin' up in there. I been around and I can tell."

"We appreciate your astuteness," Ruth said as she watched the girl pull a bobby pin from her rat's nest of a hairdo and pick at her teeth with it.

"A-tuteness better be sumpin' good or have sumpin' to do with food, I'll tell you that much, yessiree."

Ruth glanced at Mary who was rolling her eyes. Although they'd both had second, third, and fourth thoughts about this girl, they'd decided that they had run out of time for thinking. Ruth sucked her teeth, turned back to the door, and rang again.

The door swung open. Magdalena stood before them.

"Good Lord Jesus," Ruth said before she could catch herself. She looked back at Mary to make sure Mary was seeing what she was seeing. Mary's mouth was gaped wide open.

"See, I told you ain't nothing good up in here. Who she?" Emma Sue said crossing her arms. "You that *Lady* Magdalena they been talkin' so much 'bout? You don't look like no lady. You look like a mess. You been in a fight or somethin'?"

"Sisters," Magdalena said, smoothing her hair at her temples and glaring at Ruth. "How *surprising* to see you."

"We brought you a new tenant," Ruth said, glaring right back, yet quite surprised by the smattering of bruises on her neck and face. Ruth peered past Magdalena and into the home. Something in that house was awry and Ruth wasn't sure she wanted to dip into any danger right now. Ruth turned and looked back at Mary again. Mary looked like a frightened bird, just like she always did. Ruth sighed; if something was going to happen here, it was going to be up to her, as usual. Ruth wanted what was due to her and that desire burned greater than any fear. She stepped forward. "Perhaps we could come in."

Magdalena looked over her own shoulder and into the dark Manor. "Could you wait just a moment?"

Ruth jumped as the door slammed loudly in their faces. She exhaled. "Sister, can I speak with you a moment? Emma Sue, please stay here."

"Y'all better hurry up," Emma Sue said as she shifted in her shoes. "I gots to use the facilities and it ain't for number one or number two, but number three."

"Number three?" Mary said.

"Y'all two prol'ly too old to get 'number three' anymore, but I am a young woman and I still get it. And thankfully so, this month."

"Oh," Mary said.

Ruth cradled her hand and walked past the girl. A grimace stretched across her face. "'*Number three.*' For heaven's sake."

At the bottom of the stairs, Ruth grabbed hold of Mary's arm. "Mary—"

"I do not have a good feeling about this, Ruth," Mary said, clutching both of their suitcases. "This horrible new girl. Now Magdalena? I almost didn't recognize her. This is a big mistake. Big."

"Mary," Ruth tried again.

"And my good gracious. With this girl, this is the thirteenth trip. Thirteenth! I didn't realize it 'til now because it's been the shortest of the trips. Ruth—?"

"Mary—"

"We should just go back to Greensboro and count our many, many losses and—"

"Mary—Mary!" Ruth put her finger to Mary's mouth to shut her up. "Mary, I agree. I think this is a big mistake. You're right. But we need that money. We *need* that girl's check. How will we get home otherwise?"

Mary dropped her head. "You're right. I know you're right, but I don't want you to be right, sister. I don't want to go in there."

"We get in there, we tie her up, and we find that check and get out. Got it?"

"Do you still think that's a good idea, sister? We've been so peaceful in the past. This is escalating terribly fast. I don't know that I can."

Ruth held up her hand. "If I don't get real help soon, you might become an only child, Mary."

Mary nodded reluctantly. "I understand. Yes, sister. Yes. I can do it."

"Hey, I need the facilities, lady!" They both turned to see Emma Sue now banging on the door.

Ruth dropped her head in her hand. "Oh dear Lord..."

The door swung open.

Magdalena had changed into an orange silk gown that looked like she'd picked it up off the floor rather than from a hanger. "Please, do come in." She swept her arm ceremoniously, like she did every time with a new girl, but her face was stone cold. Emma Sue stampeded past Magdalena, almost knocking her and the plate of biscuits she carried over.

"Where's the facilities?" Emma Sue cried out.

"Off the kitchen," Magdalena answered, annoyed. The girl ran off as directed.

Ruth clutched for Mary's arm and they reached the top of the stairs. Ruth looked into Magdalena's bloodshot eyes; something was missing from them. Ruth figured that whatever it was, it might help her get her money back. "You're looking just as lovely as ever, Magdalena."

"*Lady* Magdalena, and I told you I never wanted to see you again. What the hell are you doing here?" Magdalena said.

"We have unfinished business, madam." Ruth said as she brushed past Magdalena while suppressing another cough. "Time to pay up. For real this time."

CHAPTER 47

Mary carried their suitcases and followed Ruth, who followed Magdalena into the Manor. As they passed through the foyer and into the dining room, Ruth motioned for Mary to pull the purple curtains closed and to draw the sliding doors, which she did.

"Wherever is little Tilda?" Mary asked, picking up just one of the suitcases and leaving the other by the sliding doors.

"Sold," Magdalena said.

"Sold?" Emma Sue said coming from the kitchen and wiping her hands on her dirty dress.

"Ah, Yes. She's out selling; she makes little trinkets and goes out to sell them. She's sold most of her things—why we say, 'sold.'" Magdalena waved her hand and led them through to her office. "Mary and Ruth, wait in my office. Emma Sue, please help yourself to some biscuits here. I'll be right back with some tea."

"Tea and biscuits?" Emma Sue said, staring at the plate on the table.

"Just formalities, dear," Ruth said.

Emma Sue plopped onto a chair, pulled her carpet bag of a purse onto the table, and put her head on it. "I do not need any more of them formalities. I'll tell you that much, yessiree. I need some real food."

Mary scanned the dining room. "*Sister*," she whispered, "is that... syrup on the wall there?" Mary pointed to the wall and picked up a bit of a broken white plate from the floor. "Whatever could have been going on here?"

"Magdalena is a volatile witch. Anything could have happened, Mary. Let's stay focused."

"And Tilda, *sold?* This is all very strange—"

Mary stopped as she entered Magdalena's office. It looked like a classroom of children had camped there and had their way with it. "What's happened here?"

Magdalena entered the office behind them and closed the door. She carried a cup of tea. "Quite a bit has happened, Mary. With some warning, perhaps I could have hired five maids and had this place cleaned to your liking. But since neither of you has any couth whatsoever, this is where we are. Please sit."

"Magdalena, are you alright?" Mary asked.

"Won't you please sit," Magdalena ignored the question and sipped the tea, looking at her watch. "I have an appointment I must keep, and I do have a Mysterie party to prepare for this evening, as you know."

"You don't look anywhere near being ready for company," Mary said. "Is that *tea* you're drinking? You never drink tea."

"I have a sore throat. Is that alright with you, Mary?"

"Mary, will you hand me my suitcase? Please," Ruth said from her chair.

Mary absentmindedly handed the suitcase to Ruth, who yanked it from her hands. "Sister, you needn't be so gruff," Mary startled, blinking at Ruth, who scowled at her. Mary remembered what they were there to do. Tie Magdalena up, get the money, and get out.

Mary walked around to Magdalena's side of the large desk.

"Mary, I've asked you to sit," Magdalena said.

"No time for sittin'," Mary replied, rushing toward Magdalena and holding her tight in the chair while Ruth came around with the large rope they'd found near a garbage can in an alley.

"Are you out of your mind?" Magdalena squirmed.

"Very much in it," Ruth said, tying her up clumsily. "Now, I want my money."

"This is absolutely asinine!" Magdalena flung her arms wildly, pushing both of them away and yanking the rope off of her. Mary kept her footing, but Ruth tripped over the rope and fell. Magdalena scoffed at the rope that was meant to hold her captive, now entangling Ruth's feet.

Ruth howled in pain.

"Sister, are you alright?" Mary ran to Ruth.

"No! I'm not alright," Ruth cried from the floor as she rocked back and forth with her hand. "I want my money!"

Magdalena stood. "Why didn't you just ask for it, you idiots!"

"We have asked, Magdalena," Mary said. "You've made us squabble and beg and beg again. And now, look at my sister. Look at her. She has been butchered by a two-bit doctor because we didn't have any money to get her cared for properly. We have slept on park benches and been thrown from Union Station benches as though we were mere vagrants. *We have eaten out of garbage cans!* My mother was the lead of her cotillion and look at what you've reduced us to! A pile of slop. Give us our money!" Mary wailed.

"Oh for goodness' sake, stop your whining. Here's your stupid money," Magdalena pulled a roll of money from the Budhai and threw it at them.

Mary crawled on all fours and scooped up the bills from the carpet, handing them to Ruth. "Here you are, sister."

Ruth held the money. "This isn't anywhere near our regular rate."

"That is what was paid for Tilda, and that is what I have."

"What about Harlem's check? Where is that?" Ruth said. She tried to stand.

Mary hurried to her sister and guided her back to the floor gently. "Sister? I'm worried. How do you feel?"

"I'm alright, Mary." Ruth turned to Magdalena. "The check?"

"It has been stolen. You see how things look here. Someone, probably an old client, beat me up, robbed me, and stole the check. It has been a true, true ordeal. So, you see, you aren't the only ones who have been inconvenienced." Magdalena rubbed her neck dramatically and pitched more tea down her throat.

"When did this happen?" Ruth asked suspiciously.

"Only just last night, really."

Mary peered at Ruth. The color had drained from her face. "Sister...?"

"Ruth, dear. You don't look well at all."

"At no thanks to you!" Mary said.

"I'm fine, Mary," Ruth said, leaning to one side. "Just a little woozy is all. Probably need a good rest to heal from this wound."

"Well," Magdalena shrugged her shoulders and downed the rest of her tea, "stealing is wrong, you know. And there are consequences, for which I am only somewhat sorry, of course."

"Now *that* was a feeble apology to my sister, Magdalena."

"When was Tilda sold?" Ruth continued. "Help me up, Mary."

Mary held onto her sister's meaty arm and got Ruth standing successfully before depositing her into an armchair. She straightened her hat and smoothed her dress and made a mental note that when they got back home, her sister was going to be put on a strict diet.

"Tilda? Last night as well. You know what, Ruth, I hadn't thought about it until now, but maybe the same *putz* who came for Tilda is the same who robbed me." Magdalena laid her head against the back of her chair and closed her eyes.

Mary looked at Magdalena. "Are you drunk in the middle of the day?"

Magdalena kept her eyes closed and shook her head slowly.

"Then I suppose we will have to stay here for tonight's party and collect from your earnings, Magdalena. We are not leaving without the full amount," Ruth said and coughed.

"That's right," Mary said, placing her palm on Ruth's forehead to check her temperature. Ruth nudged her hand away.

"Mmm, I don't know," Magdalena murmured. "I don't know that it's such a good... good idea, given your condition, Ruth. What will the guests... think? We can't have you sweating and falling all over everyone—"

Suddenly the door sprung open. "Theth bithcuits are hard as rocks," Emma Sue slurred. "I need me some more buttah…" Emma Sue pitched forward and toppled over one of the chairs to the ground.

Magdalena sprung forward in her chair. "What in the hell?"

Mary stared at the girl on the floor. She had landed face-first and her dress had flung up around her buttocks. "She is not wearing a slip!" Mary said.

"Are you surprised? Wherever did you find this oaf?" Magdalena said, standing and swaying as she side-stepped around Emma Sue.

"Does it matter?" Ruth counted the money again. As she did so, a card fell from the roll of bills onto the floor.

Mary reached for the card; the air flew out of her lungs. "The devil is coming for us." Mary looked at Ruth. "Sister, look."

Ruth took the card. She read, "Jonas Stewart."

"Who is that?" Magdalena said from the closet.

"We should be asking you the same thing," Ruth said.

"This is horrible. He was *here*?" Mary said, pacing in front of the figure sprawled on the floor. She couldn't stop her hands from fluttering and clasped her fingers tightly. "He's found us, Ruth. He's found us and it's over. We need to leave right now. You hear me? Right now."

"Who is this Jonas Stewart?" Magdalena clumsily smashed a hat on her head and fumbled as she pulled on some leather gloves.

"Trouble," Ruth said. And then she passed out.

CHAPTER 48

Magdalena adjusted her hat oddly as she pushed Amoura through the bank doors. "Hurry up and shut up. Keep your mouth closed, and I'll do all the—I'll do all the talking."

Amoura nodded. Magdalena's eyes were red and glassy and she was acting strangely. She had fallen asleep in the taxi on their way over. Only just now had she started making sense again. Amoura shuffled into the cavernous bank and couldn't help but feel like she didn't belong there. Everyone looked so smart, so cosmopolitan in their suits and ties and heels and slim-fitting outfits. There was one sole Negro woman in the bank. Waiting in line for a teller, she was decked in pearls and her bone-straight hair was coiffed perfectly into a tight victory roll. Her deep-fuchsia-colored dress with its light pink heart-shaped lapel stood out boldly amongst the other patrons who were primarily dressed in black and heathered greys. Behind cat-eye glasses, the woman's gaze landed on Amoura. For a brief moment, Amoura saw a flicker in the woman's eyes—the flicker seemed to ask, "Are you alright?" Amoura's pulse quickened, and she held the woman's gaze for probably two seconds too long, moving toward her fuchsia figure slightly. Amoura stopped. She wanted to talk to this woman. She wanted to go where she was going, and she was so very happy to have been seen.

Just then, Magdalena grabbed her by the arm and yanked her to her side, to the point where Amoura had to do a two-step skip to catch herself from tripping miserably. As she caught herself, she looked back to the woman, but she had turned away, probably back to the business that had brought her into the bank in the first place.

Amoura dropped her head and smoothed the wrinkled cotton on the shift dress she'd been wearing since yesterday, trying to walk as though she were in her glamorous, red velvet Mysterie gown. It was all she could do. She wasn't sure if she was successful. She surveyed the area, her eyes bouncing from the bank staff to patrons hurrying here and there to wait in line. No one else cared to take any notice of her at all. She felt invisible and wondered if that was a good thing or something awful.

She continued on behind Magdalena, who looked slightly ridiculous in her orange gown. Maybe they didn't notice her because Magdalena was such a sight. Some had stared at her with surprise, while others just sniffed in haughty disdain, as Amoura had seen some of the wealthier guests do at Mysterie parties. Amoura wasn't sure why Magdalena had chosen that outfit for the bank, but who was she to question anything? Magdalena had been riled up this morning after her meeting with Ruth and Mary and the new girl. She had barked for Amoura to get ready and then commanded Desire and Fury to deal with their new tenant, who was a complete mess with two left feet and a very crude mouth.

Magdalena presented herself to a clerk who asked them to wait while he went for Mr. Trieg.

"Stop fidgeting," Magdalena said.

"These shoes are too small," Amoura said, trying to wiggle her feet. "You should have just let me wear my dance shoes."

"Those dance shoes are ugly and they are for dancing, not banking. So stop fidgeting."

Amoura stopped fidgeting. Now that they were in front of Mr. Trieg's office, she was becoming increasingly nervous. She couldn't remember the last time she was out in the real world and this particular outing was so important. There was so much riding on this. She hoped she could deliver, for herself and for the girls. She still hadn't come up with a plan of her own exactly, but she was looking for an opportunity to act. *Had the Negro woman been her chance? Had she missed it?* She was hoping that she could count on Stan Trieg to do what the Negro woman had, to notice her and to give her all the courage she needed to tell someone exactly what was going on at Magdalena's. To help her sisters become women of the world rather than girls behind colored doors. Perspiration was gathering under her armpits. She tried to blow some air down the front of her dress to cool herself down. To calm herself, she focused on the din of the bank. The *ding* of the bell that announced a waiting patron's turn. A door squeaking on its hinges as a worker left the partitioned office area. A child crying as his mother leaned into the window to talk with a clerk, keeping one hand on a rocking pram. *This is what living sounds like,* Amoura thought to herself. She longed to be that woman at the window. To have a real life, with all of its problems and ups and downs and joys and daily disturbances. To maybe have a husband again, a family, something. Or to go back to school and study something so that she could be an office worker in a suit, walking efficiently from one window to the next. She'd hoped that what she was doing at that bank today was one step closer to really living.

"What is taking so long?" Amoura asked.

"I said, 'no talking.'"

Amoura bit her lip and shoved her hands in her pockets. She turned away from Magdalena and glanced behind her toward the front door. Conceivably, she could just run through them right now and never look back.

"Don't get any bright ideas like last night. I will scream 'thief' if you run and you'll be thrown in jail faster than you can figure what's happening," Magdalena said into Amoura's ear while digging her talons into her arm.

"You're hurting me," Amoura said as she pulled her arm away.

"Everything alright?" The clerk reappeared. Concerned eyes searched her own. Magdalena stared hard at her. Amoura caught her breath and nodded her head. *Dammit!* She thought. Another moment that she could have done something. *Why didn't she? Why?* Her pulse quickened again. Maybe she didn't have what it was going to take to make a move. Her mind was playing tricks with her.

"Yes, thank you. Small domestic squabble." Magdalena smiled broadly.

"Please follow me."

They followed the clerk. Magdalena turned back and pointed her finger at Amoura in warning, her green eyes blazing.

Amoura trailed behind, averting her eyes to the crying baby to avoid Magdalena's jettisoned threat. She rubbed her arm and wondered if she was bleeding.

They entered Stan Trieg's office. It was much larger than Magdalena's—cleaner, more efficient, with a stream of sunshine that flowed in from the large picture windows.

"Ah, Ms. Sapperstein," Stan Trieg smiled. He rose from his leather chair and extended his hand politely.

Amoura looked up. *Sapperstein?* She'd never heard Magdalena referred to in this way. Amoura noticed that although he was shaking Magdalena's hand, Stan Trieg was actually looking at her. Quite intently. Amoura found him to be quite striking in this light. His grey suit fit him well and showed off his premature salt n' pepper hair, offsetting the brightness in his light eyes. As he explored her with his eyes, she felt more naked than when she was partially clothed on stage. She tried to look him in the eye, but only made it to his chin and so diverted her attention to the patterns in the wood floor of his office instead.

"And you've brought along someone," he continued.

"Harlem Markeson," Magdalena said with a smile.

Suddenly, Stan Trieg stood before her quite closely. She couldn't avoid his eyes now, which were searching hers. He shook her hand warmly while holding her elbow perhaps a bit too long. "Hello," she managed.

"Harlem Markeson," Stan Trieg said. "Very interesting."

"I'm certain you recognize each other," Magdalena laughed softly. Stepping between them, she brushed a piece of lint from his suit. "But, Mr. Trieg, you've not known her true identity."

Amoura stepped back still looking at Stan Trieg. Of course, they were familiar with each other. They had passed by one another during parties. The occasional eye contact, casual small talk. However, he often bid on and spent time with Sienna; he had never chosen to be with the Brown Betties. The man seemed nice enough, though. Sienna had said he was usually gentle and kind with her. She studied him.

"Her true identity," Stan Trieg said as he broke their gaze and moved swiftly to his desk. "Well. You see, Ms. Sapperstein," he said, "I took the time to do some calling around, sent some telegrams here and there, and received this in the mail today. Just in time, really." He handed Magdalena a newspaper clipping.

Amoura watched Magdalena's smile plummet as she held the clipping in her shaking hands.

"Stan, I—I can explain, but—but what prompted you to—" Magdalena stammered.

Stan Trieg ignored her, took the clipping and handed it to Amoura. "Have you ever heard of such madness?"

Amoura glanced at the clipping. "*MURDER/SUICIDE STILL SHOCKS TOWN*" blared from the headline and there underneath it, clear as day, was a photo of Harlem. She looked so frightened, her eyes vacant and lifeless. Amoura looked up at Stan Trieg.

"So, you, my dear, although quite attractive, look nothing like this girl. Who might you be, actually?"

"I'm—"

"It doesn't matter who she is," Magdalena interrupted.

"I guess you're right," Stan Trieg returned to his desk and sat. "Where is the real Harlem Markeson?"

"What do you care?" Magdalena stood. "You clearly have gone behind my back for reasons unknown to me. I thought we had an agreement, and I see now that we do not. Amoura, let's go."

Stan Trieg held up his hand, "No need to be so rash. There is still business to be handled between us; that is not what I was implying. Please sit."

Magdalena calmed herself and sat hesitantly. "Alright," she said.

"I will ask again, as I am concerned about the whereabouts of this 'Harlem' woman. Where might she be, then?" He asked slowly.

She escaped."

"What?"

"Last night," Magdalena said as she lowered herself to perch on the edge of the chair like a wounded bird. She pulled the netting from her face. "You may have noticed my bruises. That harlot. She's clearly a brute, just a terrible, horrible, brutal human being. She nearly killed me last night, like she did her father, apparently, and, well—she escaped."

"Escaped?" Stan Trieg gazed at Amoura steadily. She felt like such a simpleton still standing there. She fidgeted in her shoes. "So, this means you lovely creatures cannot come and go as you please?" he said.

Amoura blinked. She quietly put the news clipping on Mr Trieg's desk. Her face burned like a brush fire and her fingers tingled as blood rushed through her. Time stopped. *What should she say? What should she say? This was her chance!* Magdalena turned slowly to look at her. Amoura straightened her shoulders, licked her parched lips; her thoughts trampled on her voice, which was so eager for the chance to be heard. She stared into the wells of his eyes and found what she thought to be trust.

Stan Trieg leaned forward, his elbows on his desk. "Is this true, kitten? You aren't allowed to leave?"

"Well," Amoura cleared her throat; courage found its way to her vocal cords. "We are kept—"

The door swung open, and Amoura was nearly knocked into the wall by it.

It was Lucinda, the loudmouth who came to every Mysterie party.

"Apologies for being late," Lucinda said.

Amoura steadied herself against a tall bookcase. *Why was Lucinda there?*

"Oh, pardon me," Lucinda said, patting Amoura on the shoulder as though she were a paper boy or something. "Good to see you again, Amoura." Lucinda was dressed sharply in a maroon pantsuit and a dark green hat with a plume of matching maroon. Amoura was reminded of Robin Hood by the outfit, as stylish as it was. Lucinda looked Amoura over as she continued into the room, taking it over really, with her presence. "I wanted to compliment you on a bewitching performance during the last party. You always do quite a nice job, actually. I doubt Magdalena ever tells you girls something so complimentary." Lucinda boldly grabbed a cigarette from Stan Trieg's desk and lit it with his crystal lighter.

"Amoura, is it?" Stan Trieg said, intrigued.

"Brown Bettie at your service," Lucinda said and sat in the second chair next to Magdalena, opposite Stan Trieg. She blew out a stream of smoke. "So. What did I miss?"

"What are you doing here?" Magdalena demanded.

"I'd rather chat about what this orange get up is that you're wearing, but that would most certainly be a waste of time, I gather. I think the proper response to seeing me is more like, 'Pleasure to see you, Lucinda.' But, since you've asked what I am doing here, you should know I'm here protecting my investment." Lucinda looked back at Amoura and grinned. "Isn't this an investment meeting? Mr. Trieg was gracious enough to alert me to your very, very good fortune, Maggie. He and I are business partners, you see. We have a stake in the Manor, together." Lucinda crossed her ankle over her knee, her dark green and white leather spectator loafers gleaming.

Stake in the Manor? Amoura felt a piece of herself float away like a child's circus balloon. There was no way she could say anything to Stan Trieg. He was one of them. She stared at him. He smiled slyly back at her. He was nothing more than a liar, just like

Magdalena. So was Lucinda. They were horrible, ravenous vultures, each of them, eager to pick at her bones as soon as they were given the chance. Amoura hardened, turning from his disgusting smile, and focused on Magdalena.

"You double-crossing, two-timing snake!" Magdalena stood, her face red and splotchy. Amoura had never seen her lose her wig in public. Magdalena's gown caught under her chair; as she yanked on it, she looked like a rabbit caught in a trap. "You won't get away with this," she growled.

Quite entertained by Magdalena's struggle, Stan Trieg leaned back in his chair with his hands clasped behind his head. "Magdalena has just informed me that our Harlem has escaped."

"So convenient," Lucinda said, moving the chair aside casually and freeing Magdalena. Lucinda inspected Amoura. "I assume you're here because Maggie was going to pass you off as our star, Harlem Markeson?"

Amoura darted her eyes to Magdalena and then down to her shoes. She mumbled, "I wouldn't know." She hoped the girls were ready to run. To try again what they failed at yesterday, because nothing but more trouble was coming.

Magdalena pushed Amoura aside and opened the door. "Come on, we're leaving."

Lucinda stood swiftly, pointing her cigarette at Magdalena threateningly. "Maggie. I'm done playing with you. You hear me? Done. Stan and I will be at the party tonight. Announcements will be made, so be sure to clean yourself up."

Lucinda crossed her arms, satisfied. "And Amoura, darling, I hope you're looking forward to new management."

CHAPTER 49

Harlem imagined herself back at home, in her ballet room. She placed her hand on the wall at the height the barre would be, and she began again. She pointed her foot. As though holding a pencil between her toes, she circled her ankle to the right several times and then switched the circle motion to the left. Circle, circle, circle, and then again, circle, circle, circle. For as long as she could remember, this was something she'd done before and after ballet practice to strengthen her ankles. It was all she knew to do, so she did it. No need for a sprain after all she'd been through. She pulled her spine straight, her muscles rippling with the pain of a scab torn from scraped knee. She took as deep a breath as she could and exhaled just as deeply.

'You must be strong in your body and in your mind if you want any success at all.'

George had said that to her.

'Look at the willows on this property. Been here more years than most things. These trees don't last a hundred years because they can't weather a storm. They have a

mind to last. Be strong like the willow if'n you want any success at all. Willows have strength and grace, people can too, if they put their mind to it.'

George had said that while driving her to the courthouse that very first time. His steady voice echoed in her head. Strong in the body and the mind. Strong like the willow. With a pointed foot, Harlem circled once again. She then rested her leg and foot in fourth position as best she could, balanced, and lifted her leg in a *petite battement* and continued into a *grand battement,* lifting higher and higher each time. *Battements* were warm-ups she and her mother would do together. To the front... *un, deux, trois, quatre...* to the side, one, two, three, four... to back, *un, deux, trois, quatre.*

Every tendon that hadn't been worked since the day her parents died cried out to her like a fussy child. She continued. Every muscle that had been pummeled by Magdalena resisted, not wanting to participate. She continued. Every fiber in her being that hadn't been fed howled with arresting hunger. She continued. Her body became warm. It began to shake from fatigue. She continued. *Un, deux, trois, quatre...* She kept her eyes closed, breathing deeply through her pain, using her mind to imagine the barre that was not there, the mirrors that were not there, and the light that was not there. She was enveloped in darkness, and it was almost comforting.

Although lost in her mind, she was reminded that she wasn't alone in her bedroom. The girl who lay comatose in what used to be her bed shifted and moaned. She was the new girl.

Having followed the Betties upstairs, Harlem had been sleeping when her door sprung open and Magdalena and Mary entered.

"Move," Magdalena had said.

She had.

"This is your new roommate 'til I figure something else out."

Mary and Magdalena had argued with one another about the room as they struggled to get the girl onto her bed. Apparently, Mary had thought she and Ruth should stay in Harlem's room and Harlem and the new girl should move down to Tilda's.

"That's absurd," Magdalena had said.

"Ruth needs to rest," Mary had said.

"You're such a pest, Mary," Magdalena had said. "You can both rest in Honey's room. But only while I'm away for my appointment."

And then they trudged out of the room, leaving her with the dead weight of a stranger to deal with. That had been 500 ankle circles and now 30 *battements* ago. Strong in the body and the mind. Strong like the willow. She would keep doing this until it was time for the party. Time for her to escape. Alone. She took a deep breath in and released it slowly. *Un, deux, trois, quatre...*

CHAPTER 50

Honey sat on the edge of the bed with Tilda on the floor, sitting between her knees. She finished the last braid of two neat cornrows. "There, Tilda," Honey said, kissing Tilda warmly on the head. "You look beautiful."

Tilda stood, feeling the tightness of the braids with her slender fingers. She smiled and hugged Honey before running to the bathroom to check herself in the mirror. Honey returned Jonas' brush and hair grease to his toiletry bag and closed the metal latch. She looked out the small window. The distance from the motel to the next brown brick building was less than the length of her body. Across the way, she could see into the kitchen of another apartment. A woman stood at a sink, washing dishes.

Honey moved aside and watched her. She wondered what the woman's name was. What she did all day. What she'd had for breakfast. Honey leaned into the curtains, clung to them, as she inhaled the decaying scent of them. A man entered with an empty plate and handed it to the woman. Honey thought she saw her body tense up ever so slightly as he circled his arms about her waist and kissed her on the neck; yet she smiled and turned to him. Honey turned away slowly as they kissed each other passionately.

Leaning on the windowsill, Honey's fingers went to her own lips. She closed her eyes, lost. *One day. In Chicago. One day...*

The key scratching in the front door pulled Honey from her thoughts. Jonas entered; his hands exploded with groceries. She hurried to him.

"Sorry it took so long," Jonas smiled at her broadly. "Markets were full today. Guess everybody wanted to get their Saturday shopping in."

"I imagine so," Honey said, helping him.

"Got some bread and cold cuts for sandwiches, so we don't starve ourselves to death."

Honey pulled packages wrapped in butcher paper from the bag and arranged them on the table, "It looks like we'll have a feast for sure."

"Couldn't get everything I wanted. Things are in short supply, even with the war just over. But it will get us through!" Jonas laughed.

"Jonas, I—" Honey paused as she unwrapped the cold cuts, "I wanted to apologize for everything."

"I do, too."

"Please, let me talk first, especially before Tilda comes out from the bathroom."

"Alright. Go ahead."

"I'm sorry I didn't tell you fully about the necklace. I should have. I'm sorry."

"It's okay, I understand."

"Alright. And for my tone last night. Before we fell asleep. I'm sorry for how I spoke to you."

"Thank you, I appreciate you saying so." He shifted in his shoes. "Is there more?"

"Yes. I'm so confused about so many things right now, but what I do know is that I need to start a new life. On my own. I want to know what's out there and to have the chance to do it without having to be responsible for anyone. I just want that chance now that I'm free and... when Tilda started asking me why I hadn't come back for them, I just... I wasn't prepared."

He reached inside his jacket and handed her an envelope.

"What's this?" she asked.

"Open it."

"Money?" she stared at him. His eyes looked different than they had before. Deeper, kinder; with a new understanding.

"You deserve a normal life, Honey. Or at least a chance at it. I want that for you, most definitely."

She looked down at the bills. "I want you to know that I do want to help you. And the girls."

Jonas reached for her elbow and squeezed her hand. "I know, Honey. I'm grateful to you. You have your chance. Use it. I no hero, but I can do what I can and you can go on to Chicago after this is all over. I've lived my life. You haven't. Maybe me an Arnetta can—maybe we can—"

He pulled away from her. Leaving that thought to find its own way. He wiped away at his brow. "I've come to the realization that I am being tested. More than I ever imagined. God just keeps putting obstacles in my path and then also shows me the way. You two are a part of that. Do you understand me?" He turned to the groceries.

"I do."

"And now, I've got you and Tilda—"

"To worry about," Honey finished. She looked down and traced the grain of the wood table with her finger.

"No, to guide me. I'm no longer alone. You see?"

Before she could answer, Tilda ran from the bathroom and stared at the food, her eyes wide.

Jonas looked at Honey, signaling their conversation was over, and smiled at Tilda. "You needn't be shy, Tilda. Have at it!" Jonas said, removing his hat.

"Jonas, you've been so generous to us. I don't know how we'll ever repay you," Honey said, trying to think of something to say other than what she was feeling. She slid the envelope of money under Jonas' hat so that Tilda wouldn't see it.

"There is no 'repay' around here. We'll just thank God for bringing us all together. He knew we needed one another and now here we are. So, let's make the most of it while we can."

"But how can you afford it?"

"I've taken care of what I need to take care of. Long as I got enough for a bus ticket home for me and Arnetta, I can afford it." Jonas went into the bathroom. Water ran from the faucet as he called out, "Now, Tilda, I do want to say that your hair looks right fine."

He exited the bathroom drying his hands. "Honey's done a wonderful job. Gon' have to learn how to do that greatness on your own, too."

Tilda's face beamed with a joy Honey hadn't seen in a very long while. Honey hugged her warmly and whispered in her ear, "You deserve it, Tilda. Alright now," she continued, moving the armchair to the table, "let's move this ugly table closer to the bed. You'd think they'd give you more than one chair for sitting on."

"In a place like this?" Jonas said, sinking deep into the chair. "Can you all reach? Guess it's a good thing the good Lord blessed me with long arms."

"We can reach," Honey said as she began to make their sandwiches. "I haven't had this type of sliced bologna in ages!" Honey smiled and eagerly brought a taste to her mouth.

"Shall we say grace?" Jonas looked at her.

Honey looked down. "Certainly. I'm still so out of practice."

Jonas reached for her hand and she reached for Tilda's. "Heavenly Father, thank you for these gifts you have put before us. Thank you for keeping us all safe and sound and for the many blessings you have bestowed upon us. In your name. Amen."

Honey enjoyed the courage and strength of his hand on one side and the familiarity and smallness of Tilda's on the other. She smiled at Tilda. "Amen." She picked up the meat and stuffed it in her mouth with thanks. "This is delightful!"

"I was worried if you preferred bologna over ham or vice-versa, so I'm glad I chose correctly. Tilda, make sure you get yourself one of these here pickles," Jonas said, sliding a juicy mound of them toward her. "They are *divine!*"

"And root beer, too?" Honey said. "It's heavenly!"

They chewed in silence for a moment, except for a few moans of satisfaction here and there. Honey watched Tilda. Even though she was a girl of sixteen, she completely looked and acted like a child. More like a thirteen-year-old, as though time had stopped ticking for her.

Honey sipped her root beer and thought about her bus ticket from Burle and the money hiding quietly under Jonas' hat. She wondered when she'd get to use it and what she'd do once she had. And then she thought of Tilda. What would happen to her? Honey shook her head. Too many questions and not enough answers. Providing for Tilda would now fall on her shoulders, most likely. She simply had to accept it. They were sisters, after all. But for now, she tried to stay in the moment and be content with knowing they were presently safe and cared for.

Jonas wiped his mouth with a paper napkin. "I was wondering something. Everything has a beginning. That one thing that carries or pulls you from one situation over here and positions you in another situation over here. What was that thing that happened to Magdalena? Do you know?"

Tilda tapped and looked at Honey for confirmation.

"I agree with you. It was Lon Listromski."

"Listromski. Name sounds like it should be a cut of meat for our sandwiches or somethin'," Jonas laughed.

"He would have been better as a slab of meat than as a person," Honey said.

"How so?"

"After our parents died, we were taken care of by our mother's brother, Uncle Mac. He took care of the three of us best he could, for as long as he could, but our parents had a lot of debt and didn't leave much for anybody to work with," Honey said.

"I see."

"Uncle Mac told us we needed to be on our own. I can't fully remember how old Maggie was at the time, but over twenty for certain, and considered a full adult woman, as you can imagine. But we'd been so sheltered as children. Everything had been done for us. Tilda was still a baby; I was a young teen. We didn't know soap powder from potato flakes. We were near Uncle Mac's bar today, right next to Dolly's. I didn't feel right to talk to him, looking as bad as I did."

"Umm, hmm." Jonas nodded.

"It wasn't his fault, really. He left us in the house and moved on to taking care of himself. After a while, Maggie and I ran out of things to sell or pawn and when there was nothing left to sell, Maggie sold herself."

"Hmmm," Jonas dropped his eyes and sipped some cola. "Not the first or the last to do so, I reckon."

"Yes, that's true, I suppose. Soon, Maggie found a boyfriend in the way of one Lon Listromski. He'd been an orphan too, and a two-bit thief. Lon would say that no one cared where he was or what happened to him and neither did he. Every day at mealtime, as though it were his prayer, he'd recite, 'no one cares about the unwanted.' He was right. But he was also smart. And an opportunist. Magdalena's Manor was his idea. He was the one who named her 'Lady Magdalena.' He was the one who said people would pay for entertainment in a secret place. Together, we fixed up the basement into a speakeasy club and turned it into something nice. Then, Lon went out searching for orphans to be singers or dancers and whatnot in the speakeasy. People he could sorta turn into indentured servants. People nobody cared about. Problem was, those orphans were dirty sometimes, and sometimes they'd fight or steal, and sometimes they'd just disappear. They were bad for business. Then one day Lon Listromski disappeared. He took off with the little bit of money we'd earned and all we had left to our names."

Tilda interrupted and tapped.

"That's right, and a nice cooking pot, too! And so, well. It's not a good story, Jonas, I'm afraid."

"Folks' stories aren't always good ones, Honey. That's what makes life what it is: life. Can you continue? I'd like to know more."

Honey settled on the bed. "My sister was gorgeous. She still is. She was captivating and alluring and spoke so eloquently. Mesmerizing, really. She had some of my mother's gowns but found ways to persuade shop owners and tailors like Paola to give us more gowns and jewelry and so on. And soon, well, soon she went out on the streets herself and found women who weren't so destitute, had some sort of sophistication, but had just been alone. Women who had been cared for, but now... weren't. She turned them into working girls and suddenly, we, she, was a madam. And I was helping her. But when I wanted to leave, she locked me in, afraid I would rat on her, ruin her. Then she locked in the others."

"Her own sister," Jonas said, gathering the empty wrapping paper. "What made her so heartless?"

"My sister isn't heartless. Lady Magdalena is heartless."

Jonas paused. "I apologize."

"I'm not without guilt either, Jonas. I could have done something and didn't."

He looked at her. She thought she saw something flicker in his eyes.

"Why didn't you?" he asked gruffly, avoiding her gaze.

"With what resources? Where would I have gone? How could I help any of those girls if I couldn't help myself? And you've seen now what Magdalena is capable of."

"I have t' admit that I am listening to the words you are saying, and I believe them to be true, but in my spirit, I do not understand how your own spirit didn't rise up to stop all that nonsense!"

"I can't expect you to understand. It's just—one of those things, I suppose. When someone has power over you, I..." her voice trailed off. She never could manage to explain what her life was like to anyone before and couldn't do it now, either.

Tilda stood to help Jonas with the last of the cleaning up. She paused and tapped for a long while, her face tight with anger.

"My sister, our sister, *has* hurt a lot of people. And you're correct, Tilda. She does deserve to be punished. I want that too! But what amount of punishment is going to do any good? How will she be absolved of anything? Who is going to feel better because Magdalena has been punished? Very few, Tilda. Very few."

"Listen, I'm sorry I brought it up," Jonas said.

"No. Don't apologize. We can't keep the truth locked up in ourselves or in that house any longer. My sister..." Honey buried her face in her palms. "I love her. I honestly and truly still love her. I love the girl who I knew. The one I grew up with, who was silly and laughed and took care of me and was enchanting. She was so enchanting. Everyone always said so. I miss that sister. I love that sister. She just... we just. She became something else."

Honey leaned her head back on the wall. She stared at the white ceiling with its brown water stains, signs of leaks no one had tended to or cared about. She closed her eyes and allowed her tears to fall naturally.

Tilda climbed on the bed and wrapped her arms around Honey. Honey let the warmth coming from Tilda's arms make her feel a little better. They remained like that for a while.

"God help me for saying this," Jonas exhaled heavily. "Everyone deserves a second chance. Maybe even Magdalena."

Honey opened her eyes. "Even with everything that you've gone through with Arnetta, you believe this?"

"I have to. I have got to get rid of this bitterness so that I can make room for my daughter when I finally have her in my arms again. Got to move on because, hopefully, in a few hours this will be over, and a new story can be told."

CHAPTER 51

agdalena checked her watch. Only thirty minutes more before guests would begin to arrive. Off in the dining room, her two remaining butlers moved things about. She could only afford to pay two out of the previous five. Without Tilda and any of the untrustworthy Rainbow Girls to help, it was slow going. Still, they broke down the dining-room table, and transformed the room into the great hall. She was comforted by the sounds. She inspected herself in the mirror. The long bath had done her pretty good. So had the makeup and the hairbrush and hairpins. These things artificially covered the bruises that would continue to hurt her long after they were gone. She looked like herself again, although she didn't feel it. Her stomach lurched and her hands tremored ever-so-slightly as she adjusted a pin in her hair. She reached for her glass of champagne and turned from her vanity mirror. Usually, Officer Brighton was here with her and sometimes they would rendezvous with one another for several glasses of champagne and an energizing roll in the hay. Today, there was none of that. She gathered the folds of her black velvet gown as she walked past her empty bed, neatly made for the first time in a long time. She turned off the light.

Magdalena entered her office, which had also been tidied. She placed her champagne glass on her desk and sat. Pulling two new envelopes from Budhai's belly, she began humming a tune.

"*In my solitude, you haunt me,*" she sang. The band had been warming up downstairs and had played the number. It was one of her favorites.

"*With memories of days gone by...*" Magdalena pulled the papers from the first envelope. It was her father's will. It had never occurred to her to review it again, but after the incredible disaster that occurred at Stan Trieg's office today, she started to wonder what sort of real ammunition she had over Lucinda and Stan. She had the law. Her father's will left the house to her and to Honey and then to Tilda. It was signed by a lawyer and stamped officially. Next, she pulled out the deed to the home. It, too, was legitimately signed and she even found the bill of sale that confirmed that her family paid for and entirely owned the brownstone, free and clear.

"Lucinda can go jump off a cliff," Magdalena said, putting all documents in a larger envelope. She pulled a sheet of paper from her stationary drawer. With her fountain pen from her desk set, she wrote:

June 30, 1945

Dear Honey,

I don't know if you'll ever get this. Many things have happened of which I am not proud. I did the best I could, not always through the best choices, but I tried. We're sisters. We'll always have each other and this house. That is our history and our legacy wrapped into one. I pray one day we shall be reunited here under better circumstances. With hope in my soul, I imagine you reading this with us by one another's side, with you having forgiven me. Somehow. I love you.

Yours,
Maggie

Magdalena sealed the letter, wrote *Honey Sapperstein* on it in large script, and placed it with the will and the deed.

A knock on her door interrupted her.

"Come in."

"Ma'am. Your messenger is here," her head butler, William, announced.

"Thank you, send him in."

A young man of nineteen or so entered. Magdalena sized him up. "You're to take this to the address here. It is to Mac's Bar, right next to Dolly's Diner. You're to deliver it to the man they call Uncle Mac, and no one else. Do you understand?" Magdalena sealed the envelopes and handed them over.

"Yes ma'am."

"Be quick about it. These documents are very important." The young man departed, and Magdalena finished the last of her champagne and crossed her fingers. She figured if Honey was looking for any sort of place she called home, she would go to Uncle Mac. He'd have the documents and Honey could fight for their home. She was through with it all. As soon as she and Amoura had left the bank, Magdalena had sent Uncle Mac a telegram telling him she was sending him something important. Perhaps, maybe, once more, he could save them... even if she wasn't involved. She hoped.

Magdalena moved to her desk and opened a suitcase hidden underneath it. She placed the pen in the suitcase pocket; it rested next to Harlem's check, her toiletries, and stockings. Beyond that, she had only packed what she wanted. And that wasn't much. Magdalena rose and looked around her office. "That's it. That's all I need."

She double-checked her pocketbook for her morning train ticket to Montreal. Years ago, a man had visited her Manor from there and told her she might do well in Canada. Magdalena wasn't sure if she was going to continue in this business, but at least in Montreal there was a higher demand for what she offered and maybe she could start over, or maybe not. She'd get there, pretend she was Harlem Markeson, finally cash that damned check, and begin her new life. As a black woman. As herself.

It was Ruth and Mary who had prompted this sudden change in her plans. Mary had gone on and on about how they never should have chosen Harlem, how Ruth was so greedy, how Jonas Stewart was onto them, and how this *abducting* was the thirteenth time, and so on and so on. Magdalena had made up her mind to leave right then and there. Because whoever this Jonas Stewart really was, he had Tilda and he knew about Harlem. These were two glaring strikes against her, and she didn't need to wait around for a third.

Looking around the office, she knew she was going to miss the place. Her father was still present here, as far as she was concerned. But in order to get past all the shit that was in her way now, she had to leave. Had to drop everything and just start over. She hoped this would be her home again one day, but right now it was a noose. Uncle Mac and hopefully Honey would save it and would probably do better by it too.

Lucinda could have the girls. They had become burdens, reminders of what had gone wrong in her life. She was sick to death of looking at them, hearing them talk and whine for food and this and that. Sick of policing them and keeping them in line and fighting them. Absolutely sick to death of it. Lucinda could take the headache from her and deal with it how she pleased. And that headache was all she was going to get from Magdalena.

She brushed her hands free of all of them, rose, and sauntered into the dining room. The room was just about ready for the evening.

"Lady Magdalena," William approached her. His silver hair shone with pomade.

"Yes?"

"Am I to believe that we only have fourteen bottles of champagne to get us through an entire evening?"

"Yes. Fourteen."

"A party of ten could drink fourteen bottles just themselves in under two hours, madam."

"Understood. Perhaps you could manage a little creativity, William." Magdalena left him shaking his head. She'd already consumed one bottle by herself to celebrate her closing shop, and she couldn't care less. She continued to the buffet where the lightbulbs, red dresses, costumed bustiers, and stockings were stored. She always kept a second set of dresses pressed and dry-cleaned and she took hold of this set from a drawer. She reached above in a cabinet and pulled a morphine tablet from a tin. This would be for Harlem.

The girl looked haggard, and she was needed to make the night look and feel a success.

Magdalena went upstairs. Her guests counted on seeing alluring women in alluring red dresses. That's what they were going to get. More importantly, she needed every bidder to go high this evening. Every dollar counted toward her having a certain standard of life in Canada. Putting on a shitty farewell show was not an option.

Magdalena laughed to herself; after the bidding tonight, they'd discover that they were going to get even more than usual from the Betties. Now that Honey was gone off that stage as a Brown Bettie, she didn't care what happened to the rest of them. Especially Harlem. Plus, she'd remembered how much darling Arthur had enjoyed Harlem. He would pay handsomely for her as a Bettie. Were she demoted to a Rainbow Girl, he might not dive into his wallet so deeply.

"Conniving brat," Magdalena said. She walked through the foyer carrying the dresses and one lightbulb. Magdalena walked past Tilda's room. Pain shot through her knees. She shook her leg out as if to kick off the pain. "She's better off. Good riddance," Magdalena said as she continued up the stairs. "Better off."

Her knees continued to groan as she made her way up the stairs. Her breath was short and fought with her aching stomach for attention. Now that she had decided to jump ship, Magdalena hoped she hadn't done too much damage with the tea. No longer did she have the desire to be like her father. She rubbed her stomach and took a deep breath as she unlocked the door.

"Get dressed," Magdalena coughed and handed the lightbulb and wardrobe to Harlem. She looked at Emma Sue, who was snoring loudly. "Good, still out. One less thing to worry about." Magdalena looked back at Harlem: she was sweating. Her face was gaunt and looked completely worn out. "You look terrible. Take this tablet. I can't have you lurching about like a maimed clown up there. Get yourself together. And remember to cover your bruises with makeup; get some from the girls. Hurry up! The girls will bring you down."

"But—" Harlem began.

"Shut up and do as I say," Magdalena cut her off, slamming the door shut.

Magdalena unlocked Fury's door and handed her the remaining dresses and a key from Tilda's key ring, which she pulled from her pocket. "Make sure you bring them down in one hour. Take my watch." She closed the door and moved on to Ruth and Mary. "Ladies?" she called out as she turned the knob. "Guests will arrive—Oh." Ruth and Mary were primping themselves. Unsuccessfully. Ruth's hair was in ringlets, Mary's was plastered to her forehead and her lipstick seemed to be everywhere but on her lips. "Is that the best you could do?"

Ruth slammed the door in her face.

"Idiots!" Magdalena huffed as she returned down the stairs. "*Idiots!*" She couldn't wait to be free of all of them. She stopped to inspect the stained glass the harlots had broken while trying to escape. She had repaired the broken window herself. She'd done a horrible job with the glue paste she'd found under the kitchen sink, and it was completely noticeable. "Idiots!" she shouted.

Music travelled up from downstairs. She took a breath in to calm herself and get her mind right as she continued down to the speakeasy with a mind to check on the band and the Rainbow Girls. Her heels chimed on the stairs as she descended. They were playing a new tune she didn't recognize. She hummed along with its rhythmic baseline.

"Hey, Joe," Magdalena called out. "Glad to see you could join us this week."

He steadied his upright bass and tipped his hat at her. "Ma'am. Happy to oblige." A cigarette dangled from his lips.

"Got an extra for me, Joe?" her stomach was churning. The tea was calling for her. A cigarette would have to do.

He handed her a cigarette and lit it for her.

"Thank you, Joe," she said. She exhaled deeply and waved at the rest of the band with her cigarette. "Same to the rest of you, of course."

"Lady Magdalena," they said back. The drummer nodded to her and counted the band in with his sticks before they rehearsed another number.

The girls were dressed and some were stretching or going over moves. She motioned them to come near. They looked like they wanted to spit on her, but she didn't care. She was through with them after tonight anyway. Icicles hung from her words. "Infidels, tonight is a special night. I expect your performances, your behavior, and your bedside manner to be impeccable this evening. I don't want to hear any complaints from my guests about what you will and won't do behind those closed doors. You have been paid for and it's your job to perform."

She looked toward Sapphire's door. "We're obviously down one girl, which means less money in my pocket, but luckily we should more than make up for it with Harlem and the Betties working tonight. Lucky for you. Be sure to congratulate them when they're through."

"And what about Sapphire? We got the bleeding to stop, but she wakes up every now and then. What the hell are you goin' to do about her?" Ruby said, wringing her hands.

"Maybe there will be a doctor in the house. Why don't you ask around in between your duties?"

Magdalena smoothed a tablecloth and straightened a candle as she returned upstairs. She was strangely happy. Tonight was going to be a good night. Because it was her last.

CHAPTER 52

rthur straightened his bowtie and repositioned his cufflinks as he walked into the enticing folds of the Mysterie party. His shoes were gleaming, having just been freshly polished. He smoothed his hair, pushing it neatly against his head. It was important to him to look immaculate when he attended these parties. There was no excuse to look slackish or off-color at such an upscale event where he would rub elbows with peers.

"Good evening, gentlemen," he said, smiling up at the statuesque Mr. Rathbourne and his pack of high-class associates.

"Arthur," the man said and turned his back. Arthur refused to participate in playground games with these men. They often shunned him from their little machismo-drenched elite circles. He was fine to not be included, especially tonight. He patted his breast pocket. Tonight, he'd brought along an extra sum. Insurance. Tonight, he wanted more than a few stolen moments with a girl; he wanted to take one home. After some gentle pestering through the grapevine and a bit of mild threatening, he discovered that the sweet, sweet dessert he loved was available for sale.

Had he known this earlier on, he may have indulged sooner. But, he knew, as he did with most things, patience had its rewards. And the timing was now perfect. He had recently come into some money through a lucrative investment and it gave him a large cushion on which to build his future. And that is what he saw this purchase as: an investment in his future. Through his travels, he had learned that in the old countries most women never even saw their husbands until their wedding. His own mother and father had had an arranged marriage while still in Poland. That was normal. Her dowry had gotten their family started here in America. But that kind of match-making was old fashioned. He had a mind to secure a wife through other means, and he was quite accepting of this one—he wanted to experience her first, for starters. And he was as determined as he was prepared. He had already purchased a larger bed with new linens and new dishes that had yet to be unpacked (he would leave that to his new bride). He had even shopped for a dog at the pound, just this morning. He would return with his new wife-to-be, ensure that she liked the beast, and bring it home. He had enough room in his home for a child's room too: everything was set. The only thing he needed now was the bride.

He saw her. Ann Smith. She was huddled with the other three women who wore the red dress. The Brown Betties. Her back was to him, but he knew her body well. How she moved and carried herself. He moved toward her. Mesmerized. Elated. Excited.

"My dear," he whispered into her ear as he approached her from behind and touched her elbow.

The girl flinched.

He stepped back, dropping his hand from her elbow. Up close, his Ann looked so much more radiant the first time he met her, but he attributed that to the rapture he felt by her pure energy. Heavy makeup covered her radiant skin now. It didn't matter. Smiling at her, he remembered his time with her. How wonderful she had felt. Only one week ago she was beneath him, behind the yellow door. "You look brilliant, *mon cheri,*" he said, beaming.

She said nothing.

The girl seemed to be shaking. He reached for her again, to calm her this time. "Are you alright, Ms. Smith? Here, let me give you my suit coat."

She shook her head no.

One of the Brown Betties, Amoura, the plump one with the full, inviting figure, took Ann's hand and led her away from him.

"Amoura? That's not polite now, is it?" Arthur smiled tightly.

"You can't have Ann all to yourself now, can you, Arthur? You know the rules."

Arthur did know the rules; everyone was to mingle and to not spend too much time with just one girl. He didn't believe in rules when it came to Ann Smith. "Wait, my precious. Wait." He put his arm around her waist as he stepped in front of her. "You needn't be shy with me." He lifted her chin with his finger. "I have a surprise for you this evening. One that I think will make you very, very happy."

"I have to go now," she said.

"Of course. Of course. You must get ready. I will see you later, downstairs." He held and kissed her trembling hand warmly. "*Tout a l'heure, mon cheri. Tout a l'heure.* Later, later for us."

Quite pleased, Arthur helped himself to a champagne from a passing butler. He sipped it and grimaced. "Not to Lady Magdalena's usual standard," he muttered.

He searched for Magdalena to discuss her taste in quality. As he did so, he was surprised to see a Negro man enter the party with a Negro woman. He immediately remembered the young woman. She was a Bettie and once wore the red dress that signaled that role. Her name was Honey, as he recalled, or something sweet like that. She was dressed simply now and wore little makeup; her lack of glamour sharply contrasted the other women present. Arthur wondered if the man had made an investment in the girl and had brought her to show off his spoils.

"Well, well, what a surprise," he heard from his colleague, a Mr. Ihlenfelter, who owned an advertising outfit in Manhattan. He too was staring at the tall Negro man.

"I guess the party has been integrated," Arthur said.

"It appears so. I imagine there is enough pussy to go 'round as long as his dollar is as long as ours!" The man slapped Arthur on the back and rejoined his chums, both men and women, who were also enthralled by the presence of the anomaly amongst them.

"Only time will tell," Arthur laughed. His smile disappeared. His Ann Smith was talking to the man, animatedly. Exclamations seemed to fly from her entire being, actually. And then, she was hugging him. *Closely.* He didn't like that one bit. Not one bit. He slammed his empty champagne glass onto a passing tray, nearly knocking the whole thing over. He stormed over to Magdalena.

"Magdalena, since when have Negroes been allowed into this party?" he demanded.

"Arthur, some of my girls are Negroes. Whatever do you mean?" Magdalena said.

"That one. That one over there. He is here and I want to know why."

Magdalena looked to where he was pointing and reached for his shoulder as she spoke, "I—I—don't know. But, Arthur, thank you for alerting me to this...

occurrence." She brushed past him and approached the man who was still embracing his Ann.

Magdalena appeared irate that the man had arrived, as well she should. If this event was to remain exclusive, letting just anyone in wouldn't do. Magdalena's back was to him, but even from behind he could tell she wasn't happy. He had seen Lady Magdalena become less than a lady only once before—when one of the girls tried to leave with one of the guests. Of course, that had been eons ago, and nothing like that had ever happened again.

Arthur watched Madgalena talking to the Negro, Ann, and the fair-skinned Brown Bettie who was absent last party and who'd never spoken to him. His eye caught two more Negro women as they entered the party. Their attire was barely appropriate. They clearly were out of place. "What *is* this?" he said aloud. He crossed his arms and stamped his foot.

"What is it, Arthur?" a voice said.

Arthur turned and saw it was Lucinda. He flung his hand toward the two new Negro women. "Them. I—I'm just. I don't know what they're doing here."

"Arthur, stop stammering. It is unbecoming. Didn't you, only last Mysterie, have relations with a Negro woman? The new girl, I believe. You outbid all of us so that you could have her. I didn't think you had a problem with Negroes."

"That's different," Arthur huffed.

"Is it, old boy? This isn't the eighteen hundreds. You may want to think about where you slip your pecker at night if you can't handle a cordial conversation during the day. However, I will say there is a line we must not cross. I think the establishment here is best run by someone who is one of us, wouldn't you agree? Just to keep things running properly, you know."

"Well, that is a given. Who in their right mind would frequent a Negro-run establishment? Excuse me." He marched over to the group of Negroes.

He extended his hand abruptly to the man. "Hello, I am Mr. Arthur Penn."

They all turned and looked at him. Their faces looked like they'd been slapped and subsequently sprayed with foul-smelling water. Arthur dropped his hand. "Perhaps—perhaps I am interrupting something."

"Not a' tall. Nice to meet you, Mr. Penn. I am Mr. Stewart. Jonas Stewart."

The man extended his large brown hand and Arthur shook it as confidently as he could. "Wel—wel—welcome to Mysterie."

"Thank you," he said.

"And the rest of you? You are...?" Arthur tried hard to smile.

"Where are my manners? Mr. Penn, this is Ruth and Mary."

"The Fisherman sisters," the larger one said, offering her fingertips. Arthur stared at her as she fixed her curls, which looked like they belonged on a six-year-old girl.

"This is Honey—"

"They've met," Lady Magdalena said tightly. Arthur noticed her face was covered in red splotches and she seemed to be electrified with anger.

"Hello Arthur," Honey said. "Are you ready for an eventful evening?"

"That I am," Arthur said.

Lady Magdalena grabbed his elbow roughly. "Arthur, might we make our way—"

He held his ground. He had no intention of leaving his lovely with these unsavories. "And Miss Ann Smith, I already know," he smiled tightly at Ann. He pulled on his sleeves. Suddenly his jacket felt quite snug. "Darling. How do you know these people?"

"Arthur, could you possibly excuse us for a moment?" Magdalena asked with a tone that was as gripping as her elbow grab.

"Actually," Jonas Stewart said, clapping him strongly by the shoulder, "I'd like to share a cocktail with the man who was kind enough to come over here and introduce himself."

Arthur stumbled a bit as they walked away. This Jonas Stewart was much larger than him. "What, umm —what line of business are you in, Mr. Stewart?"

"Accounting," Jonas handed him a card.

"Accounting. Fine business," Arthur placed the card in his pocket. "Been at it long?"

"Longer than I care to admit," Mr. Stewart said, looking around.

"First time here?"

"Yes. You?"

"I like to think I'm a regular. No other place in town with this type of party."

"Is that so," Mr. Stewart said. His face seemed to lose some of its color. His breath seemed to stop too.

"Girls here are quite nice. Later, I can tell you which ones are better than the others, if you like."

The man fell into a fit of coughs. "Would you excuse me?"

"Certainly," Arthur exhaled.

"See, that wasn't so bad now, was it?" Lucinda was by his side.

"That man was awkward. All of them were. That wasn't the best experience of my life, I'll tell you that much. I don't understand Negroes much."

"Arthur, you funny little man. Can't you see something is brewing? You must make yourself more aware, my friend." The lights flashed. "Come. I think we might be in for some theatrics this evening," Lucinda said as she led him downstairs.

Arthur craned his neck to get a glimpse of his new bride. She seemed quite upset. What had he missed? He hoped that Jonas Stewart wasn't the cause of his love's distress. He had no problem punching that Negro in the nose if he needed to.

CHAPTER 53

Tilda hid in her old room. When she, Jonas, and Honey arrived at the party, she had tucked herself behind the two of them so no one would see her. While they both distracted the doorman, she had dashed toward the room and darted into it, unseen.

She crouched on her bed and waited. It was strange to be back so soon. When it was time to come to the house, she had been real worried she was going to be afraid to step foot in this place at all. But Mr. Jonas had assured her that he would let nothing happen to her. Plus, she had Honey by her side. They were a team, with a real live mission, and there was no room for fear. That's what Honey had said, and she believed it.

Even though she'd spent so many years in this room, she felt like a stranger to it now. She looked around her; she was more than this place now. She was more than the hard, old cot. More than the dust that hid under it. More. She didn't know how she knew this, or how quickly, but the minute she'd been thrown into Jonas's arms, and he had looked at her with how somebody is supposed to look at you when you're scared, she knew she was going to be alright. And when she fell into Honey's arms, she just about thought God had made two miracles happen in one night. Nothing was impossible now and she felt tingly and sparkly just thinking about it.

The muffled sounds of the band playing below carried into her bedroom and made her concentrate again on what needed to be done. She didn't realize she could hear the band from here. She'd always been downstairs during the party and only returned to her make-believe bed once everyone was gone and everything was cleaned up and forgotten.

Tilda clamped her palms around a box of matches. The plan was for her to run on stage after the first dance and act like there was a fire. She was to yell *"FIRE!"*, even though no sound was going to come shooting out of her mouth. But just acting like she was yellin' would make everyone run. Then Honey and Jonas could grab the girls and run with them straight to the outside where Magdalena could no longer have them. It was a messy plan, but it was the easiest and the quickest, they'd decided. Tilda was happy to do it. She wanted her girls to get out of there, to feel the air on their faces, like she had. She wanted them to get out of that place and to not be afraid to leave, to know that the sky wasn't going to fall, and that their breath wouldn't stop knowing how to move, and that all the bad guys weren't going to come rushing to get them the minute they walked off the stoop. She knew she was still afraid of lots of things, even with what she had to do, but Jonas and Honey made her not so scared. Honey had left. She had left. They were both alive to talk about it. Tilda smiled knowing the rest of the girls would be next. That they'd all be free, and that life could begin. For real this time.

She stood quietly and cracked the door, then peeked through it and listened. The crowd's chatter had died down and she could hear them clomping their way down the stairs. Tilda sat back down and waited. It wouldn't be long now.

CHAPTER 54

Harlem blinked quickly, trying to focus as she peeped through the curtains from backstage. The guests had taken their seats. The piano man played a pleasing number that got toes tapping and shoulders swaying. Glowing candles sat atop the tables and put everybody in a cozy, profiled silhouette. Harlem surveyed them as they leaned forward to whisper to one another, with their glowing cigarettes raised and left on pause for a moment. Diamonds sparkled, creating those little prisms of light she liked. Top hats shadowed pert noses and dimpled chins, seemingly to hide them rather than to make them look more sophisticated.

Harlem looked back behind her at the Betties. The three girls had been huddled together and brewing like storm clouds since Magdalena had forced them backstage. Honey's arrival had gotten them all bent out of shape, and full of excitement, really, but Harlem didn't have time for any of that. She'd learned well and good that excitement got you nowhere. Calm and focus did.

Harlem held onto the curtain. She felt like she was on a boat, rocking. Her body was floating and tingling at the same time. She wondered if this was how her mother had felt after taking her nerve pills. Harlem remembered her mother falling off her chair in the parlor once. One minute her mother was sitting there, staring ahead with glassy eyes; the next, she was on the ground. Harlem had run from the room, yelling for anyone who could hear her to come help.

Harlem tried to recall the events of the evening in relation to the timeline of her high. The feeling had hit her gradually at first. When she'd seen that slimy, crumby Arthur, she'd only thought she was going to pass out from fright the way he was holding onto her like she was some toy puppet. A puppet he was afraid of leaving behind at the fairgrounds.

By the time Amoura had taken her to meet Honey who'd *escaped*, Harlem had started to feel funny. She'd asked the girl how her tooth was, and the girl, who was really quite beautiful, looked at her like she had two heads. Harlem had explained, "Magdalena told me you needed a dentist and that's why you were being taken away..." Honey had said that wasn't true. Harlem had gotten closer to her and had taken her by the shoulders to ask her why she had come back to this place and if she could get them all out, and everyone had shushed her like it was some secret they couldn't leave.

She realized she was in la-la-land when she had noticed Mr. Stewart, whom Honey was with. Because she had blurted out, "It's *you!*" and everyone had shushed her again. Harlem had exclaimed, "He's a wanted man! He's wanted back in Greensboro for *murder!*" Amoura had put her hand on Harlem's mouth to quiet her, and Harlem had wanted to bite her to get her to stop. But Amoura pulled her into a corner in the dining room and explained it all to her: the sisters had framed the man and had lied on him something good. He had been trailing Harlem to try to protect her. Of course, the sisters knew about it and had to do *something* to get rid of him; they'd wanted Harlem for themselves to bring to Magdalena. Once Amoura had told her everything, Harlem had rushed from their corner in the dining room and back to Mr. Jonas Stewart and fallen tearfully into his arms with gratitude.

She looked at him now through the curtains. She blinked again while euphoria bubbled through her like a water fountain. "That man is such a nice man. Jonas Stewart is a nice, nice man!" she exclaimed to the girls behind her.

"Harlem! You're too loud," Amoura said, hushing her.

"It's the morphine kicking in," Fury said. "She'll come down soon."

Harlem looked at Fury. "I've never felt so good in my life!" She clapped her hands. "When do we go on?

When? I am so ready. I am so ready to dance and to get out of here. I'm never coming back. No offense ladies, but I hope I never see you, or this place, or this dress, or anything else around here *ever* again. Do you hear me?"

"Get ready, Harlem. Honey's music is coming."

"I'm going to dance like a—"

"Harlem, the sax is blowing. Go!"

Harlem flicked apart the red curtain, making an entrance, which she'd never made before. With the spotlight on her face, she smiled at her audience and began pulling them in, distracting them with all that she'd been given by God for her first and last dance. She sashayed off the stage and across the room, gracefully. As she walked, she felt no pain. None anywhere. She felt like she was in another world, just looking at this one. She felt the heat of the lights on her face. She smelled the perfume of the women before her. She felt the softness of her gown as she slid her palms along it. She was there. Present. And she was going to escape.

She approached a table and smiled at the guests seated around it as she leaned over them to coyly move the center candle aside. She then crawled onto the table, stretching across it like a feline bathing in the sun. She turned to her back, and kicked her legs up sweetly, letting her dress fall around her hips. Harlem noticed some bruises on her legs that she hadn't covered with Amoura's make up; to hide them she quickly pulled herself to her knees and lifted her arms above her head. Her fingers languished in the heat of an unseen sun. Then they slid down her face and neck like dripping honey; her movement let the saxophone know that she heard it and let the audience know that she felt it. With her hands on her knees, she whipped her head in a big circle, allowing her curls to break free and land on her face like the women on magazine covers. Dizzy, she righted her head and caught up to herself for a moment. In spite of everything, *everything* that happened to her, in this moment, she felt alive. Untouched, awakened. She felt new. A euphoric pulse shot through her insides and she whipped her head again, then happily played with this joy from the outside, tickling her fingers along her body almost as though she herself was the upright bass.

She then threw her arms out like an airplane and whipped her head back to allow laughter she hadn't experienced in such a long time. And laugh she did. A big loud laugh that came from the little girl trapped inside her. She pulled herself round to the front of the table and the girls were there to lift her. Like a floating ballerina with butterfly wings, they carried her to the stage where she was deposited gracefully. She leaned as demurely as she could against the wall, aware of all that surrounded her and caught her labored breath while the others took their solos.

Amoura skipped amongst the tables to the spritely *plink plunk* of the piano, playfully rubbing the faces of gentlemen and some women into her plump bosom. She hopped onto a chair and played with the fabric of her dress, raising it higher and higher and higher from her calves to above her knees. She pulled her dress to her thighs to display her garters and then the bottom tip of her tap pants before she pushed it back down in a tease. With a loud "Wheeee!", she put her foot on the top of the chair's back and in an acrobatic teeter-totter, sent it gently to the ground, and stepped away from it while swirling her hips around and around and around. She moved like that until she found herself on stage, buoyed by whistles and whoops from the audience. She kissed Harlem on the cheek while smiling out at the crowd, then leaned on a wall opposite Harlem. Her breasts heaved as she winked at Harlem before letting herself catch her breath during Desire's solo.

The clarinet called for Desire by her first name with its beguiling summons. Desire emerged from the shadows, her slender arms played the air like a harp as she slinked and intertwined herself between imaginary lines. She moved with a fluidity that matched the gorgeous, exotic notes floating from the clarinet. With her hands on the back of a chair, she leaned forward and lifted her leg back and up into a hypnotizing arabesque that seemed to touch the sky; as she turned to extend and glide out of it, the man who was sitting in the chair she had balanced on held her wrists and kissed her hand. Harlem watched as a cloud darkened Desire's face. She was already rattled. This kiss pulled her from her private place. Her leg dropped like a bird shot from the sky. She stood motionless in the light—her eyes wide with fear and confusion, a look Harlem fully recognized. Harlem scowled and pushed herself from the wall, but Fury was already at Desire's side and pulled her into a tango that whisked them between the tables; Fury pulled her close and whispered something into her ear. Desire held on to her dancing partner tightly as they spun about until Fury dipped and dangled her friend for the enticement of the audience, using Desire as a prop so that the frightened girl had only to smile. Fury finally whisked them onto the stage, again to delighted applause.

Harlem took her place center stage next to Amoura as all four of them joined as one in a choreographed bond that became stronger and stronger with each tiptoe, each swing of the hip, each turn of the head. Harlem stared out at an audience of eyes that were drinking in their every move. When the clarinet said so, Harlem reached across her chest, held the top of her dress, just as the Betties did, and unzipped the side of it. They peeled their red dresses down in soothing unison to reveal golden bustiers with sequins that shone as bright as their smiles. As they stepped forward from the dresses that lay on the stage, she was high with the secret that she'd just discovered: that she would always know pain, but pain was temporary. A dress from which one can step.

Harlem looked right and left at the girls. The three Brown Betties stepped backwards as one, leaving her alone as she took her moment in the spotlight. She moved her hips like she was stirring the sweetest, thickest cake batter in a bowl of jazz. She dipped low and back up again, swirling something within. With her hands on her hips and with a wink of an eye, there, in her golden glory, she confirmed to herself that she had a gift. And it wasn't dancing. It was knowledge—knowledge that there was a part of her that no one could ever touch. Or tarnish. That part was wrapped tight in a silk bow of her favorite color, pale blue. She was protected. She made her strength brilliantly known under the spotlight she'd been given. The girls rejoined her and weaved around her in undulating moves that ebbed and flowed and ebbed again in response to the beckoning band's magic. It was magic. They were magic and it showed.

Back in one line, they slowly turned their backs to the audience. They deftly unhooked and flung off their bustiers to the beat of the drummer's 1-2-3 command and covered their bare bosoms with the teasing delight Harlem had learned from the girls. She looked at each one of them and smiled. For the first time, she felt like one of them. A Brown Bettie. She realized there'd always been space for her between

Amoura, Fury and Desire; she simply had not walked into it. She'd been angry with them, hurt by their inability to help her when she really needed it. Looking into their eyes, her body still feeling wonderfully zingy, she knew forgiveness was their new bond.

With their bare, brown, supple, glistening backs turned to the downtown elite, they crossed arms in victory behind each other's backs, feeling the energy and warmth of one another. They leaned forward quickly and sent their backsides to the audience in a Bettie bow.

The well-heeled men and women cheered wildly.

Harlem and the girls rose from their bow, waiting for Magdalena to take the stage behind them and begin the bidding. Harlem heard sniffling to her right. Desire was crying.

"It's over. Someone's gonna—" Tears covered her cheeks.

"Don't worry. We won't let anyone touch you," Harlem promised.

"Not today," Fury whispered.

Amoura smiled, "Not ever."

"Okay," she sniffled.

Harlem nodded. "Those stairs out of here are waiting for us. After the Rainbow Girls' dance, it's over."

Still connected, they sauntered backstage as one. Magdalena took the stage, swept her arms again and called out, "The Brown Betties, everyone!"

CHAPTER 55

Jonas clutched his empty champagne glass. With his head low, he stared out at the laughing faces of the white men and women clapping and stomping their feet. They were congratulating some fellow who'd bid the highest to spend time with the Brown Betties. He watched the man embrace Magdalena, wave to the crowd with the lighted "Lady M's Mysterie" sign shining bright above him, and walk off into the folds of the backstage where Harlem and the other girls had gone. It was barbaric. Even in their fine clothes and fine furs and things, they were horrifically barbaric. To him, they were predators with jagged, razor-sharp teeth who had lost their moral way in this underground society that was supposedly so elite.

"That was something," Jonas said.

"Wasn't it?" Honey beamed, clapping wildly.

"Never seen anything like it in my life," Jonas responded, setting down the champagne glass.

"They were exquisite. I'm so proud of them."

"What?"

"Did you see how the girls pulled together? That doesn't happen all the time. It's magic. Truly. The new girl was really quite good."

"I don't understand," Jonas said as he rubbed his forehead roughly. "What did they do to that young girl? The paint on her face? All done up like a harlot. That was not the girl I met in Greensboro! I don't think I can take this much longer."

"I know, Jonas. This is our world. I can't say anything other than that," Honey said, patting his arm. "Are you ready? Tilda should be coming down any minute."

"I don't know if I'm ready. I'm not made of steel, Honey," he said as he slammed his hands on his knees. His stomach was in knots. The smoke. The music. The people. It was all getting to his nerves.

Honey held his hand. "Yes, you are, Jonas. In fact, you're a hero. You didn't give up. You cared about Harlem enough to risk your own freedom, even with the hopes of finding your daughter. Because of you, these girls just might get out of here. We need more heroes like you."

"Right. Right," he exhaled. Her hands were cool and reassuring compared to his, soothing. He focused on his breathing and got his mind right. As he fixated on the folks again, Jonas caught the eye of the Joe fellow at the stage. Joe gave him a discrete nod as though to welcome him into some kind of club; Jonas reluctantly nodded back as Joe bent his head back down to the bass.

"Now, just so you are aware," Honey said, directing his gaze to the left, "You've got Officer Brighton over there by the door. That's obstacle number one. Lucinda, sitting just over there with Arthur and Mr. Trieg, she likes this place, and she could be obstacle number two. Then there's Ruth and Mary, who you know. That's three and four. And Magdalena makes five. That's five people who will try to stop us. I truly hope that after Tilda motions 'fire', they all just all run out and we don't have to deal with them."

"Right," he said and clasped his hands together. He rested his forehead there and squeezed his eyes shut.

"Jonas?"

"When do the Rainbow Girls come out? I want to see Arnetta."

Honey put her hand on his shoulder. "Here they come, Jonas. Here they come."

Jonas swallowed his heart back into his chest, opened his eyes, and stood up. Honey gently sat him back down. He looked at her and she gave him a nod that was sure to mean that he should sit down, and everything was going to be okay. He sat. Six women holding hands filed onto the stage. They each wore masks of different colors.

Honey gasped. "There's only six. There should be seven. Sapphire is missing." She looked at him gravely. "Something's wrong."

"What do you mean? And I cannot see their faces. For the Lord's sake, why do they have those masks on?"

"Jonas, wait here. I'm going to check on Sapphire," Honey said as she scanned the room. "I'll be right back. Watch for Arnetta. You can tell who a girl is from more than her face. Look, Jonas. Look at them."

CHAPTER 56

From backstage, Magdalena had peered through the curtains at her sister. Honey always had a peacefulness about her, even when agitated. It was something Magdalena often envied about her baby sister. But even with all that peace, Magdalena wondered what was going on inside the girl's head. *How could she come back here like this? What had that man said or done to bring her here? She wasn't supposed to be here!* Magdalena was so incensed that she was shaking.

"And all that I did for you!" she growled.

When Honey ran from her table and darted behind the Rainbow Girl's curtain, she chased after her.

Magdalena ran into the small space behind the curtain. In the limited light that shone down on them, she was surprised by her sister's calm expression, as well as the bruises that still lined her neck. "What do you think you're doing, Honey?"

Honey reached for Sapphire's door handle. "Why isn't Sapphire dancing?

Magdalena slapped her hand away, "That's no longer any of your business."

"Thanks to you. Throwing me out of my own house. And for what? For what, Magdalena?" Honey's eyes filled with resentment; her chin quivered with it. Her body shook. For the first time, that peace that Magdalena relished was gone.

"I—I—," Magdalena faltered.

"Why must you destroy everything you touch? You can't seem to exist without making bad things worse." Honey swiped tears from her cheeks. Her eyes, filled with pain, questioned Magdalena. "Wasn't I enough? You had to go and hurt this girl, too?"

"...What do you want, Honey? Why are you back here?" Magdalena asked, wishing somehow that they were talking about something else. That she could turn back the clock to them arguing over hair ribbons, or pretty glass beads, or anything but this. That she could hug her sister and end it. But she couldn't.

Honey looked hard at her. "I'm here because *I'm* trying to help someone. I'm doing something right for a change." She reached again for the door handle.

"And what is that?"

"That man out there is looking for his daughter, Arnetta," Honey hissed. "Which of the girls is Arnetta, Magdalena? Is Sapphire named Arnetta?"

"How would I know?" Magdalena said

"Think, Magdalena. You go through everyone's things. You keep records. Is she Arnetta or not?"

"Maybe. I don't know," Magdalena said and threw up her arms, hitting the curtain in the cramped space. "Maybe!?"

Honey stared at her. "You're useless, Magdalena. Go on back to your party."

"Honey, wait!" Magdalena reached for her sister. A scream from the party stopped her.

CHAPTER 57

He couldn't stand it any longer. His head swiveled on his neck toward Ruth and Mary's table where they sat in the shadows. Before he knew it, he was on his feet, knocking over a chair in the process. Someone screamed as he charged them like a monster. Jonas grabbed Ruth by the collar and snatched her up to her feet. Her face was inches from his. "Where is she?" he snarled. He shook her like a rag doll; his strength was coming from a place he hadn't known. "Where is my daughter? *What have you done with her!?*"

When the girls in the colored masks had taken the stage, he had scanned them, desperately. Their legs had been kicking and bodies moving fast and slow and fast again; they'd turned round and sideways and forwards, but even with all those views, he knew.

His daughter was not there.

"Tell me!" Everyone was staring at him, including the man, Arthur, whose thin lips were as stiff as his starched bowtie. Jonas didn't care. He kept shaking Ruth; his rage wanted an answer.

Mary stood and slapped at his arms. "Stop! Stop it, Mr. Stewart!"

"Tell me what you've done with my daughter! Where is Arnetta?" Jonas stared into Ruth's wide brown eyes, rimmed with guilt and creases. They were vaults of information, and he wanted answers. "Tell me!"

CHAPTER 58

agdalena ran from behind the curtain with Honey in tow and took the stage in front of the frozen Rainbow Girls. "Please, everyone, if you could remain calm and remember that this is a sophisticated event—"

Jonas whipped around to her, letting go of Ruth. "Sophisticated event? Do you people realize that these young women *belong* to someone? They have people. Somebody somewhere is missing them. That girl up there is someone's *daughter*. You're sick. Each and every one of you is sick in the head."

"Officer Brighton, if you could please escort Mr. Stewart—"

Arthur stood. "You see! This is what happens when you integrate Negroes into fine establishments!"

"Arthur, let's keep our comments to ourselves," Magdalena said.

"Fine establishment?" Jonas yelled. "Sick. You're sick!"

"Ladies and gentlemen, I apologize for this outburst and assure you that the evening will resume in just one moment, after we remove this gentleman from the party. Officer Brighton!" Magdalena looked toward the stairs to where Brighton usually held his post. He wasn't there. Magdalena looked to Lucinda's table; he had joined her. They both sat there with their arms crossed, looking spitefully smug.

"Magdalena, you should be ashamed of yourself. Ashamed," Jonas yelled at her. "I hope you rot in jail!"

Magdalena smoothed the hair away from her face. *Jail.* There was no way she was going back to jail. She looked out at the crowd with their painted faces, pursed lips, and hardened eyes. Had they turned on her? *Did they all know?* Their accusing eyes looked like they were looking at a Negro woman, the type of woman most of them hated, ignored, were jealous of or spat on when not doing something else to them. She'd seen that look many times before.

Nervous laughter bubbled from her. She knew what kind of jury she stood before. If it were up to them, she would not go to jail for providing girls. For being a Negro woman when they thought she were otherwise—that would be the bigger offense.

But maybe they hadn't turned against her. Maybe all they wanted was for the show to go on and they were only hardened because there had been an interruption to them getting their jollies.

She wasn't going to wait to find out.

"Ladies and gentlemen, I do apologize for this strange outburst," she said quickly as she thought through her next move. She was going to grab her things and run from this place. Now. She was going to catch the very next train to Montreal, and this was all going to be over. The Rainbow Girls would be her cover. She needed them dancing again. Immediately.

"Sir, if you'll join me over there by the stairs to discuss your grievance, we'll get this party started again, and our girls will dance, and—"

A woman wrapped in mink shouted, "Oh my God!"

Magdalena looked behind her to where the woman was pointing, and there was little Tilda on the stage. She was hopping up and down like a jumping bean, her arms flinging hysterically about her head.

"What!?" Magdalena stared at her. "What are you doing here? What is it?"

Tilda pointed to the hem of her dress, which was literally on fire. "Fire?" Magdalena stepped back from her.

Tilda's silent mouth gaped open, mouthing with no sound: "*FIRE!*"

Magdalena heard screams from the crowd as they rushed to exit the speakeasy. "Fire? What in the world, Tilda! Just stomp it out!" Magdalena pushed Tilda against the wall as the huddled Rainbow Girls scattered. "*What are you doing?*"

Magdalena tore the dress off Tilda. She beat it on the stage, trying to put out the flame. The flames grew with each swing. Fire ripped at her fingertips and she flung the garment from her hands with a loud yelp of pain. The dress landed along the wall near the edge of the stage. With a fiery lick, it ignited the silk folds of the gold curtain that framed the stage. As though stuck in a dream, she watched the curtain burst into flames, almost like it was opening its mouth in some sort of raptured joy, with her in the center of it. It laughed out loud in a breathy *hah!* and a brilliant, almost gorgeous cyclone of color carried itself up the curtain in an ecstasy that only took seconds to reach.

The fire took her breath with it.

"Good God," she whispered.

Just then, Mr. Rathbourne ran from backstage, his pants falling from him. He ran off the stage through the blazing gold mouth and hollered, "Fire!"

Slower than caramelized molasses, she turned and yelled, "*Run!*"

CHAPTER 59

66 *Run!*"

As soon as Mr. Rathbourne had walked behind the stage curtain, unbuttoned his pants, and stared at them with a wide, silly grin that betrayed his lust, Harlem had made a run for it. He had tried to grab for her, and she had dodged his grasp, knowing that if he touched any part of her it was over. The other girls had joined in the game of keep-away, leaving him with nothing to hold onto but his sliding pants.

Desire had just picked up the Derringer that they'd hidden backstage and was pointing it at Mr Rathbourne when little Tilda had magically appeared down their backstairs, matches in hand. She had motioned for them to leave, to get out, to "Run!"

"*Tilda!*" they screamed. The gun and Mr Rathbourne forgotten, they'd hurled questions at her —what happened that night? How had she gotten back in the house? So many questions they had asked amidst hugs that left no room for breathing. Tilda had rapped the whole thing to them, telling them that Honey had come back for them, that Jonas was looking for Harlem and his daughter, that the plan was she would pretend there was a fire and Jonas and Honey would get them out.

"This way!" Amoura had shouted at her, pointing up the backstairs. "We have keys, we can get out!"

"It's faster this way," Harlem had said and directed them toward the curtains. Her plan had been to run through Mysterie, up the main stairs, and out—and she was sticking to that plan. "I'm going this way!"

Mr. Rathbourne had been staring at them, not knowing what was going on when Fury had pointed at Tilda, eyes wide with fear. "Fire! Tilda is on fire."

"Fire?" Harlem had said. And sure enough, Tilda was walking through the curtains. On fire.

Mr. Rathbourne ran out. Harlem ran right behind him. The girls ran left.

CHAPTER 60

Fury whimpered from a recess of the pitch-black stairway. "I can't. I can't do this," she cried.

"You'll have to, Fury!" Amoura pleaded.

"Fire eats people. People die in the fire. I'm going to die by the fire. I'm going to die by it. Just like my momma. Like my daddy. I'm going to die by it!"

"Do you *want* to die by it?" Amoura said. "C'mon, my love, we've got to go now. Right now."

"Can't you hear them screaming down there?" Desire begged. "Can't you smell the smoke?"

Fury felt little hands on her arms tugging at her. She knew the hands to be Tilda's. She'd joined them.

"We must go now!" Desire said, pulling Fury by the arm and up the stairs.

Fury sank to the steps beneath her, "The dark. The dark. The dark. I can't...!"

Amoura commanded, "Close your eyes. Tilda and I will lead you. We have to go."

Desire shouted, "Get up NOW or we're going to *die!*"

She closed her eyes, and they carried her—they took care of her like Brown Betties do.

CHAPTER 61

Honey cringed at the bloodcurdling screams radiating throughout the room. She pushed herself against the red velvet curtain, backed against the wall of rainbow-colored doors. "Oh no," she covered her face with her hands. "This wasn't supposed to happen!" Thick, gigantic, orange flames were leaping up the gold curtains and happily licking the ceiling. As though released from a witch's cauldron, ribbons of ghostly smoke wisped and snaked stealthily along the ceiling like an army of pythons looking for a hole to retreat into. They fanned and spread and spilled, ravenously searching for prey. She pulled her dress collar up to her nose.

A vulgar crackling filled the air, punctuating the crescendo of hysterical screams that filled the room as densely as the smoke.

Lucinda stood on a table. "People! You must calm down. You must!"

Officer Brighton was near Lucinda trying to direct people in some kind of orderly fashion. "One line, yous! One line!"

Joe, the bass player, scrambled over Lucinda's table like a rabid dog, knocking her off her pedestal and onto Brighton. He threw people aside with brute force, forging a path for himself that went nowhere. He was sucked into the mass of people.

Honey froze at the spectacle of it all. A woman had fallen into a crumpled ball and was crying hysterically, "We're not going to get out! We're trapped!" Honey recognized her as Mrs. Clarke. Her husband, Mr. Clarke, jerked her up. "Get it together, Eleanor. We've got to get out! We can't be seen here!" They scampered past Honey pathetically and joined the herd jammed into the staircase. There was no way they were going to make it. And neither was she.

She felt herself shaking. She looked to her left and saw a hand on her shoulder, gripping her. "Honey! Honey!"

It was Jonas, his face etched with fear.

"We need to get Sapphire. Come with me to her room!"

"I'll get her! Go, Honey, go!" Jonas yelled as he barreled toward the room.

"But wait—!"

"Just *go!*"

Honey ran.

CHAPTER 62

Magdalena felt like she was slowly sinking deeper and deeper in the center of a hot liquid mass. Heavy and gripping, the heat touched every part of her being, working to steal what belonged to her and claim it as its own. It seeped sneakily into her nostrils and spread into her mind, pouring itself behind her eyeballs before closing off the sound in her eardrums and spilling down into her throat. It expanded as it went along, stealing what it really wanted: her breath. She gasped for air. She stumbled from the shock of it all. Her tortured breathing echoed in the scorched chamber of her body. She fell to her hands and knees. Something in the fall released its grip for a moment. Air found its way into her body. She coughed, welcoming it. Suddenly a rush of sound shook her core. Over the din, she heard her name.

"Magdalena, help me! Help me!"

She rose to her knees. "Honey?"

Honey was pulling down the curtain that lined the rainbow rooms; it was alive with fire. The flames charged along the dips in the fabric where it clung by its rings to the hanging rod. The curtain's fire had become monstrous and was devouring the rainbow color from the metal doors it covered in massive licks. It was growing larger and more powerful behind Honey as she ran through the wreckage that was Lady M's Mysterie.

Magdalena rose as the curtain came crashing down in a fiery cloak. Honey screamed and fell out of sight. Magdalena charged blindly through the landmine of toppled tables and chairs and fought her way through the smoke that had descended upon them with lightning speed. Her sister was entangled in the red fabric and flailed wildly against it like some fantastic monster coming to life. The flames illuminated the whole thing as it became a flesh-eating organism that turned itself on Honey. Magdalena sprang to her sister. "Honey! Honey!" she screamed as Honey stood, hopped, sprung, and thrashed about, ricocheting from walls and doors and tables and chairs, twisting herself further into the burning firestorm. Sounds of terror sprang from her sister. Sounds Magdalena couldn't tolerate.

"*Honey!*" Magdalena hysterically ripped away at the fiery cloth trapping her sister, scorching her own fingers as she did so. The flames were stronger and quicker than her. Hungrier. Angrier. Smarter. She tore blindly for her only sister. "*Honey!*" From beneath the stinking velvet, Magdalena grabbed Honey in a tight hug, wanting to help but wanting to go with her, wherever she was going. She felt her own flesh burning and she screamed in agony until the sound once again disappeared from her consciousness. Her legs buckled; she closed her eyes and swore she saw her mother and father's faces melt before her as she and Honey succumbed to a force stronger than them both. *Momma, Papa...* she thought as she drifted toward them. Finally.

CHAPTER 63

From under a table, Ruth hoped not to die. The heat and smoke strangled her. "Mary! Help me!" Ruth yelled out hysterically, blindly. "Mary! Mary!"

"Ruth!"

On the floor, the smoke wasn't as thick. She could see. She looked up and was eye-to-eye with Mary who was scrambling on all fours toward her. "Mary!"

Mary's face was frozen in terror. "Ruth!"

Ruth grabbed for her sister and clutched her as Mary climbed chaotically past her. "Can we get out? Can we?" Ruth cried.

"I think we can," Mary said breathlessly as she stood. "I think—"

Ruth reached for sister, to pull her back down, just as the Lady M's Mysterie sign came crashing down on top of them, its burned, jagged edges abruptly ending whatever Mary was going to say.

Mary landed heavily on top of her. Ruth stared into Mary's brown eyes. She saw the light go out of

them and trickle out of her mouth, a trail of blood as
thin as a hair pin.

CHAPTER 64

Jonas frantically scooped his arms underneath the girl's shoulders and lifted her. He could barely see her in the darkness. The fire that crashed about him outside the door provided some light as he stole a glance at the girl in his arms. He saw the outline of her face. Her nose was his. Her chin was his. His. He traced her eyebrows with his fingertips, as he had done when she was new to him. *"Baby?"* His fingers were frozen by her face, unsure what to do. He had waited so long to touch her, to hold her, to see her. Now that she was here, in front of him, he was afraid to touch her. Every hour, every minute, every moment of worry and anguish for her poured out of him first as a whimper and then as a mournful howl, worse than any wounded beast.

Jonas looked down at her. Her head rolled on her neck.

"Arnetta!" he screamed. He felt wetness where her body slumped against his. He moved her away and his shirt was soaked with her blood.

"*No!*" Jonas faltered at the sight of it. He stared once more out into the cackling beast of fire; with the smoke hovering around him like death, he put his daughter back on her cot. He closed the metal door, took off his jacket, and blocked the bottom of the door with it. He crawled onto the small cot, and held his daughter, his Arnetta.

"Daddy's here, baby girl. Daddy's here."

CHAPTER 65

Harlem had gotten to the stairs and had tried to turn back when she saw Tilda laying on the stage. That brief, selfless moment of hesitation had been her downfall. Had she not stopped, she would have cleared the pack of animals she was now trapped in.

These people who were supposed to be so posh and collected had turned into savages. They had trampled each other, pulling one another back to make room for themselves. Harlem had tried to tunnel through their pulling and trampling like a rat digging its way through a wall, but she was having trouble. She was caught. Her face was smashed against the back of a taller man. They were moving through the dark, narrow tube that was their staircase as a mass of sludge. A sludge that had no control over its movement and was to be squeezed and pushed until it found a release.

The screams reverberating in her head rose to a frenzied state. People were being crushed and so was she. Harlem tried to disappear. She closed her eyes and thought of nothing but the front door. Of seeing the front door and running through it. Through that door. Through it. "Please, God," she sighed. "Help me get through it." She tried to take a deep breath, but she was having trouble doing so. The sludge from behind was pushing too hard on the sludge at the front. Keeping her eyes closed, she tried again to focus. Tried not to panic. But the panic was winning. It was strangling her, just as sure as if someone had their hands around her neck. "I can't breathe!" she panted. "I can't breathe!"

CHAPTER 66

Arthur had crouched low on the cement floor and had crawled into the yellow room where he'd had Ann, his love. He had scuttled under their cot and taken out his kerchief from his pocket, covering his mouth to breathe. To take seconds to think. To cut through the fiery chaotic hell. And then he remembered. He'd been to enough parties to know that the Brown Betties often disappeared backstage, never to be seen again during the party. There had to be another way out. He had to go now. He had to run through the fire out there. He had to. If he wanted his Ann, if he wanted to live, to love, to have the life he came here for, there was no other choice but to run.

He got to his knees and scampered toward the stage. He crawled over bodies that weren't moving, bodies that were obscured by smoke, faces he couldn't see. He'd been here enough times. He knew the layout. He knew what to do. He did it. He crawled through fire. His hands burnt, but he did it. He found the dark corridor he was looking for. He bumbled around in the darkness, falling his way up the oddly-spaced stairs on all fours, his shoes scuffing against wood, not knowing where he was going other than up. Voices seemed to be coming from somewhere ahead of him but then stopped, as though vanished.

He'd run out of stairs and fell onto a landing in a heap. Frantically, he picked himself up, fixed his cuffed shirt sleeves, and smoothed back the hair that had fallen out of place. "Hello!?" he screamed. There was nothing there. No exit. No one. Where had they gone? "Hello?" He slapped against the walls. Darkness enveloped him, offering him no clues. Smoke filled his nostrils with each heaving breath he took. He felt dizzy. He walked again, straight, and ran into a wall. He turned. Ran his hands along the wall. Nothing. He spun again. He spread his body against the wall. Searching. Nothing. He coughed. His lungs burned. A tightness gripped his chest. He thought of that time when he was twelve years old in Brooklyn; his younger brother had thrown a wooden airplane into the stove-pipe oven, left open to heat the home in the dead of winter. They'd loved the plane and so quickly pulled it out of the fire, setting it on the rug to blow out the flames. They'd almost burnt the house down until a neighbor came to their rescue. He felt like that now. He pulled his shirt to his nose. "*Hello!*"

He had to go back down. There was no way out this way. He began his clumsy descent, skidding along with no railing. He noticed he could see the outline of the steps now. There was a glow, a light that hadn't been there before.

The fire had reached the bottom of the stairs; it was coming for him, creeping into the passageway like a glowing orange and black tiger who'd escaped its cage with intentions of its own.

CHAPTER 67

In the dark of their room, Amoura kneeled on the ground and hugged Fury tightly, "We made it, we made it, honey. Are you alright?"

"I'm scared," Fury whimpered.

Desire and Tilda moved in closer to wrap their arms around Fury too. "We're safe, Fury. You've got to believe that."

Amoura rocked Fury and kept talking, hoping her voice would sooth her into the here and now. "We're going to be fine. We're going to be fine. There's no fire up here, there's no smoke—"

"But it's dark, it's still dark...!"

Amoura continued, "We're going to have to work through that. You know that we're here for you and there's nothing here that can hurt you; the danger is gone and—"

Suddenly, candlelight flickered, illuminating the room. "Oh Tilda, you sweet girl. You've always made sure there was a candle! Thank you."

Tilda stood there in a new undershirt and knee-length knickers.

Desire whistled. "Where'd you get those new threads?"

Tilda used her fingers to tap along the door.

"Mr Stewart and Honey took you shopping this morning? Well, isn't that something. You must feel like a brand-new girl," Desire said.

Tilda nodded emphatically. She tapped some more.

Amoura listened to Tilda tap. "I guess they are, Tilda. Fire and light are becoming your secret weapon. I'm glad you had an extra candle in your britches, but what you did down there was truly bizarre!"

Tilda tapped in agreement, her wide smile beaming with pride and bewilderment.

"I don't know that you shoulda done all that, Tilda. I can smell a lot of smoke, what if you burned the place down? Right before we reached the stairs, I saw Magdalena try to put out the fire with your dress, but what if she didn't do it all the way? I'm worried, girls. I think we need to get out of here—can't you hear them down there?" Desire said, leaning her ear to the door. "What if there is a real fire and it got too big? What if it's reached upstairs? We're going to be trapped in here!"

"No, we're not," Fury mustered. "Magdalena gave me the key earlier; I never gave it back to her. It's under the mattress.

Desire exclaimed, "You had the key all along?"

"It was a contingency plan; if tonight didn't work out the way we'd planned." Fury smiled faintly. Her voice was becoming lighter. She was back.

Amoura rubbed her back. "I guess you planning ahead helped us out after all!"

"I found it," Desire said, letting the mattress flop back to the bedframe. "Let's get out of here."

Amoura stopped her. "Hang on a minute, what's that banging?"

They listened and heard a muffled voice yelling, "Let me outta here!"

"Oh, my stars. Emma Sue! That's Emma Sue! She's still next door in Harlem's room!" Amoura said. "We've got to get her; she must be terrified."

Desire opened their door, and they spilled out of the room and onto the landing that led down to the stairs.

The girls all froze at the disaster that lay below them, "Oh my god," Fury said. "What's happening?"

"They're trampling each other! Dear Jesus!" Amoura screamed and turned away, certain she saw a woman dead or dying.

A banging from the door behind them startled them back into action. "Emma Sue!" Desire let Emma Sue out; the girls all took a step back. The newest girl was sweating, her hair standing completely on end and every which way. She held what appeared to be the leg of a chair in her hands, looking bewildered.

—

"What in the tarnation is going on up in here?" she asked. "That door was locked! I started screamin' and there was no light in that place. I started throwin' the chair 'gainst the door. Ain't nobody lockin' me into nothin'! I'll tell you that much, yessiree." She peered over the railing, "What in the—?" The sight below cut off any other words she had to say.

"There's Harlem!" Amour cried. Some of the people blocked the front door, trying frantically to get out of it. Others had reached the stairs and were out of harm's way, but most of the crowd had bottlenecked between the dining room and the foyer area. They were a mass of arms and legs and heads and shoulders with nowhere to go, and Harlem was right in the middle of it. "We've got to move girls! Now!"

Amoura gathered the folds of her red gown and ran down the stairs with the rest of the girls trailing behind her, including Emma Sue with her chair leg raised for battle.

CHAPTER 68

Harlem gasped for air. She could barely touch the floor. The crowd was carrying her, buoying her from one step to the next. She pried one arm free and grabbed onto the shoulder of the man in front of her who she was being squeezed against.

"Help," she gasped.

The man reached up to his shoulder, clasped her hand, and held on.

Suddenly she pitched forward and the wall of people she had been smashed against, including the man who'd taken her hand, gave way. She had nothing to anchor her, nor did they, and they all fell forward as they spilled into the foyer. Someone fell on top of her and she screamed out in agony. Something told her to move. To move and move now or be crushed. She rolled from under the fallen body, dragged herself from the pack, and crawled through the crowd of people. There were more screams. Horrific screams. She looked toward the scream and saw a woman reduced and compacted into something that was no longer her body, but a grotesque version of it. The three layers of people atop her writhed about in selfishness, completely unaware of the damage they had done to the creature below them. Her brown eyes bulged from her head, filled with a vacant stare. A blond curl lay limp across her perfectly mascaraed eyelashes. Harlem turned away from her, sickened.

Harlem clambered her way to the back of the foyer near Tilda's bedroom door where there was room to breathe. She pulled her knees to her chest, with the red gown bunched around them. She looked about her. Frantic. Her chest heaved. She took in the mounting chaos around her. Screaming. Crying. Confusion. But she, she had clarity. She had been here before, in what had, unbelievably, been a mere dress rehearsal. She knew what she needed to do. What she hadn't done the other night. She rose to her feet.

From above her, on the stairs, she heard more screams and saw Amoura leading Tilda, Emma Sue, and the Betties down the stairs.

"*I've got to go; go now!*" she said to herself. Many of the people, stunned and confused, had fanned out toward the stairs and were sitting on them, gasping for air unaware they were soon to be bombarded by Betties rolling down the stairs. Others clung to the banister as they vomited the cheap champagne they had consumed earlier. Harlem looked for her path through the battlefield of fallen tuxes and shredded silk gowns in front of her. Of silver trays and toupees. Of smashed crystal mingled with pearls and cufflinks stained with blood. The wave from the left was coming down the stairs. The wave from the right was not stopping and more were coming from the dining room; an army of soldiers, fighting for their own lives. Harlem rose against the wall, using it for support. She took a deep breath. *Now!*

Harlem barreled through the people, just obstacles now, not caring about who or what she hit. As she shoved her way to the door, people grabbed at her, wanting her to take them with her. They knew she knew how to get out. To escape. She flung them from her. Kicking at their longing, which would become her demise if she let it. She hurdled over bodies. Selfish now, bent on surviving, she pushed, screamed, and clawed at anything in her way. She was not going to end up like the lifeless woman buried behind her. She reached the door, the frame splintered from the force of people trying to push through it. Harlem felt the stained glass, like fingers, tugging at her dress and tearing into her flesh, trying pull her back. She ripped through it, not caring how much of her was left behind in that place so long as the majority of her made it out. "You won't get me!" she hollered.

Harlem looked above into the night sky and saw the moon. It called to her. She kept pushing. She cried. She struggled through blindly until she felt herself catapulted down the concrete steps. When she landed, she ran. She ran as fast as she could for as long as she could, her shoes slapping the pavement, her torn dress flailing behind her. She left the madness, the epidemic of sins trying to claim her. She left the sirens coming to save those that did not deserve to be saved—and the girls that did. She left it all behind. She didn't look back. She didn't slow down. She ran like the wind, floating on the pale blue silk that had become pretty, pretty ribbons. She was free.

Acknowledgements

While writing can be incredibly solitary, getting a book completed is not. With deepest gratitude I offer thanks to my mom, Vicki Rogers for being my 1940s guru, guide and "first responder" to my initial and subsequent "sh*tty drafts". To Ruthy Hope and Becca Samson for editing and providing invaluable feedback and direction on the middle-year drafts while I was writing away in Prague. To my last stretch editors and amazing writers themselves, Auburn Scallon and Kathryn H. Ross; your artful technique and encouraging insight gave me the confidence I needed to keep going. (You both also taught me how to be a better editor to others!) To Ashley Girty for expertly copyediting and proofing this bad girl; you rock. To Les and Tyree Wieder and Marvin Zuckerman for love and cultural support. To Jennifer Farmer for being a leader in the "fight" and helping me with tools whenever needed. To LaShawn Harris for writing *Sex Workers, Psychics and Numbers Runners: Black Women in New York City's Underground Economy*, and Willard B. Gatewood for *Aristocrats of Color: The Black Elite 1880-1920*, which both became excellent resources to the proof I knew to be true. To Benjamin Mills for the beautiful cover design and lastly, to the fearless Nate Ragolia for believing in me and publishing this labor of love. Huzzah!

Now to my loves. To the Brown Betties for being my muses and my real-life girlfriends (Crescent, Keena, Danielle, Tanya, Christy, Kalia, Tina, Deonna, Nicole, Ally, Aly, Amanda and Siti). To my family (Roscoe, Darnell, Brooke, Shakir, Kennedy, Baron, Steve and Althea) for being cheerleaders and safety nets when I needed you. And to my husband Matthew for being my anchor, encourager, and provider of late-night wine.

To Matt and Parul, founders of the London Writers Salon who led me and my comrades in daily Zoom Writers Hour where a majority of this book was written...I thank you. You all saved me when I was looking for accountability and structure to my writing life. I offer special thanks to my Gold writers who talked me down from many writerly ledges of anxiety and overwhelm as I navigated through the jungle toward publication. I would be facing empty pages if it weren't for all of you. I'm so grateful.

If I forgot anyone, please forgive me.

That is all.

Except this: if you are a writer, go write. It's your turn. You got next. You can do it.

Love,
Peppur

About the Author

PEPPUR CHAMBERS is an international writer/producer/educator.

She is the founder of Brown Betties®, a women's empowerment brand and the namesake to the sultry, sassy, sophisticated characters who appear in her books (*Harlem's Awakening, Harlem's Last Dance*; Spaceboy Books/Amazon), on stage in *Harlem's Night: A Cabaret Story*, and in her "Be Your Own Bettie" Workshops where she teaches women how to be. Under this brand, she is currently working on the second Brown Betties Guide series book, *Knowing Your NO*, with the first being *How to Look for Love in All the Wrong Places*, which was also developed into an award-winning webseries.

An alum of Circle X Emerging Playwrights Group, Moving Arts MADLab, and Antaeus Playwrights Lab, she uses her voice to amplify women's issues, social justice and love. Find her radio plays *End of the Line, The Fire In-Between* and *The Boll Weevil & Chester Higgensworth* wherever you listen to podcasts. Her social justice film *DO SOMETHING* can be found streaming on Tubi.com.

A former Chicago Bulls and Milwaukee Bucks NBA dancer, she pulls from those experiences – and her years living in LA, New York and abroad – to tell many of her stories. She uses her skills as a film and theater director as well. A Marquette

University graduate and Kenosha, Wisconsin native, she currently lives in Arizona with her husband Matthew and their two rescue dogs, Molly and Vivian.

Learn more:

penandpeppur.com

brownbetties.com

peppurchambers.com

Social: @peppurthehotone @thebrownbetties

About the Artist

Benjamin Mills is an illustrator based in London, UK. Learn more at www.benjamintmills.co.uk

About the Publishing Team

Nate Ragolia is a lifelong lover of science fiction and its power to imagine worlds more hopeful and inclusive than the real one. His first book, *There You Feel Free*, was published by 1888's Black Hill Press in 2015. Spaceboy Books reissued it in 2021. He's also the author of *The Retroactivist*, published by Spaceboy Books. He founded and edited *BONED*, a literary magazine, has created webcomics, currently hosts a podcast, and pets dogs.

Shaunn Grulkowski has been compared to Warren Ellis and Phillip K. Dick and was once described as what a baby conceived by Kurt Vonnegut and Margaret Atwood would turn out to be. He's at least the fifth best Slavic-Latino-American sci-fi writer in the Baltimore metro area. He's the author *Retcontinuum*, and the editor of *A Stalled Ox* and *The Goldfish* for 1888/Black Hill Press.